Volume
ONE

Created by:

Christy Lijewski

TOKYOPOP®

HAMBURG // LONDON // LOS ANGELES // TOKYO

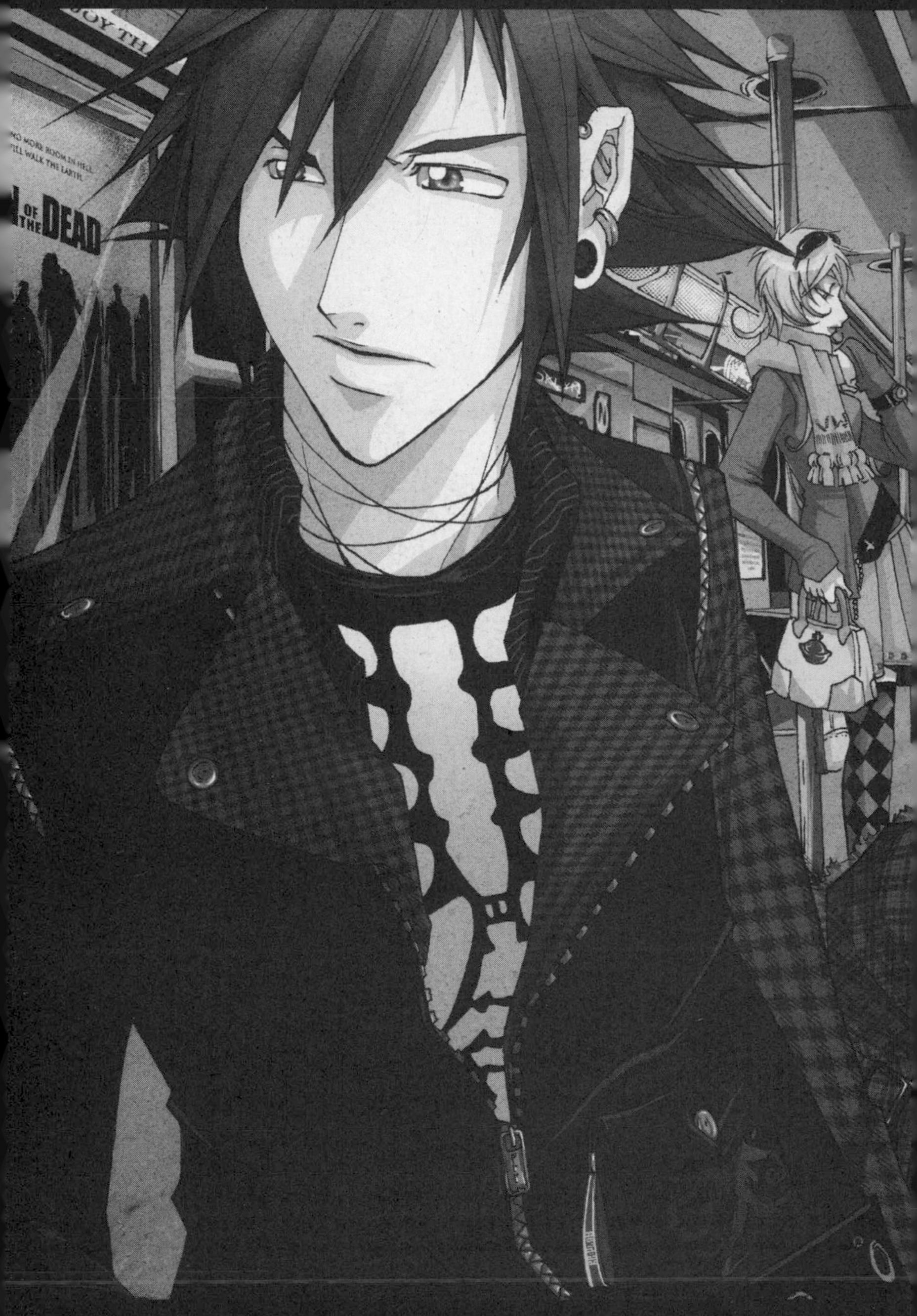
NO MORE ROOM IN HELL
WILL WALK THE EARTH
OF THE DEAD

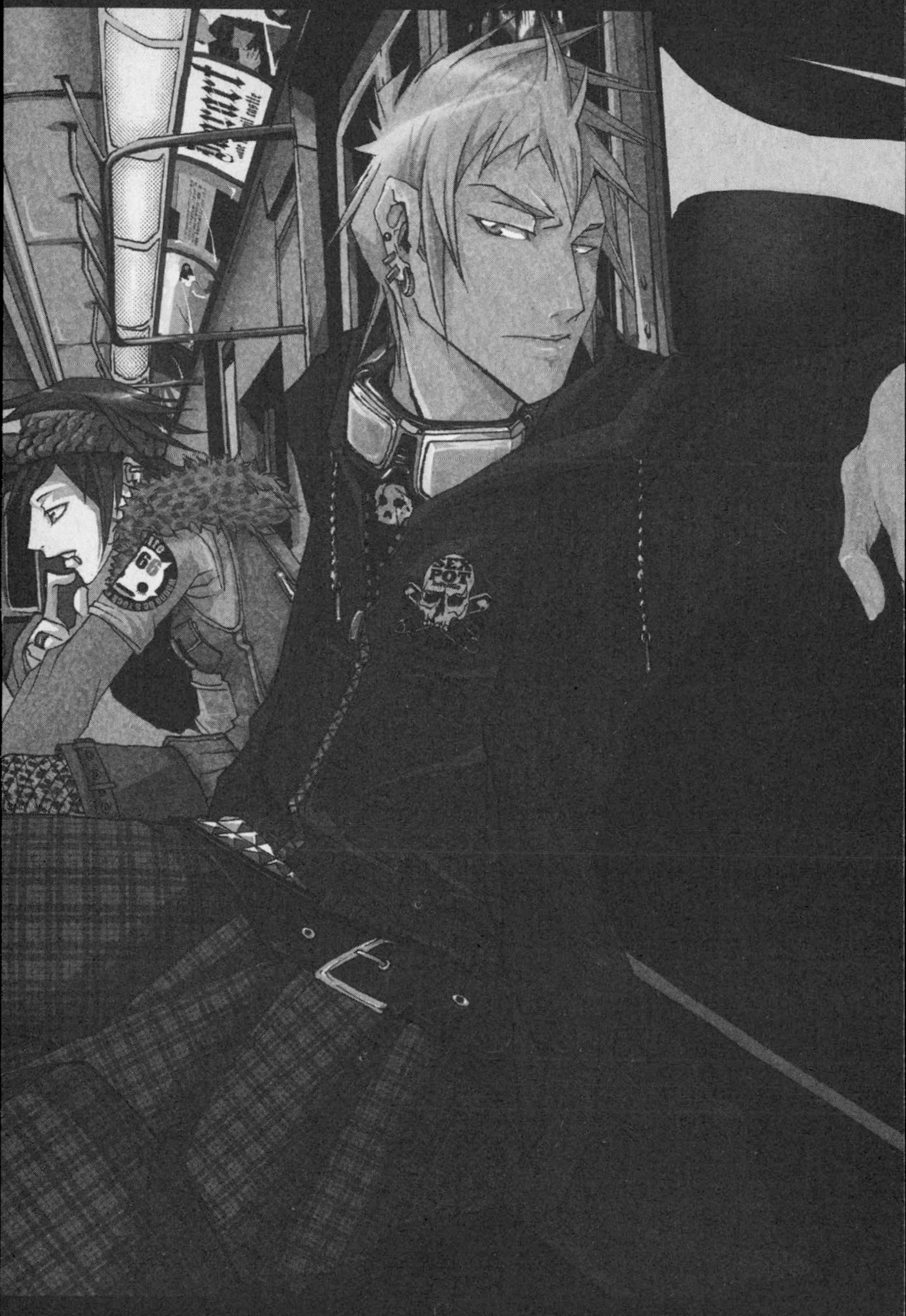
SEX POT
66

Re:Play Volume 1
Created by Christy Lijewski

Tones - Catarina Sarmento
Lettering - Fawn Lau
Cover Designer - Jason Milligan

Editor - Julie Taylor
Digital Imaging Manager - Chris Buford
Production Manager - Elisabeth Brizzi
Art Director - Anne Marie Horne
Editorial Director - Jeremy Ross
VP of Production - Ron Klamert
Editor in Chief - Rob Tokar
Publisher - Mike Kiley
President and C.O.O. - John Parker
C.E.O. and Chief Creative Officer - Stuart Levy

A 🐾 **TOKYOPOP**® Manga

TOKYOPOP Inc.
5900 Wilshire Blvd. Suite 2000
Los Angeles, CA 90036

E-mail: info@TOKYOPOP.com
Come visit us online at www.TOKYOPOP.com

ISBN: 1-59816-737-5

First TOKYOPOP printing: August 2006
10 9 8 7 6 5 4 3 2 1
Printed in the USA

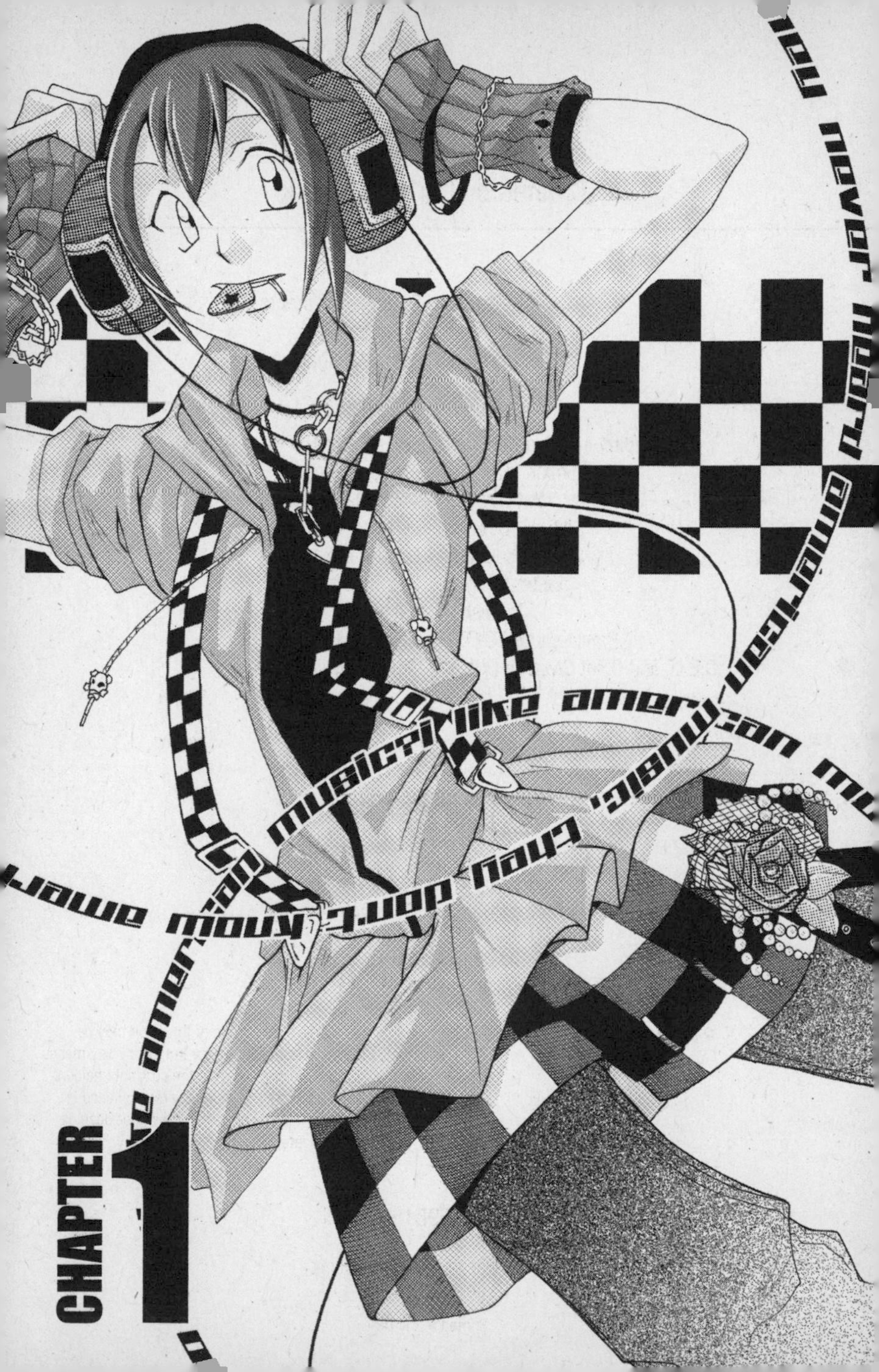
CHAPTER 1
they don't know
music? I like american

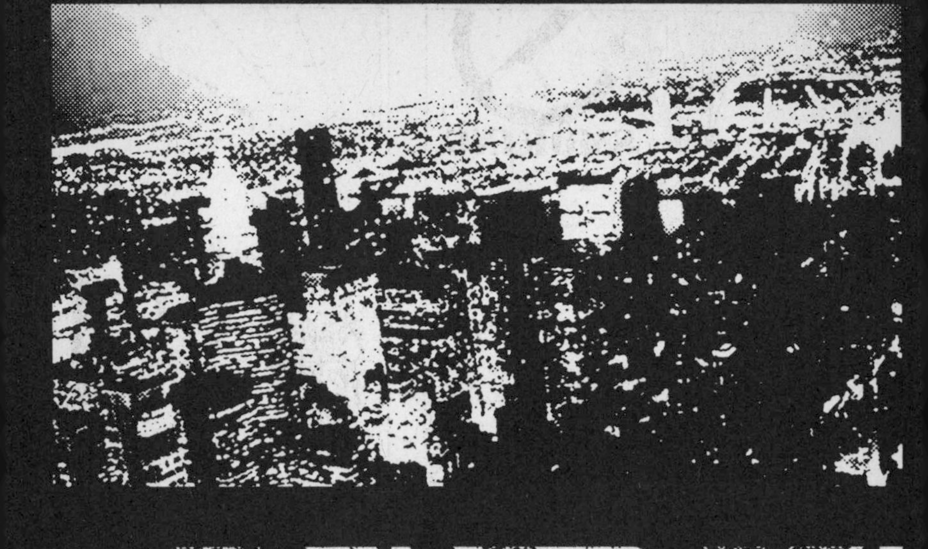

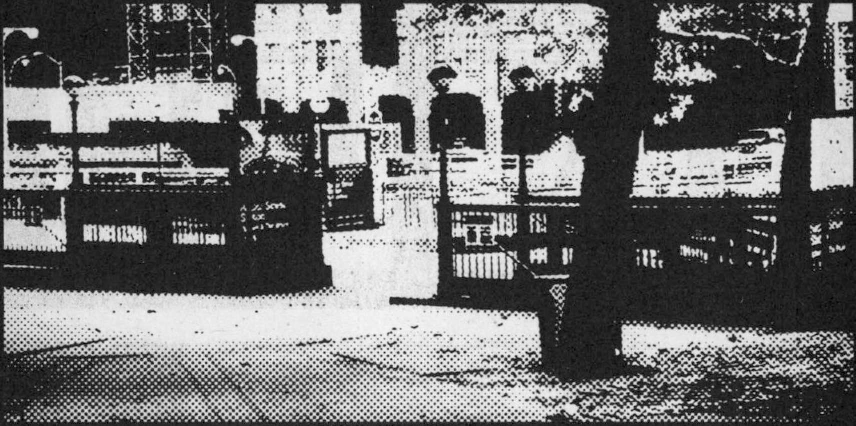

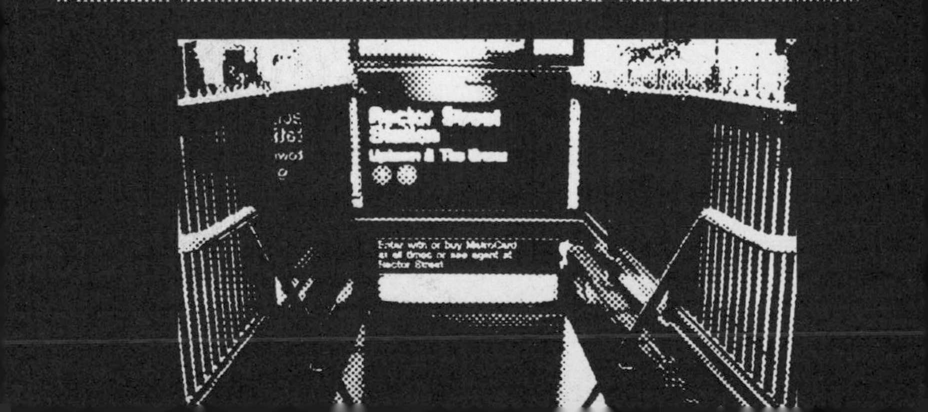

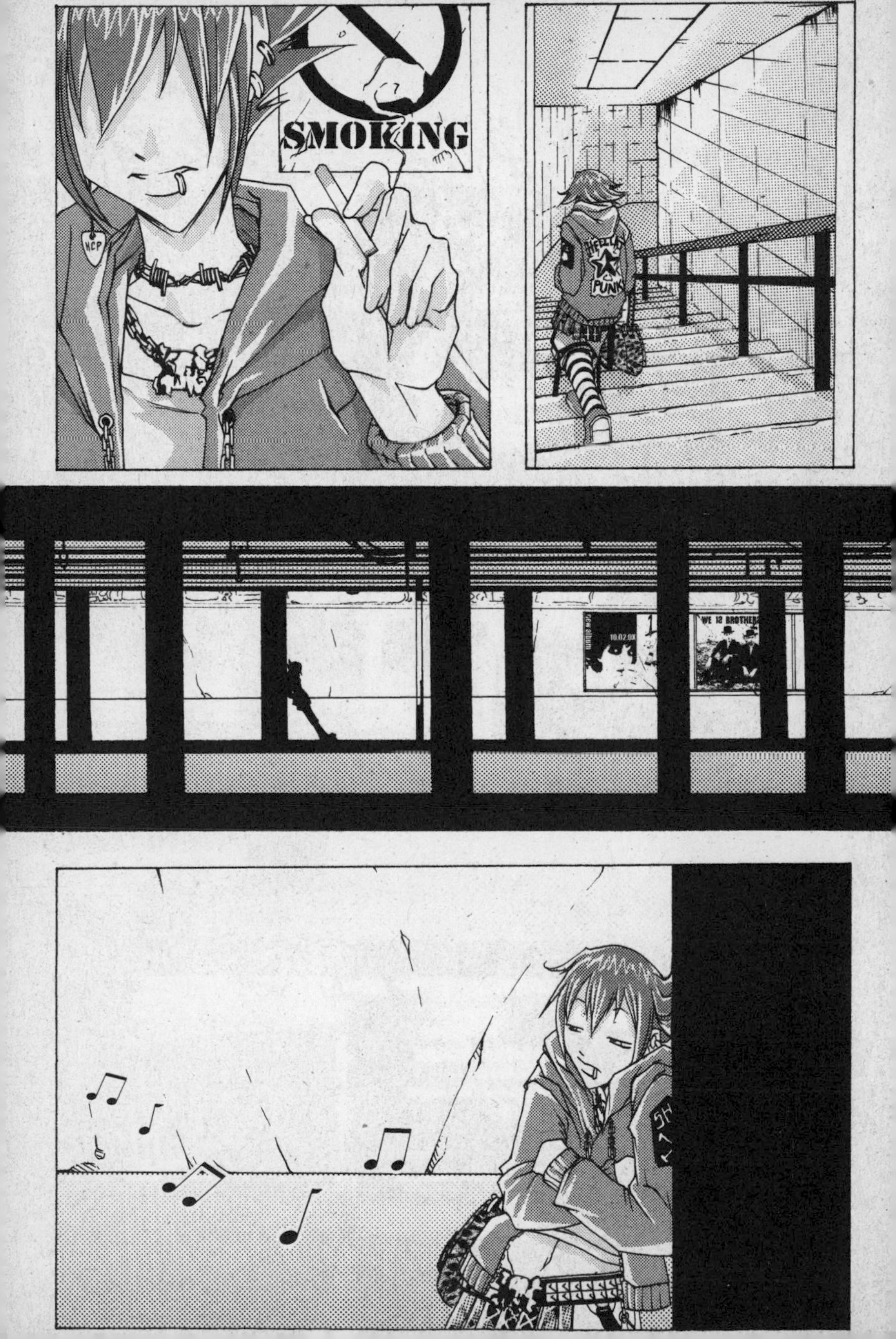
SMOKING
HCP
new album
10.02.0X
WE 12 BROTHERS

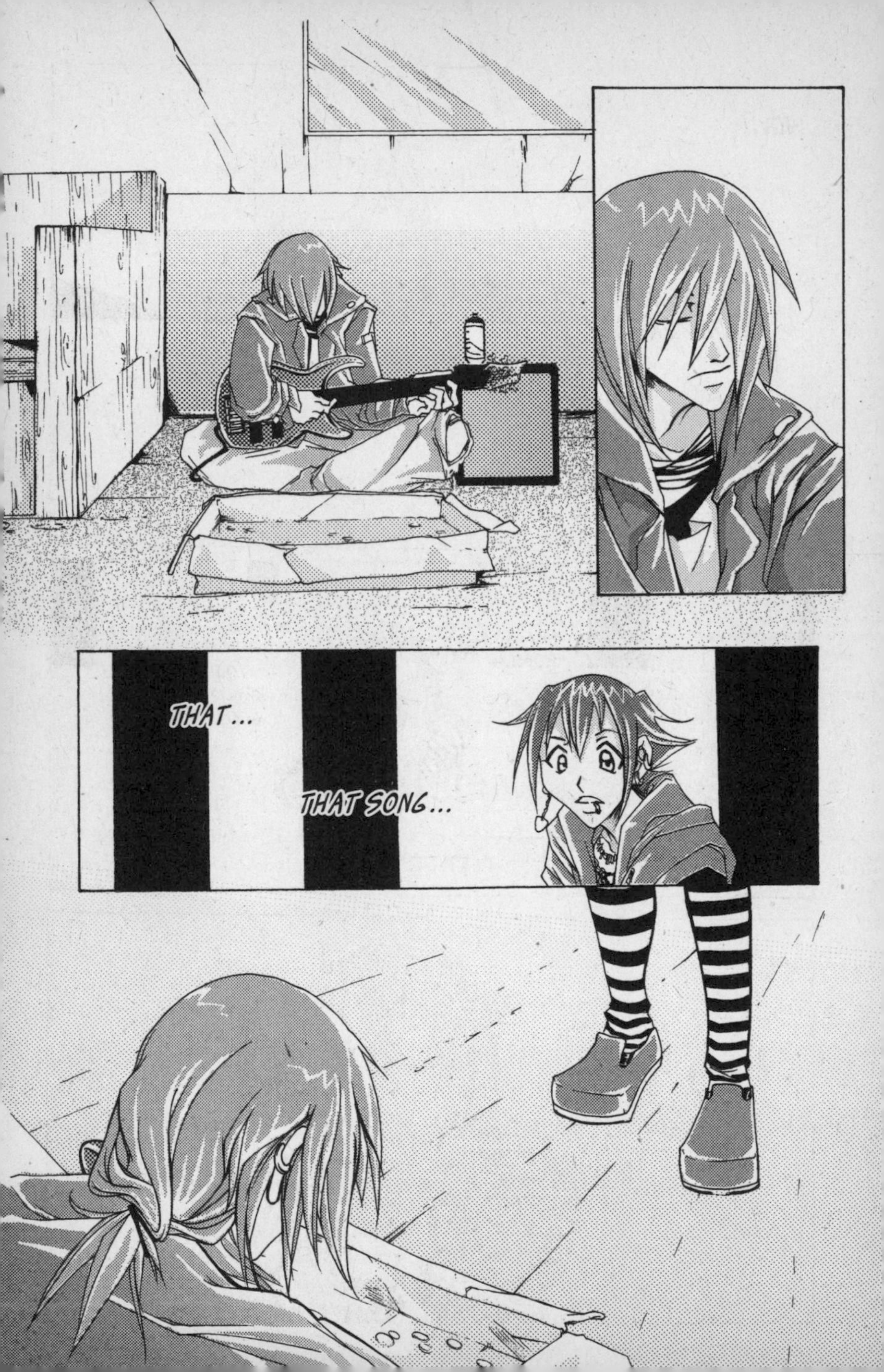
THAT...
THAT SONG...

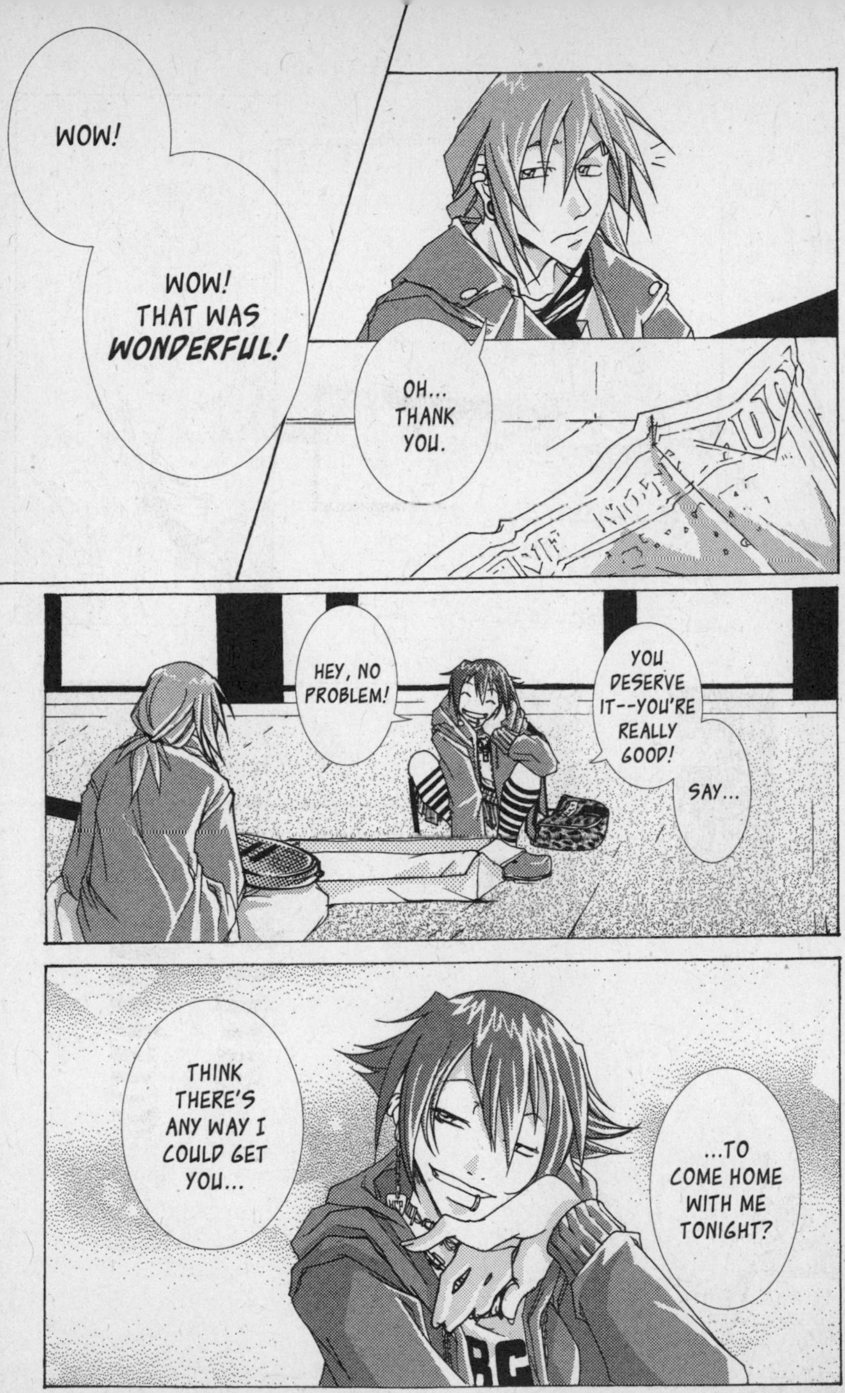
WOW!
WOW! THAT WAS WONDERFUL!
OH... THANK YOU.
HEY, NO PROBLEM!
YOU DESERVE IT--YOU'RE REALLY GOOD!
SAY...
THINK THERE'S ANY WAY I COULD GET YOU...
...TO COME HOME WITH ME TONIGHT?

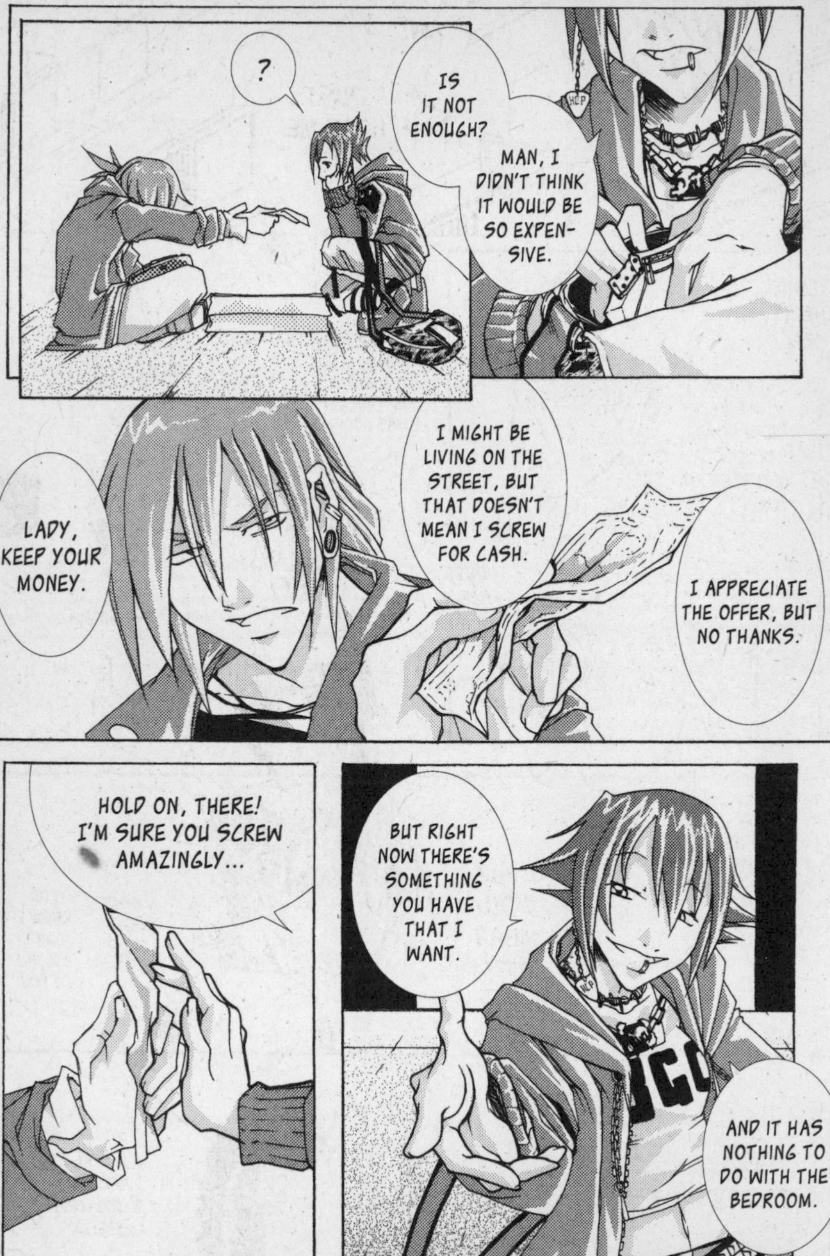
?
IS IT NOT ENOUGH?
MAN, I DIDN'T THINK IT WOULD BE SO EXPEN-SIVE.
LADY, KEEP YOUR MONEY.
I MIGHT BE LIVING ON THE STREET, BUT THAT DOESN'T MEAN I SCREW FOR CASH.
I APPRECIATE THE OFFER, BUT NO THANKS.
HOLD ON, THERE! I'M SURE YOU SCREW AMAZINGLY...
BUT RIGHT NOW THERE'S SOMETHING YOU HAVE THAT I WANT.
AND IT HAS NOTHING TO DO WITH THE BEDROOM.

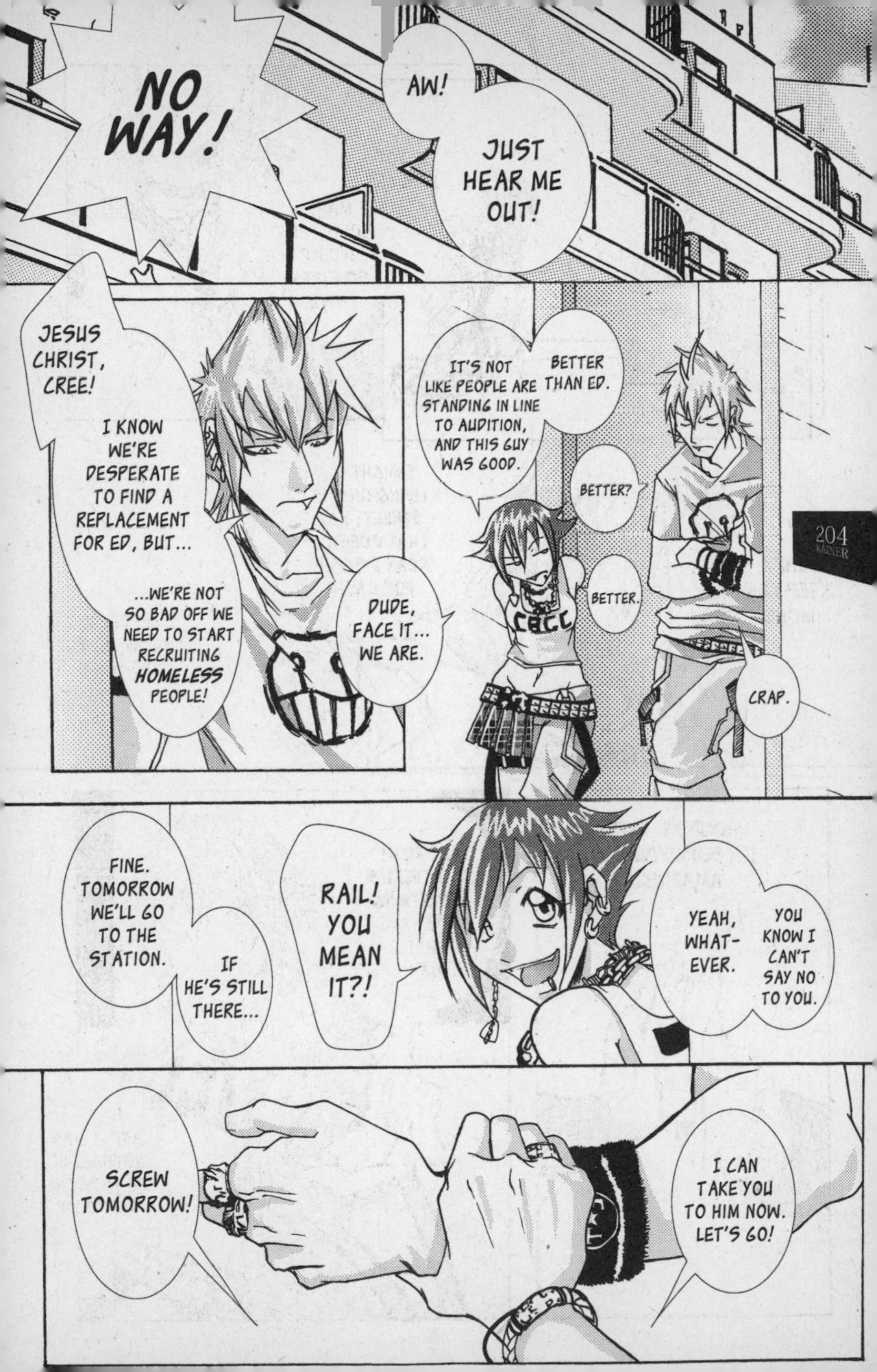
NO WAY!
AW!
JUST HEAR ME OUT!
JESUS CHRIST, CREE!
I KNOW WE'RE DESPERATE TO FIND A REPLACEMENT FOR ED, BUT...
...WE'RE NOT SO BAD OFF WE NEED TO START RECRUITING HOMELESS PEOPLE!
DUDE, FACE IT... WE ARE.
IT'S NOT LIKE PEOPLE ARE STANDING IN LINE TO AUDITION, AND THIS GUY WAS GOOD.
BETTER THAN ED.
BETTER?
BETTER.
CRAP.
FINE. TOMORROW WE'LL GO TO THE STATION.
IF HE'S STILL THERE...
RAIL! YOU MEAN IT?!
YEAH, WHAT-EVER.
YOU KNOW I CAN'T SAY NO TO YOU.
SCREW TOMORROW!
I CAN TAKE YOU TO HIM NOW. LET'S GO!

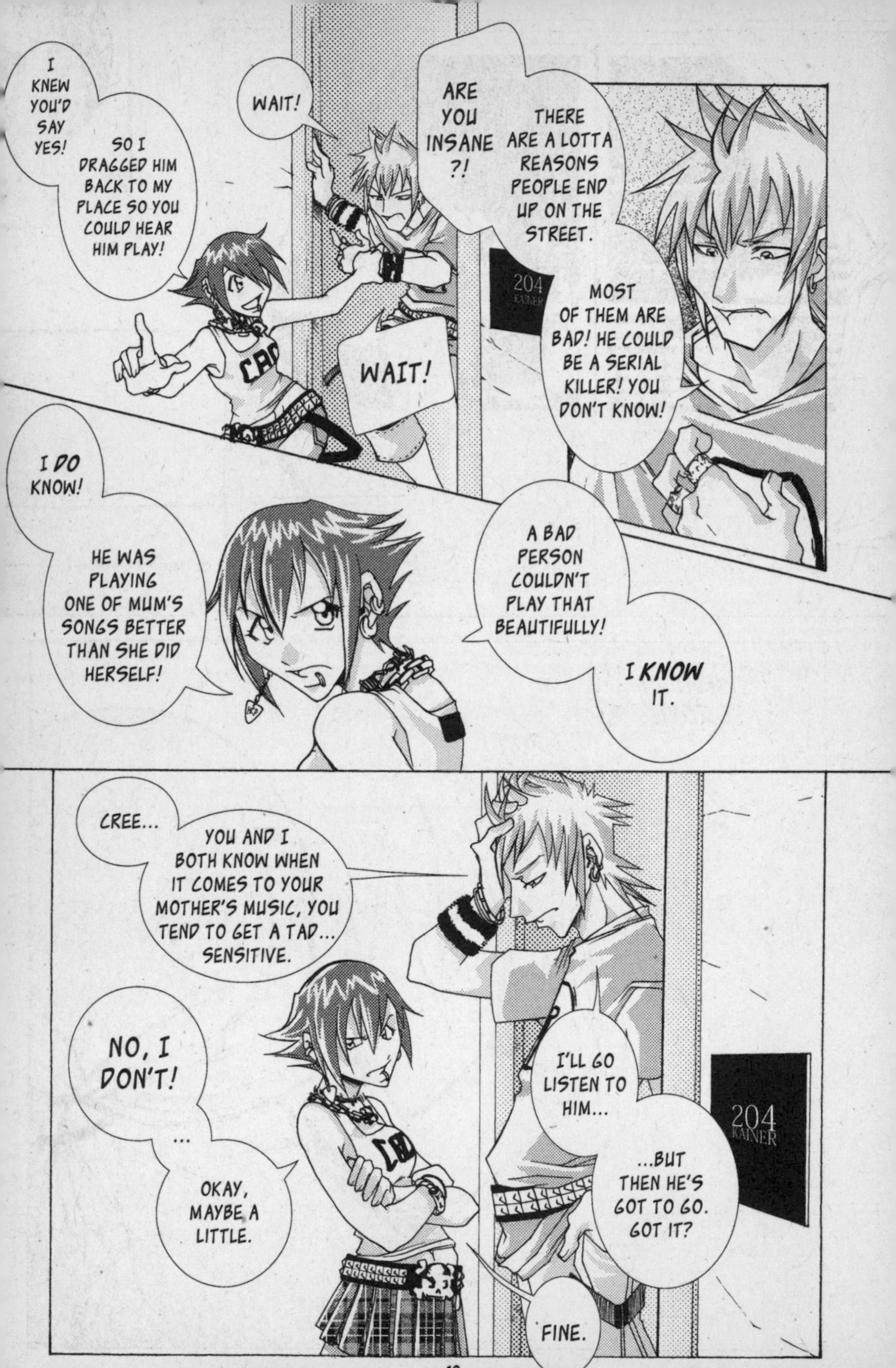
I KNEW YOU'D SAY YES!
SO I DRAGGED HIM BACK TO MY PLACE SO YOU COULD HEAR HIM PLAY!
WAIT!
WAIT!
204 KAINER
ARE YOU INSANE?!
THERE ARE A LOTTA REASONS PEOPLE END UP ON THE STREET.
MOST OF THEM ARE BAD! HE COULD BE A SERIAL KILLER! YOU DON'T KNOW!
I *DO* KNOW!
HE WAS PLAYING ONE OF MUM'S SONGS BETTER THAN SHE DID HERSELF!
A BAD PERSON COULDN'T PLAY THAT BEAUTIFULLY!
I *KNOW* IT.
CREE...
YOU AND I BOTH KNOW WHEN IT COMES TO YOUR MOTHER'S MUSIC, YOU TEND TO GET A TAD... SENSITIVE.
NO, I DON'T!
...
OKAY, MAYBE A LITTLE.
I'LL GO LISTEN TO HIM...
204 KAINER
...BUT THEN HE'S GOT TO GO. GOT IT?
FINE.

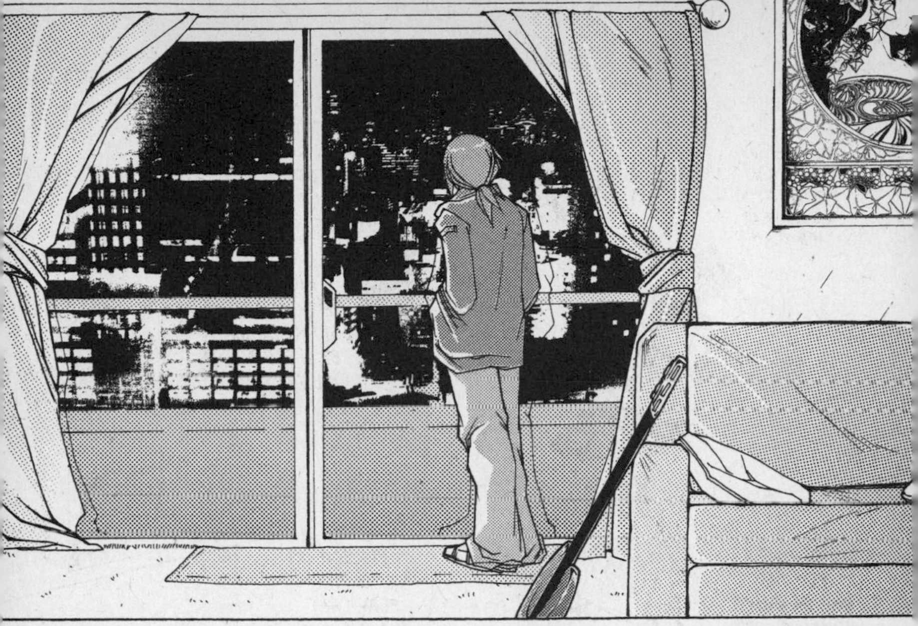

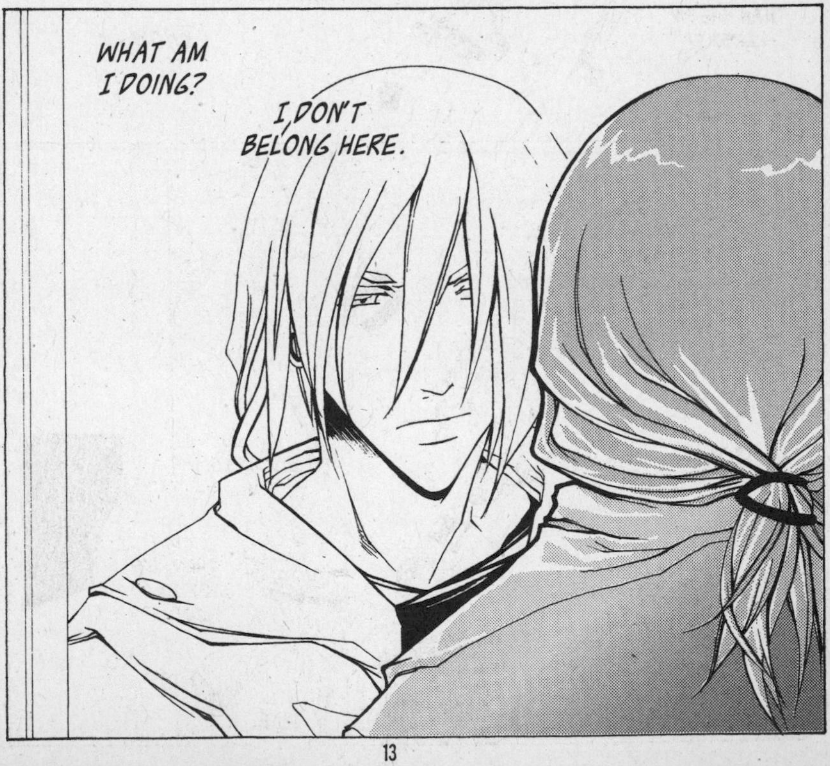
WHAT AM I DOING?
I DON'T BELONG HERE.

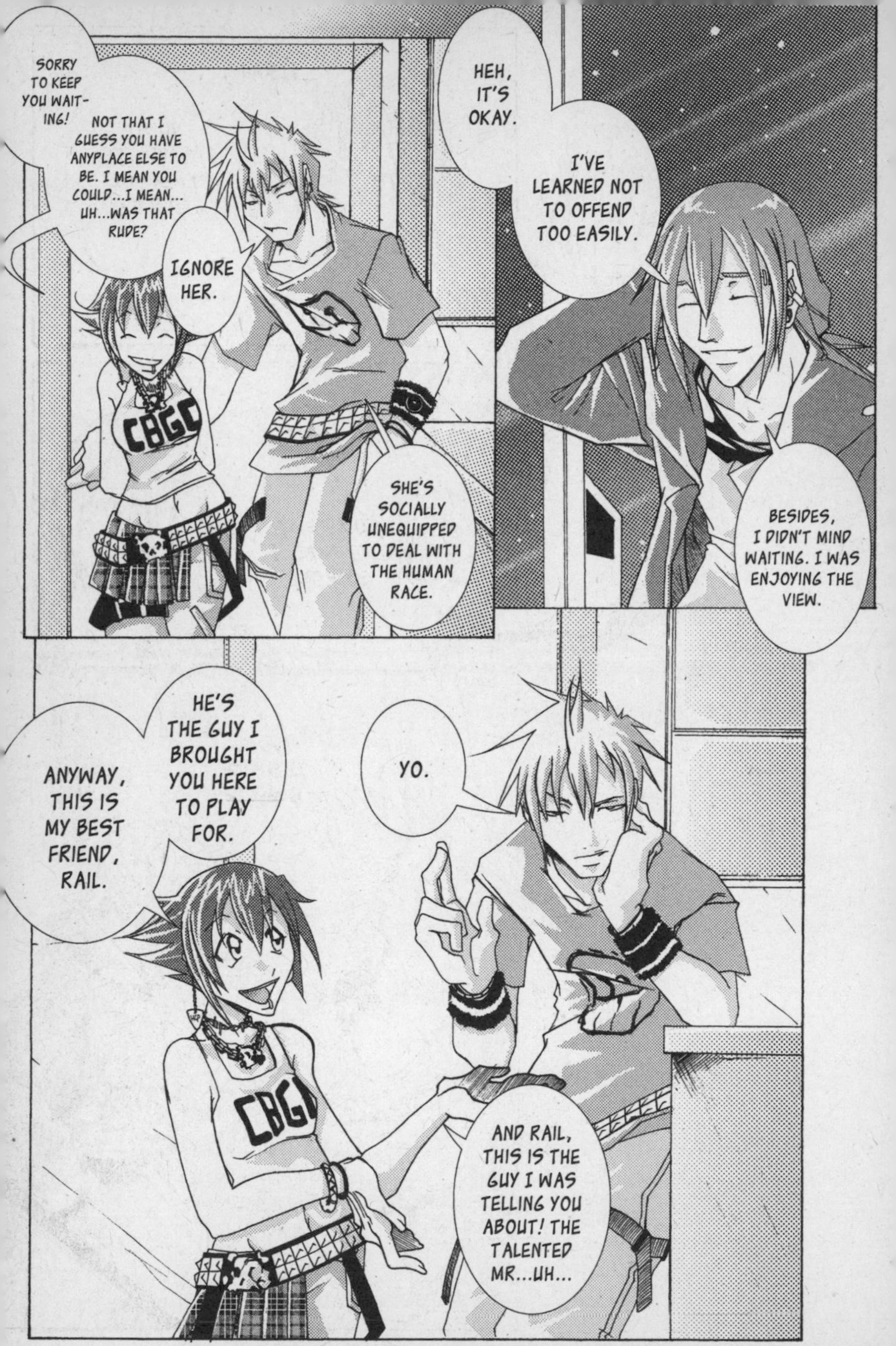
SORRY TO KEEP YOU WAIT-ING!
NOT THAT I GUESS YOU HAVE ANYPLACE ELSE TO BE. I MEAN YOU COULD...I MEAN... UH...WAS THAT RUDE?
IGNORE HER.
SHE'S SOCIALLY UNEQUIPPED TO DEAL WITH THE HUMAN RACE.
HEH, IT'S OKAY.
I'VE LEARNED NOT TO OFFEND TOO EASILY.
BESIDES, I DIDN'T MIND WAITING. I WAS ENJOYING THE VIEW.
ANYWAY, THIS IS MY BEST FRIEND, RAIL.
HE'S THE GUY I BROUGHT YOU HERE TO PLAY FOR.
YO.
AND RAIL, THIS IS THE GUY I WAS TELLING YOU ABOUT! THE TALENTED MR...UH...

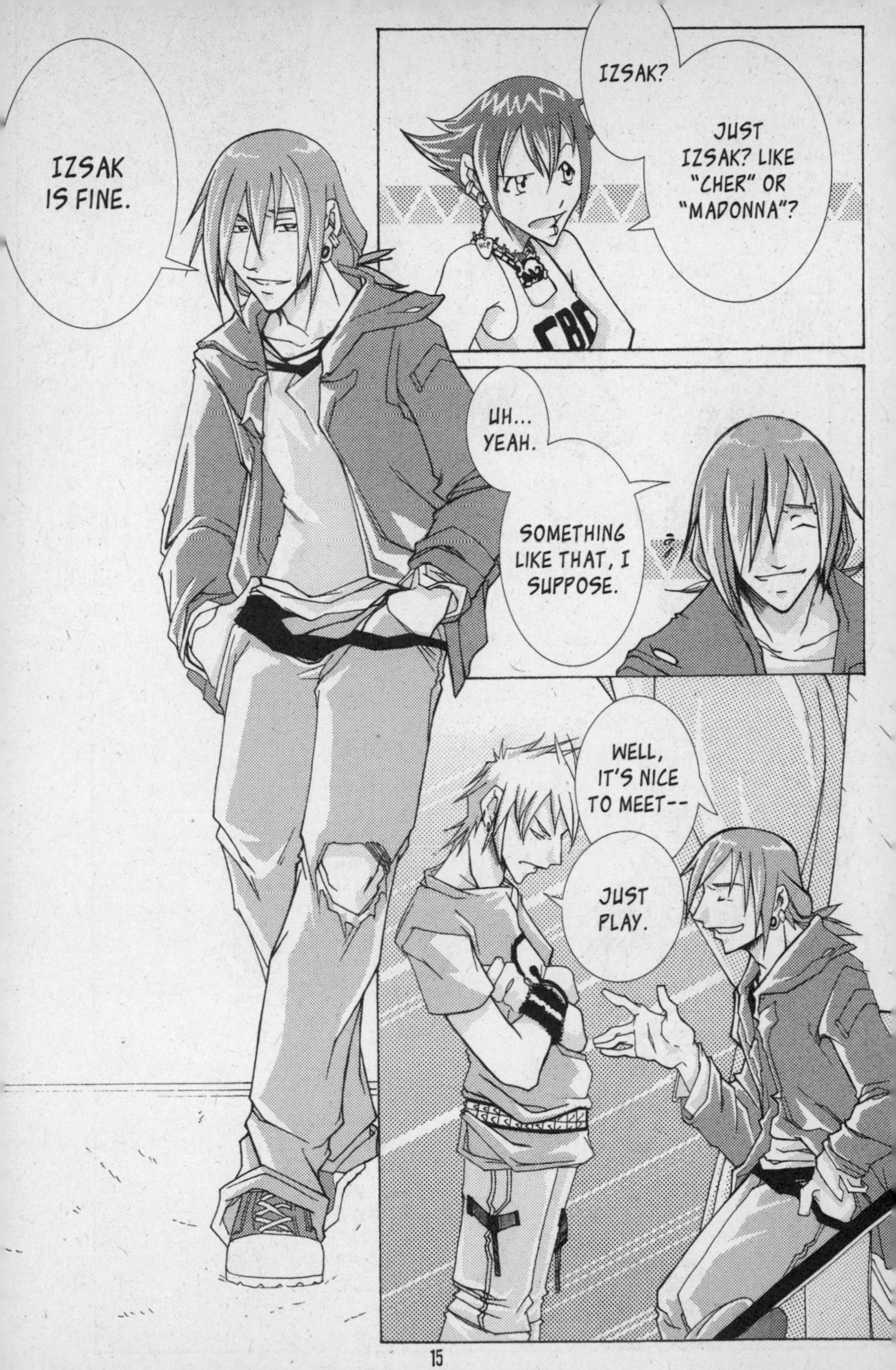
IZSAK IS FINE.
IZSAK?
JUST IZSAK? LIKE "CHER" OR "MADONNA"?
UH... YEAH.
SOMETHING LIKE THAT, I SUPPOSE.
WELL, IT'S NICE TO MEET--
JUST PLAY.

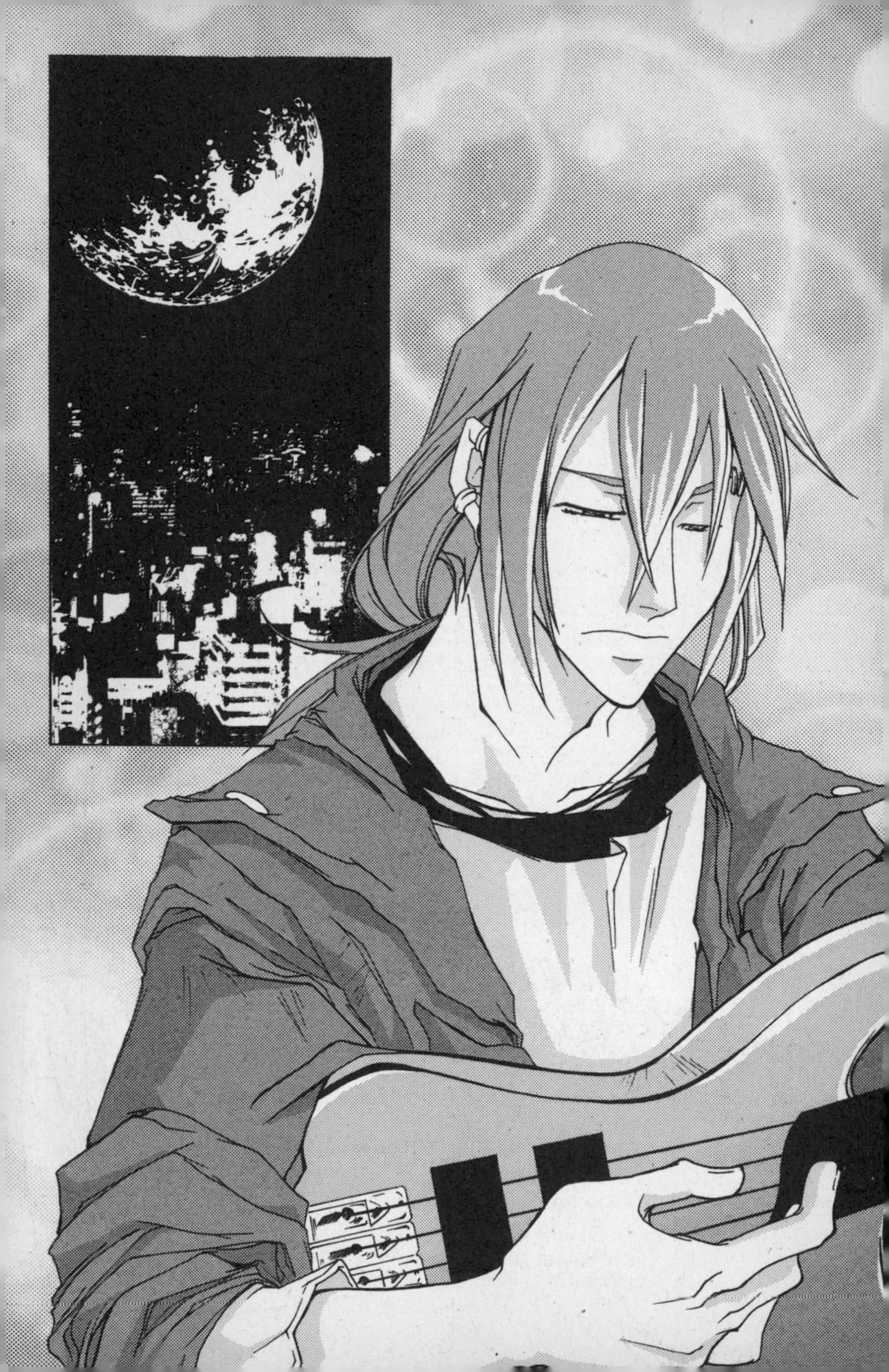

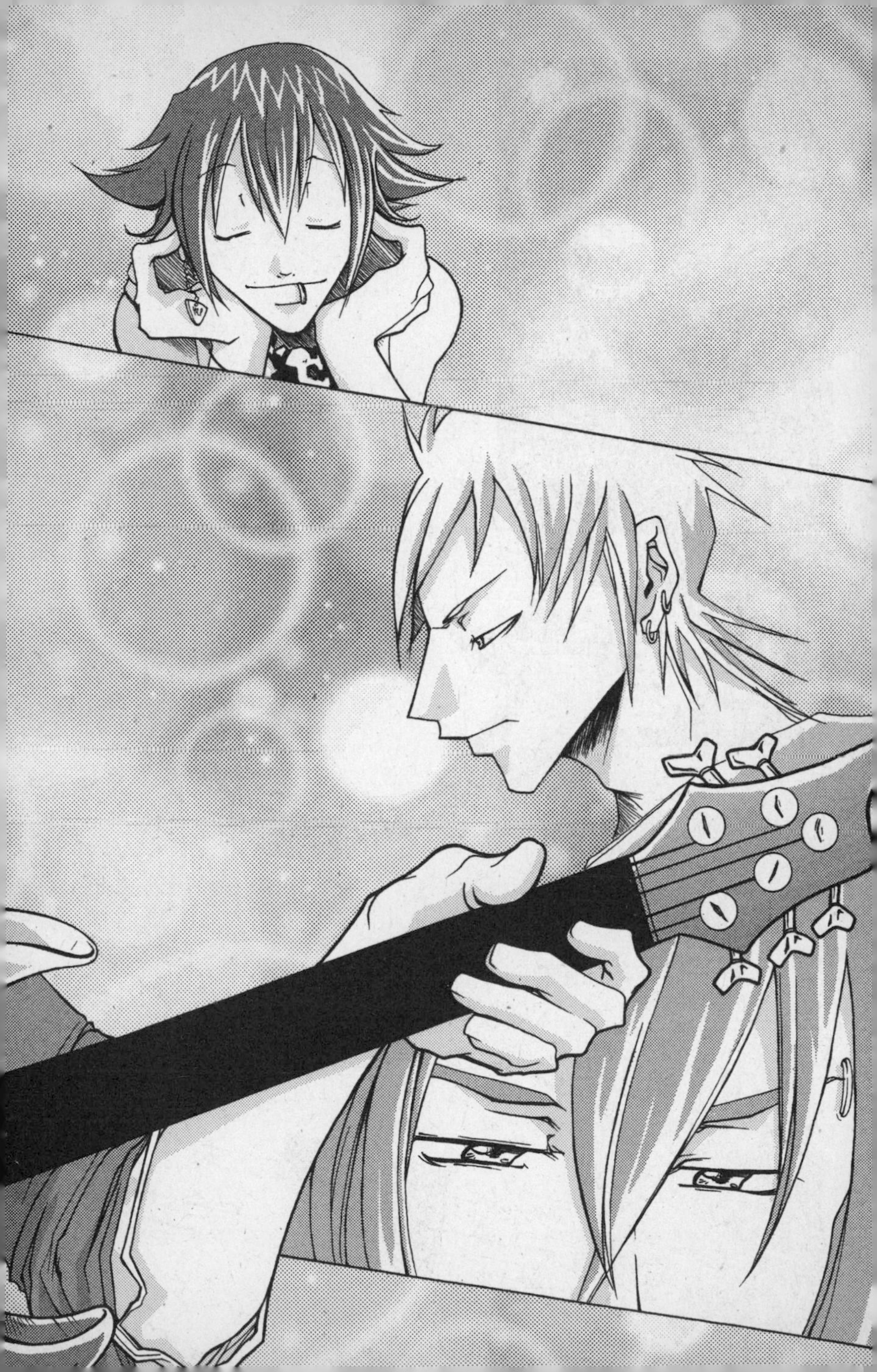

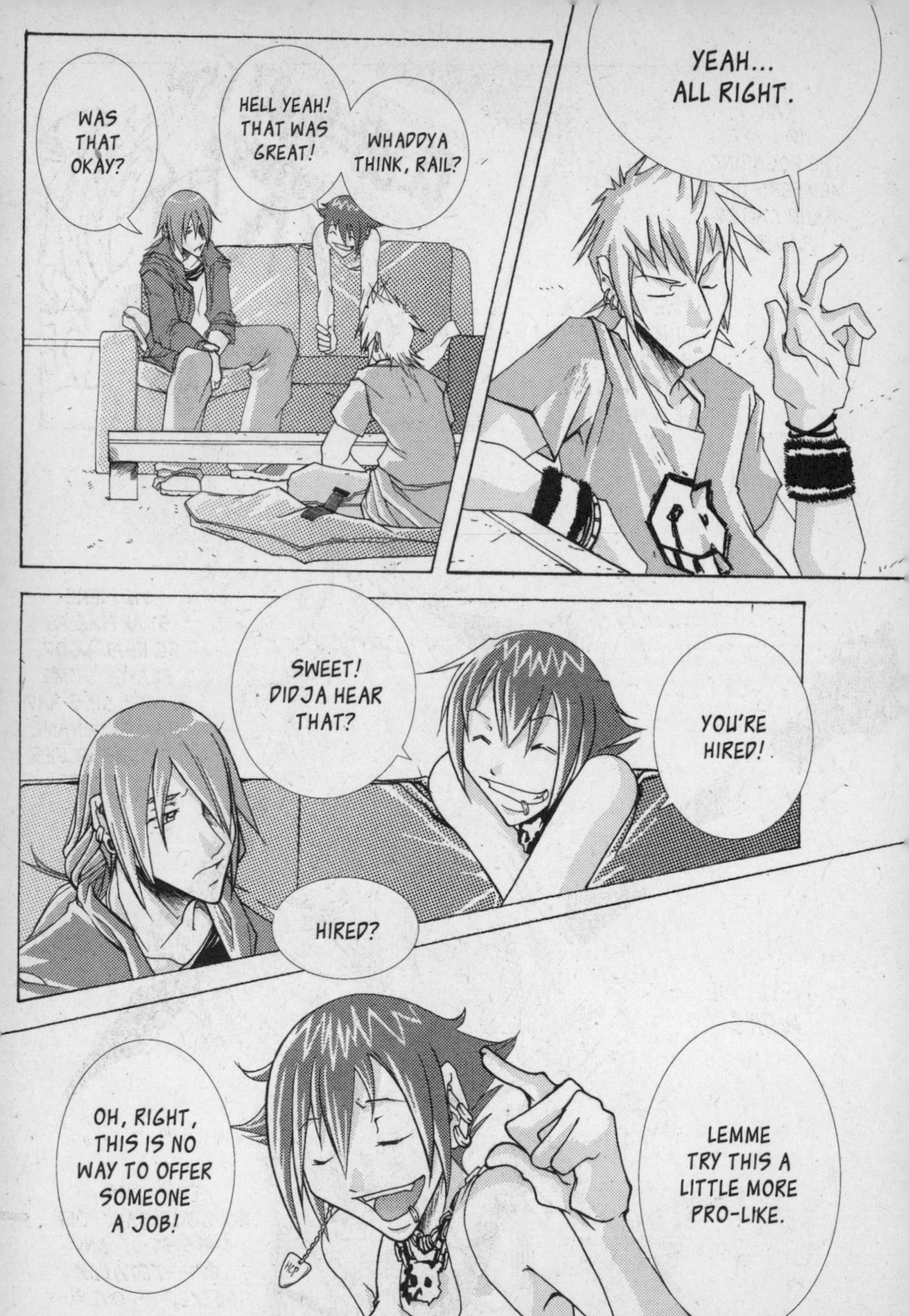
WAS THAT OKAY?
HELL YEAH! THAT WAS GREAT!
WHADDYA THINK, RAIL?
YEAH... ALL RIGHT.
SWEET! DIDJA HEAR THAT?
YOU'RE HIRED!
HIRED?
OH, RIGHT, THIS IS NO WAY TO OFFER SOMEONE A JOB!
LEMME TRY THIS A LITTLE MORE PRO-LIKE.

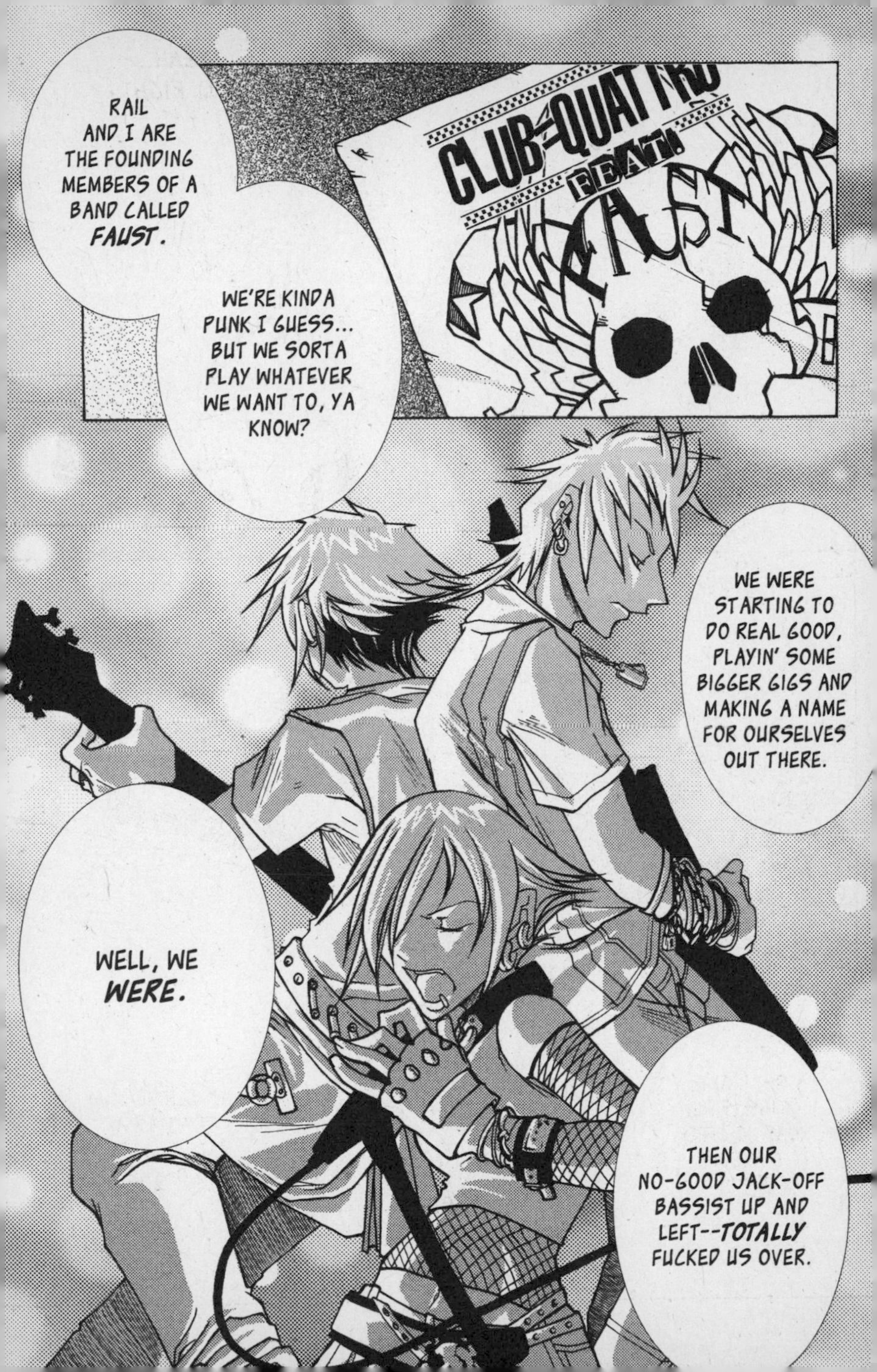
RAIL AND I ARE THE FOUNDING MEMBERS OF A BAND CALLED *FAUST*.
WE'RE KINDA PUNK I GUESS... BUT WE SORTA PLAY WHATEVER WE WANT TO, YA KNOW?
CLUB-QUATTRO
FEAT!
FAUST
WE WERE STARTING TO DO REAL GOOD, PLAYIN' SOME BIGGER GIGS AND MAKING A NAME FOR OURSELVES OUT THERE.
WELL, WE *WERE*.
THEN OUR NO-GOOD JACK-OFF BASSIST UP AND LEFT--*TOTALLY* FUCKED US OVER.

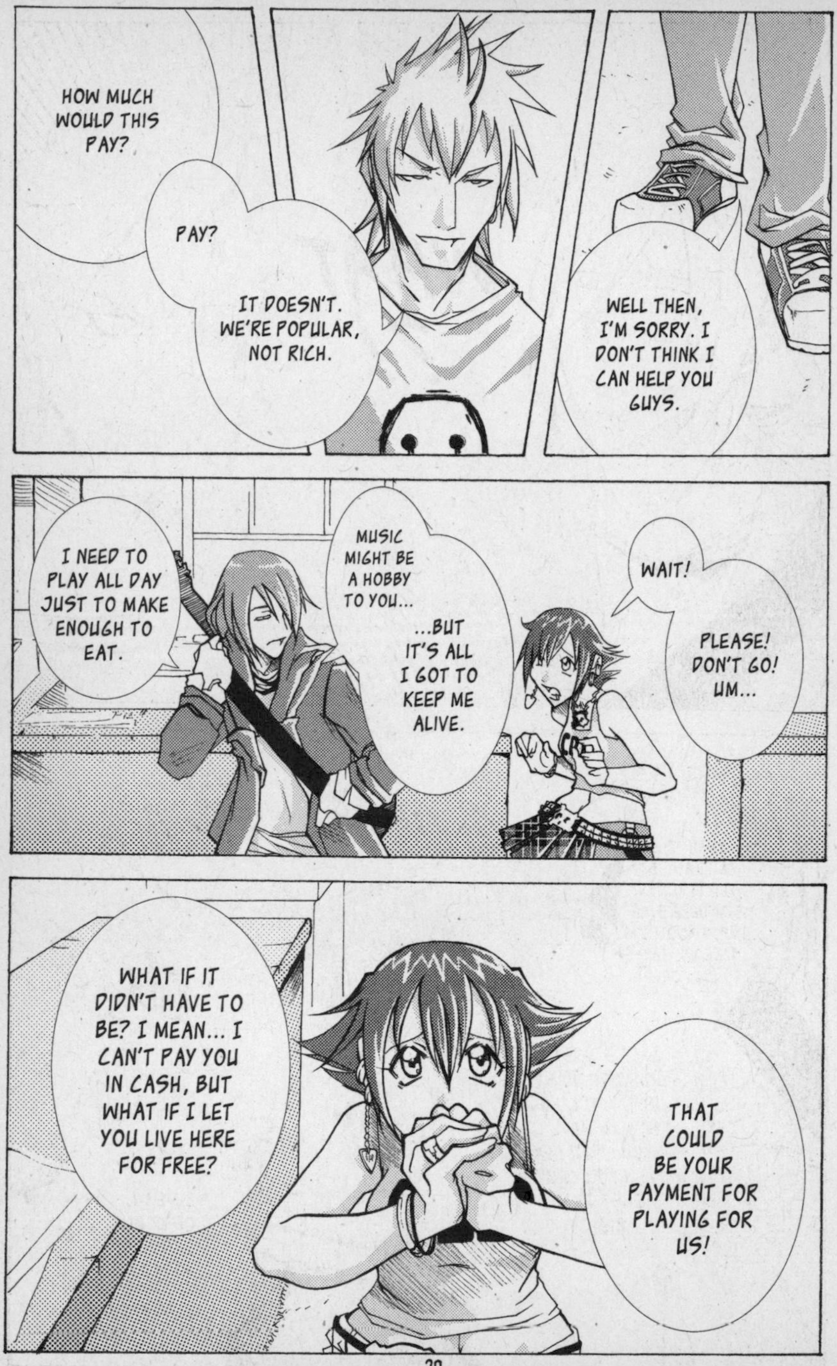
HOW MUCH WOULD THIS PAY?
PAY?
IT DOESN'T. WE'RE POPULAR, NOT RICH.
WELL THEN, I'M SORRY. I DON'T THINK I CAN HELP YOU GUYS.
I NEED TO PLAY ALL DAY JUST TO MAKE ENOUGH TO EAT.
MUSIC MIGHT BE A HOBBY TO YOU...
...BUT IT'S ALL I GOT TO KEEP ME ALIVE.
WAIT!
PLEASE! DON'T GO! UM...
WHAT IF IT DIDN'T HAVE TO BE? I MEAN... I CAN'T PAY YOU IN CASH, BUT WHAT IF I LET YOU LIVE HERE FOR FREE?
THAT COULD BE YOUR PAYMENT FOR PLAYING FOR US!

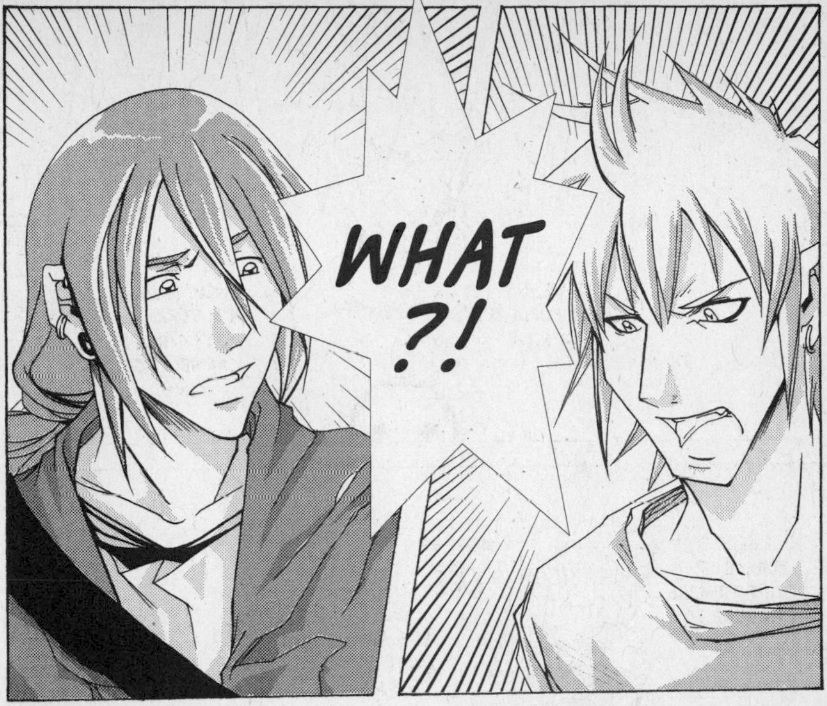
WHAT?!

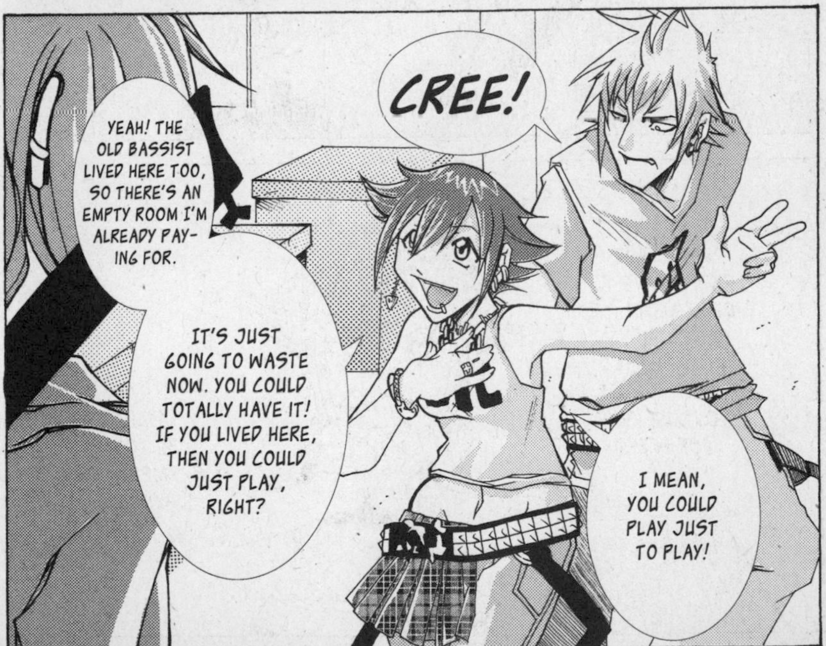
YEAH! THE OLD BASSIST LIVED HERE TOO, SO THERE'S AN EMPTY ROOM I'M ALREADY PAY-ING FOR.
CREE!
IT'S JUST GOING TO WASTE NOW. YOU COULD TOTALLY HAVE IT! IF YOU LIVED HERE, THEN YOU COULD JUST PLAY, RIGHT?
I MEAN, YOU COULD PLAY JUST TO PLAY!

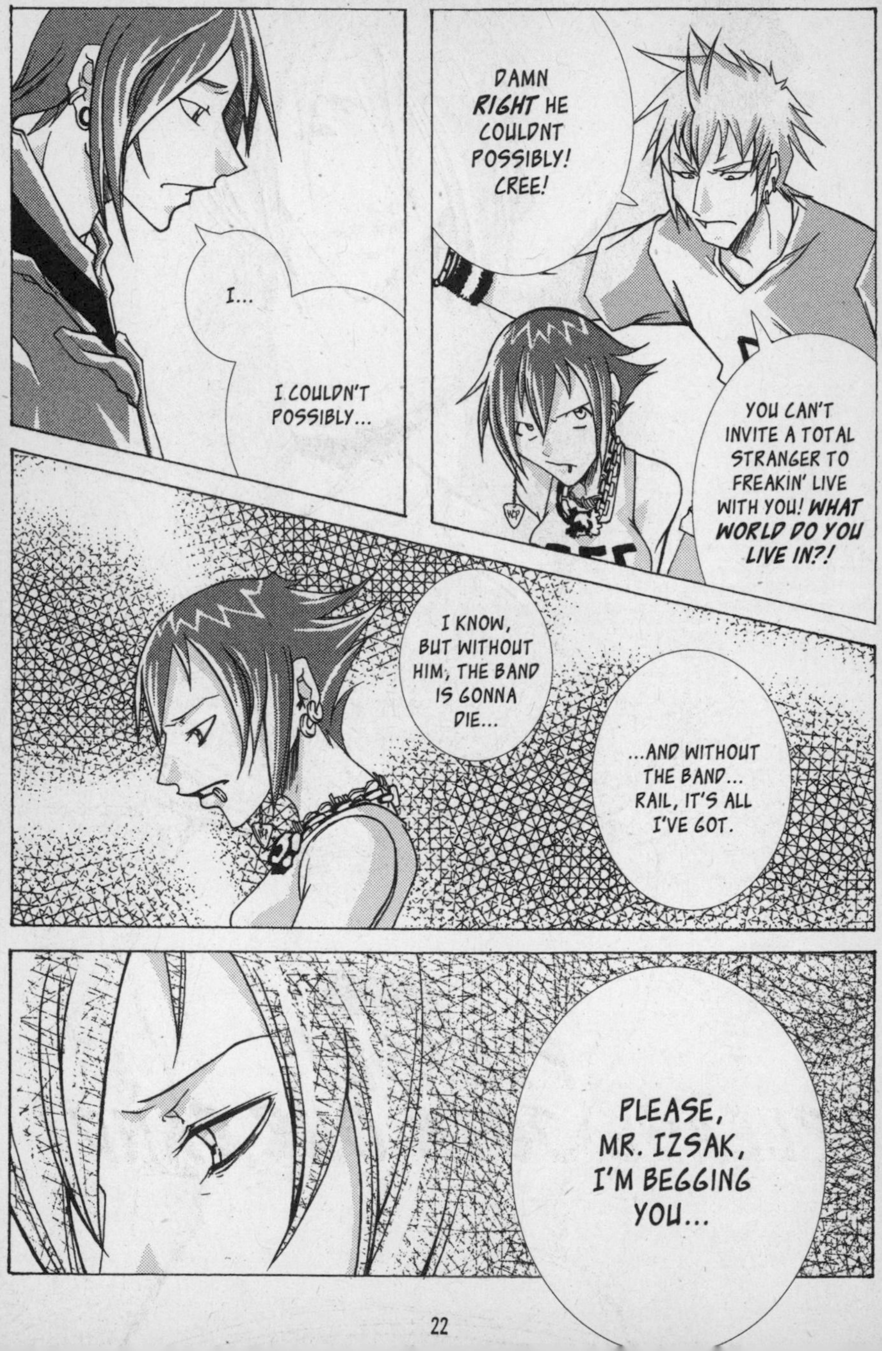
I...
I COULDN'T POSSIBLY...
DAMN **RIGHT** HE COULDNT POSSIBLY! CREE!
YOU CAN'T INVITE A TOTAL STRANGER TO FREAKIN' LIVE WITH YOU! ***WHAT WORLD DO YOU LIVE IN?!***
I KNOW, BUT WITHOUT HIM, THE BAND IS GONNA DIE...
...AND WITHOUT THE BAND... RAIL, IT'S ALL I'VE GOT.
PLEASE, MR. IZSAK, I'M BEGGING YOU...

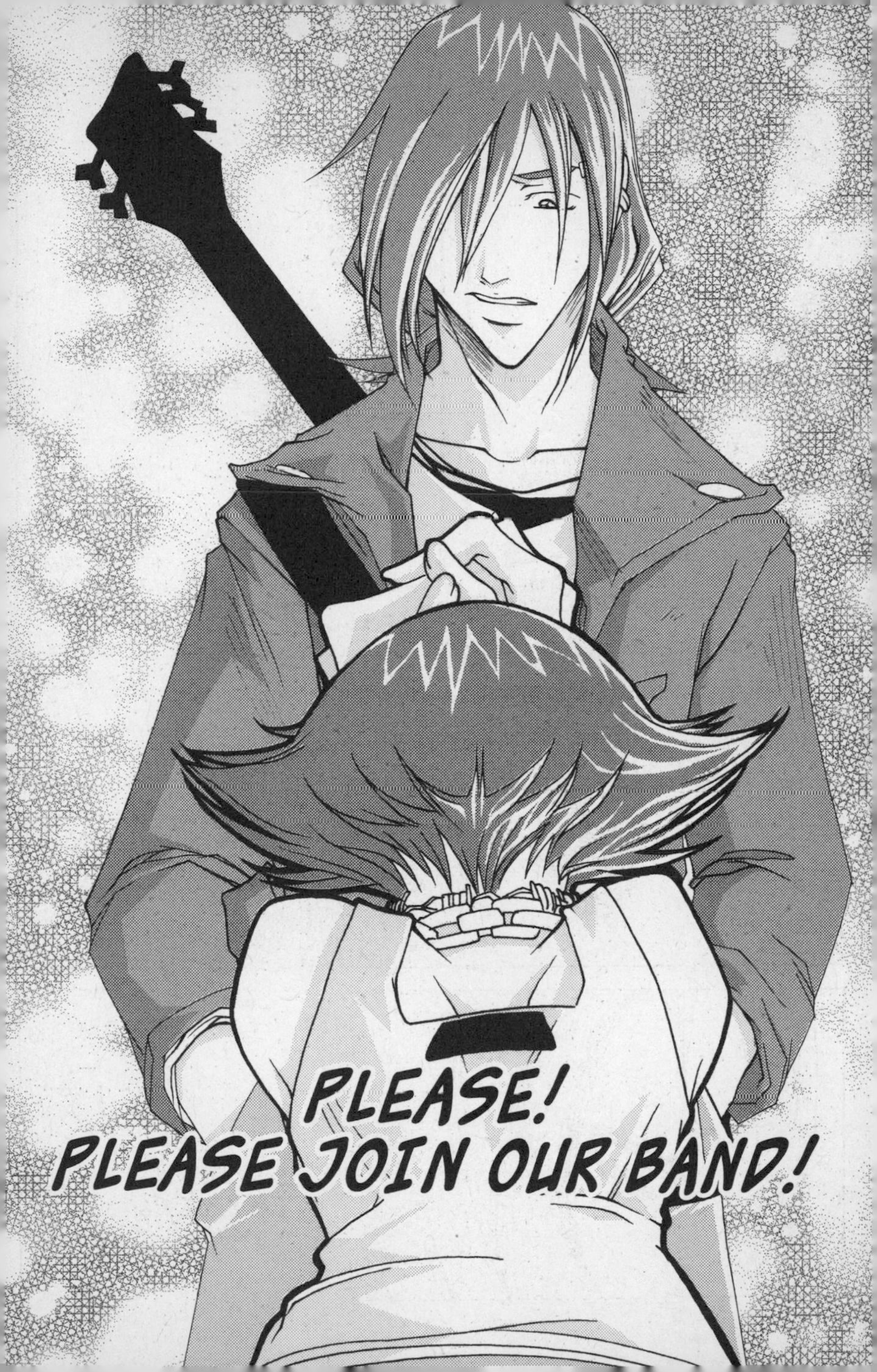
PLEASE!
PLEASE JOIN OUR BAND!

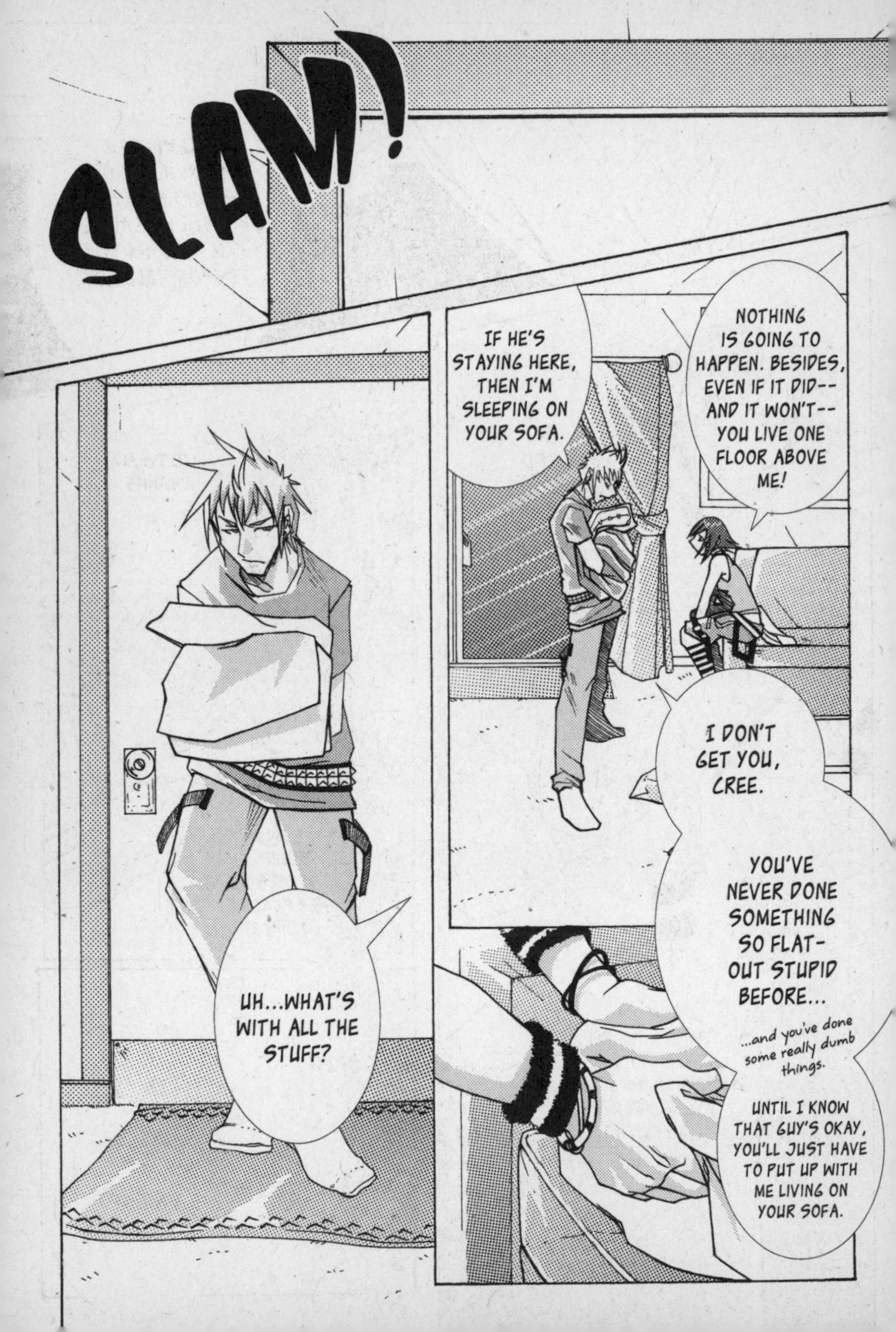
SLAM!
UH...WHAT'S WITH ALL THE STUFF?
IF HE'S STAYING HERE, THEN I'M SLEEPING ON YOUR SOFA.
NOTHING IS GOING TO HAPPEN. BESIDES, EVEN IF IT DID--AND IT WON'T--YOU LIVE ONE FLOOR ABOVE ME!
I DON'T GET YOU, CREE.
YOU'VE NEVER DONE SOMETHING SO FLAT-OUT STUPID BEFORE...
...and you've done some really dumb things.
UNTIL I KNOW THAT GUY'S OKAY, YOU'LL JUST HAVE TO PUT UP WITH ME LIVING ON YOUR SOFA.

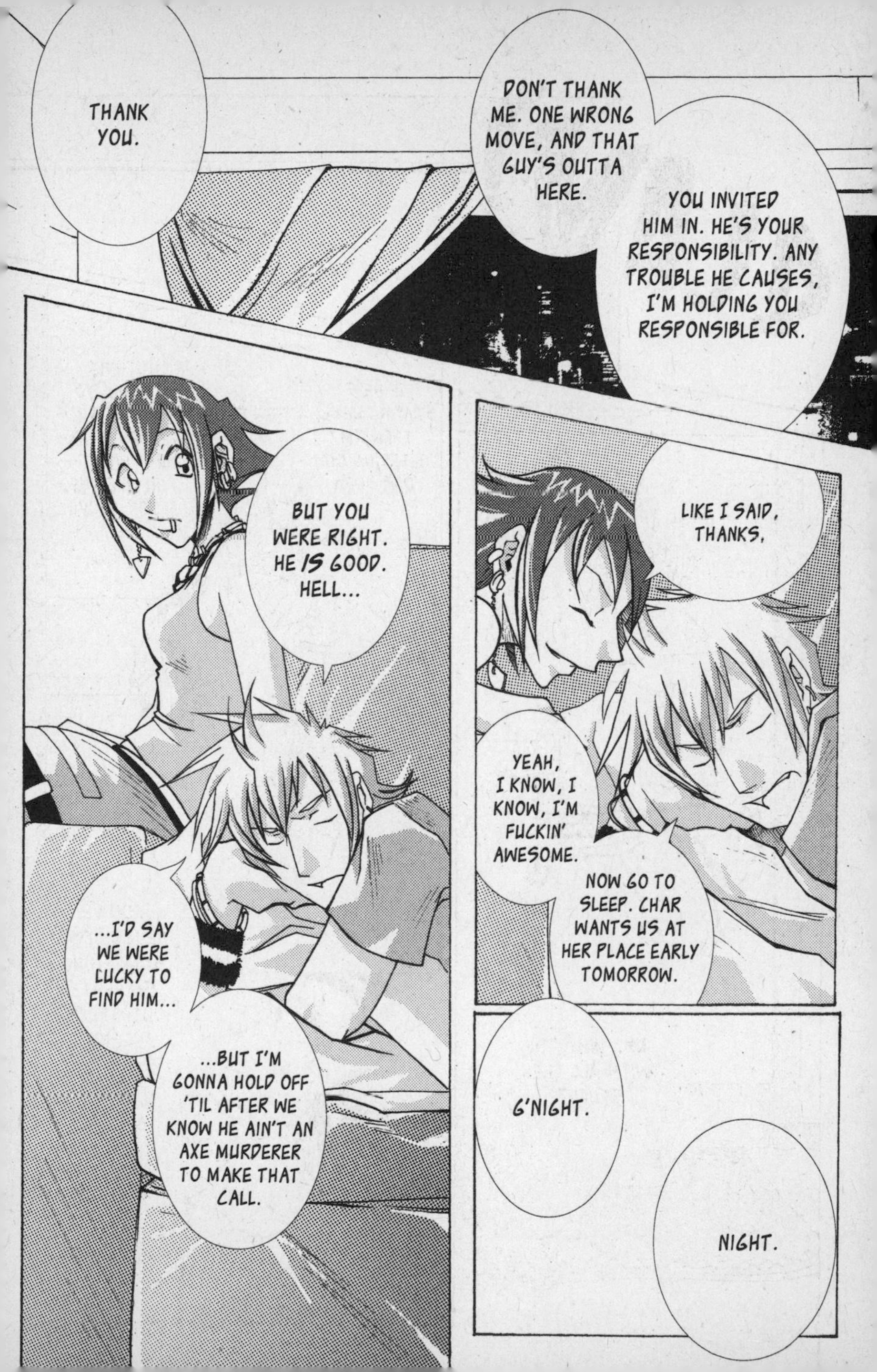
THANK YOU.
DON'T THANK ME. ONE WRONG MOVE, AND THAT GUY'S OUTTA HERE.
YOU INVITED HIM IN. HE'S YOUR RESPONSIBILITY. ANY TROUBLE HE CAUSES, I'M HOLDING YOU RESPONSIBLE FOR.
BUT YOU WERE RIGHT. HE *IS* GOOD. HELL...
...I'D SAY WE WERE LUCKY TO FIND HIM...
...BUT I'M GONNA HOLD OFF 'TIL AFTER WE KNOW HE AIN'T AN AXE MURDERER TO MAKE THAT CALL.
LIKE I SAID, THANKS.
YEAH, I KNOW, I KNOW, I'M FUCKIN' AWESOME.
NOW GO TO SLEEP. CHAR WANTS US AT HER PLACE EARLY TOMORROW.
G'NIGHT.
NIGHT.

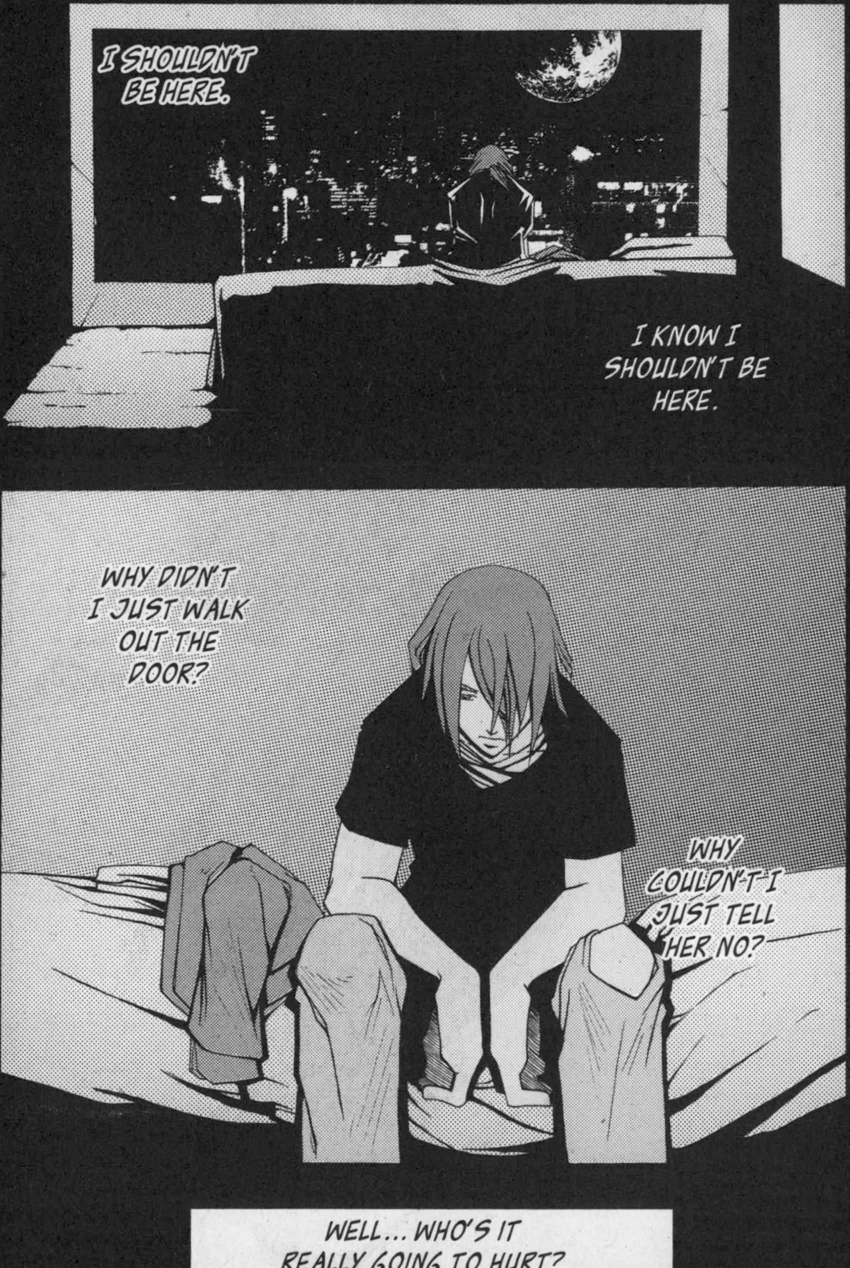
I SHOULDN'T BE HERE.
I KNOW I SHOULDN'T BE HERE.
WHY DIDN'T I JUST WALK OUT THE DOOR?
WHY COULDN'T I JUST TELL HER NO?
WELL... WHO'S IT REALLY GOING TO HURT?

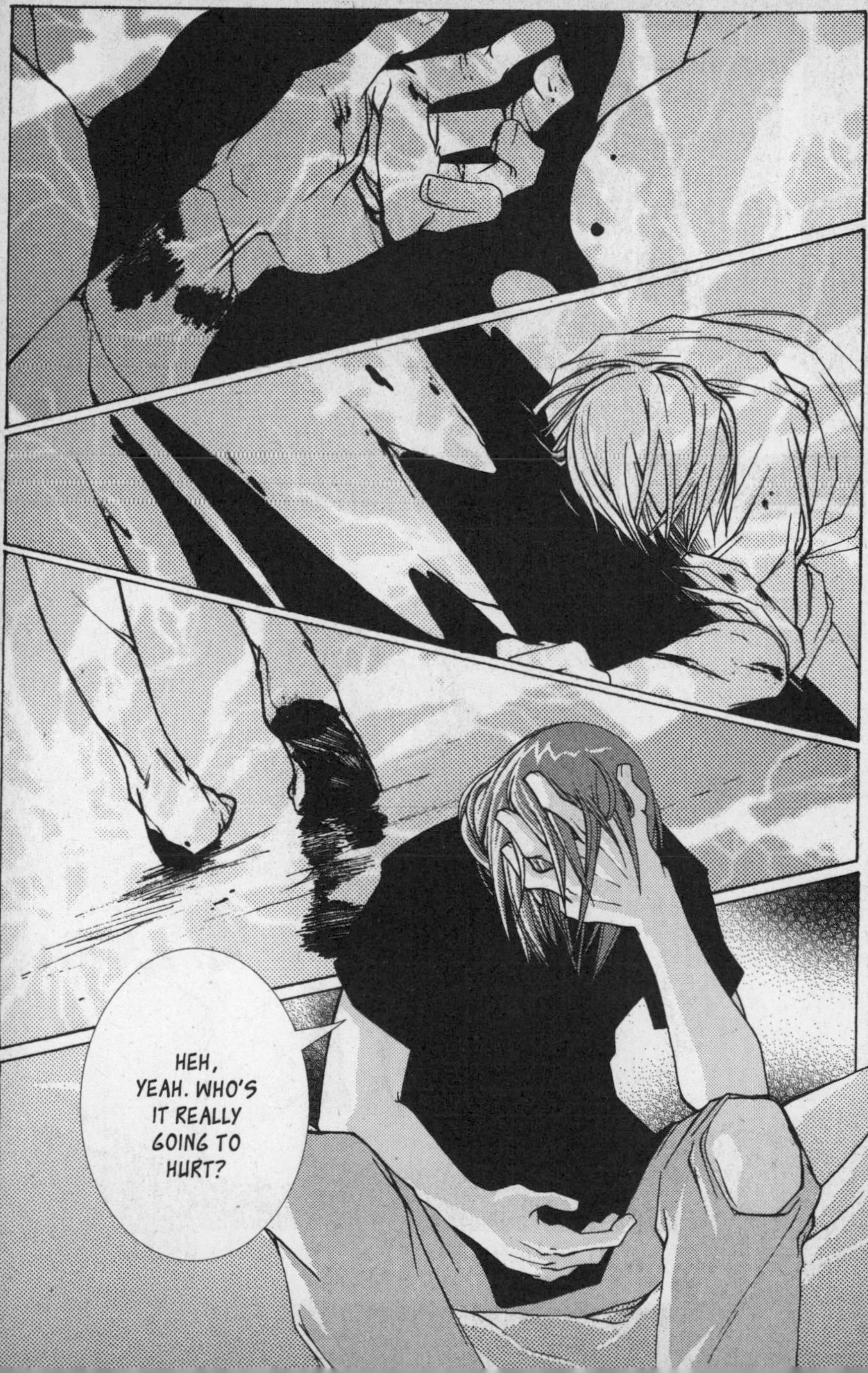
HEH, YEAH. WHO'S IT REALLY GOING TO HURT?

CHAPTER 2

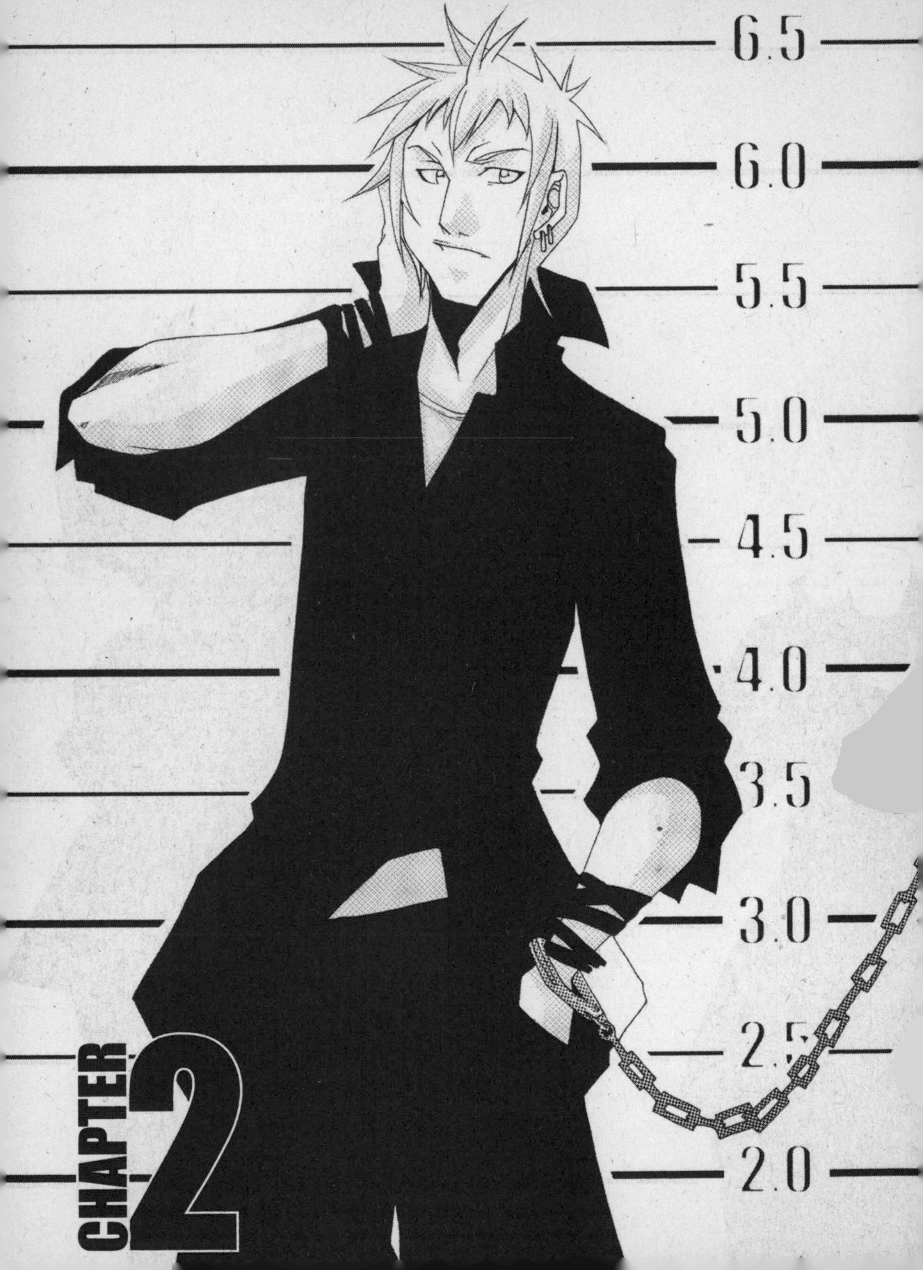
6.5
6.0
5.5
5.0
4.5
4.0
3.5
3.0
2.5
2.0

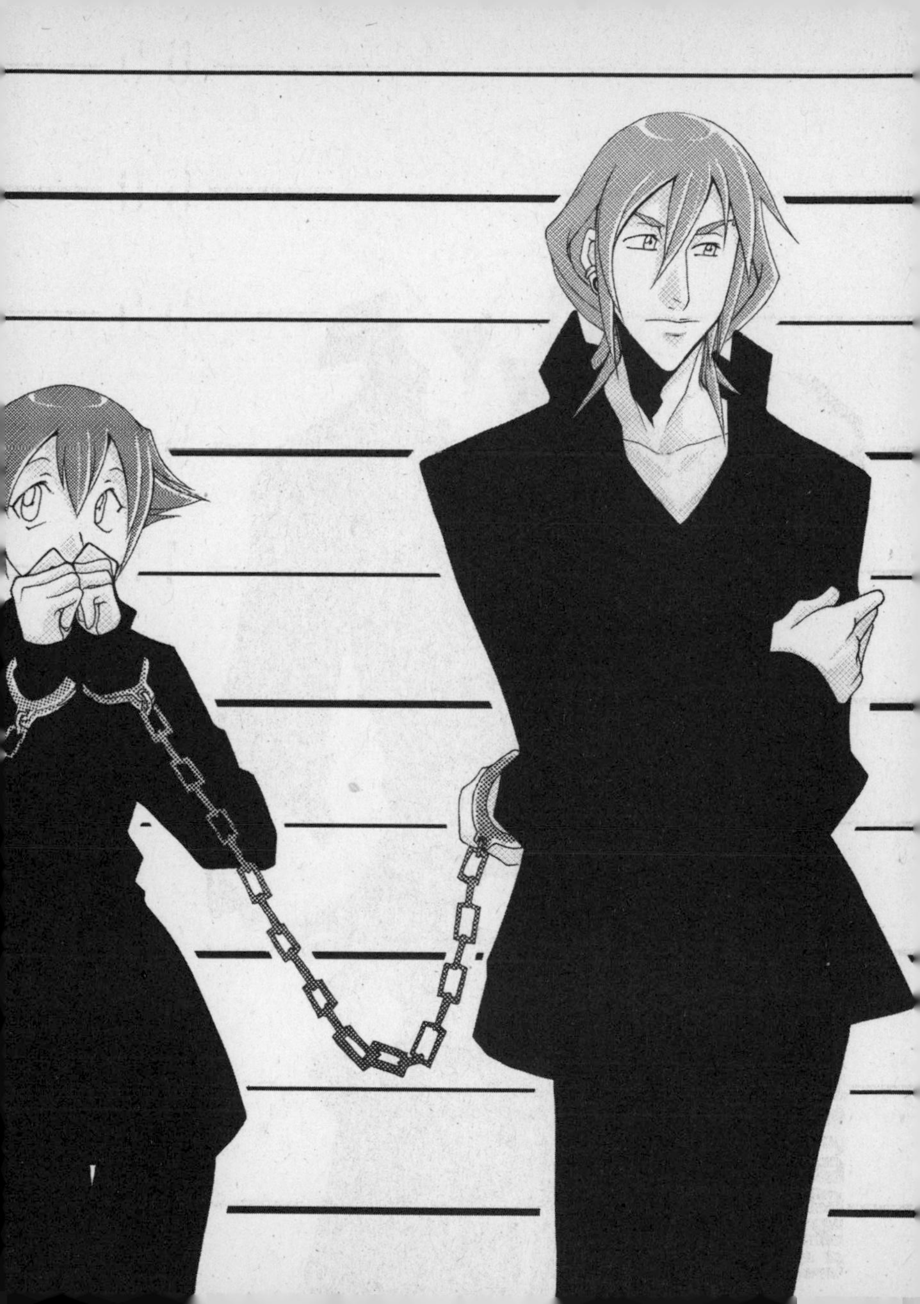

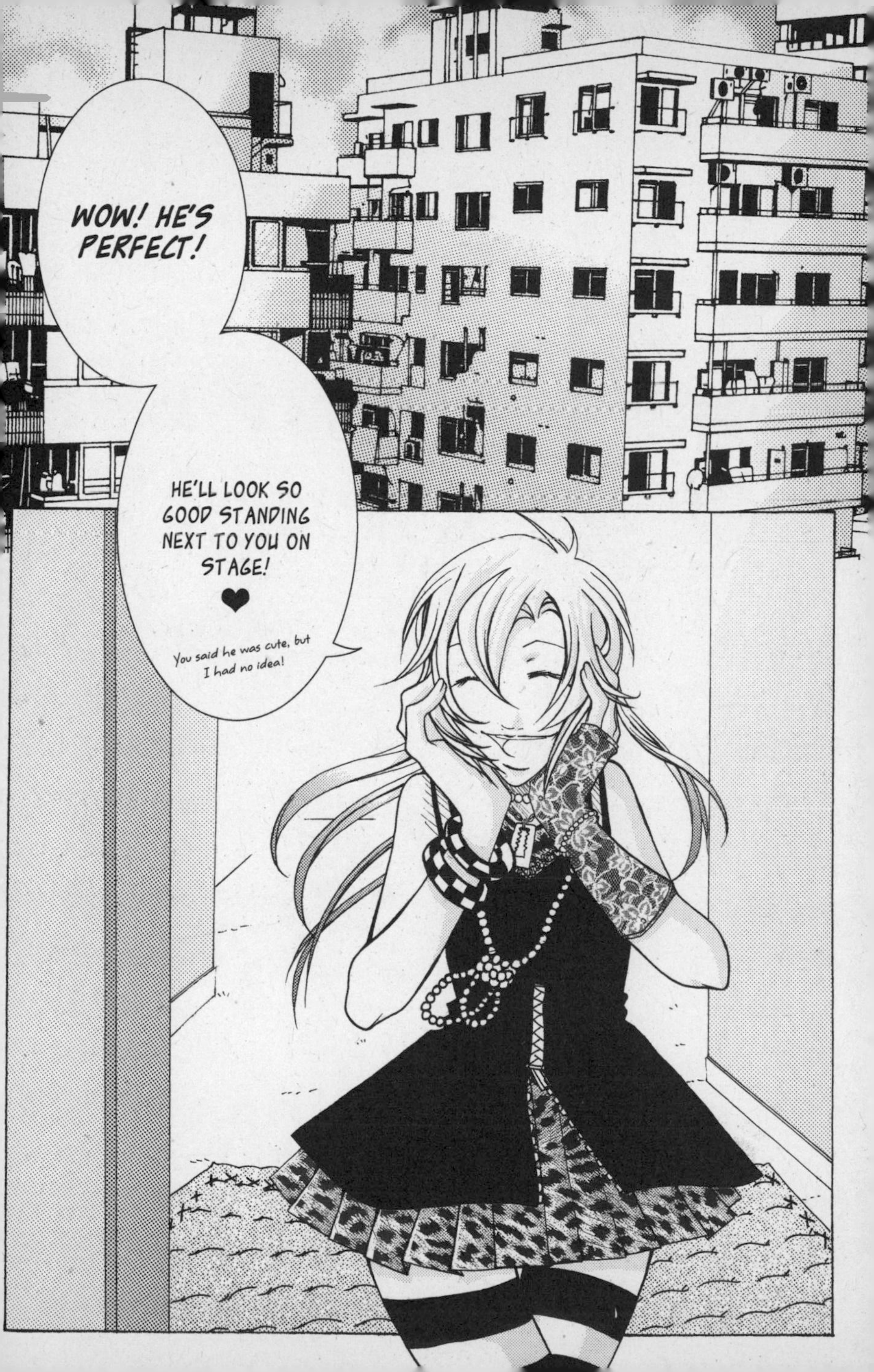
WOW! HE'S PERFECT!
HE'LL LOOK SO GOOD STANDING NEXT TO YOU ON STAGE! ❤
You said he was cute, but I had no idea!

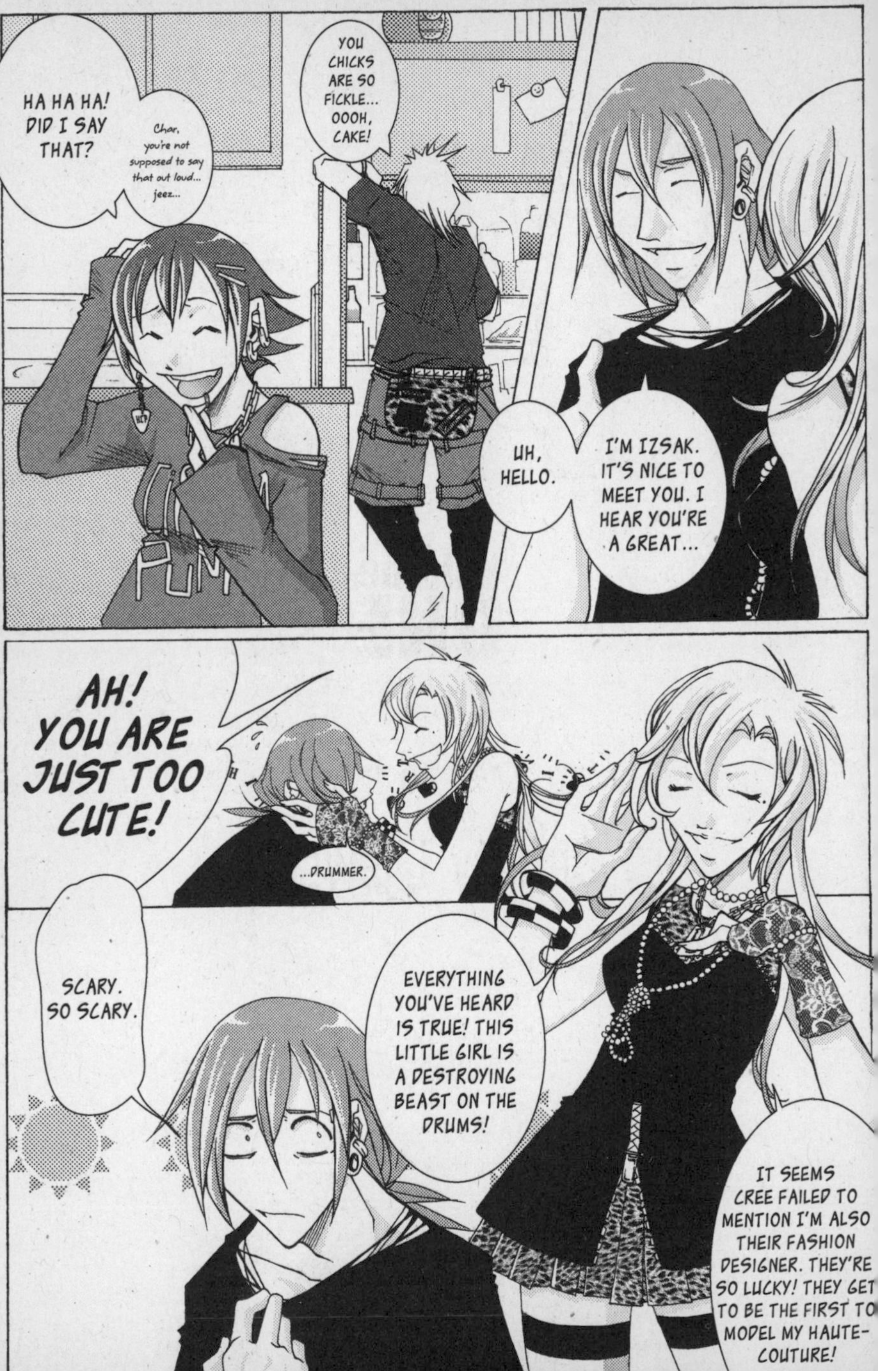
HA HA HA! DID I SAY THAT?
Char, you're not supposed to say that out loud... jeez...
YOU CHICKS ARE SO FICKLE... OOOH, CAKE!
UH, HELLO.
I'M IZSAK. IT'S NICE TO MEET YOU. I HEAR YOU'RE A GREAT...
AH! YOU ARE JUST TOO CUTE!
...DRUMMER.
SCARY. SO SCARY.
EVERYTHING YOU'VE HEARD IS TRUE! THIS LITTLE GIRL IS A DESTROYING BEAST ON THE DRUMS!
IT SEEMS CREE FAILED TO MENTION I'M ALSO THEIR FASHION DESIGNER. THEY'RE SO LUCKY! THEY GET TO BE THE FIRST TO MODEL MY HAUTE-COUTURE!

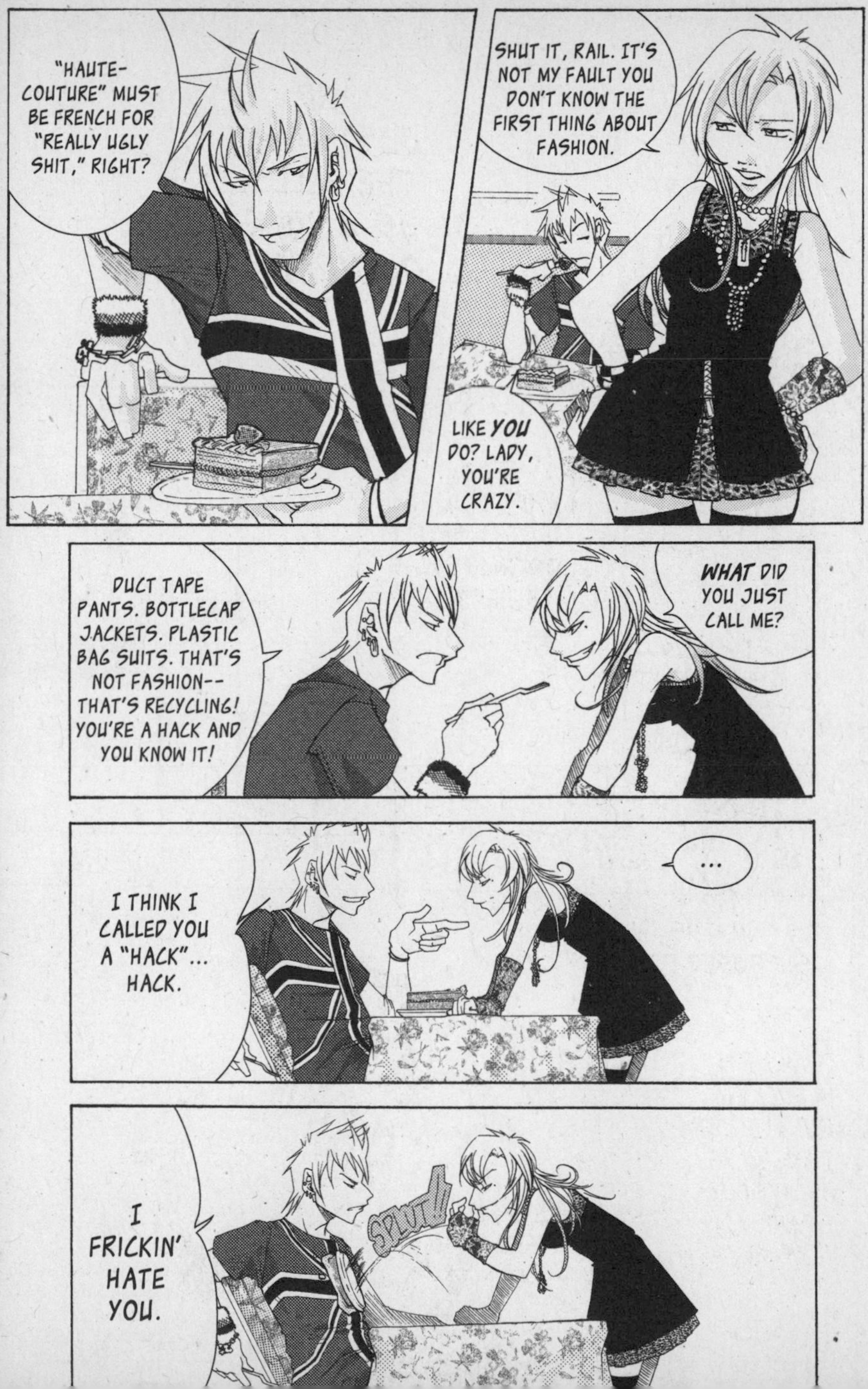
"HAUTE-COUTURE" MUST BE FRENCH FOR "REALLY UGLY SHIT," RIGHT?
SHUT IT, RAIL. IT'S NOT MY FAULT YOU DON'T KNOW THE FIRST THING ABOUT FASHION.
LIKE *YOU* DO? LADY, YOU'RE CRAZY.
DUCT TAPE PANTS. BOTTLECAP JACKETS. PLASTIC BAG SUITS. THAT'S NOT FASHION--THAT'S RECYCLING! YOU'RE A HACK AND YOU KNOW IT!
WHAT DID YOU JUST CALL ME?
I THINK I CALLED YOU A "HACK"... HACK.
...
I FRICKIN' HATE YOU.
SPLUT!!

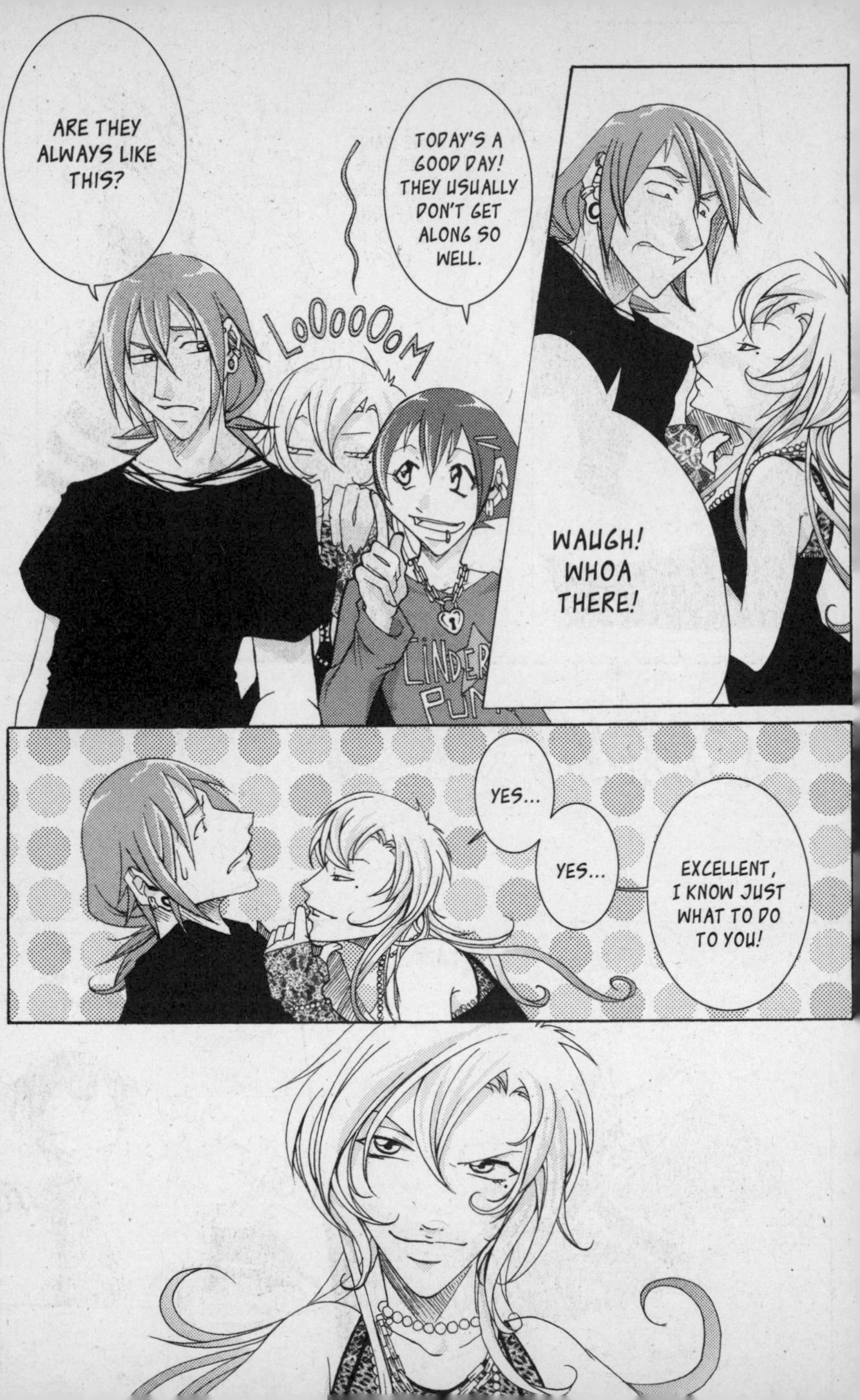
ARE THEY ALWAYS LIKE THIS?
TODAY'S A GOOD DAY! THEY USUALLY DON'T GET ALONG SO WELL.
LOOOOOOM
WAUGH! WHOA THERE!
YES...
YES...
EXCELLENT, I KNOW JUST WHAT TO DO TO YOU!

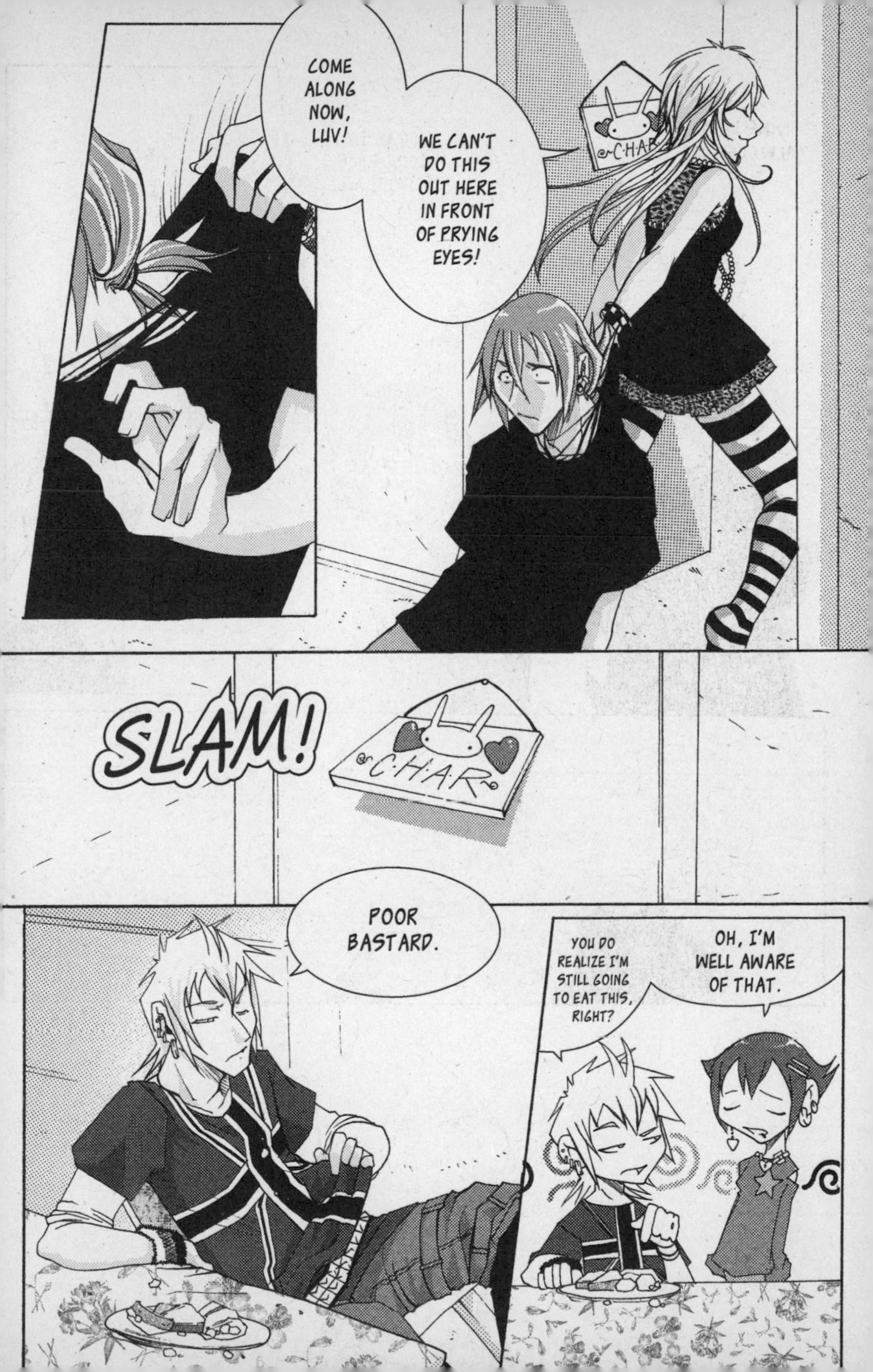
COME ALONG NOW, LUV!
WE CAN'T DO THIS OUT HERE IN FRONT OF PRYING EYES!
C·H·A·R
SLAM!
C·H·A·R
POOR BASTARD.
YOU DO REALIZE I'M STILL GOING TO EAT THIS, RIGHT?
OH, I'M WELL AWARE OF THAT.

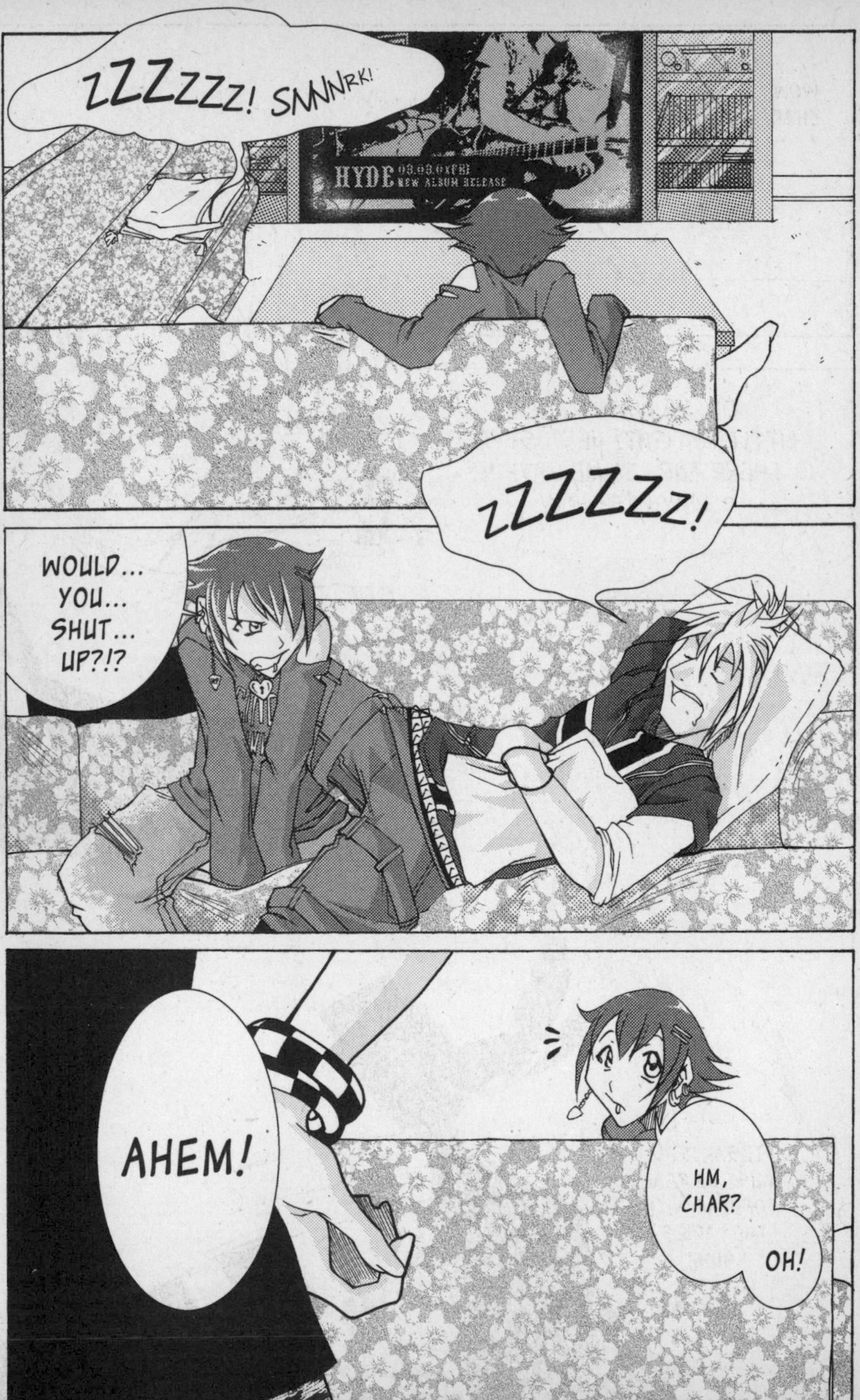
ZZZzzzz! SNNNRK!
HYDE
NEW ALBUM RELEASE
zZZZZZz!
WOULD... YOU... SHUT... UP?!?
AHEM!
HM, CHAR?
OH!

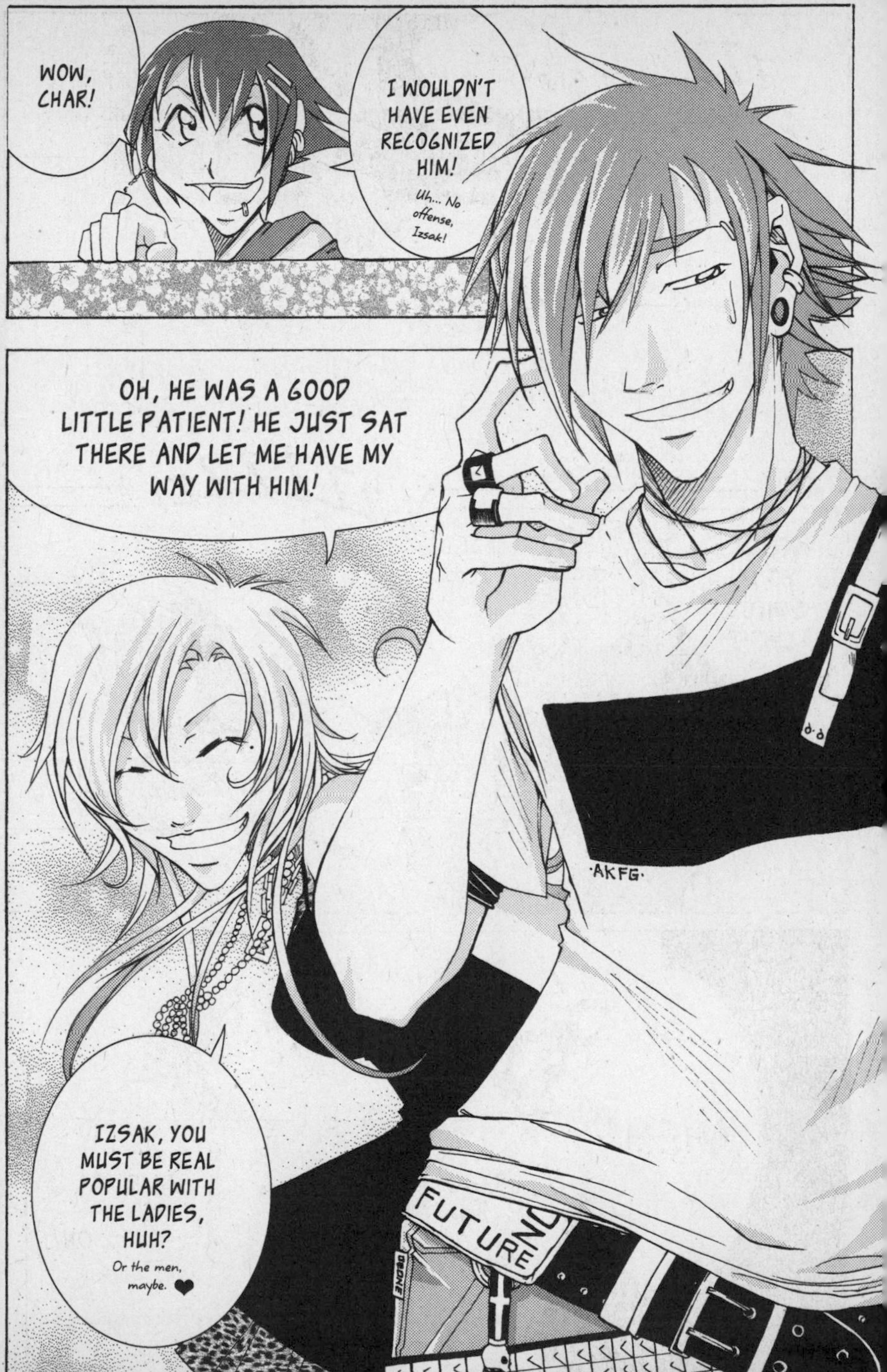
WOW, CHAR!
I WOULDN'T HAVE EVEN RECOGNIZED HIM!
Uh... No offense, Izsak!
OH, HE WAS A GOOD LITTLE PATIENT! HE JUST SAT THERE AND LET ME HAVE MY WAY WITH HIM!
·AKFG·
IZSAK, YOU MUST BE REAL POPULAR WITH THE LADIES, HUH?
Or the men, maybe. ❤
FUTURE

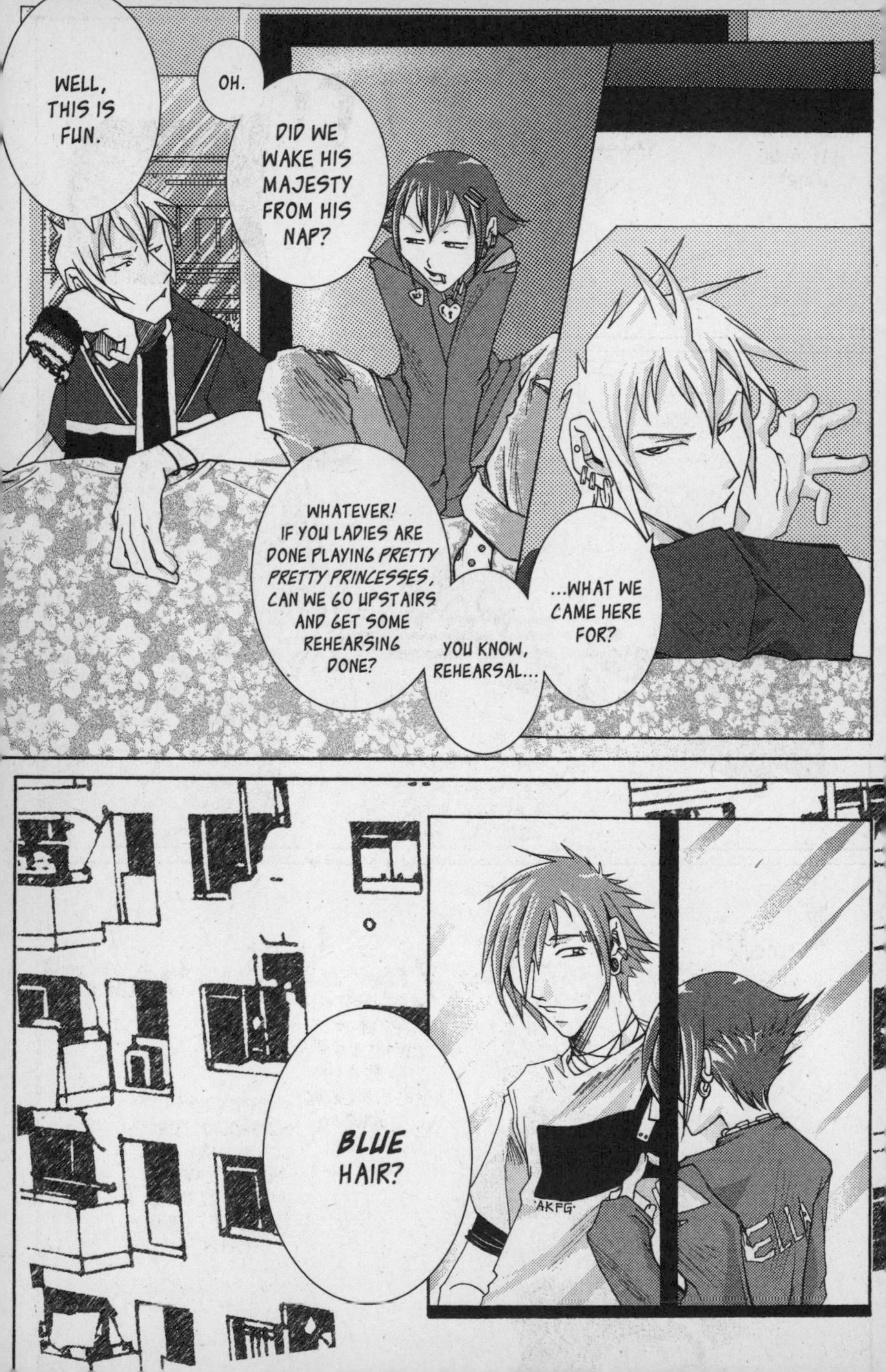
WELL, THIS IS FUN.
OH.
DID WE WAKE HIS MAJESTY FROM HIS NAP?
WHATEVER! IF YOU LADIES ARE DONE PLAYING *PRETTY PRETTY PRINCESSES*, CAN WE GO UPSTAIRS AND GET SOME REHEARSING DONE?
YOU KNOW, REHEARSAL...
...WHAT WE CAME HERE FOR?
AKFG
BLUE HAIR?

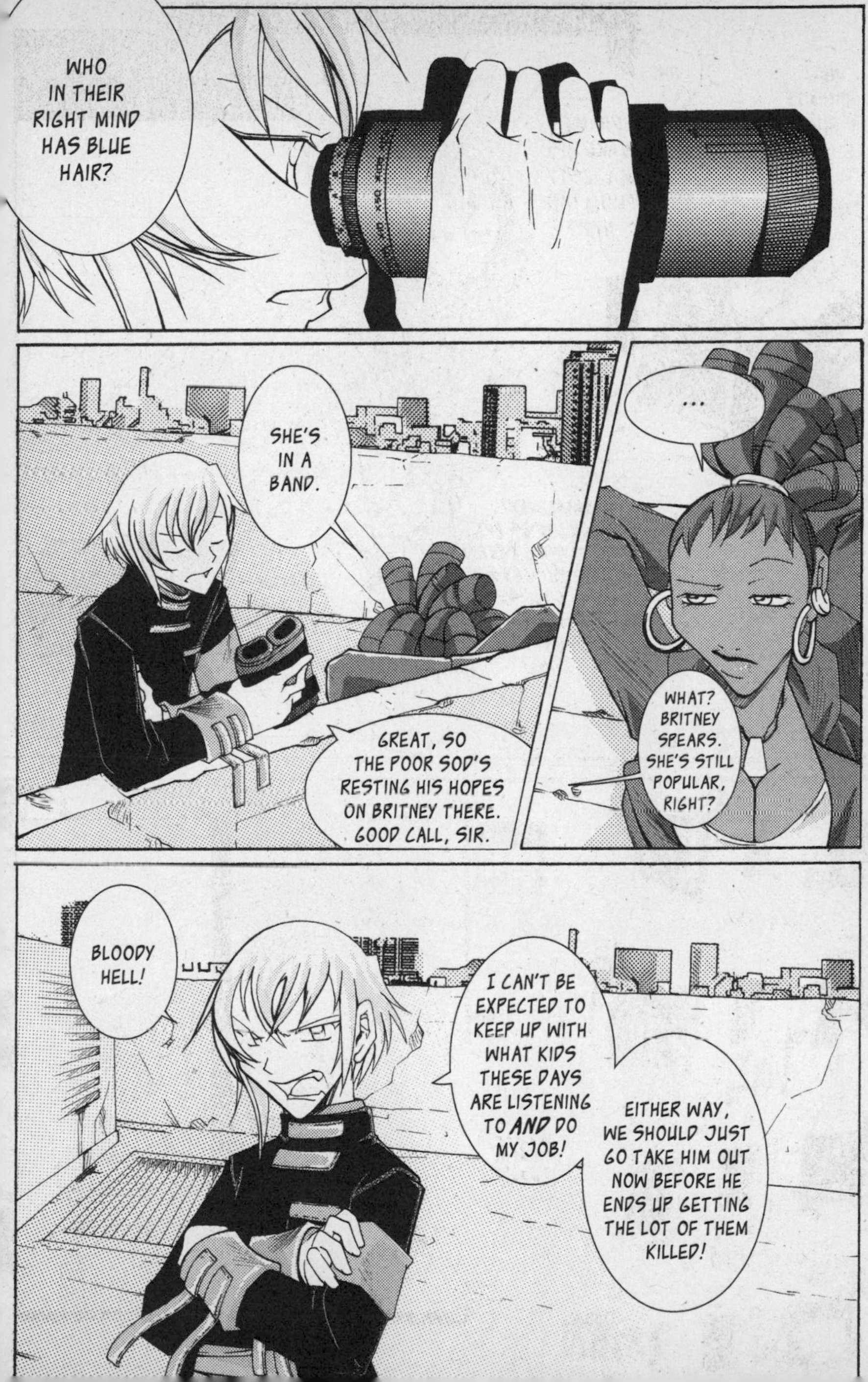
WHO IN THEIR RIGHT MIND HAS BLUE HAIR?
SHE'S IN A BAND.
GREAT, SO THE POOR SOD'S RESTING HIS HOPES ON BRITNEY THERE. GOOD CALL, SIR.
...
WHAT? BRITNEY SPEARS. SHE'S STILL POPULAR, RIGHT?
BLOODY HELL!
I CAN'T BE EXPECTED TO KEEP UP WITH WHAT KIDS THESE DAYS ARE LISTENING TO *AND* DO MY JOB!
EITHER WAY, WE SHOULD JUST GO TAKE HIM OUT NOW BEFORE HE ENDS UP GETTING THE LOT OF THEM KILLED!

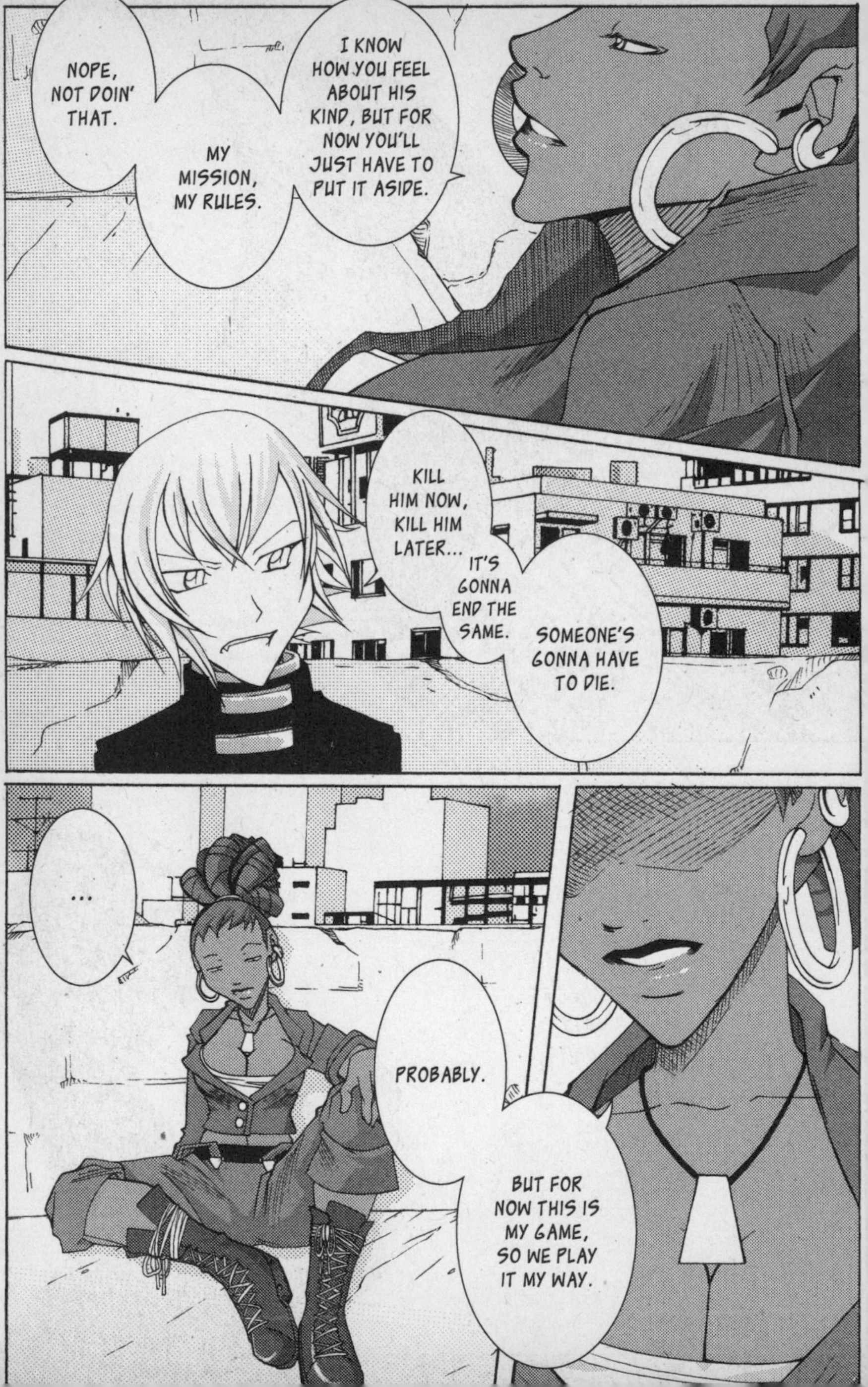
NOPE, NOT DOIN' THAT.
MY MISSION, MY RULES.
I KNOW HOW YOU FEEL ABOUT HIS KIND, BUT FOR NOW YOU'LL JUST HAVE TO PUT IT ASIDE.
KILL HIM NOW, KILL HIM LATER...
IT'S GONNA END THE SAME.
SOMEONE'S GONNA HAVE TO DIE.
...
PROBABLY.
BUT FOR NOW THIS IS MY GAME, SO WE PLAY IT MY WAY.

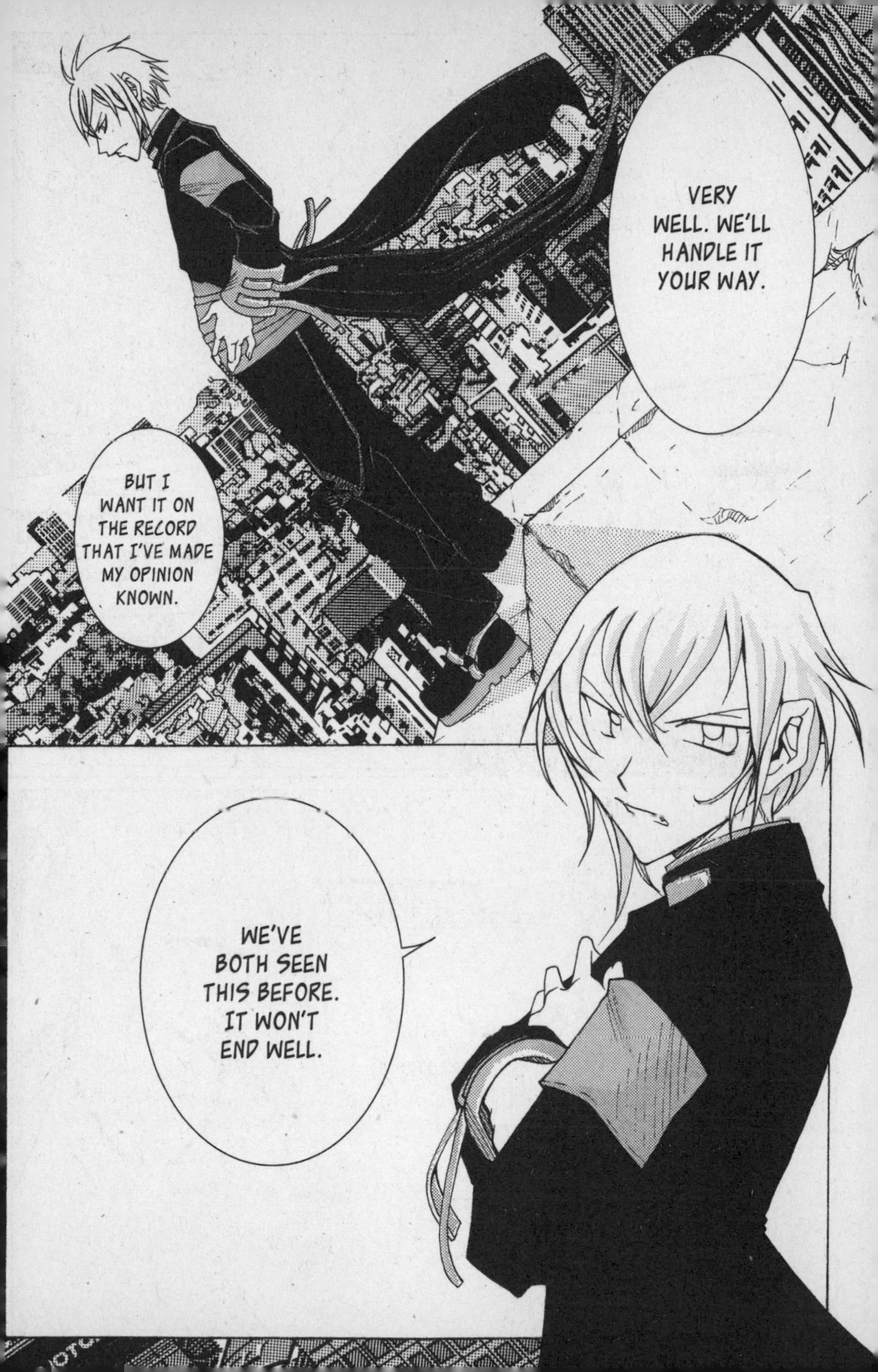
VERY WELL. WE'LL HANDLE IT YOUR WAY.
BUT I WANT IT ON THE RECORD THAT I'VE MADE MY OPINION KNOWN.
WE'VE BOTH SEEN THIS BEFORE. IT WON'T END WELL.

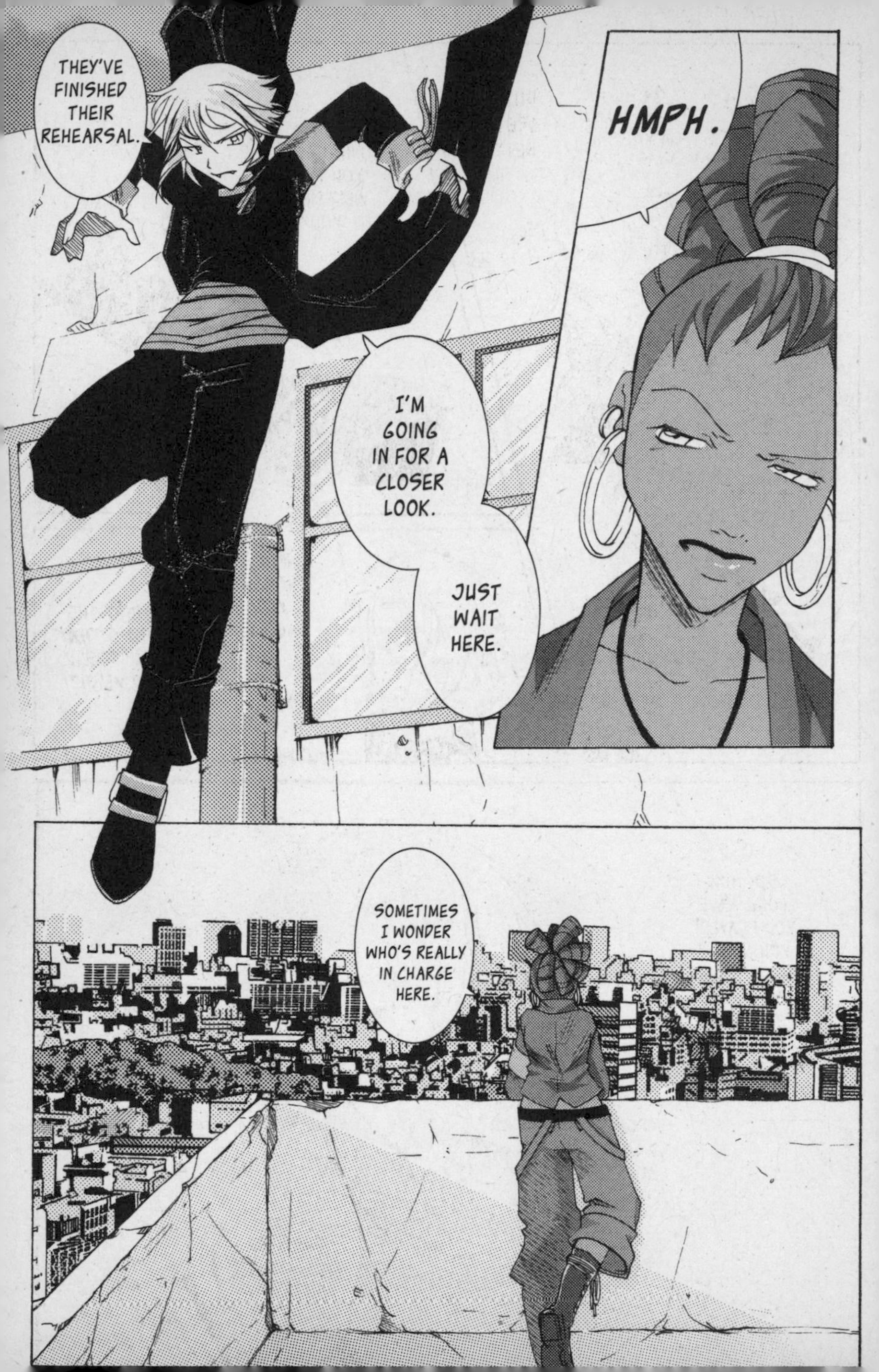
THEY'VE FINISHED THEIR REHEARSAL.
I'M GOING IN FOR A CLOSER LOOK.
JUST WAIT HERE.
HMPH.
SOMETIMES I WONDER WHO'S REALLY IN CHARGE HERE.

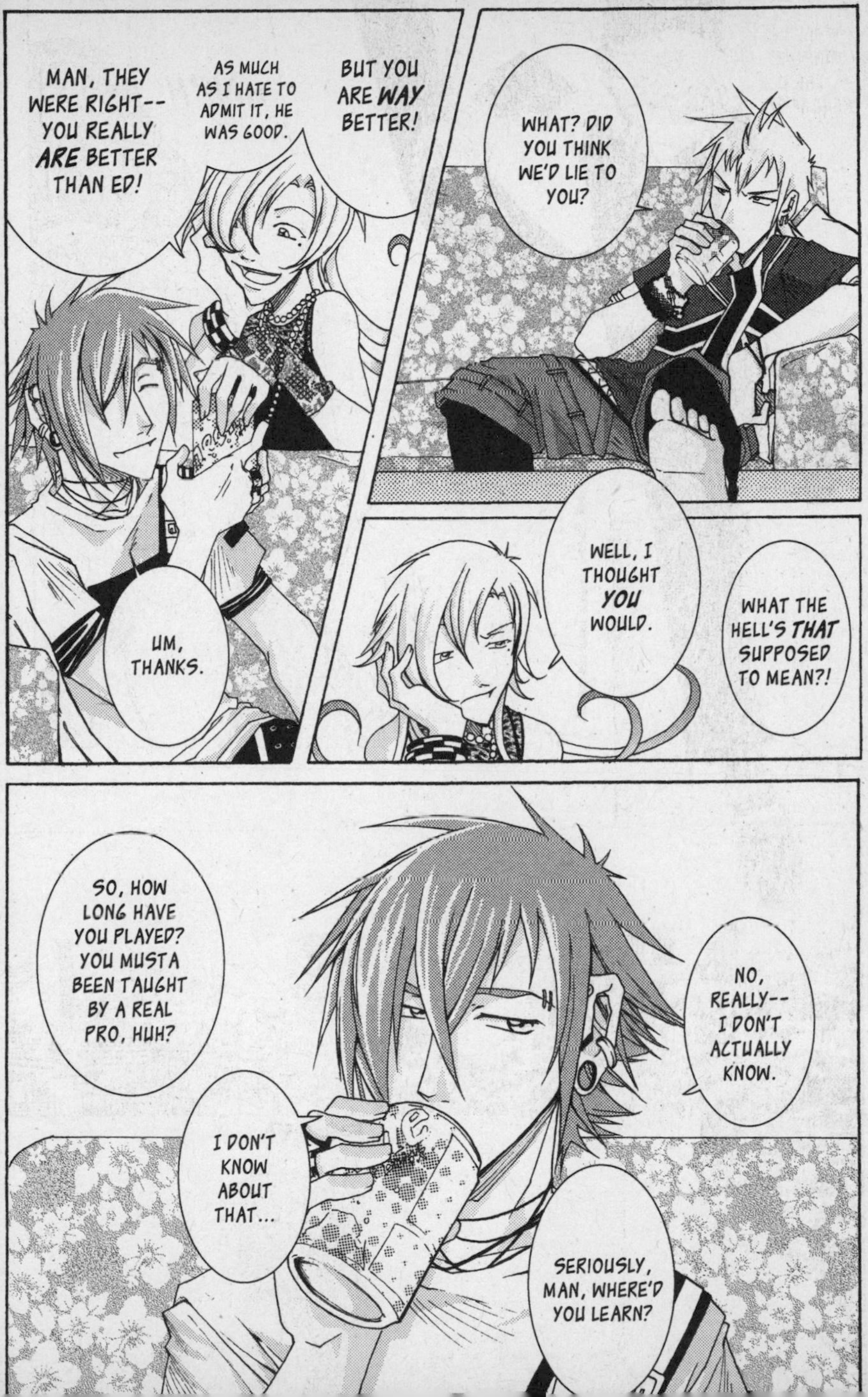
MAN, THEY WERE RIGHT-- YOU REALLY ARE BETTER THAN ED!
AS MUCH AS I HATE TO ADMIT IT, HE WAS GOOD.
BUT YOU ARE WAY BETTER!
UM, THANKS.
WHAT? DID YOU THINK WE'D LIE TO YOU?
WELL, I THOUGHT YOU WOULD.
WHAT THE HELL'S THAT SUPPOSED TO MEAN?!
SO, HOW LONG HAVE YOU PLAYED? YOU MUSTA BEEN TAUGHT BY A REAL PRO, HUH?
I DON'T KNOW ABOUT THAT...
NO, REALLY-- I DON'T ACTUALLY KNOW.
SERIOUSLY, MAN, WHERE'D YOU LEARN?

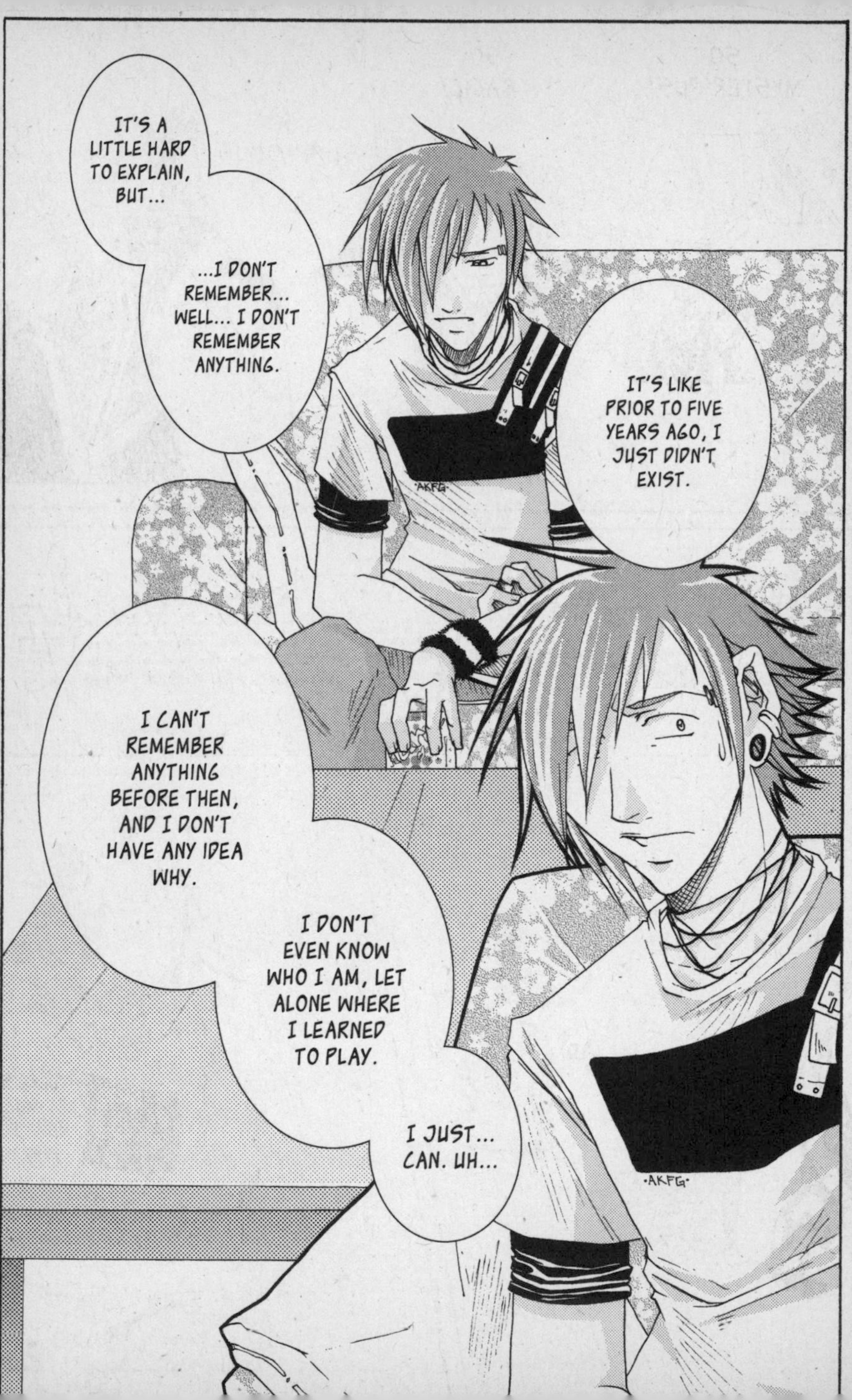
IT'S A LITTLE HARD TO EXPLAIN, BUT...
...I DON'T REMEMBER... WELL... I DON'T REMEMBER ANYTHING.
IT'S LIKE PRIOR TO FIVE YEARS AGO, I JUST DIDN'T EXIST.
I CAN'T REMEMBER ANYTHING BEFORE THEN, AND I DON'T HAVE ANY IDEA WHY.
I DON'T EVEN KNOW WHO I AM, LET ALONE WHERE I LEARNED TO PLAY.
I JUST... CAN. UH...
·AKFG·
·AKFG·

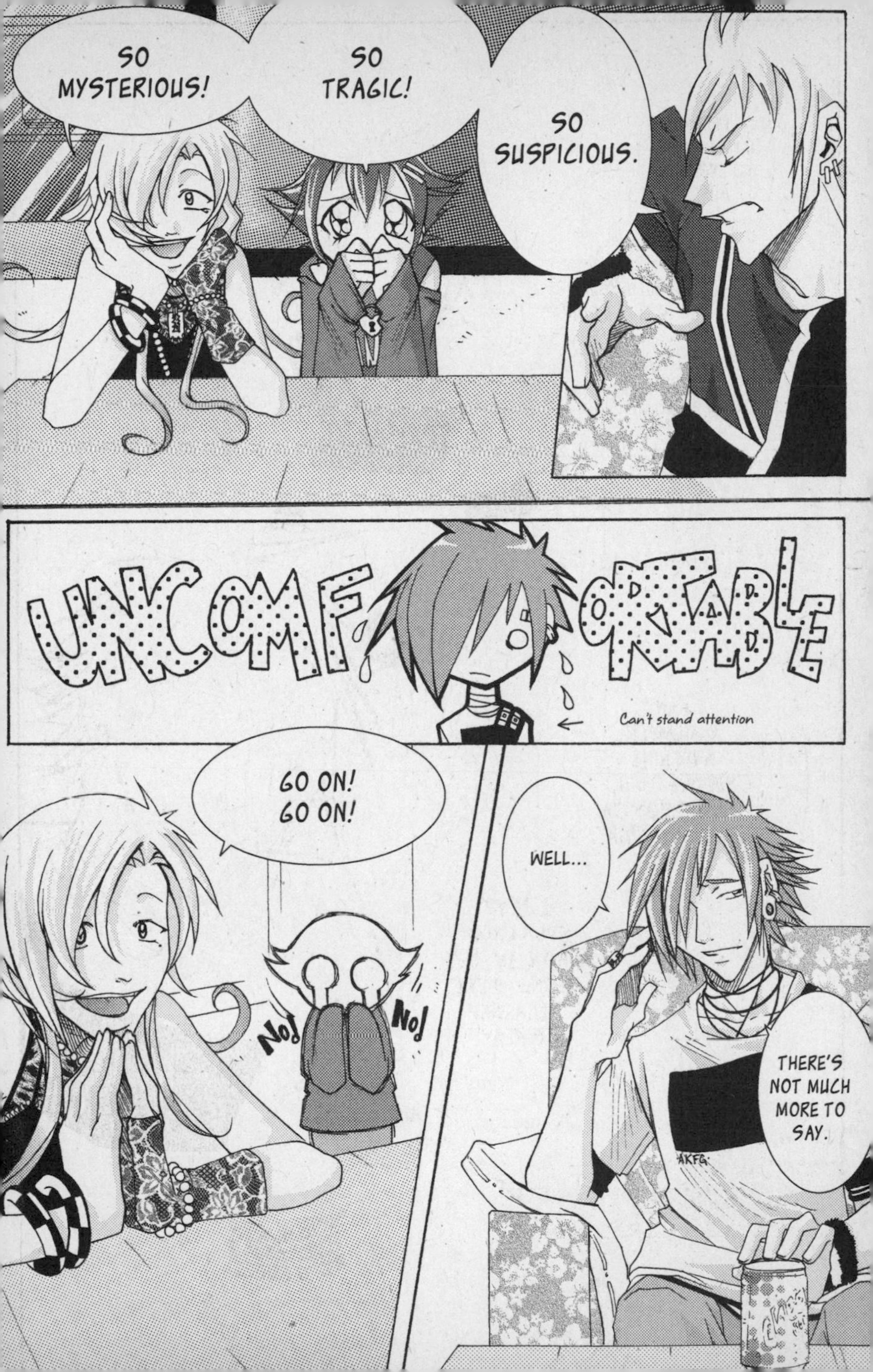
SO MYSTERIOUS!
SO TRAGIC!
SO SUSPICIOUS.
UNCOMFORTABLE
Can't stand attention
GO ON! GO ON!
No! No!
WELL...
AKFG
THERE'S NOT MUCH MORE TO SAY.

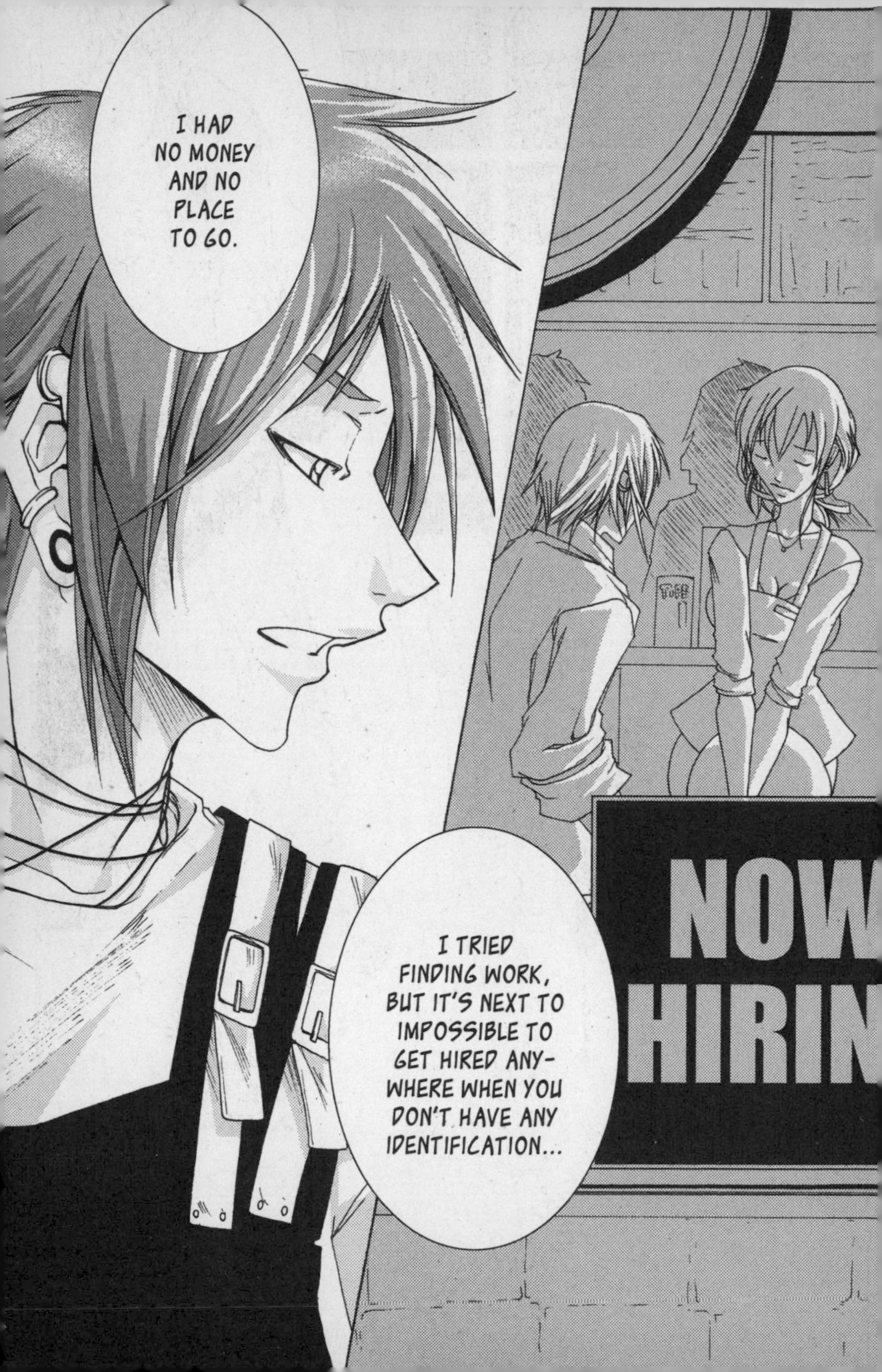
I HAD NO MONEY AND NO PLACE TO GO.
I TRIED FINDING WORK, BUT IT'S NEXT TO IMPOSSIBLE TO GET HIRED ANY-WHERE WHEN YOU DON'T HAVE ANY IDENTIFICATION...
NOW HIRIN

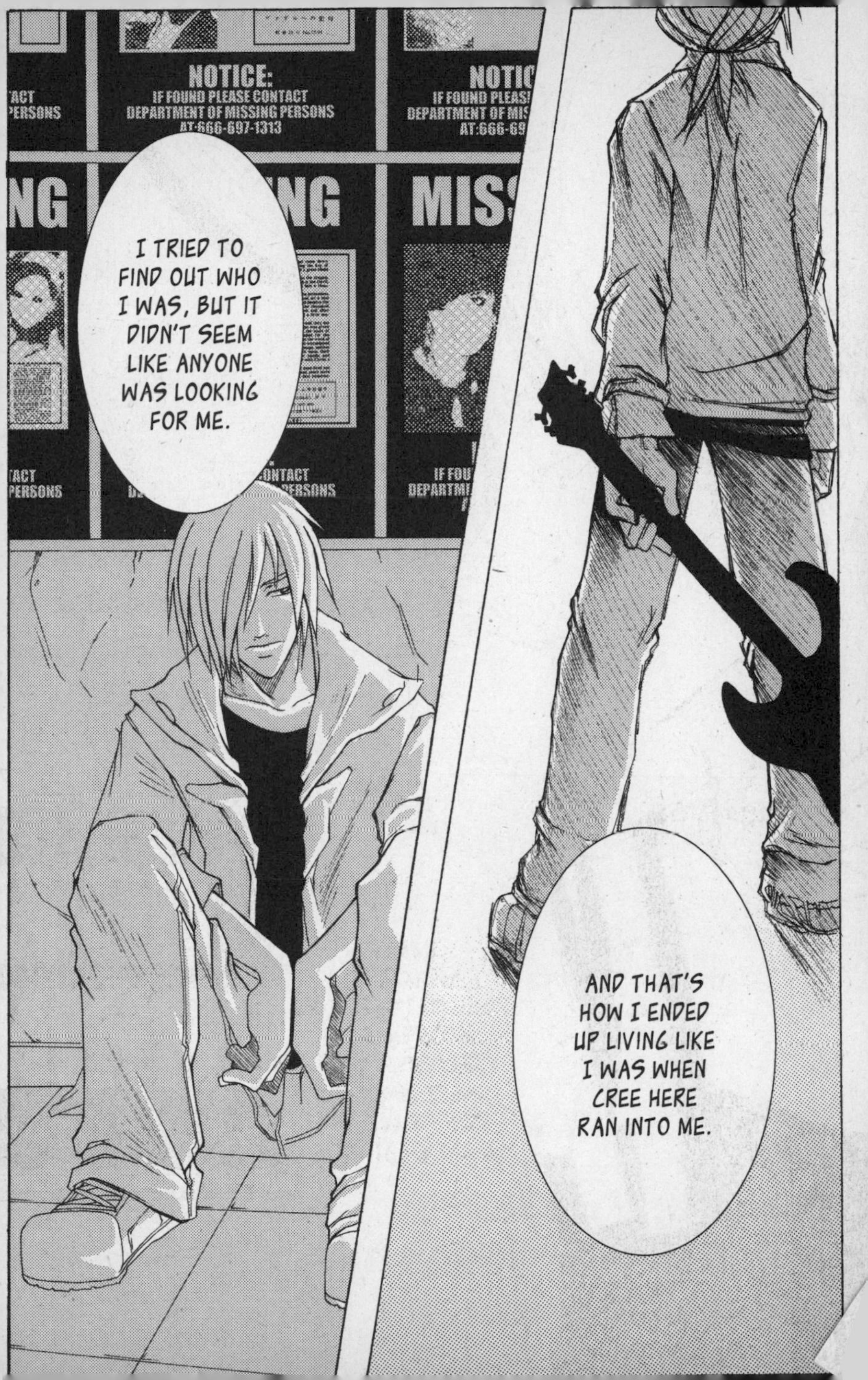
NOTICE:
IF FOUND PLEASE CONTACT
DEPARTMENT OF MISSING PERSONS
AT:666-697-1313
I TRIED TO FIND OUT WHO I WAS, BUT IT DIDN'T SEEM LIKE ANYONE WAS LOOKING FOR ME.
AND THAT'S HOW I ENDED UP LIVING LIKE I WAS WHEN CREE HERE RAN INTO ME.

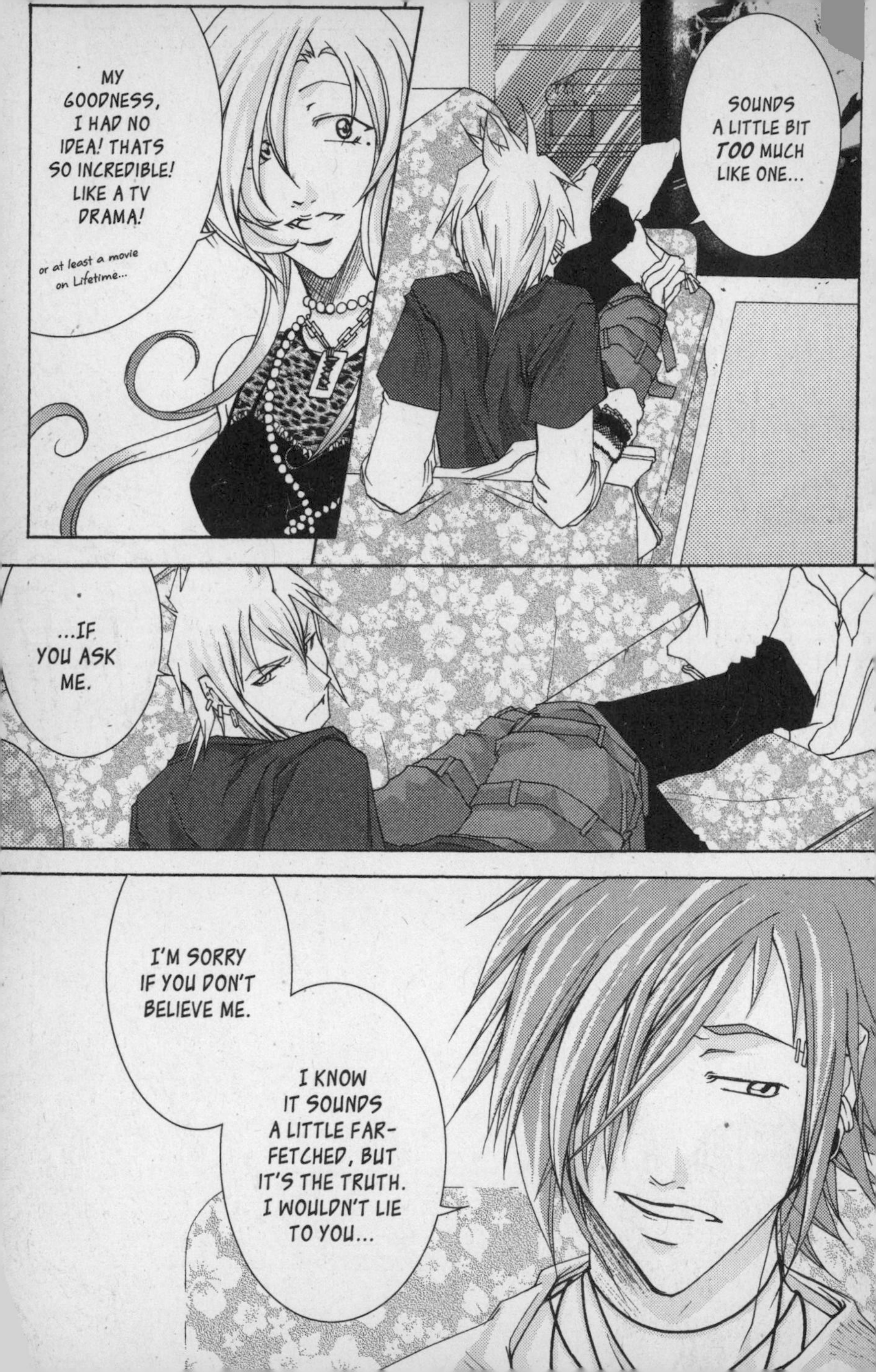
MY GOODNESS, I HAD NO IDEA! THATS SO INCREDIBLE! LIKE A TV DRAMA!
or at least a movie on Lifetime...
SOUNDS A LITTLE BIT TOO MUCH LIKE ONE...
...IF YOU ASK ME.
I'M SORRY IF YOU DON'T BELIEVE ME.
I KNOW IT SOUNDS A LITTLE FAR-FETCHED, BUT IT'S THE TRUTH. I WOULDN'T LIE TO YOU...

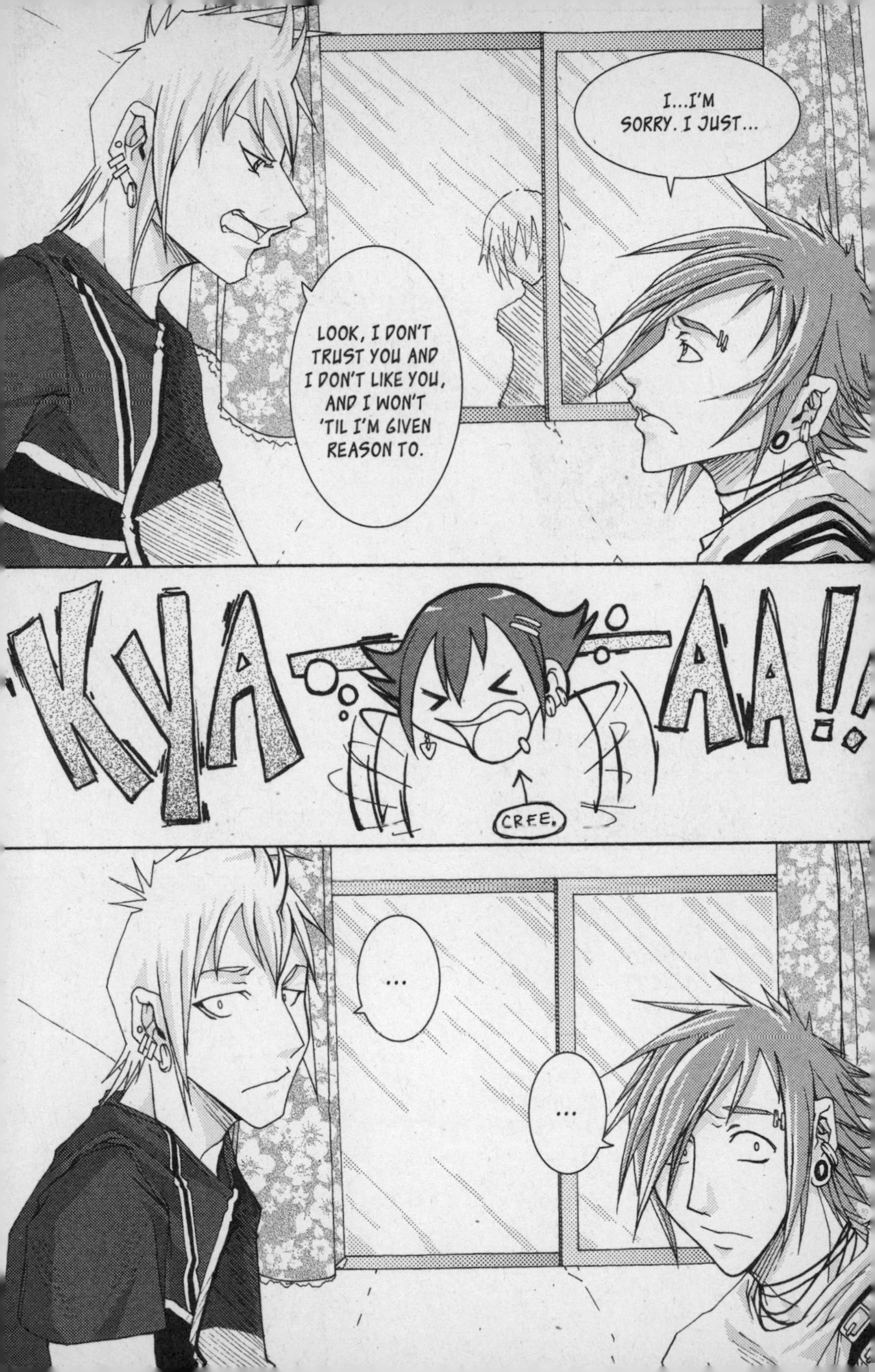
LOOK, I DON'T TRUST YOU AND I DON'T LIKE YOU, AND I WON'T 'TIL I'M GIVEN REASON TO.
I...I'M SORRY. I JUST...
KYAAA!!
CREE.
...
...

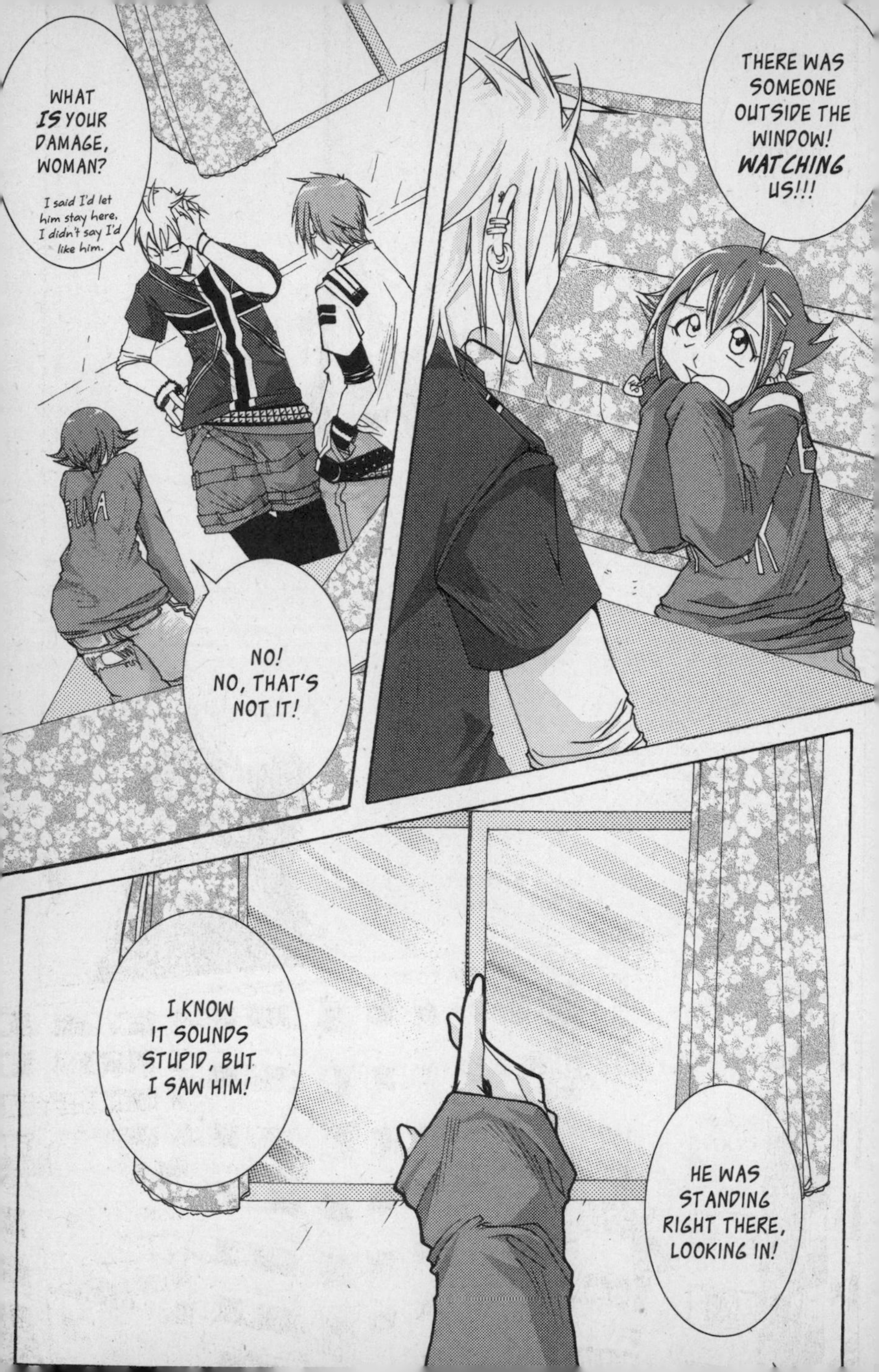
WHAT IS YOUR DAMAGE, WOMAN?
I said I'd let him stay here, I didn't say I'd like him.
NO! NO, THAT'S NOT IT!
THERE WAS SOMEONE OUTSIDE THE WINDOW! WATCHING US!!!
I KNOW IT SOUNDS STUPID, BUT I SAW HIM!
HE WAS STANDING RIGHT THERE, LOOKING IN!

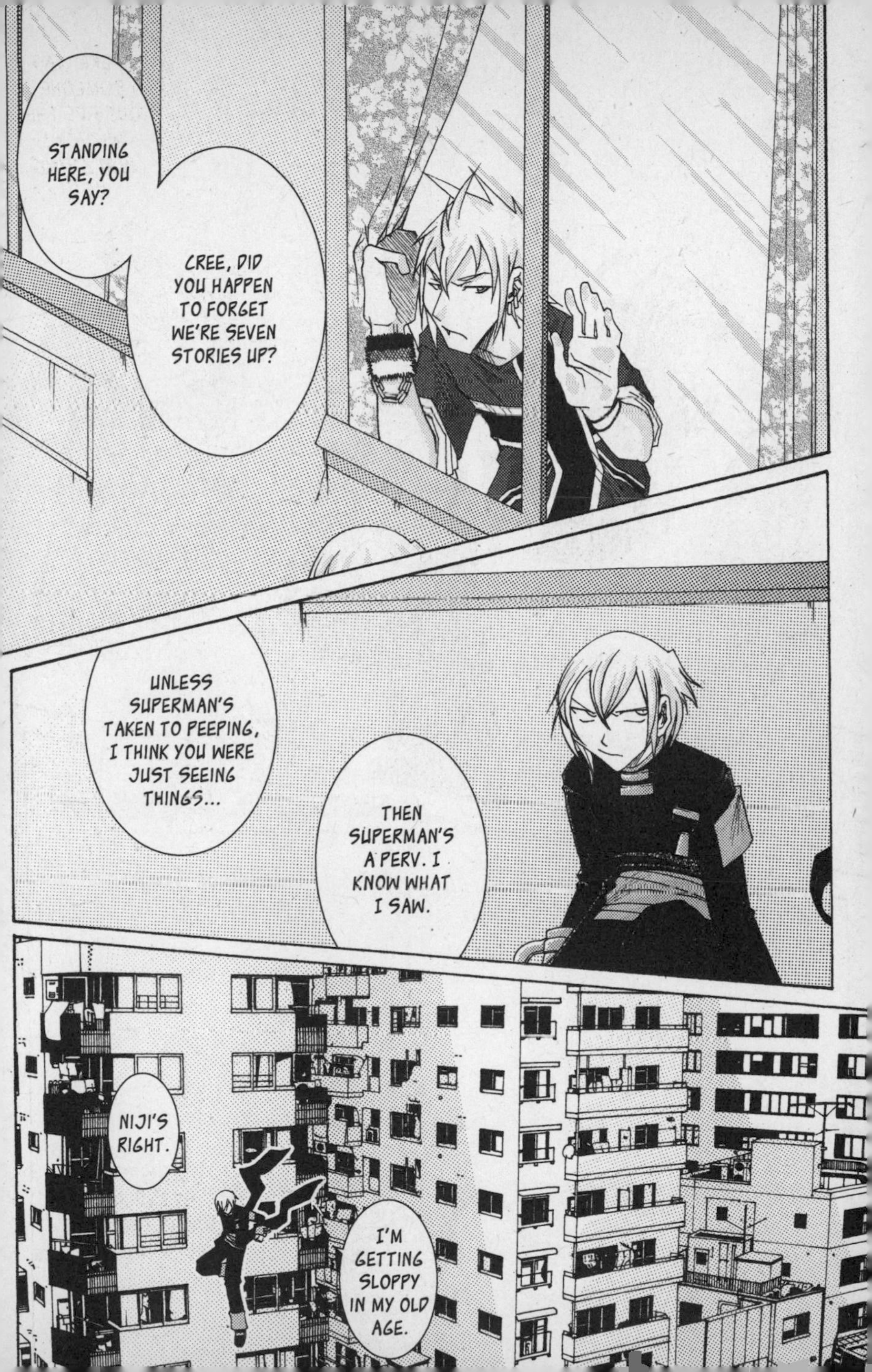
STANDING HERE, YOU SAY?
CREE, DID YOU HAPPEN TO FORGET WE'RE SEVEN STORIES UP?
UNLESS SUPERMAN'S TAKEN TO PEEPING, I THINK YOU WERE JUST SEEING THINGS...
THEN SUPERMAN'S A PERV. I KNOW WHAT I SAW.
NIJI'S RIGHT.
I'M GETTING SLOPPY IN MY OLD AGE.

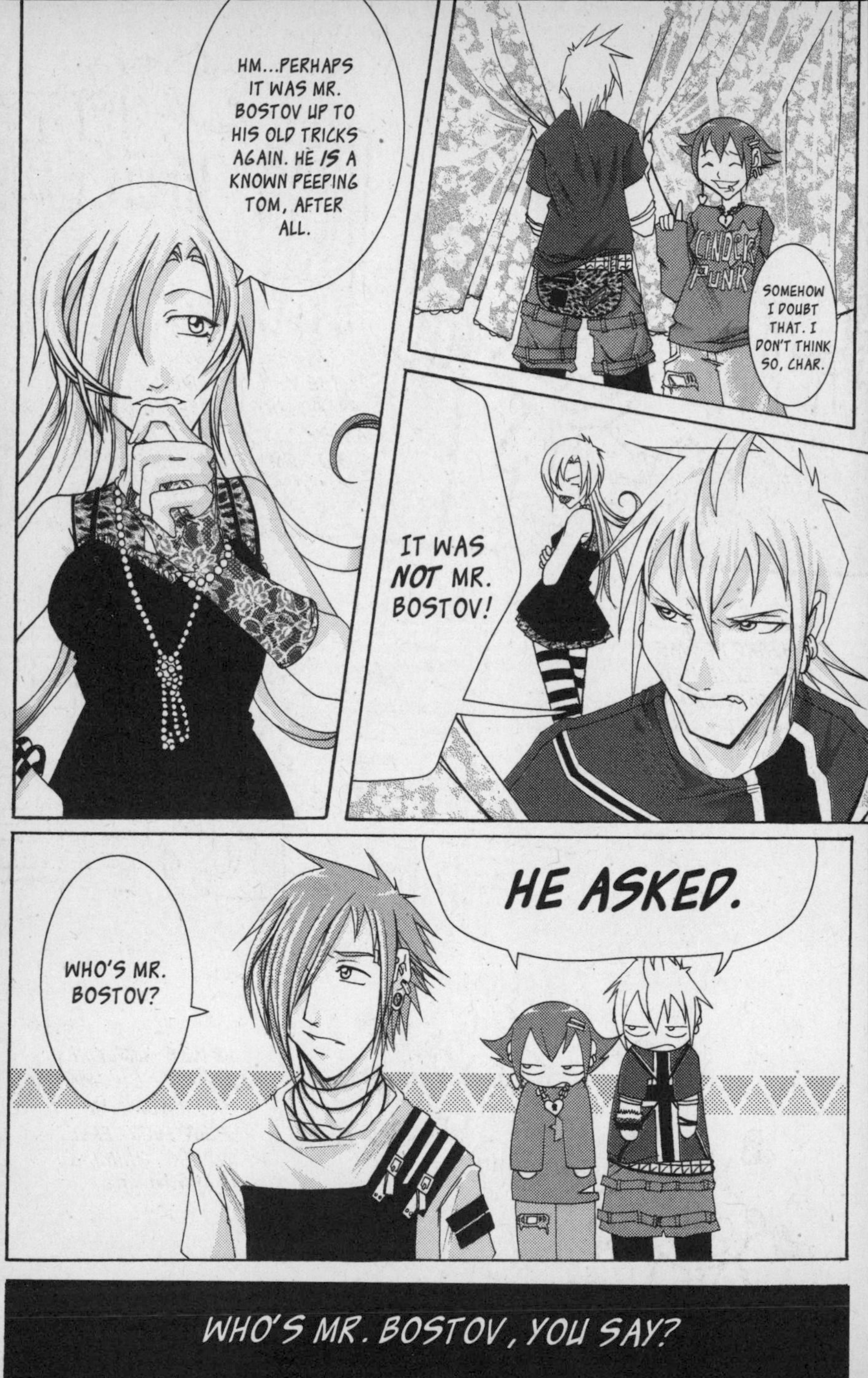
HM...PERHAPS IT WAS MR. BOSTOV UP TO HIS OLD TRICKS AGAIN. HE *IS* A KNOWN PEEPING TOM, AFTER ALL.
CINDER PUNK
SOMEHOW I DOUBT THAT. I DON'T THINK SO, CHAR.
IT WAS *NOT* MR. BOSTOV!
WHO'S MR. BOSTOV?
HE ASKED.
WHO'S MR. BOSTOV, YOU SAY?

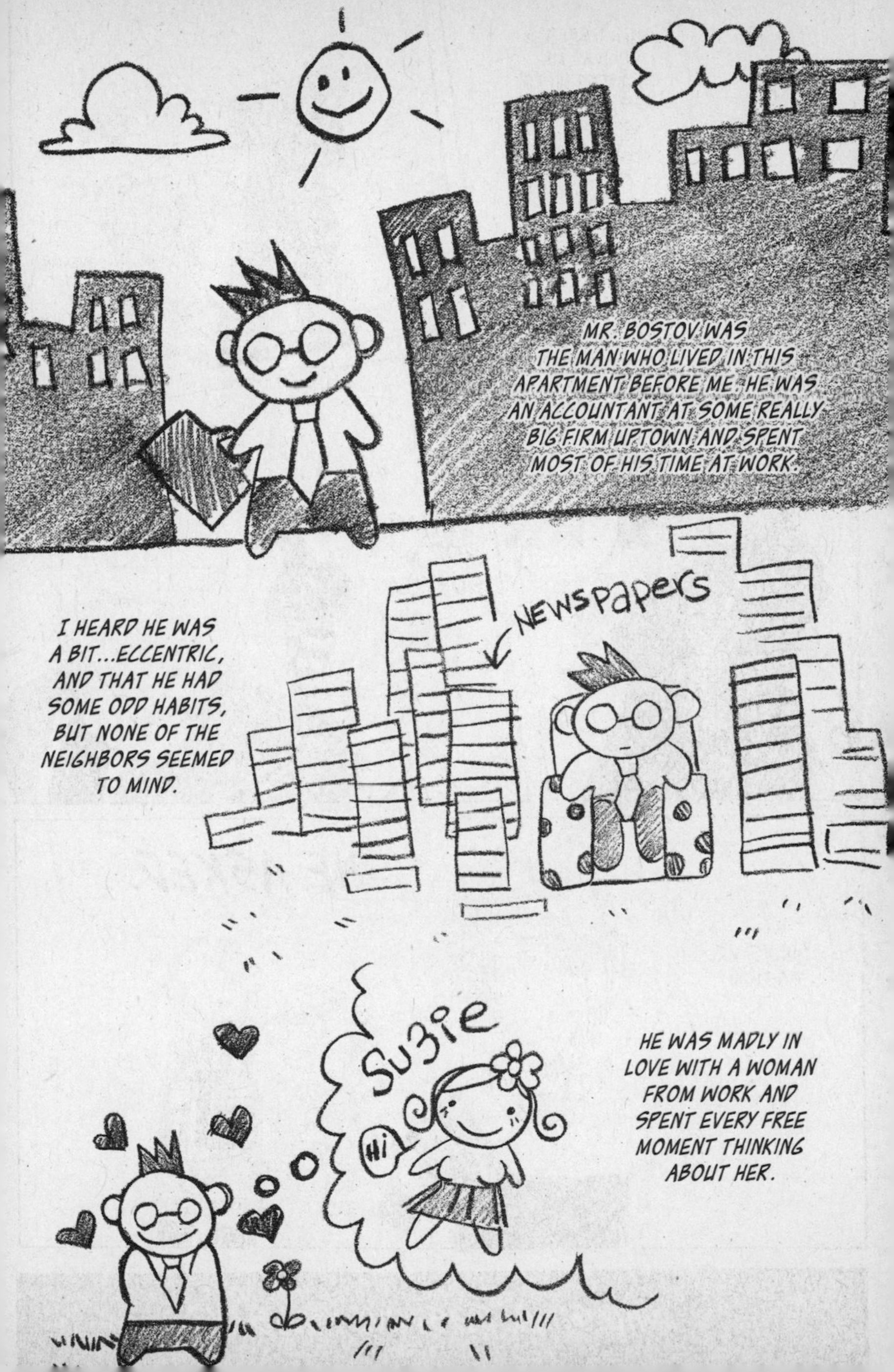

MR. BOSTOV WAS THE MAN WHO LIVED IN THIS APARTMENT BEFORE ME. HE WAS AN ACCOUNTANT AT SOME REALLY BIG FIRM UPTOWN AND SPENT MOST OF HIS TIME AT WORK.
I HEARD HE WAS A BIT...ECCENTRIC, AND THAT HE HAD SOME ODD HABITS, BUT NONE OF THE NEIGHBORS SEEMED TO MIND.
NEWSPAPERS
Suzie
Hi
HE WAS MADLY IN LOVE WITH A WOMAN FROM WORK AND SPENT EVERY FREE MOMENT THINKING ABOUT HER.

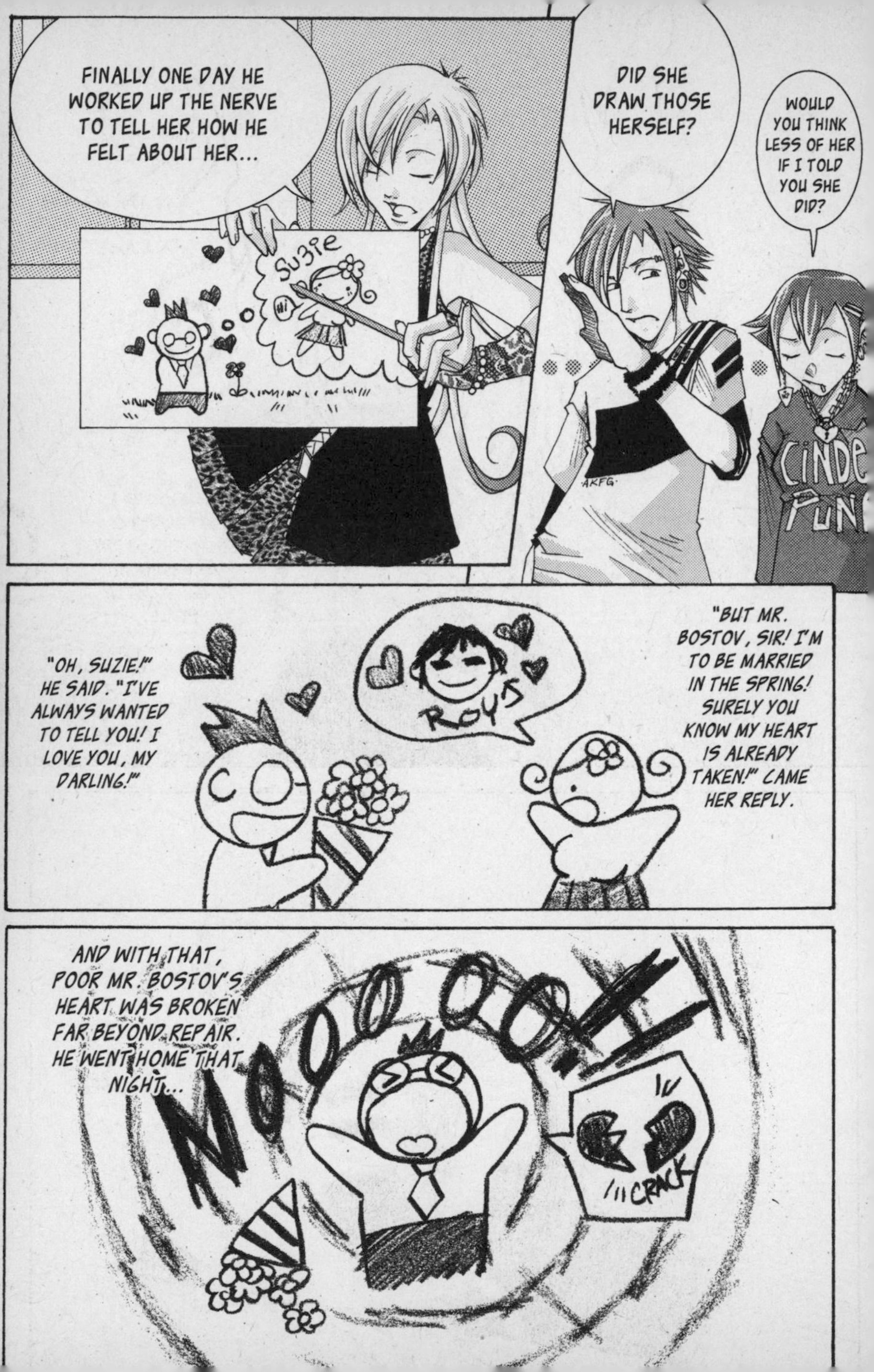

FINALLY ONE DAY HE WORKED UP THE NERVE TO TELL HER HOW HE FELT ABOUT HER...
SUZIE
HI
DID SHE DRAW THOSE HERSELF?
WOULD YOU THINK LESS OF HER IF I TOLD YOU SHE DID?
AKFG.
"OH, SUZIE!" HE SAID. "I'VE ALWAYS WANTED TO TELL YOU! I LOVE YOU, MY DARLING!"
ROYS
"BUT MR. BOSTOV, SIR! I'M TO BE MARRIED IN THE SPRING! SURELY YOU KNOW MY HEART IS ALREADY TAKEN!" CAME HER REPLY.
AND WITH THAT, POOR MR. BOSTOV'S HEART WAS BROKEN FAR BEYOND REPAIR. HE WENT HOME THAT NIGHT...
NOOOOOOOH
CRACK

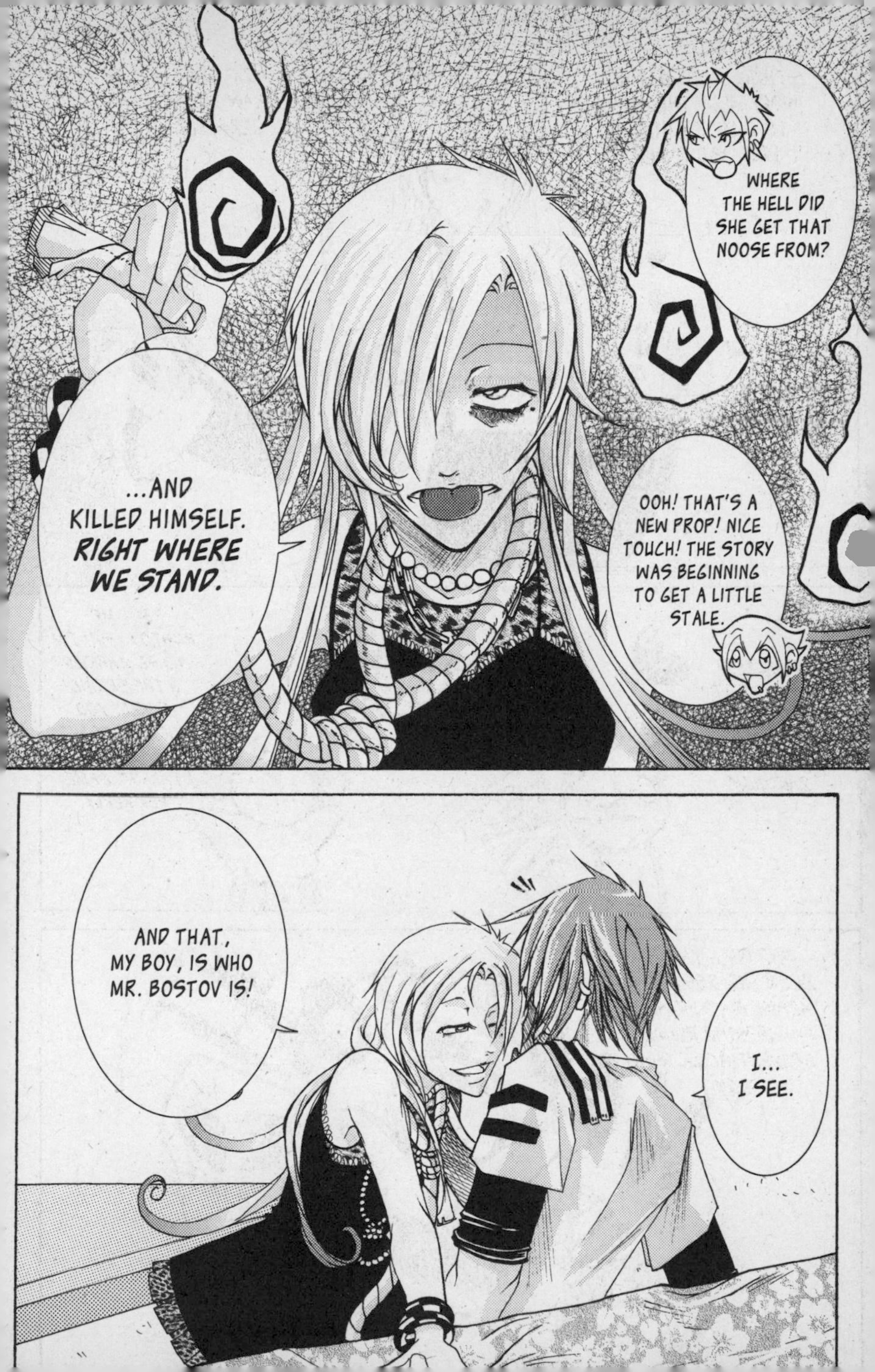
...AND KILLED HIMSELF. *RIGHT WHERE WE STAND.*
WHERE THE HELL DID SHE GET THAT NOOSE FROM?
OOH! THAT'S A NEW PROP! NICE TOUCH! THE STORY WAS BEGINNING TO GET A LITTLE STALE.
AND THAT, MY BOY, IS WHO MR. BOSTOV IS!
I... I SEE.

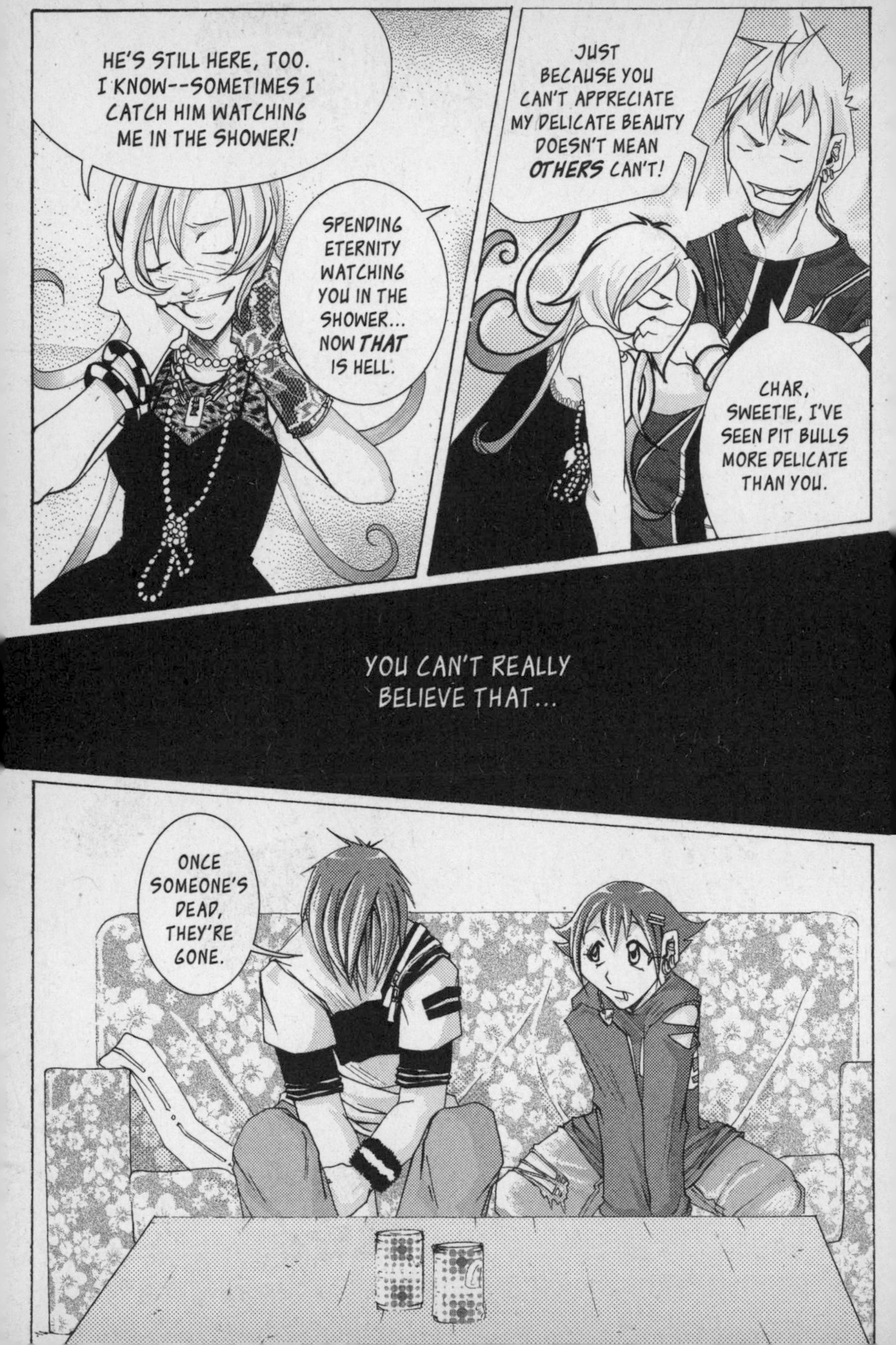
HE'S STILL HERE, TOO. I KNOW--SOMETIMES I CATCH HIM WATCHING ME IN THE SHOWER!
SPENDING ETERNITY WATCHING YOU IN THE SHOWER... NOW THAT IS HELL.
JUST BECAUSE YOU CAN'T APPRECIATE MY DELICATE BEAUTY DOESN'T MEAN OTHERS CAN'T!
CHAR, SWEETIE, I'VE SEEN PIT BULLS MORE DELICATE THAN YOU.
YOU CAN'T REALLY BELIEVE THAT...
ONCE SOMEONE'S DEAD, THEY'RE GONE.

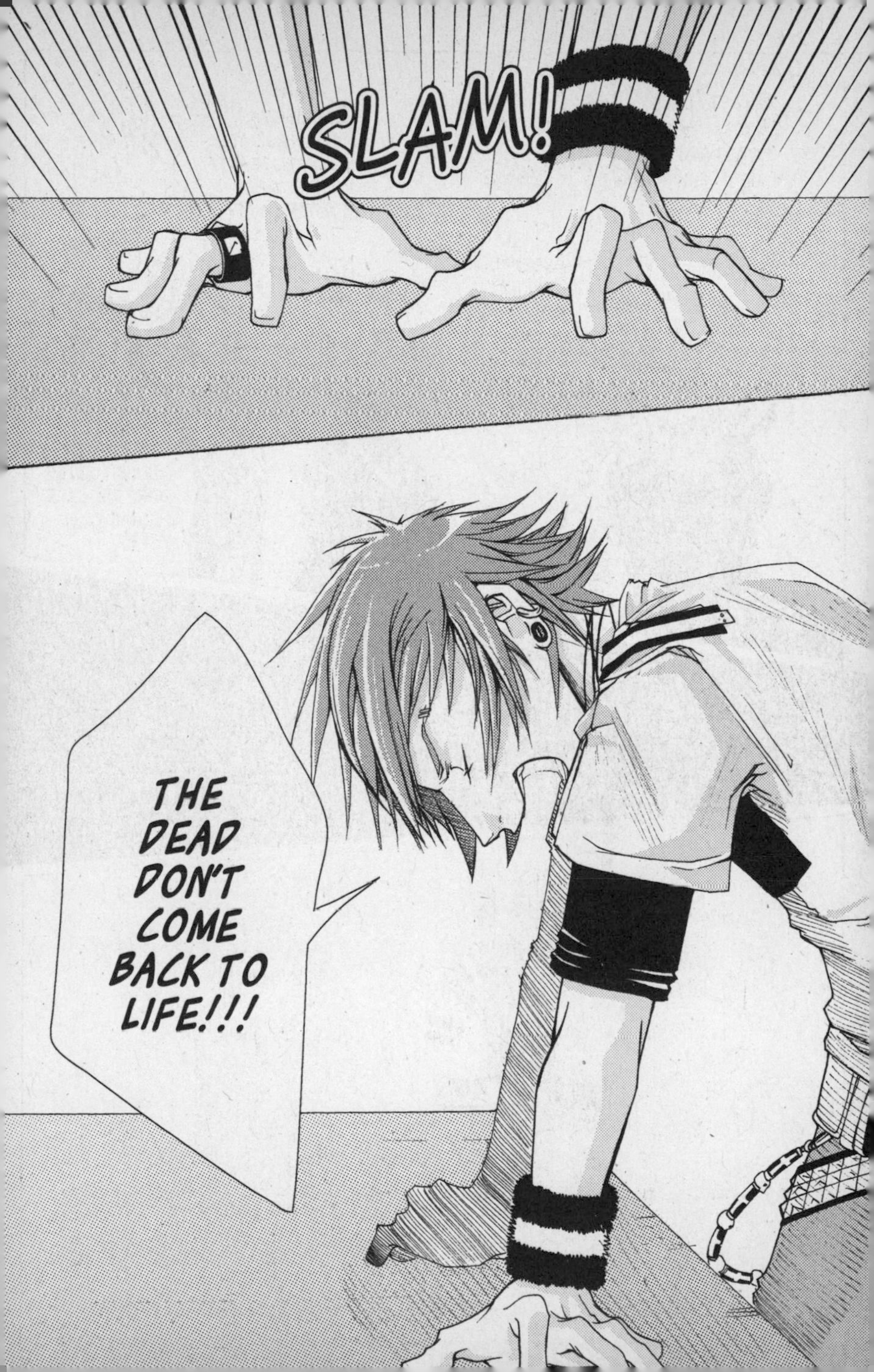
SLAM!
THE DEAD DON'T COME BACK TO LIFE!!!

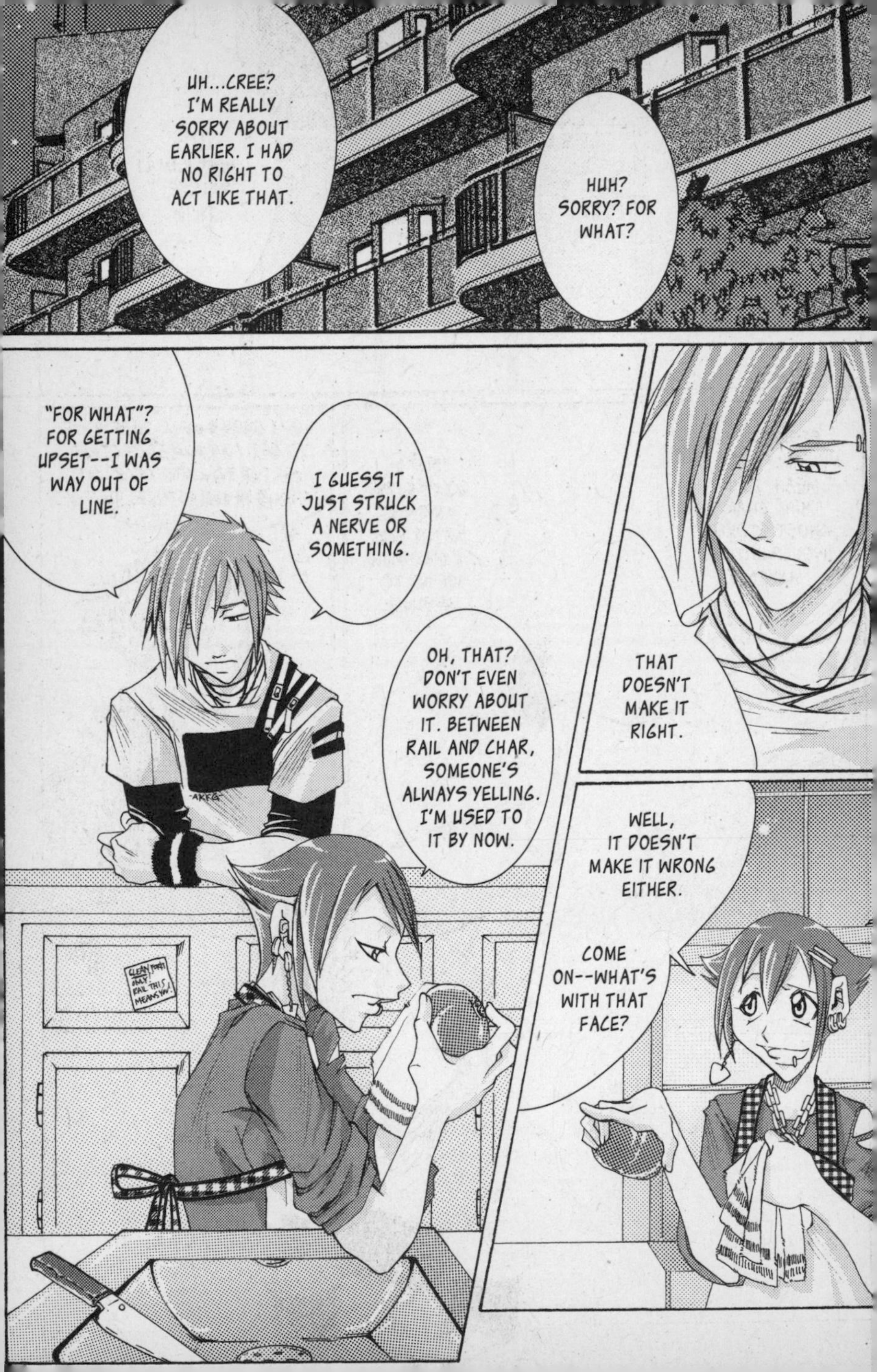
UH...CREE? I'M REALLY SORRY ABOUT EARLIER. I HAD NO RIGHT TO ACT LIKE THAT.
HUH? SORRY? FOR WHAT?
"FOR WHAT"? FOR GETTING UPSET--I WAS WAY OUT OF LINE.
I GUESS IT JUST STRUCK A NERVE OR SOMETHING.
OH, THAT? DON'T EVEN WORRY ABOUT IT. BETWEEN RAIL AND CHAR, SOMEONE'S ALWAYS YELLING. I'M USED TO IT BY NOW.
THAT DOESN'T MAKE IT RIGHT.
WELL, IT DOESN'T MAKE IT WRONG EITHER.
COME ON--WHAT'S WITH THAT FACE?

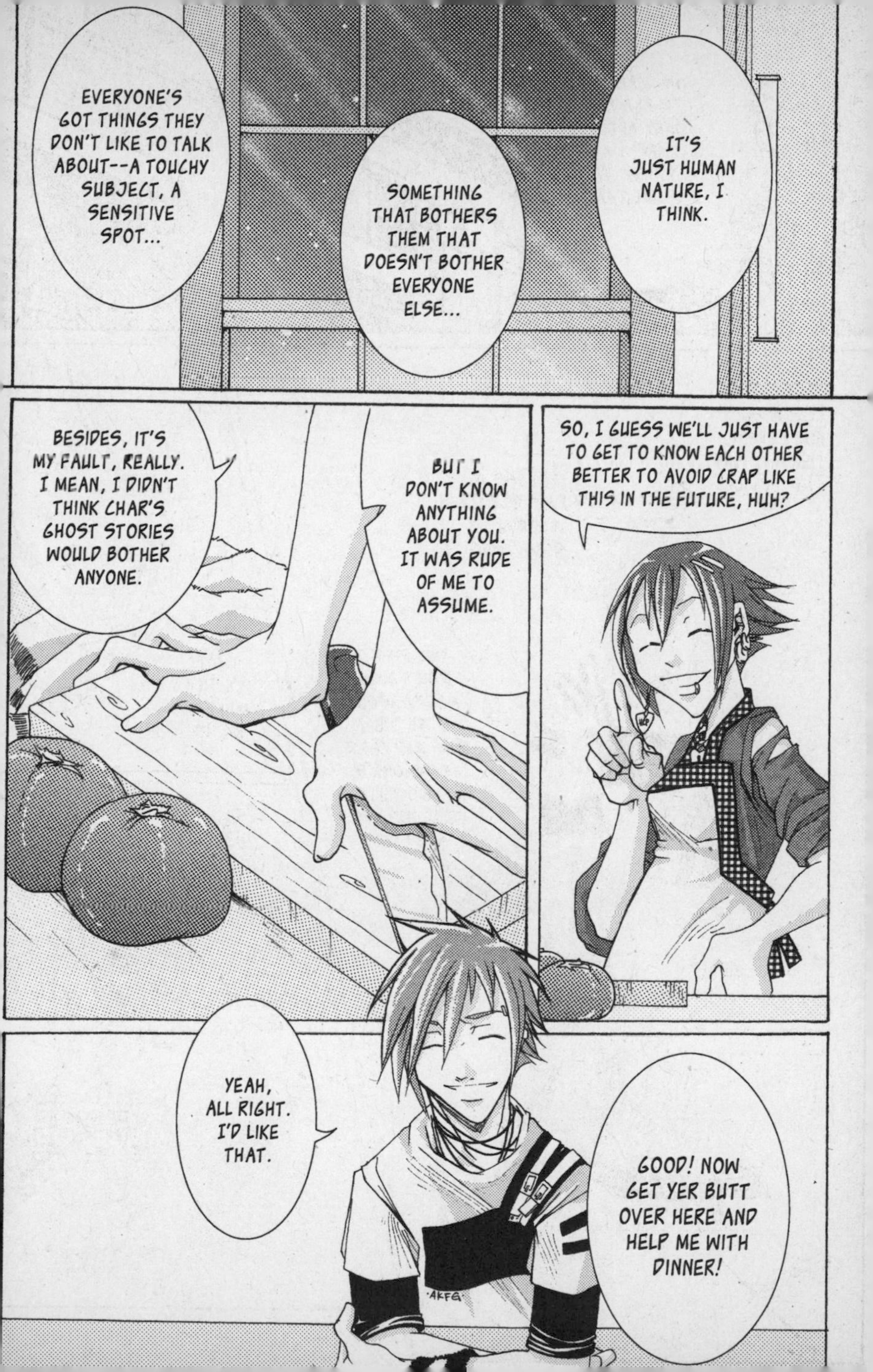
EVERYONE'S GOT THINGS THEY DON'T LIKE TO TALK ABOUT--A TOUCHY SUBJECT, A SENSITIVE SPOT...
SOMETHING THAT BOTHERS THEM THAT DOESN'T BOTHER EVERYONE ELSE...
IT'S JUST HUMAN NATURE, I THINK.
BESIDES, IT'S MY FAULT, REALLY. I MEAN, I DIDN'T THINK CHAR'S GHOST STORIES WOULD BOTHER ANYONE.
BUT I DON'T KNOW ANYTHING ABOUT YOU. IT WAS RUDE OF ME TO ASSUME.
SO, I GUESS WE'LL JUST HAVE TO GET TO KNOW EACH OTHER BETTER TO AVOID CRAP LIKE THIS IN THE FUTURE, HUH?
YEAH, ALL RIGHT. I'D LIKE THAT.
GOOD! NOW GET YER BUTT OVER HERE AND HELP ME WITH DINNER!

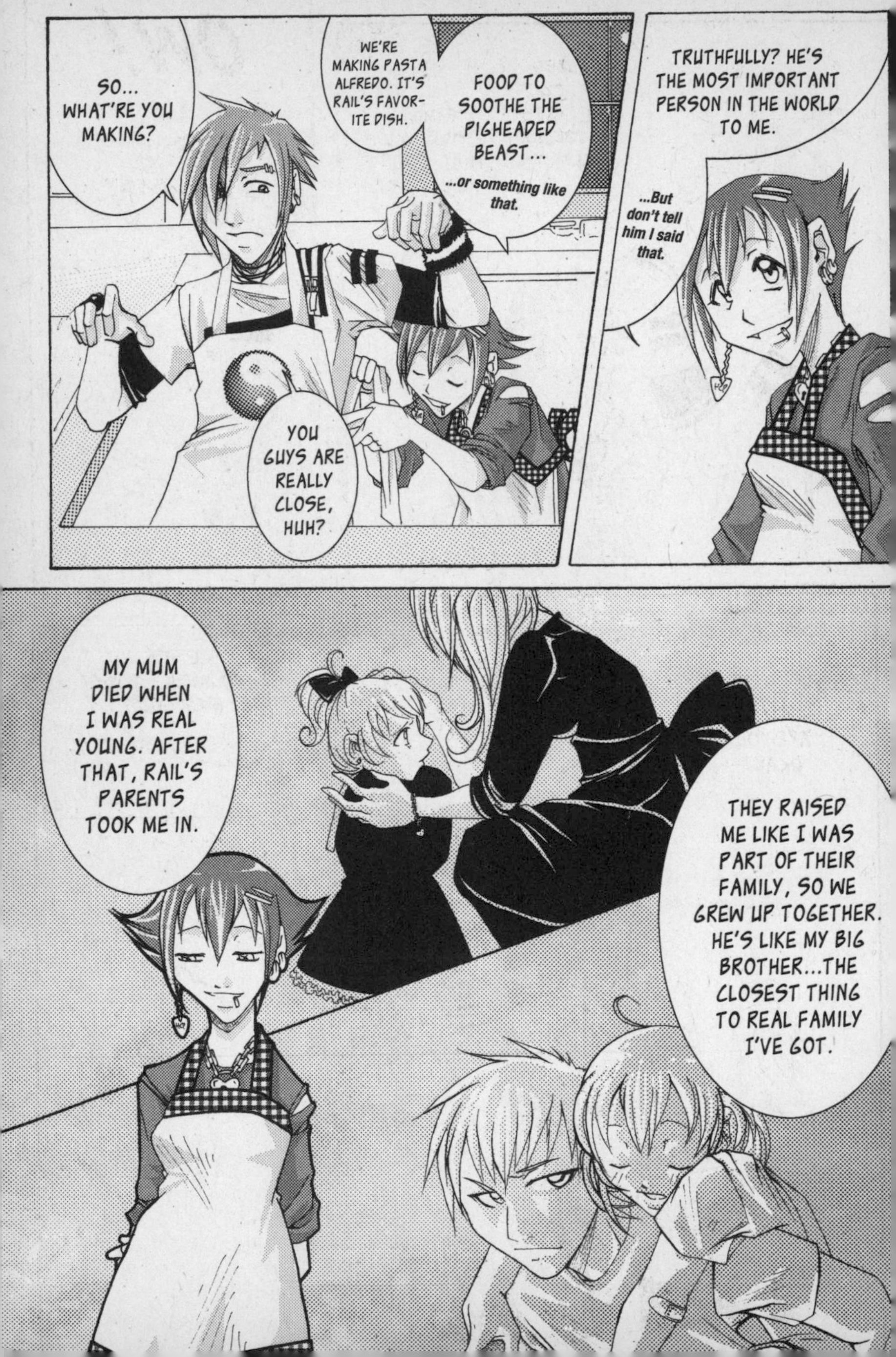
SO... WHAT'RE YOU MAKING?
WE'RE MAKING PASTA ALFREDO. IT'S RAIL'S FAVOR-ITE DISH.
FOOD TO SOOTHE THE PIGHEADED BEAST...
...or something like that.
YOU GUYS ARE REALLY CLOSE, HUH?
TRUTHFULLY? HE'S THE MOST IMPORTANT PERSON IN THE WORLD TO ME.
...But don't tell him I said that.
MY MUM DIED WHEN I WAS REAL YOUNG. AFTER THAT, RAIL'S PARENTS TOOK ME IN.
THEY RAISED ME LIKE I WAS PART OF THEIR FAMILY, SO WE GREW UP TOGETHER. HE'S LIKE MY BIG BROTHER...THE CLOSEST THING TO REAL FAMILY I'VE GOT.

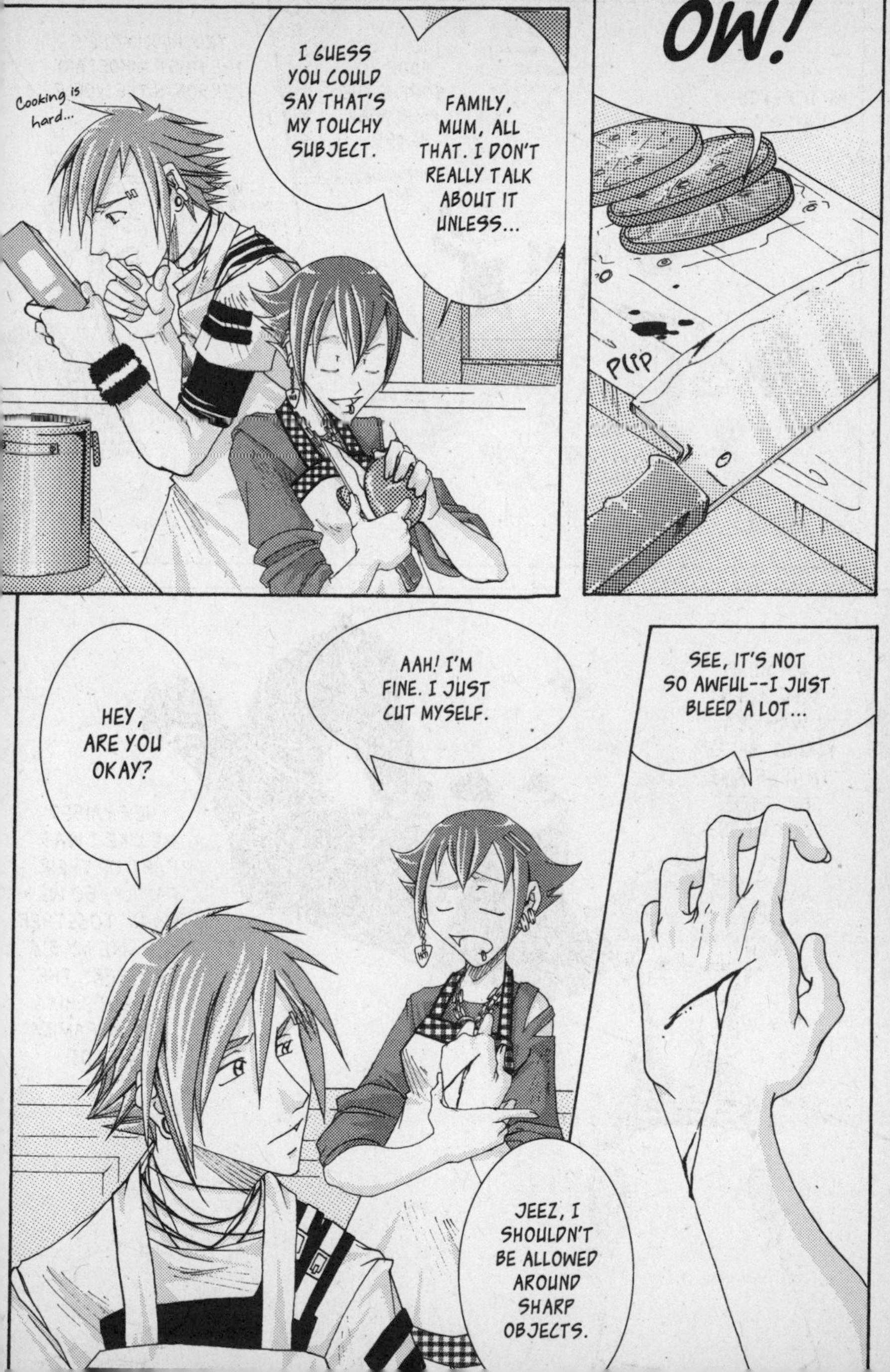
Cooking is hard...
I GUESS YOU COULD SAY THAT'S MY TOUCHY SUBJECT.
FAMILY, MUM, ALL THAT. I DON'T REALLY TALK ABOUT IT UNLESS...
OW!
PLIP
HEY, ARE YOU OKAY?
AAH! I'M FINE. I JUST CUT MYSELF.
SEE, IT'S NOT SO AWFUL--I JUST BLEED A LOT...
JEEZ, I SHOULDN'T BE ALLOWED AROUND SHARP OBJECTS.

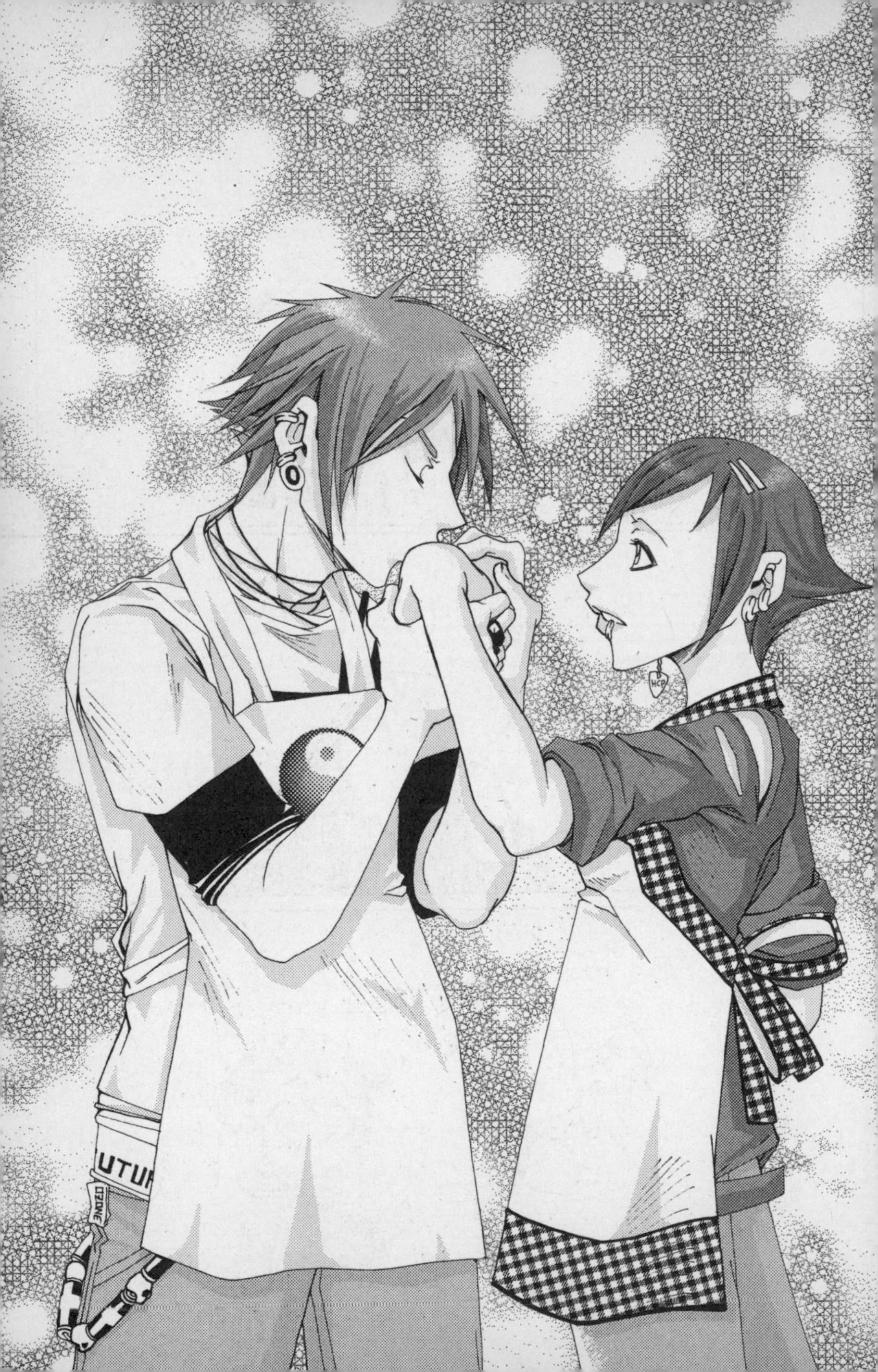

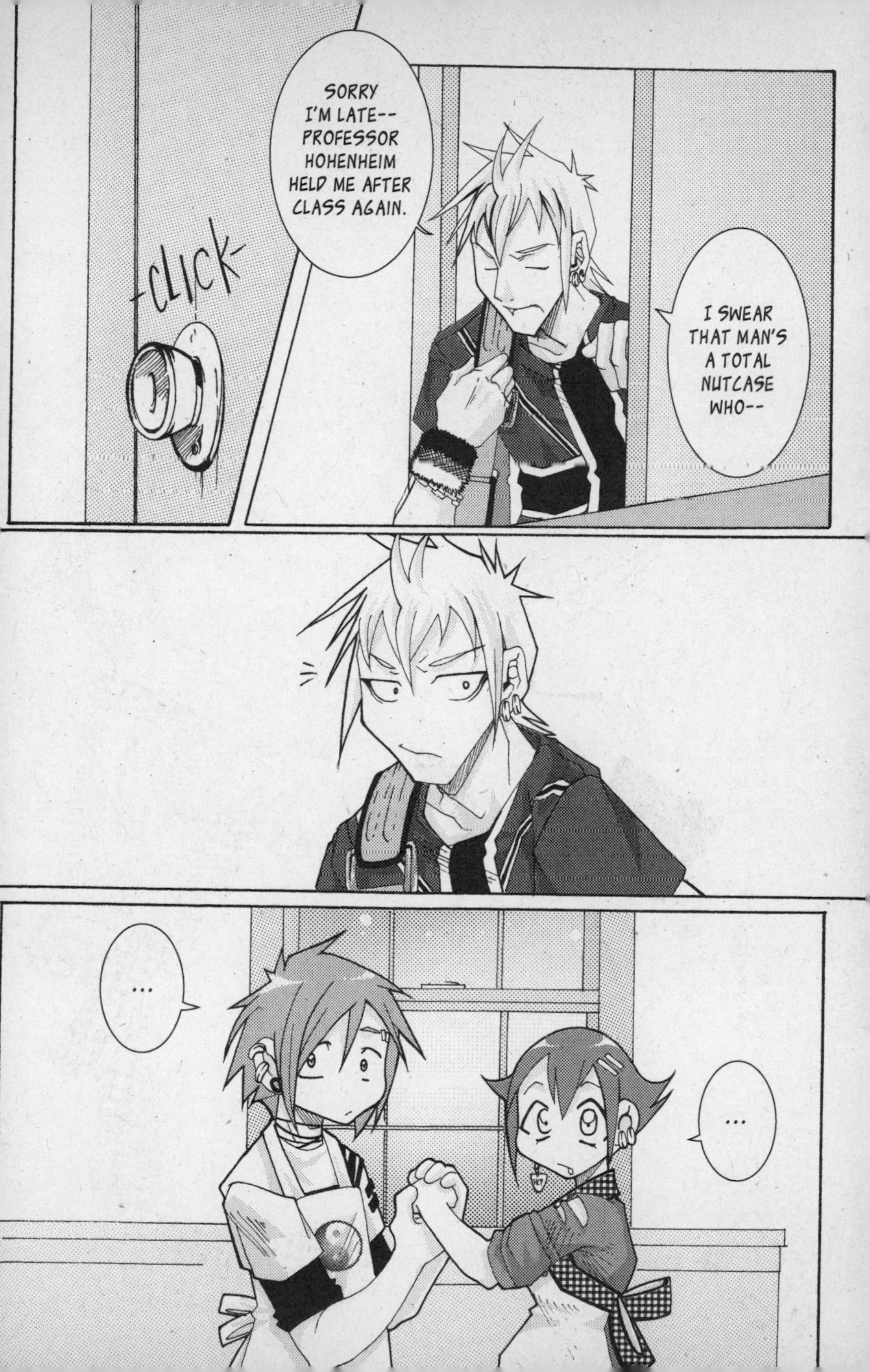
SORRY I'M LATE-- PROFESSOR HOHENHEIM HELD ME AFTER CLASS AGAIN.
CLICK
I SWEAR THAT MAN'S A TOTAL NUTCASE WHO--
...
...

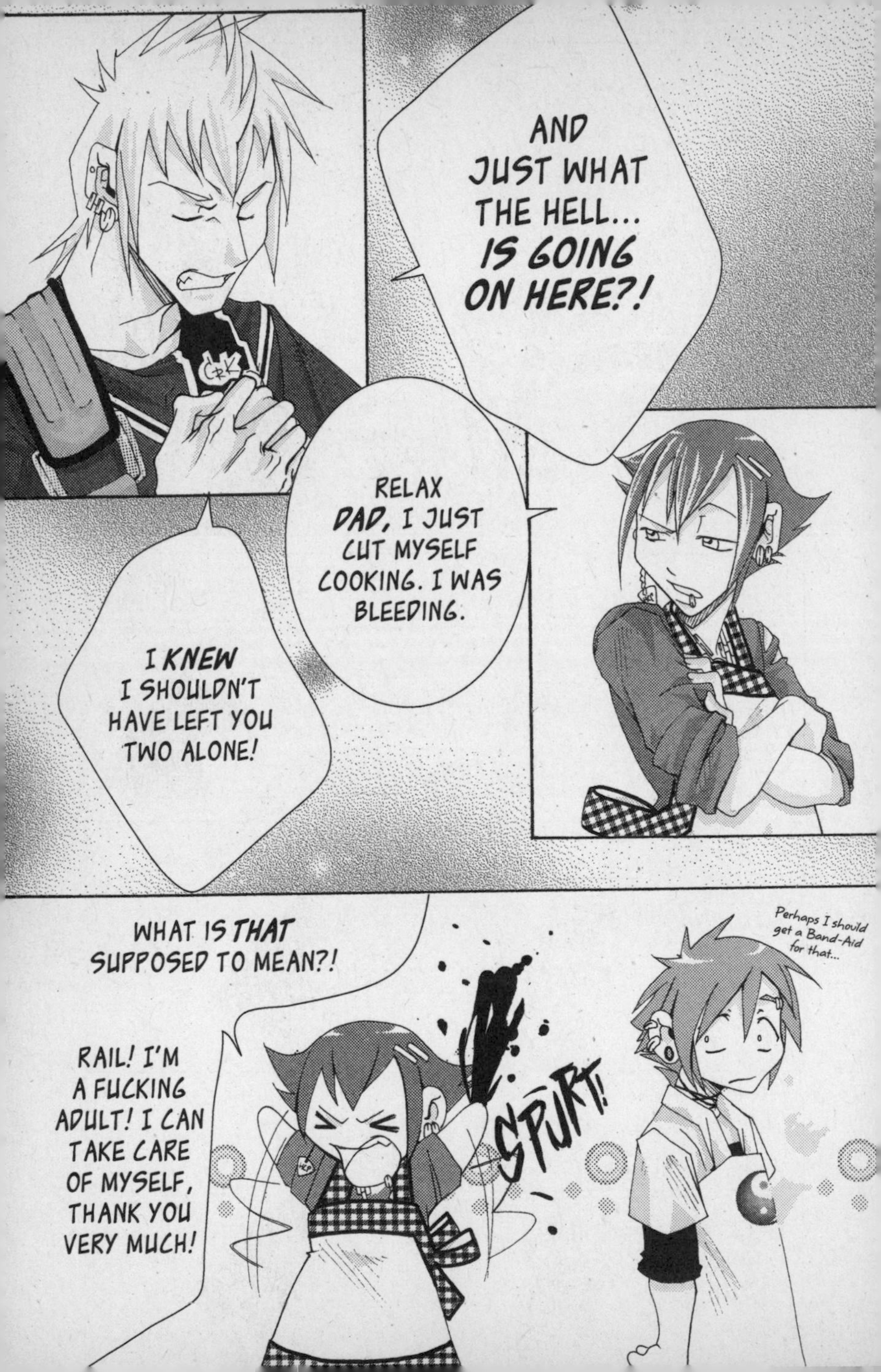
AND JUST WHAT THE HELL... IS GOING ON HERE?!
RELAX DAD, I JUST CUT MYSELF COOKING. I WAS BLEEDING.
I KNEW I SHOULDN'T HAVE LEFT YOU TWO ALONE!
WHAT IS THAT SUPPOSED TO MEAN?!
RAIL! I'M A FUCKING ADULT! I CAN TAKE CARE OF MYSELF, THANK YOU VERY MUCH!
SPURT!
Perhaps I should get a Band-Aid for that...

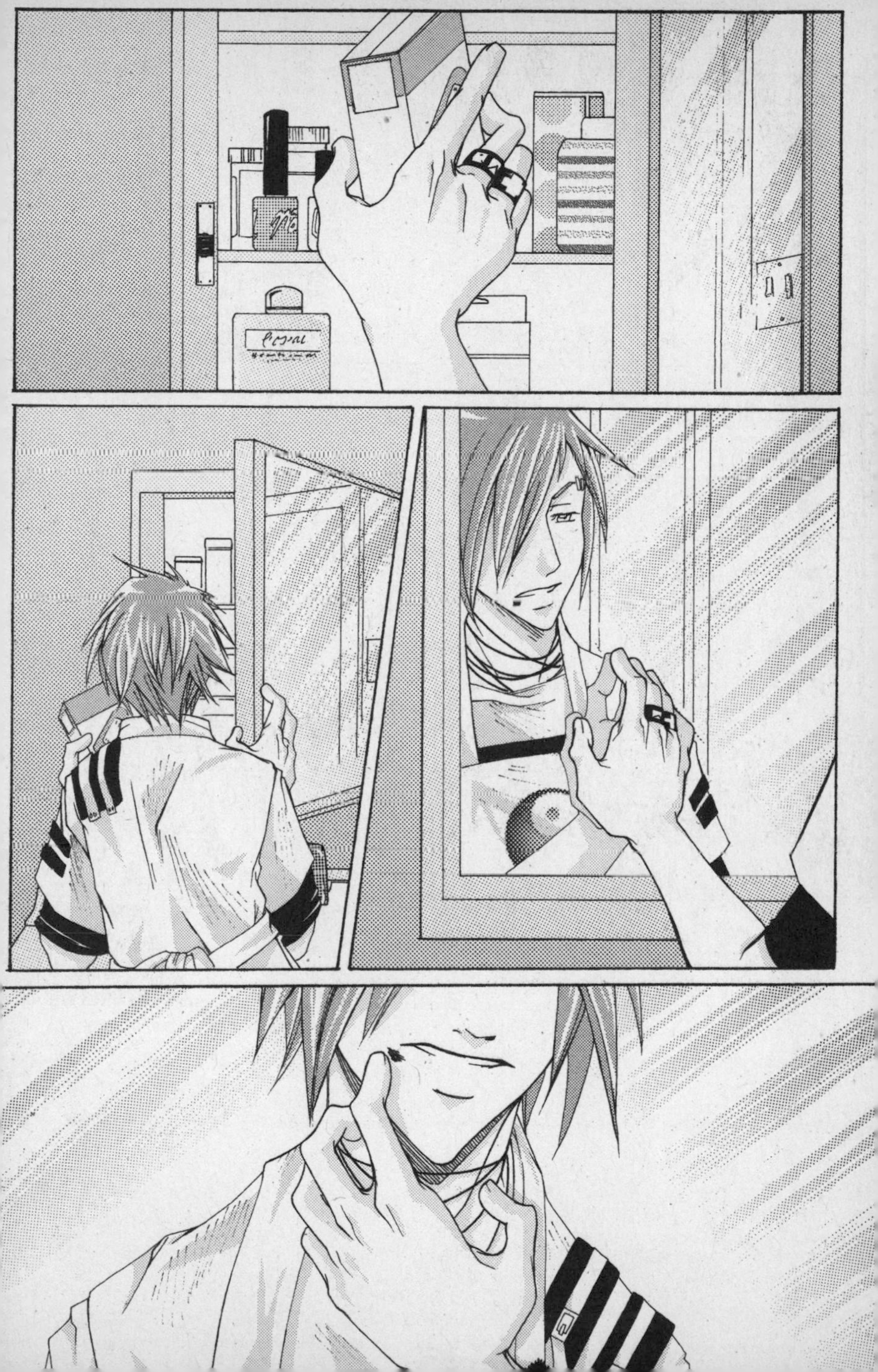

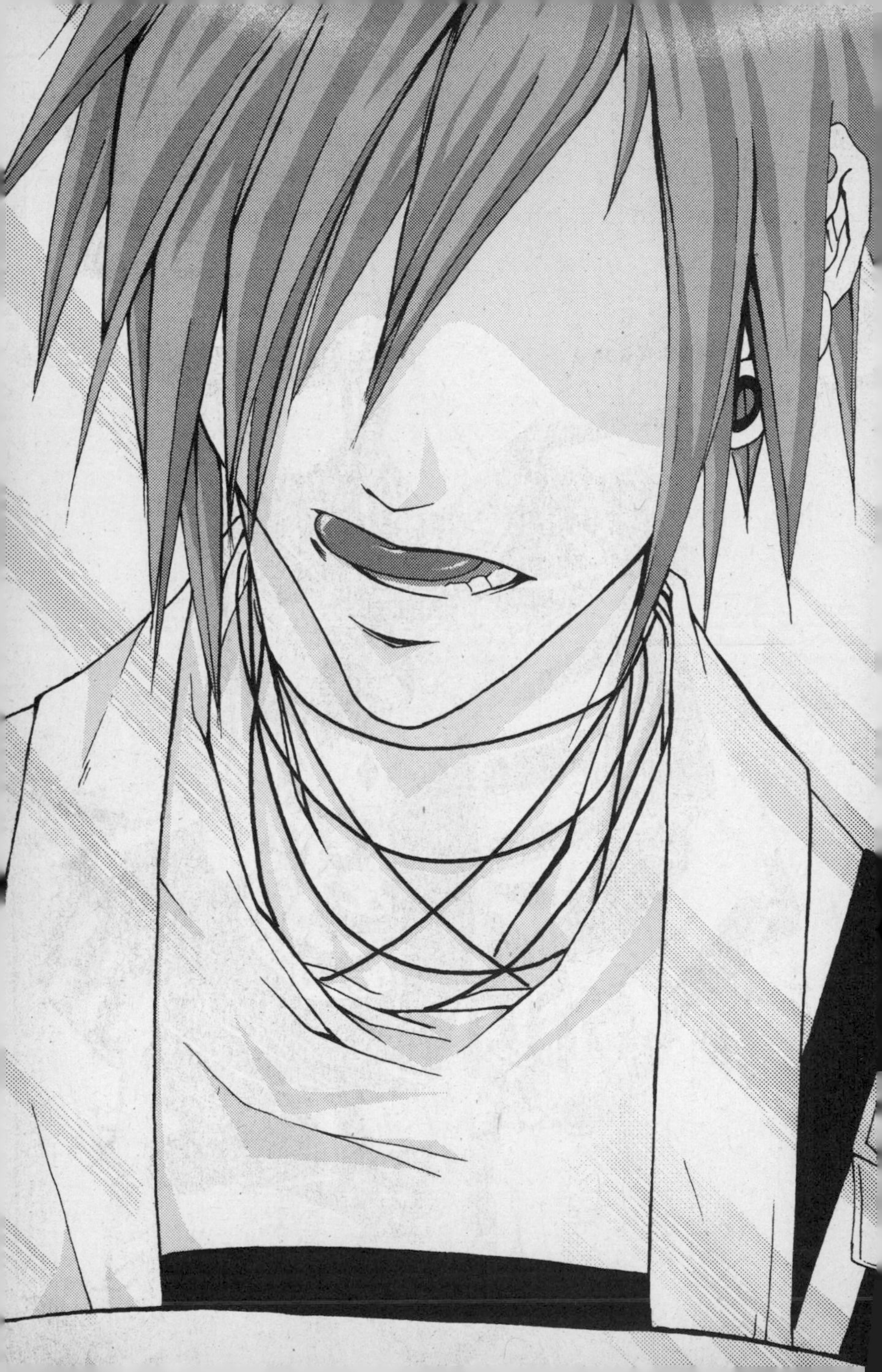

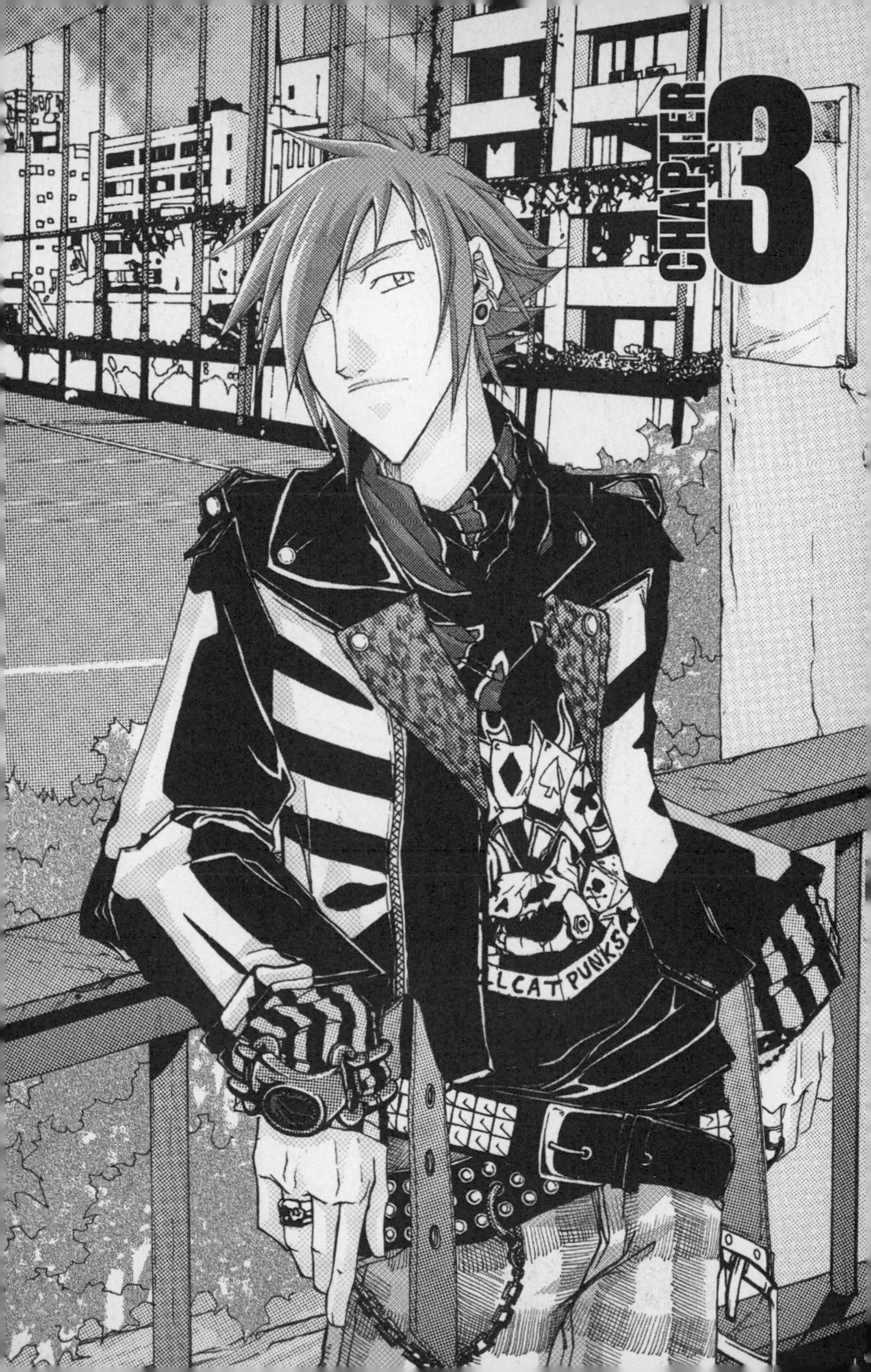
CHAPTER 3

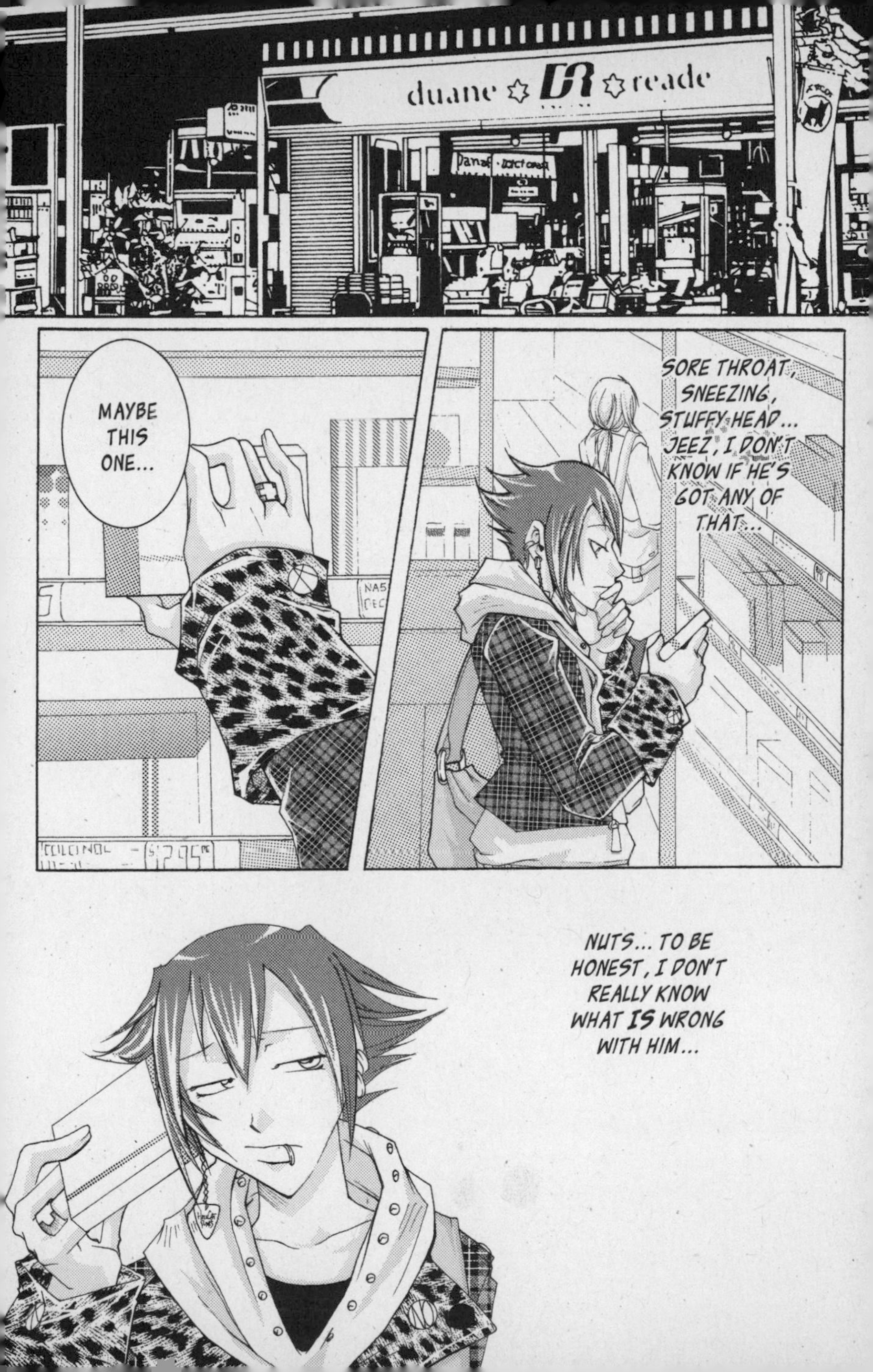
duane reade
MAYBE THIS ONE...
SORE THROAT, SNEEZING, STUFFY HEAD... JEEZ, I DON'T KNOW IF HE'S GOT ANY OF THAT...
NUTS... TO BE HONEST, I DON'T REALLY KNOW WHAT **IS** WRONG WITH HIM...

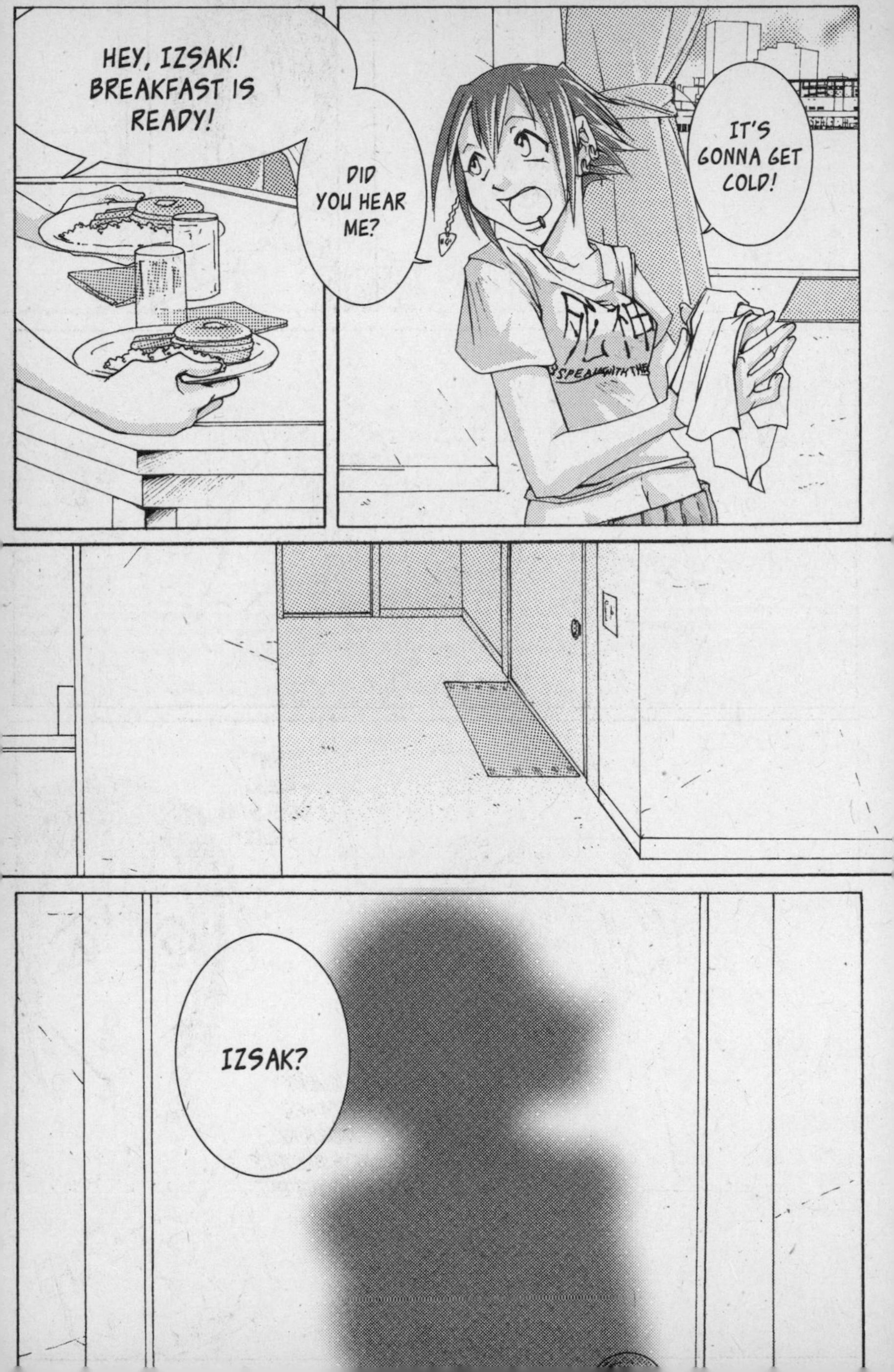
HEY, IZSAK! BREAKFAST IS READY!
DID YOU HEAR ME?
IT'S GONNA GET COLD!
IZSAK?

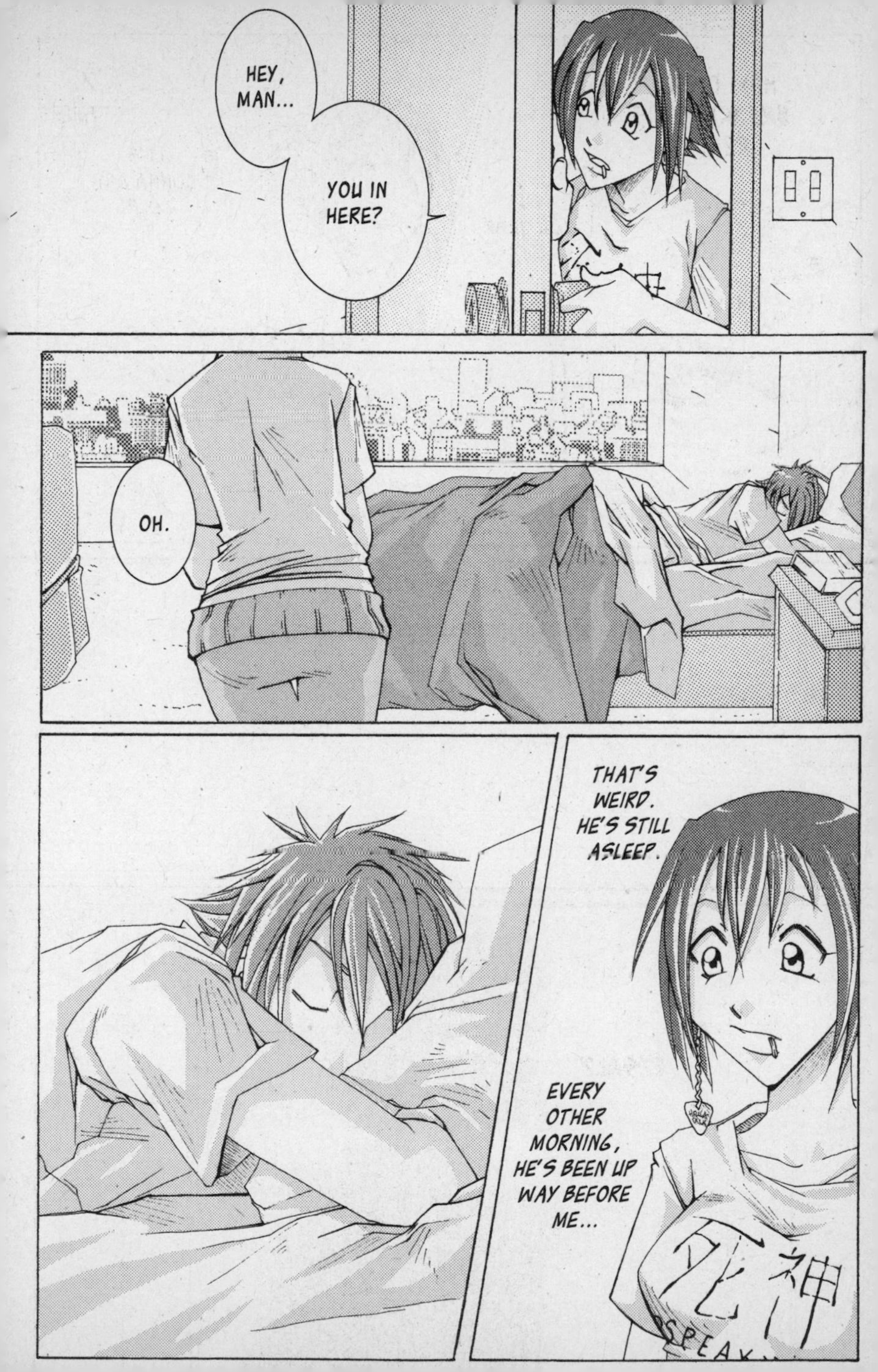
HEY, MAN...
YOU IN HERE?
OH.
THAT'S WEIRD. HE'S STILL ASLEEP.
EVERY OTHER MORNING, HE'S BEEN UP WAY BEFORE ME...

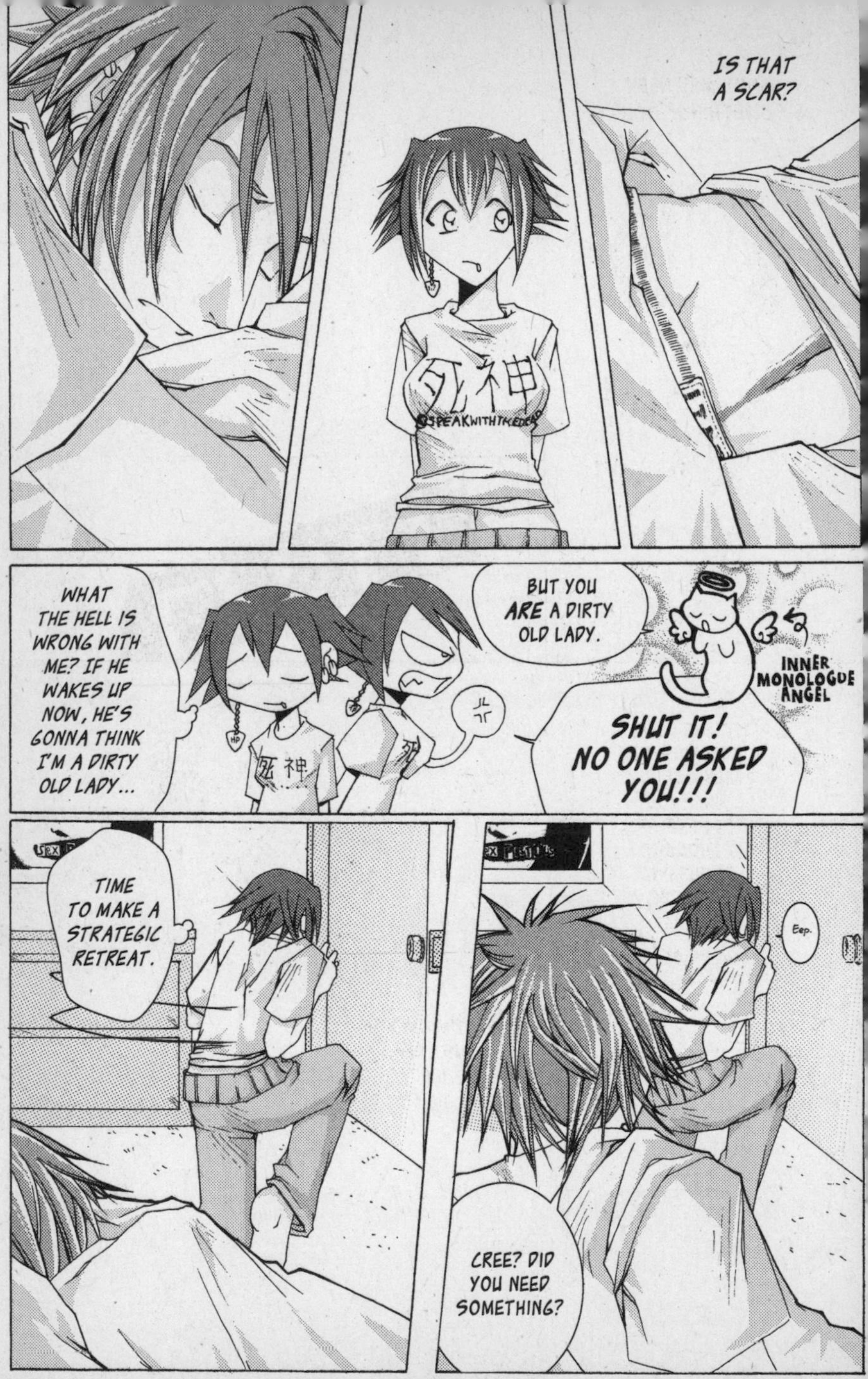
IS THAT A SCAR?
WHAT THE HELL IS WRONG WITH ME? IF HE WAKES UP NOW, HE'S GONNA THINK I'M A DIRTY OLD LADY...
BUT YOU **ARE** A DIRTY OLD LADY.
INNER MONOLOGUE ANGEL
SHUT IT! NO ONE ASKED YOU!!!
TIME TO MAKE A STRATEGIC RETREAT.
Eep.
CREE? DID YOU NEED SOMETHING?

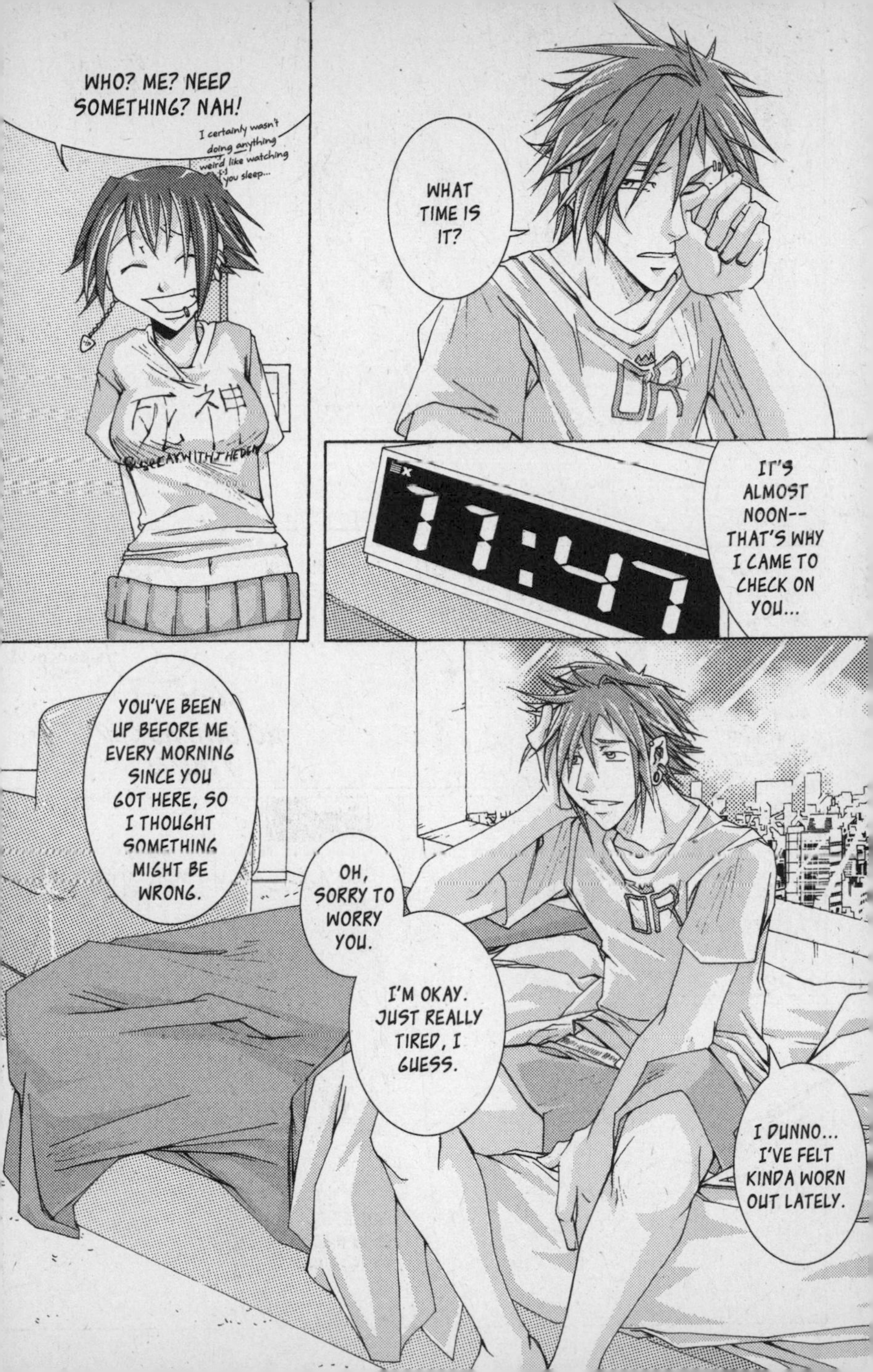
WHO? ME? NEED SOMETHING? NAH!
I certainly wasn't doing anything weird like watching you sleep...
WHAT TIME IS IT?
11:47
IT'S ALMOST NOON-- THAT'S WHY I CAME TO CHECK ON YOU...
YOU'VE BEEN UP BEFORE ME EVERY MORNING SINCE YOU GOT HERE, SO I THOUGHT SOMETHING MIGHT BE WRONG.
OH, SORRY TO WORRY YOU.
I'M OKAY. JUST REALLY TIRED, I GUESS.
I DUNNO... I'VE FELT KINDA WORN OUT LATELY.

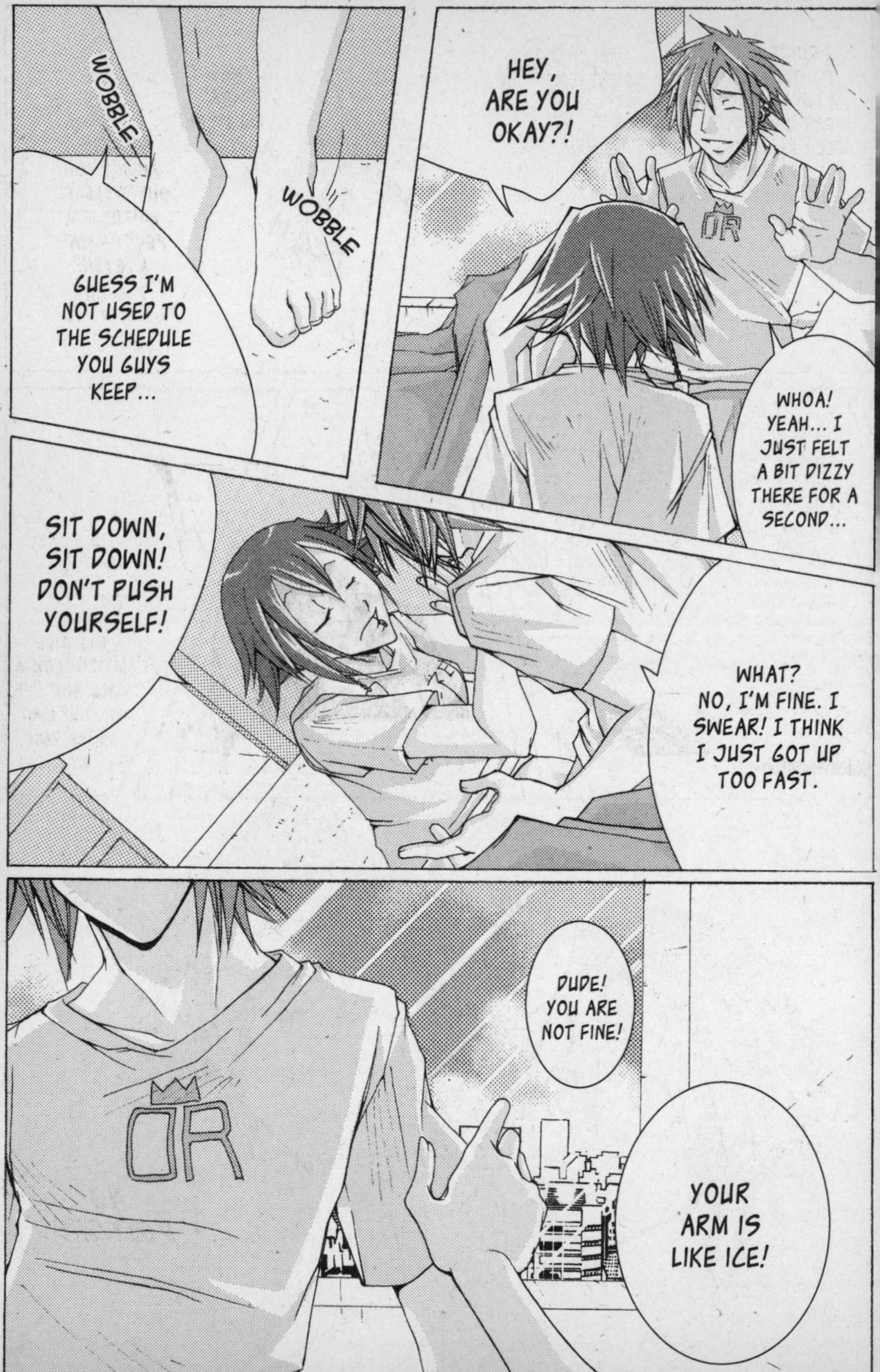
WOBBLE
WOBBLE
GUESS I'M NOT USED TO THE SCHEDULE YOU GUYS KEEP...
HEY, ARE YOU OKAY?!
WHOA! YEAH... I JUST FELT A BIT DIZZY THERE FOR A SECOND...
SIT DOWN, SIT DOWN! DON'T PUSH YOURSELF!
WHAT? NO, I'M FINE. I SWEAR! I THINK I JUST GOT UP TOO FAST.
DUDE! YOU ARE NOT FINE!
YOUR ARM IS LIKE ICE!

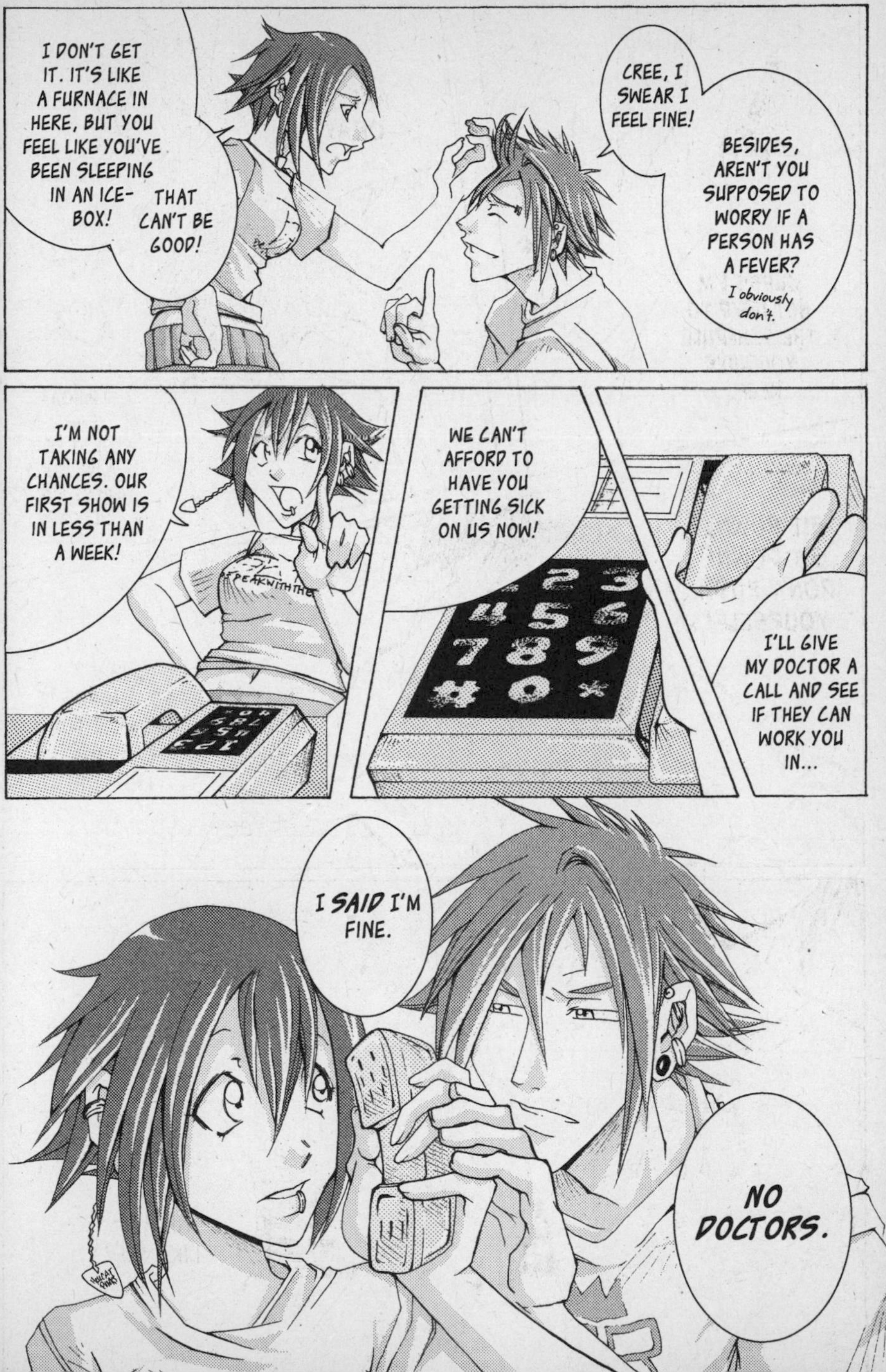

I DON'T GET IT. IT'S LIKE A FURNACE IN HERE, BUT YOU FEEL LIKE YOU'VE BEEN SLEEPING IN AN ICE-BOX!
THAT CAN'T BE GOOD!
CREE, I SWEAR I FEEL FINE!
BESIDES, AREN'T YOU SUPPOSED TO WORRY IF A PERSON HAS A FEVER?
I obviously don't.
I'M NOT TAKING ANY CHANCES. OUR FIRST SHOW IS IN LESS THAN A WEEK!
WE CAN'T AFFORD TO HAVE YOU GETTING SICK ON US NOW!
I'LL GIVE MY DOCTOR A CALL AND SEE IF THEY CAN WORK YOU IN...
I SAID I'M FINE.
NO DOCTORS.

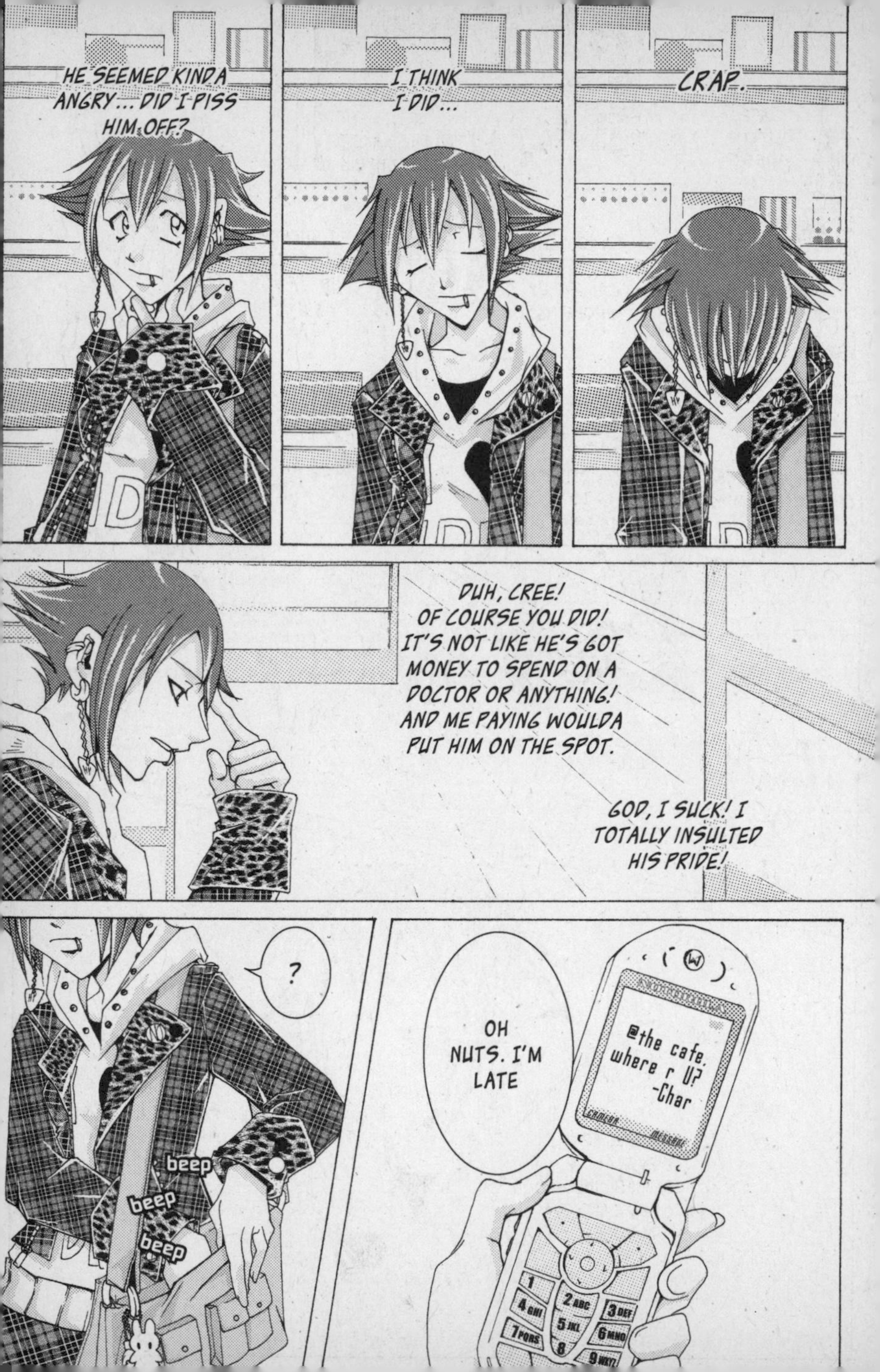
HE SEEMED KINDA ANGRY... DID I PISS HIM OFF?
I THINK I DID...
CRAP.
DUH, CREE! OF COURSE YOU DID! IT'S NOT LIKE HE'S GOT MONEY TO SPEND ON A DOCTOR OR ANYTHING! AND ME PAYING WOULDA PUT HIM ON THE SPOT.
GOD, I SUCK! I TOTALLY INSULTED HIS PRIDE!
?
beep
beep
beep
OH NUTS. I'M LATE
@the cafe. where r U? -Char

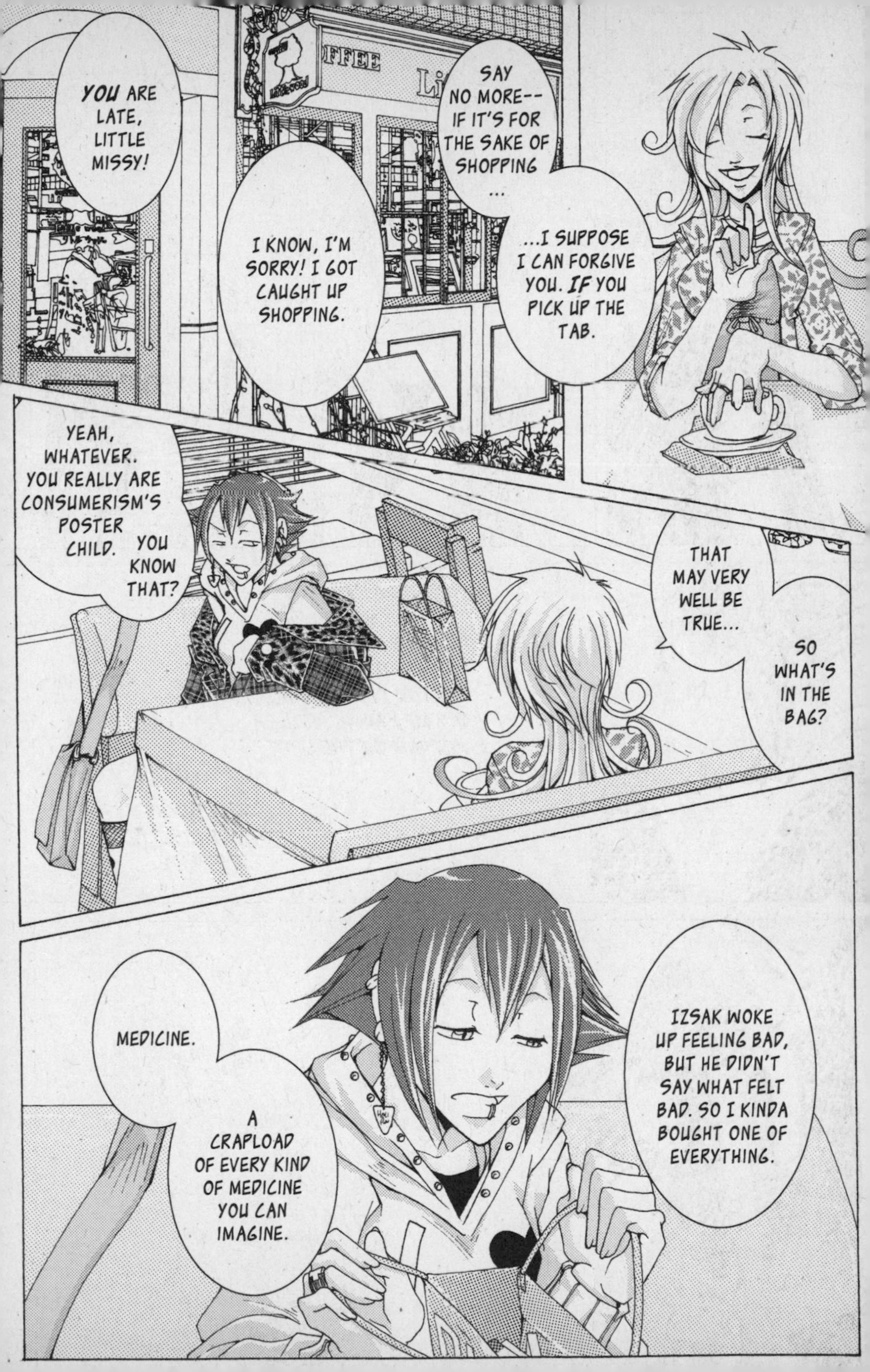

YOU ARE LATE, LITTLE MISSY!
I KNOW, I'M SORRY! I GOT CAUGHT UP SHOPPING.
SAY NO MORE-- IF IT'S FOR THE SAKE OF SHOPPING ...
...I SUPPOSE I CAN FORGIVE YOU. *IF* YOU PICK UP THE TAB.
YEAH, WHATEVER. YOU REALLY ARE CONSUMERISM'S POSTER CHILD.
YOU KNOW THAT?
THAT MAY VERY WELL BE TRUE...
SO WHAT'S IN THE BAG?
MEDICINE.
A CRAPLOAD OF EVERY KIND OF MEDICINE YOU CAN IMAGINE.
IZSAK WOKE UP FEELING BAD, BUT HE DIDN'T SAY WHAT FELT BAD. SO I KINDA BOUGHT ONE OF EVERYTHING.

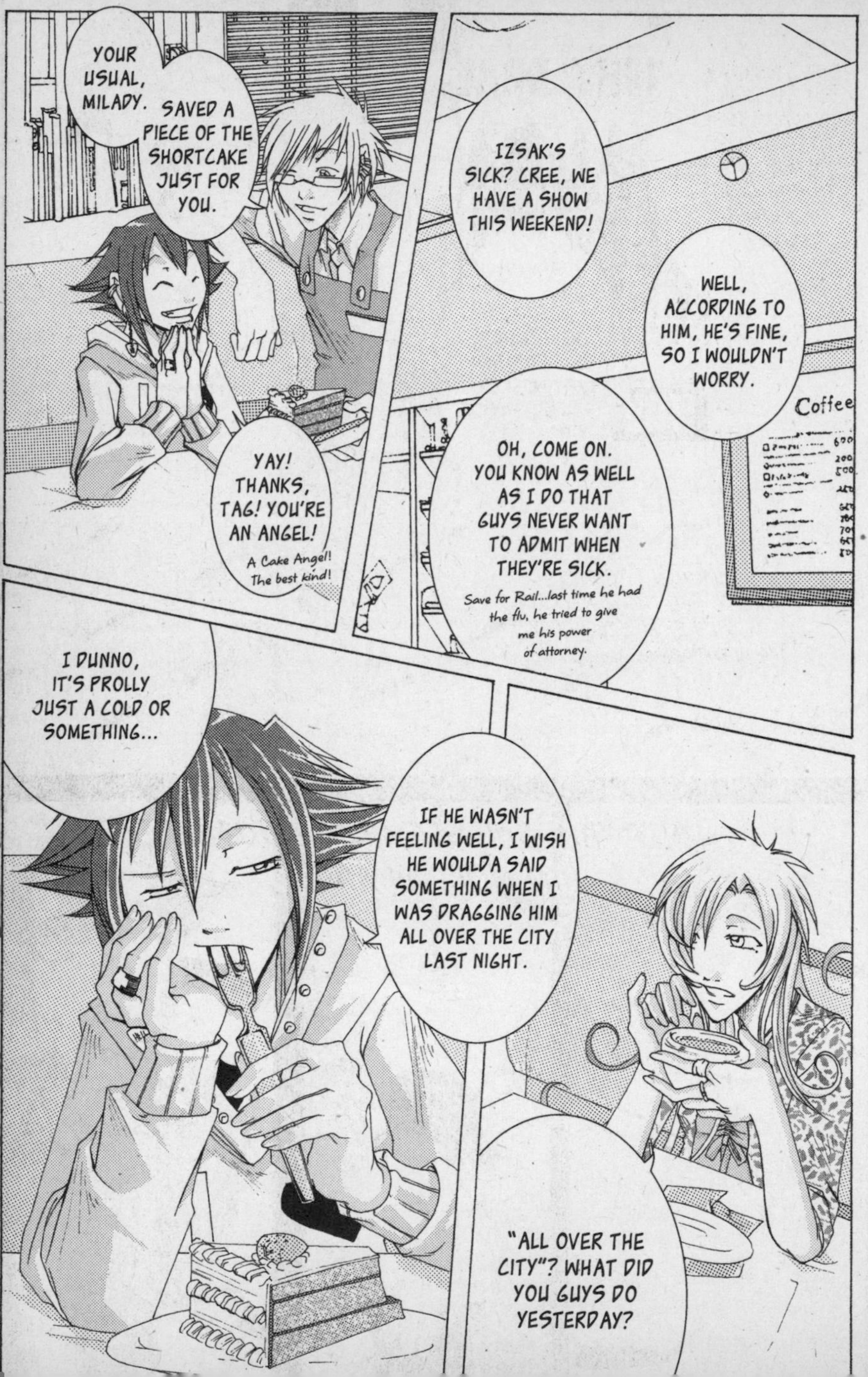
YOUR USUAL, MILADY.
SAVED A PIECE OF THE SHORTCAKE JUST FOR YOU.
YAY! THANKS, TAG! YOU'RE AN ANGEL!
A Cake Angel! The best kind!
IZSAK'S SICK? CREE, WE HAVE A SHOW THIS WEEKEND!
WELL, ACCORDING TO HIM, HE'S FINE, SO I WOULDN'T WORRY.
Coffee
OH, COME ON. YOU KNOW AS WELL AS I DO THAT GUYS NEVER WANT TO ADMIT WHEN THEY'RE SICK.
Save for Rail...last time he had the flu, he tried to give me his power of attorney.
I DUNNO, IT'S PROLLY JUST A COLD OR SOMETHING...
IF HE WASN'T FEELING WELL, I WISH HE WOULDA SAID SOMETHING WHEN I WAS DRAGGING HIM ALL OVER THE CITY LAST NIGHT.
"ALL OVER THE CITY"? WHAT DID YOU GUYS DO YESTERDAY?

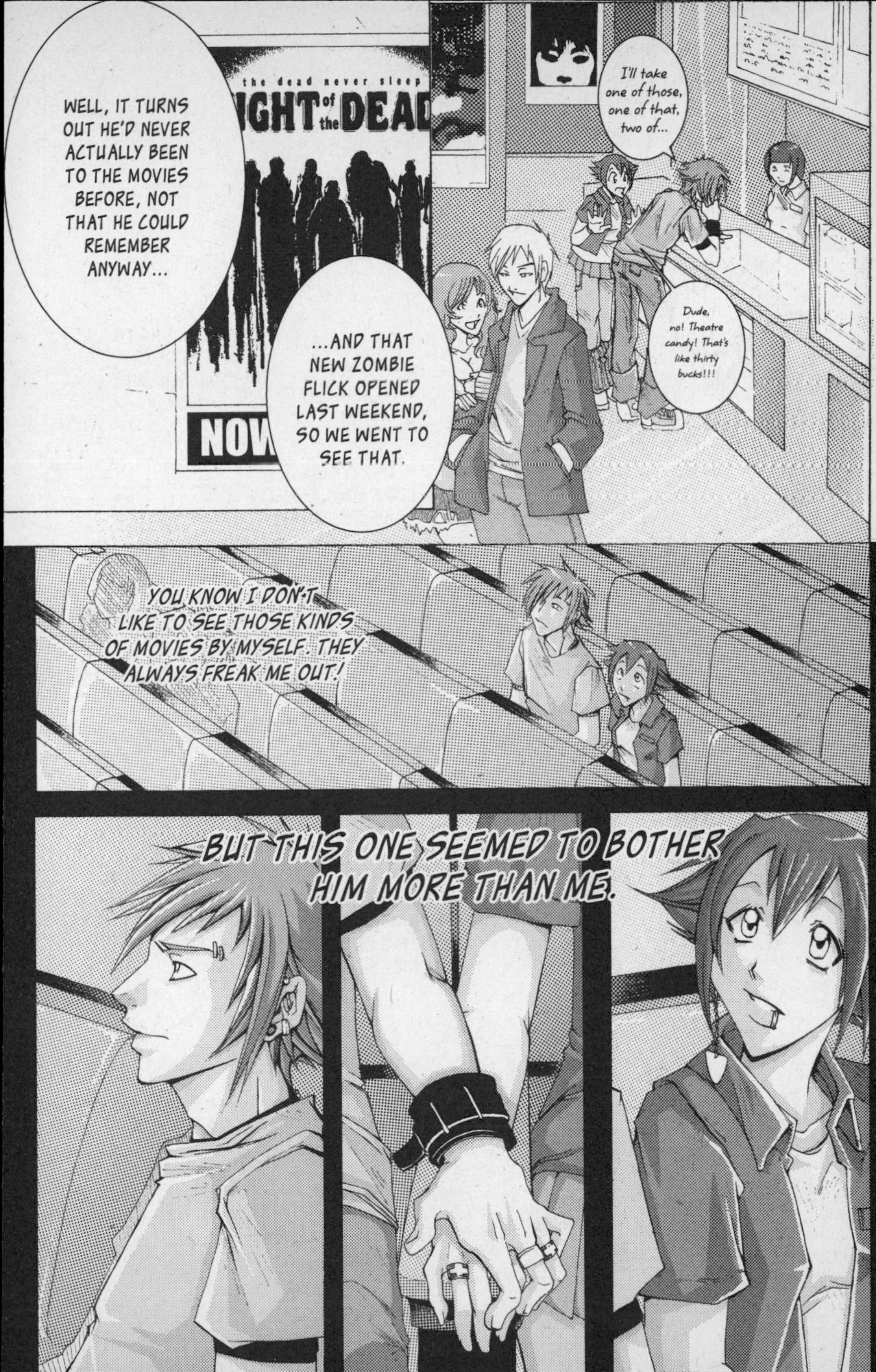
WELL, IT TURNS OUT HE'D NEVER ACTUALLY BEEN TO THE MOVIES BEFORE, NOT THAT HE COULD REMEMBER ANYWAY...
the dead never sleep
IGHT of the DEAD
NOW
...AND THAT NEW ZOMBIE FLICK OPENED LAST WEEKEND, SO WE WENT TO SEE THAT.
I'll take one of those, one of that, two of...
Dude, no! Theatre candy! That's like thirty bucks!!!
YOU KNOW I DON'T LIKE TO SEE THOSE KINDS OF MOVIES BY MYSELF. THEY ALWAYS FREAK ME OUT!
BUT THIS ONE SEEMED TO BOTHER HIM MORE THAN ME.

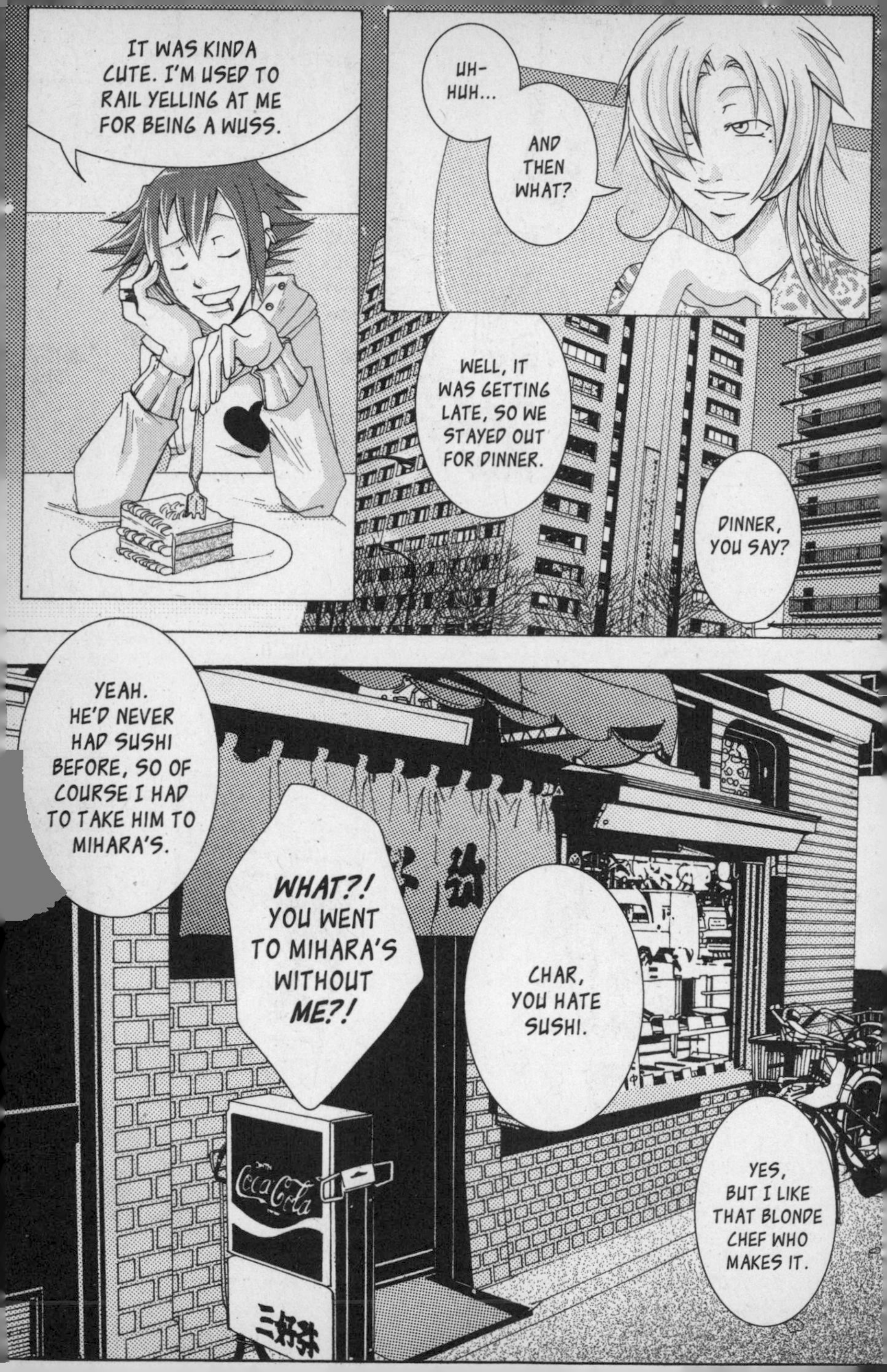
IT WAS KINDA CUTE. I'M USED TO RAIL YELLING AT ME FOR BEING A WUSS.
UH-HUH...
AND THEN WHAT?
WELL, IT WAS GETTING LATE, SO WE STAYED OUT FOR DINNER.
DINNER, YOU SAY?
YEAH. HE'D NEVER HAD SUSHI BEFORE, SO OF COURSE I HAD TO TAKE HIM TO MIHARA'S.
WHAT?! YOU WENT TO MIHARA'S WITHOUT *ME?!*
CHAR, YOU HATE SUSHI.
YES, BUT I LIKE THAT BLONDE CHEF WHO MAKES IT.
Coca-Cola

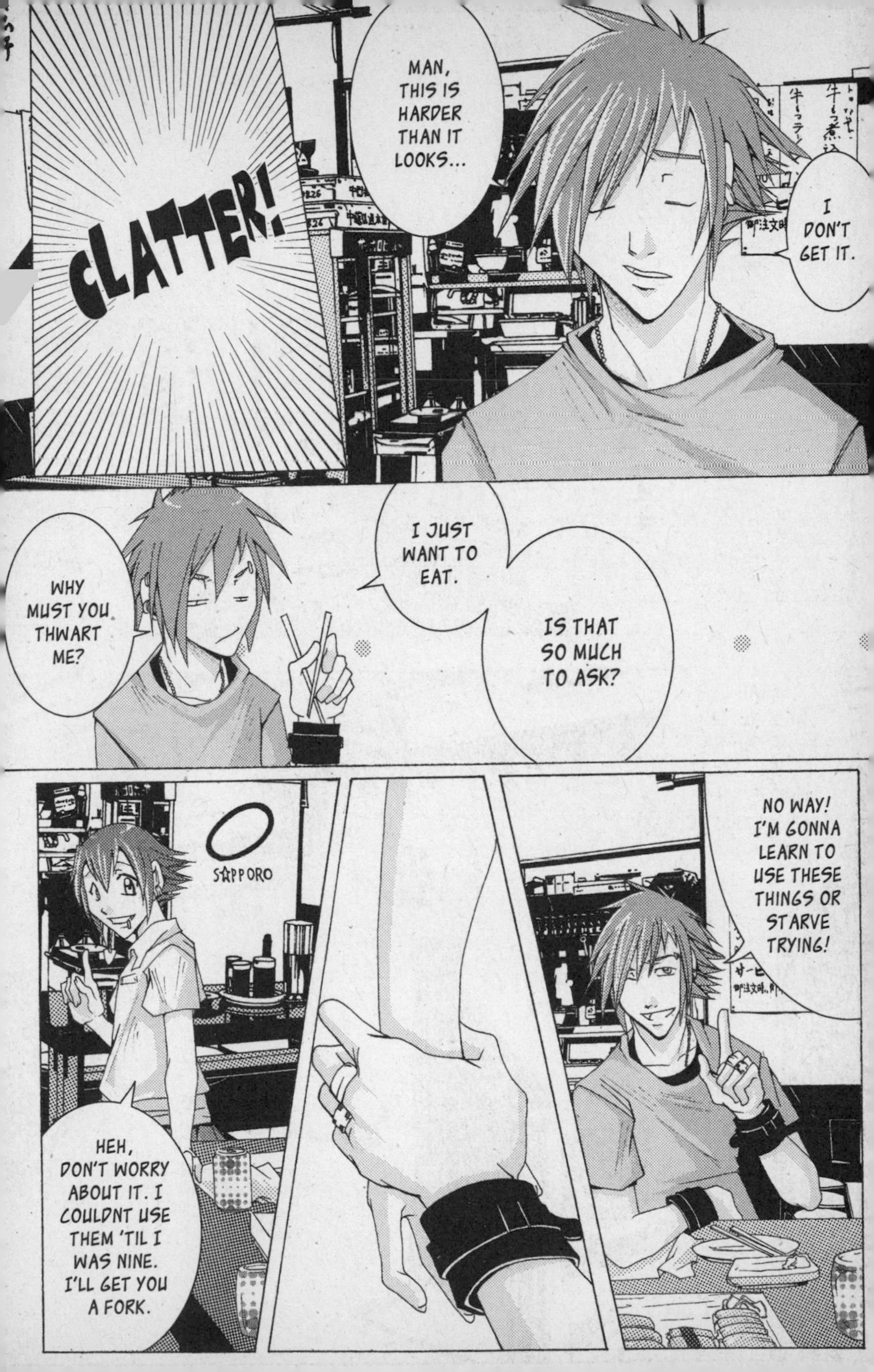
CLATTER!
MAN, THIS IS HARDER THAN IT LOOKS...
I DON'T GET IT.
WHY MUST YOU THWART ME?
I JUST WANT TO EAT.
IS THAT SO MUCH TO ASK?
SAPPORO
HEH, DON'T WORRY ABOUT IT. I COULDNT USE THEM 'TIL I WAS NINE. I'LL GET YOU A FORK.
NO WAY! I'M GONNA LEARN TO USE THESE THINGS OR STARVE TRYING!

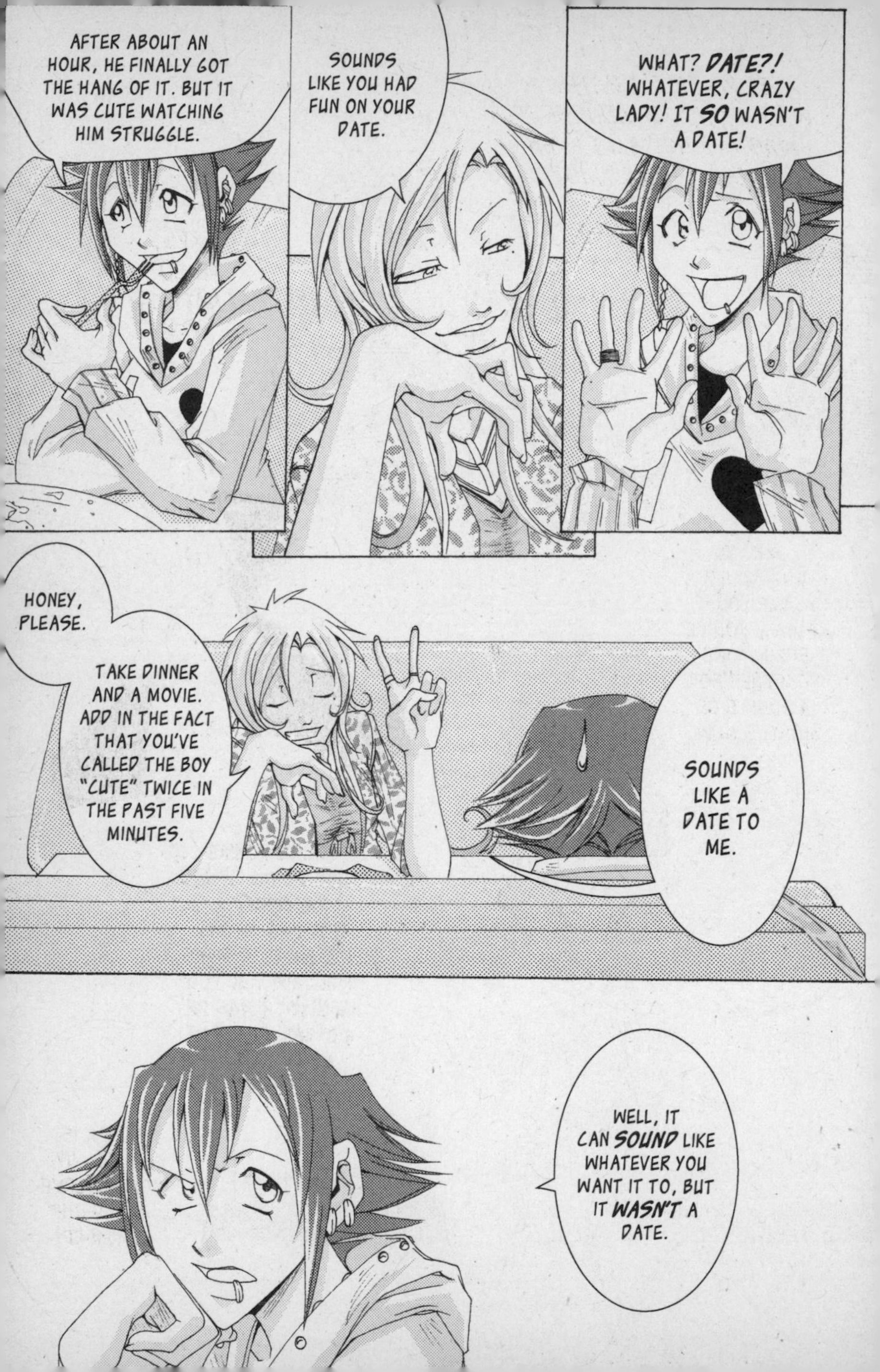
AFTER ABOUT AN HOUR, HE FINALLY GOT THE HANG OF IT. BUT IT WAS CUTE WATCHING HIM STRUGGLE.
SOUNDS LIKE YOU HAD FUN ON YOUR DATE.
WHAT? DATE?! WHATEVER, CRAZY LADY! IT SO WASN'T A DATE!
HONEY, PLEASE.
TAKE DINNER AND A MOVIE. ADD IN THE FACT THAT YOU'VE CALLED THE BOY "CUTE" TWICE IN THE PAST FIVE MINUTES.
SOUNDS LIKE A DATE TO ME.
WELL, IT CAN SOUND LIKE WHATEVER YOU WANT IT TO, BUT IT WASN'T A DATE.

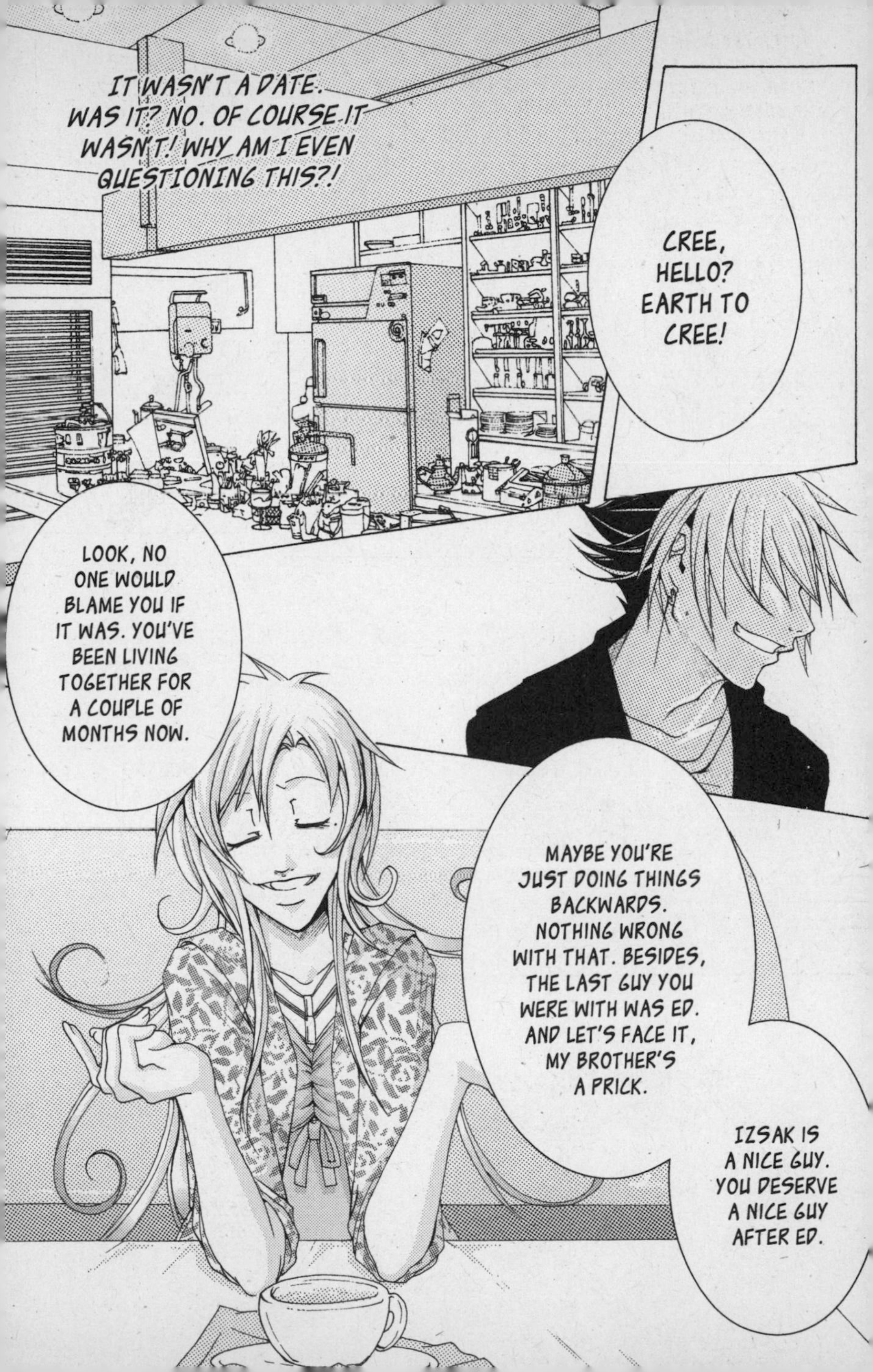
IT WASN'T A DATE. WAS IT? NO. OF COURSE IT WASN'T! WHY AM I EVEN QUESTIONING THIS?!
CREE, HELLO? EARTH TO CREE!
LOOK, NO ONE WOULD BLAME YOU IF IT WAS. YOU'VE BEEN LIVING TOGETHER FOR A COUPLE OF MONTHS NOW.
MAYBE YOU'RE JUST DOING THINGS BACKWARDS. NOTHING WRONG WITH THAT. BESIDES, THE LAST GUY YOU WERE WITH WAS ED. AND LET'S FACE IT, MY BROTHER'S A PRICK.
IZSAK IS A NICE GUY. YOU DESERVE A NICE GUY AFTER ED.

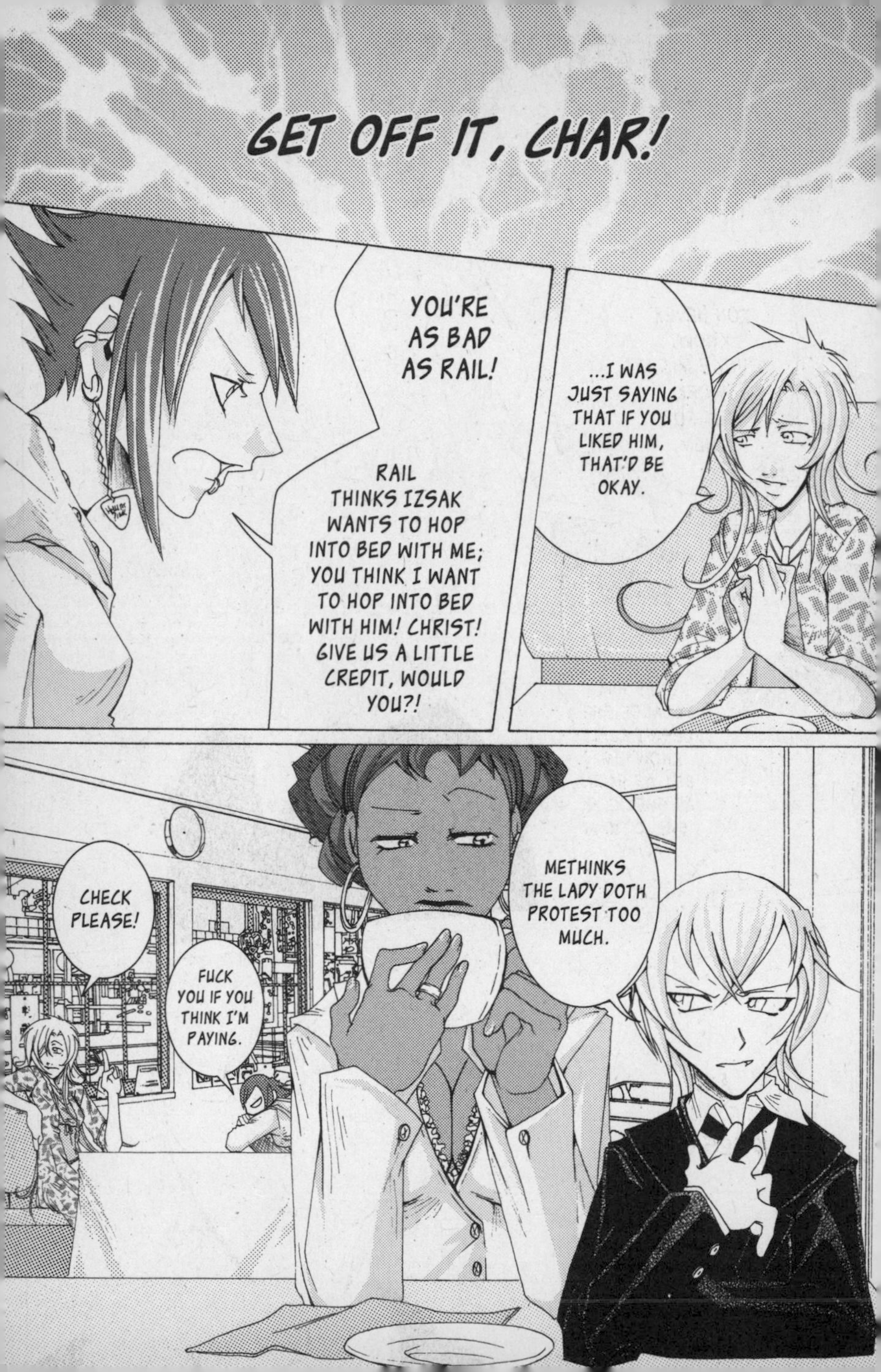

GET OFF IT, CHAR!
YOU'RE AS BAD AS RAIL!
RAIL THINKS IZSAK WANTS TO HOP INTO BED WITH ME; YOU THINK I WANT TO HOP INTO BED WITH HIM! CHRIST! GIVE US A LITTLE CREDIT, WOULD YOU?!
...I WAS JUST SAYING THAT IF YOU LIKED HIM, THAT'D BE OKAY.
CHECK PLEASE!
FUCK YOU IF YOU THINK I'M PAYING.
METHINKS THE LADY DOTH PROTEST TOO MUCH.

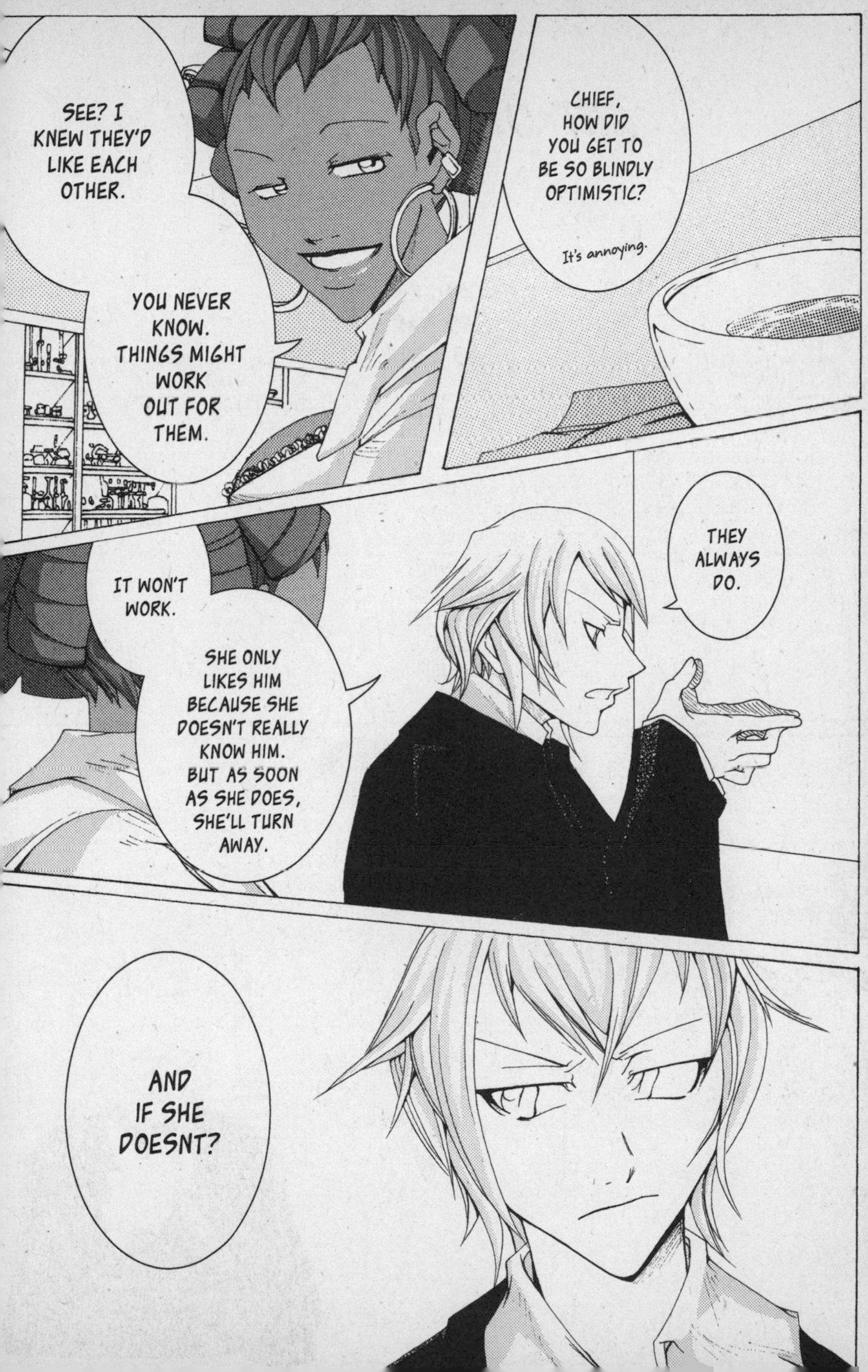
SEE? I KNEW THEY'D LIKE EACH OTHER.
YOU NEVER KNOW. THINGS MIGHT WORK OUT FOR THEM.
CHIEF, HOW DID YOU GET TO BE SO BLINDLY OPTIMISTIC?
It's annoying.
IT WON'T WORK.
SHE ONLY LIKES HIM BECAUSE SHE DOESN'T REALLY KNOW HIM. BUT AS SOON AS SHE DOES, SHE'LL TURN AWAY.
THEY ALWAYS DO.
AND IF SHE DOESNT?

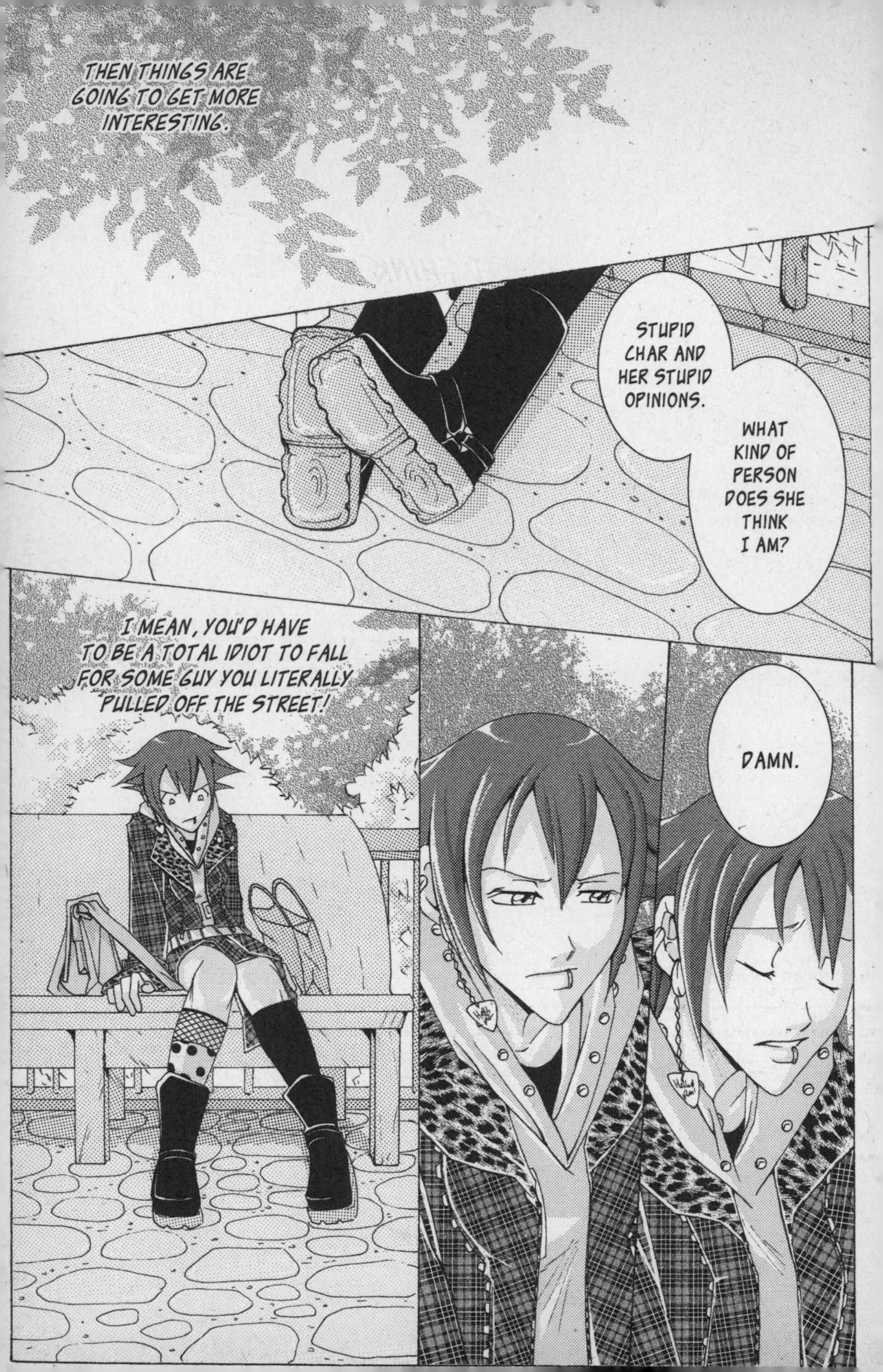
THEN THINGS ARE GOING TO GET MORE INTERESTING.
STUPID CHAR AND HER STUPID OPINIONS.
WHAT KIND OF PERSON DOES SHE THINK I AM?
I MEAN, YOU'D HAVE TO BE A TOTAL IDIOT TO FALL FOR SOME GUY YOU LITERALLY PULLED OFF THE STREET!
DAMN.

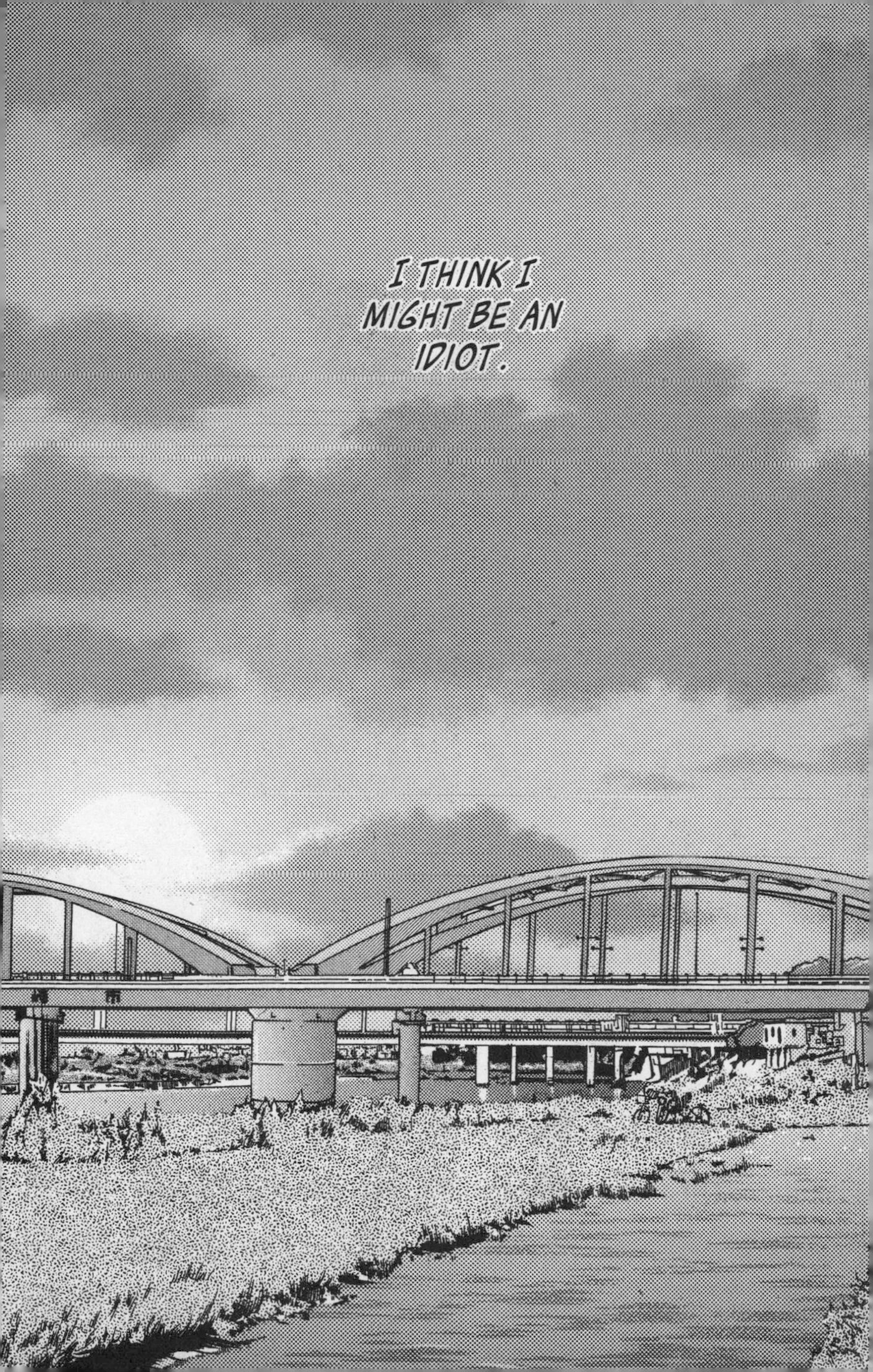
I THINK I MIGHT BE AN IDIOT.

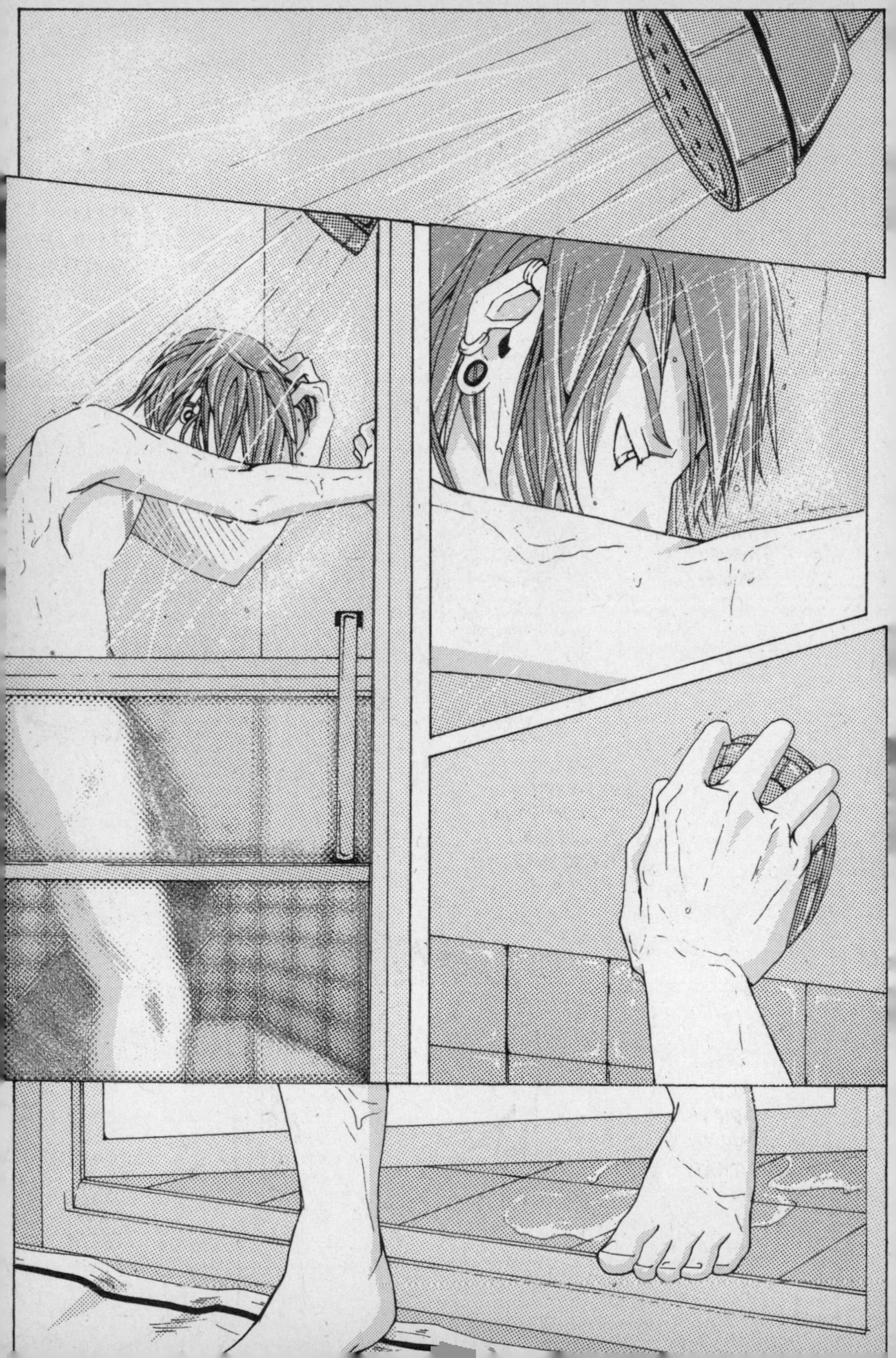

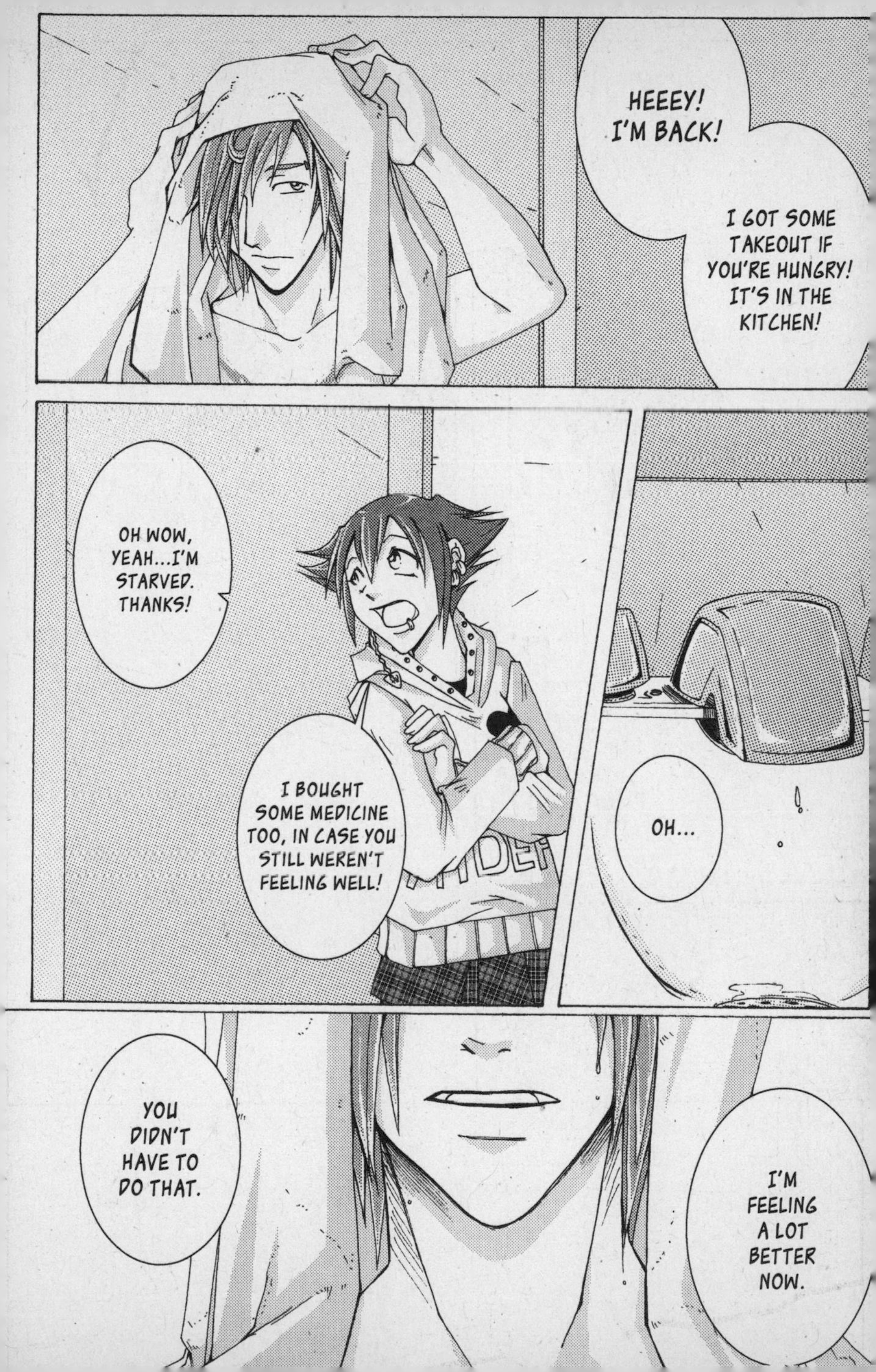
HEEEY! I'M BACK!
I GOT SOME TAKEOUT IF YOU'RE HUNGRY! IT'S IN THE KITCHEN!
OH WOW, YEAH...I'M STARVED. THANKS!
I BOUGHT SOME MEDICINE TOO, IN CASE YOU STILL WEREN'T FEELING WELL!
OH...
YOU DIDN'T HAVE TO DO THAT.
I'M FEELING A LOT BETTER NOW.

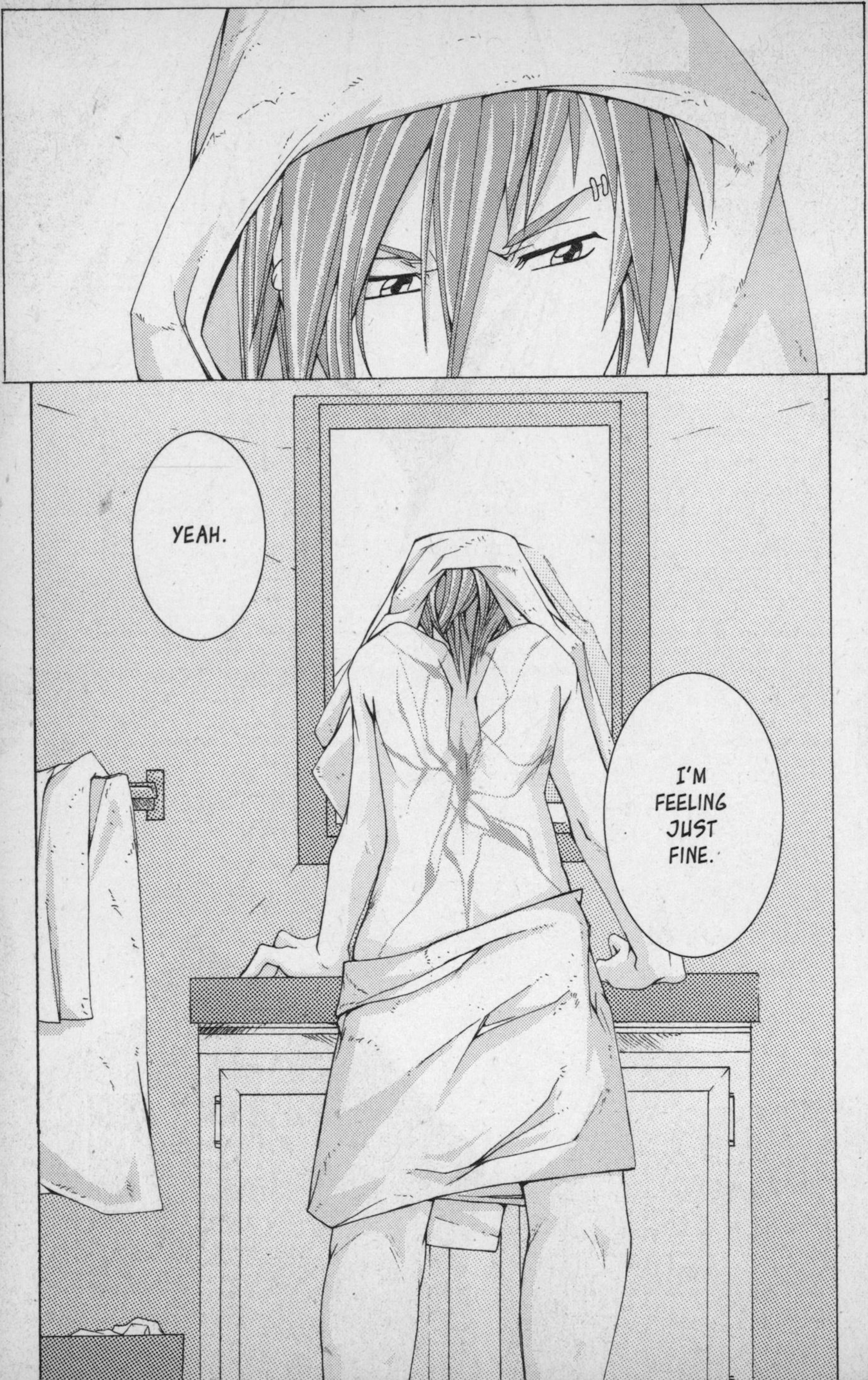
YEAH.
I'M FEELING JUST FINE.

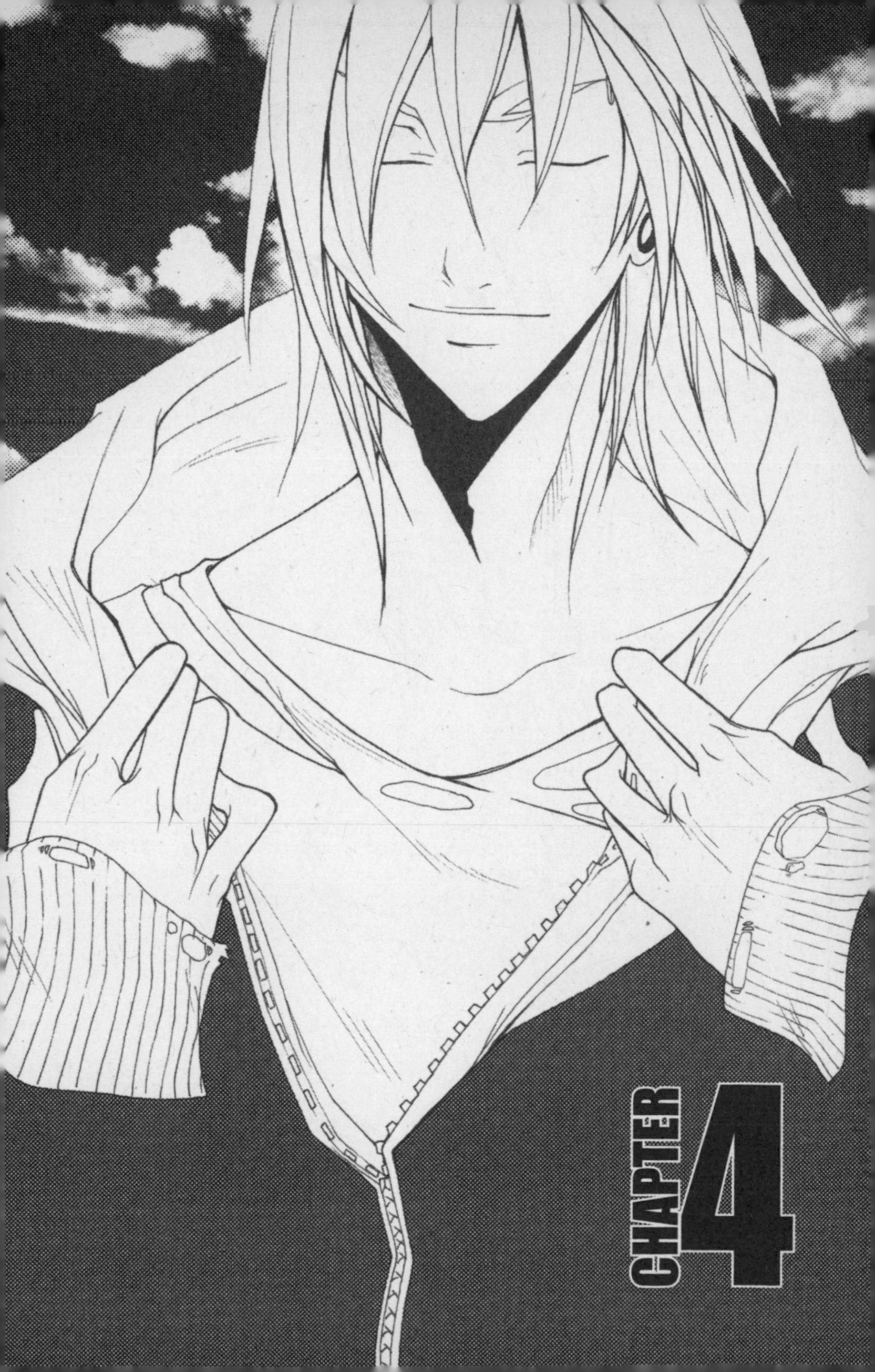
CHAPTER 4

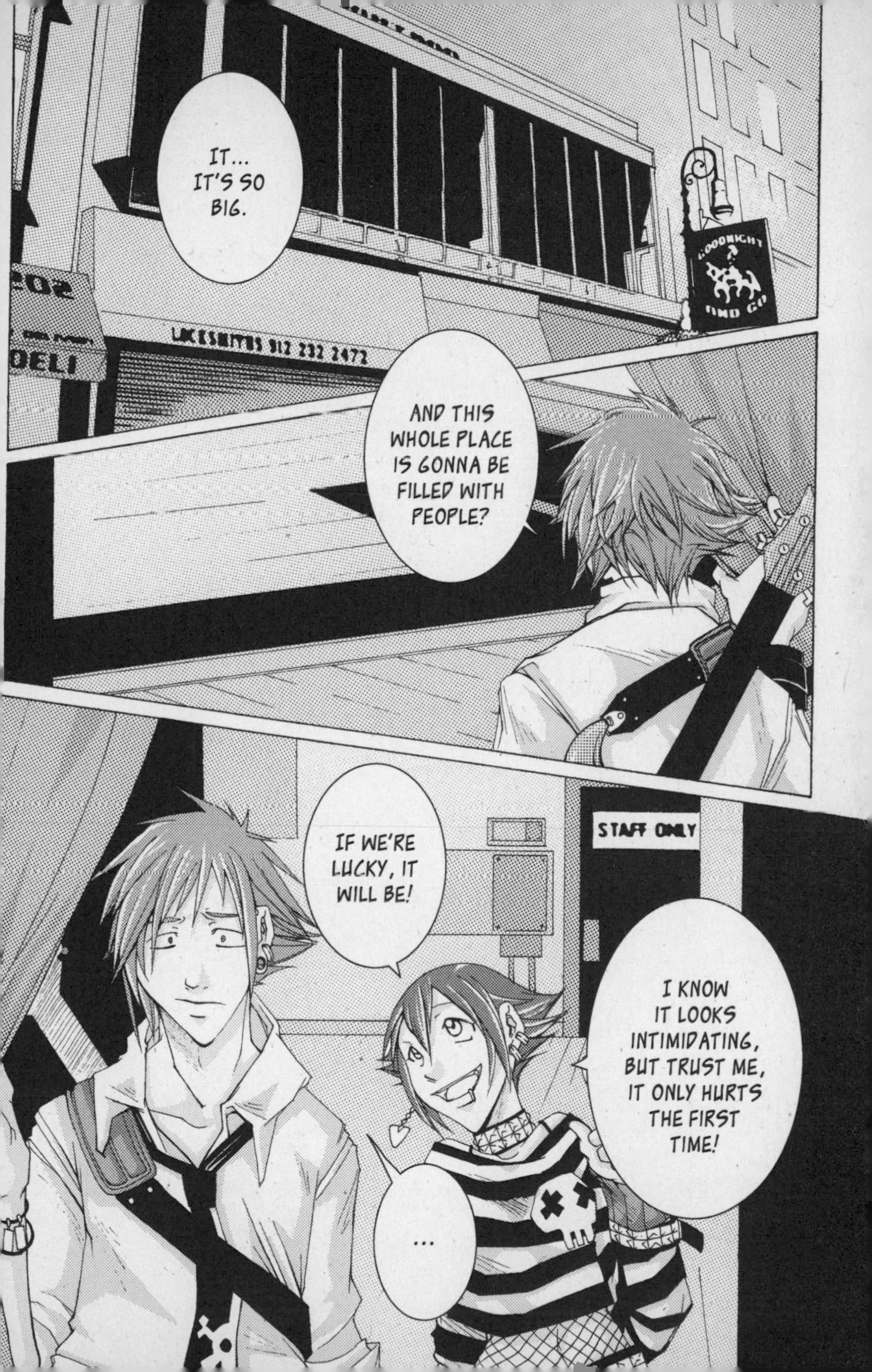
IT... IT'S SO BIG.
GOODNIGHT AND GO
DELI
LOCKSMITHS 912 232 2472
AND THIS WHOLE PLACE IS GONNA BE FILLED WITH PEOPLE?
IF WE'RE LUCKY, IT WILL BE!
STAFF ONLY
I KNOW IT LOOKS INTIMIDATING, BUT TRUST ME, IT ONLY HURTS THE FIRST TIME!
...

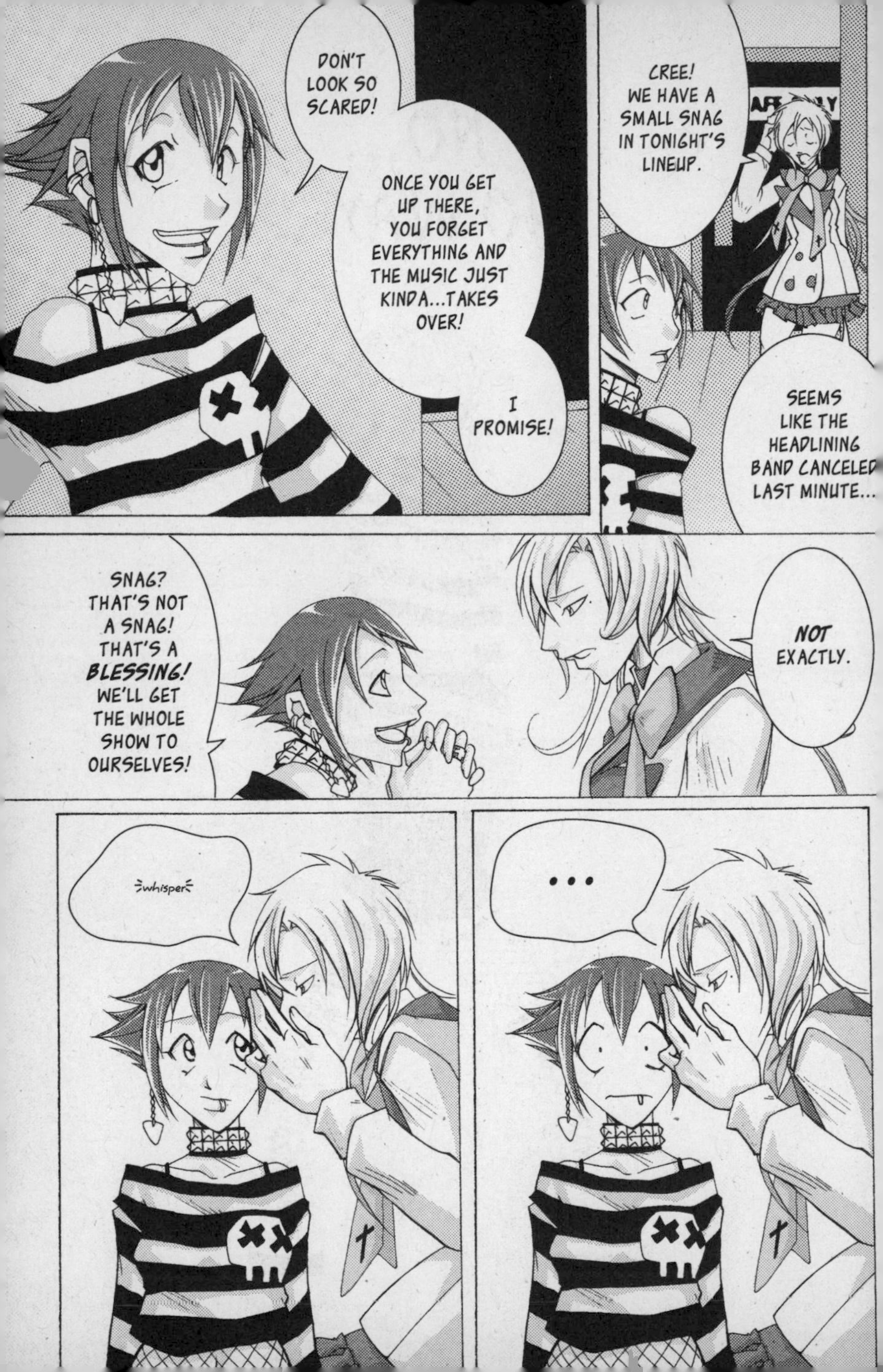
DON'T LOOK SO SCARED!
ONCE YOU GET UP THERE, YOU FORGET EVERYTHING AND THE MUSIC JUST KINDA...TAKES OVER!
I PROMISE!
CREE! WE HAVE A SMALL SNAG IN TONIGHT'S LINEUP.
SEEMS LIKE THE HEADLINING BAND CANCELED LAST MINUTE...
SNAG? THAT'S NOT A SNAG! THAT'S A *BLESSING!* WE'LL GET THE WHOLE SHOW TO OURSELVES!
NOT EXACTLY.
whisper
...

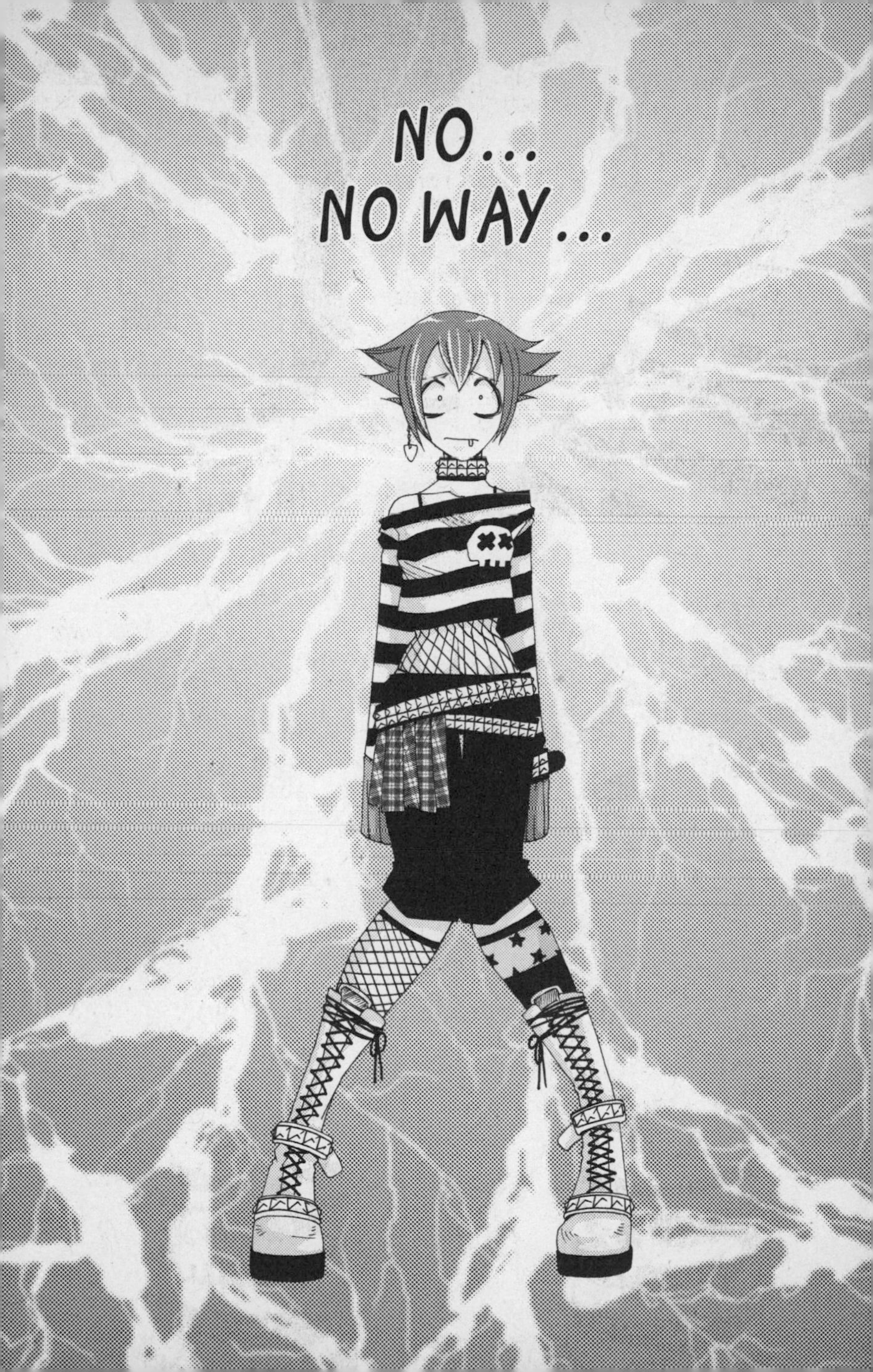
NO...
NO WAY...

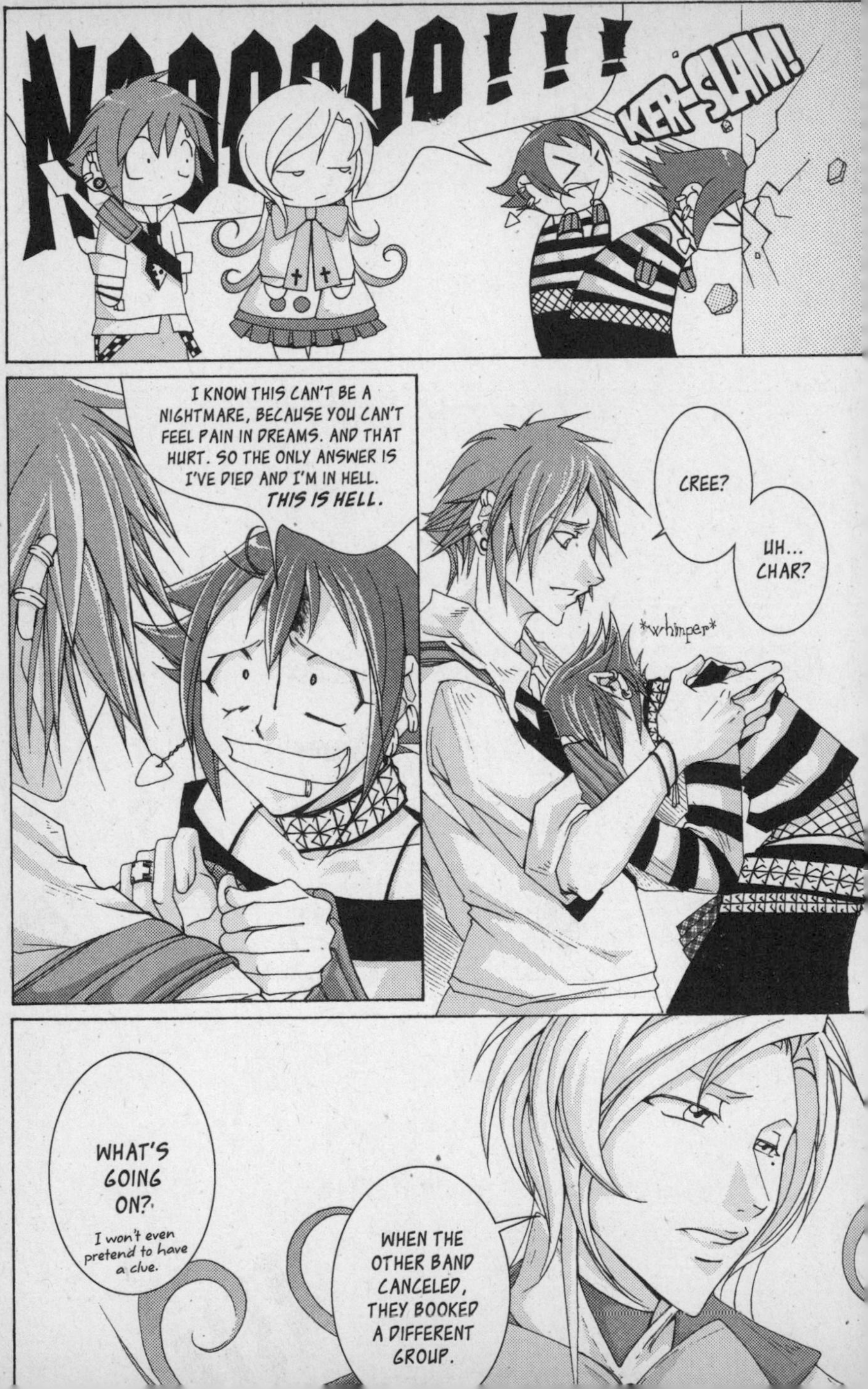
NOOOOOO!!!
KER-SLAM!
I KNOW THIS CAN'T BE A NIGHTMARE, BECAUSE YOU CAN'T FEEL PAIN IN DREAMS. AND THAT HURT. SO THE ONLY ANSWER IS I'VE DIED AND I'M IN HELL. THIS IS HELL.
CREE?
UH... CHAR?
whimper
WHAT'S GOING ON?
I won't even pretend to have a clue.
WHEN THE OTHER BAND CANCELED, THEY BOOKED A DIFFERENT GROUP.

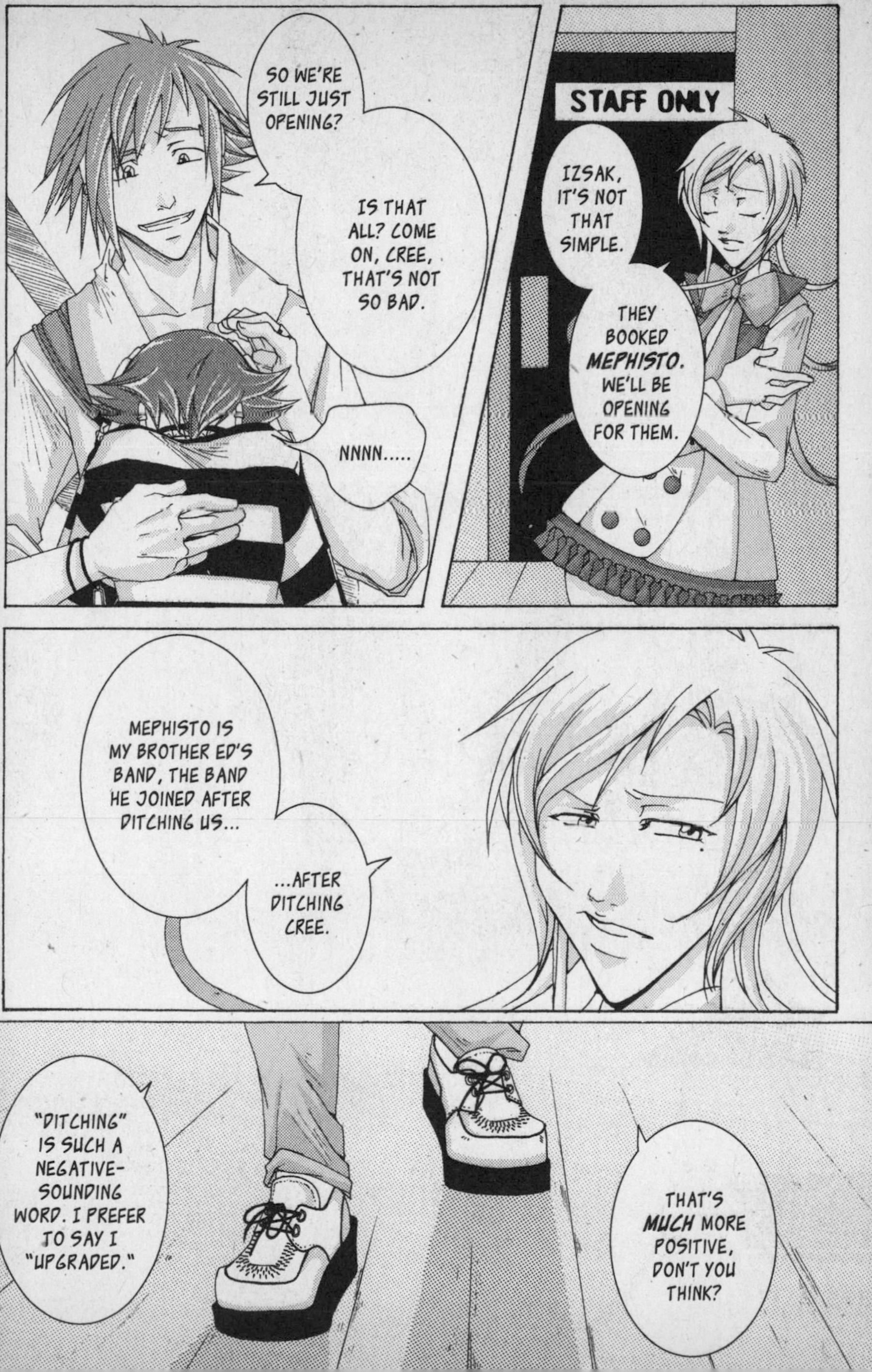
SO WE'RE STILL JUST OPENING?
IS THAT ALL? COME ON, CREE, THAT'S NOT SO BAD.
NNNN.....
STAFF ONLY
IZSAK, IT'S NOT THAT SIMPLE.
THEY BOOKED MEPHISTO. WE'LL BE OPENING FOR THEM.
MEPHISTO IS MY BROTHER ED'S BAND, THE BAND HE JOINED AFTER DITCHING US...
...AFTER DITCHING CREE.
"DITCHING" IS SUCH A NEGATIVE-SOUNDING WORD. I PREFER TO SAY I "UPGRADED."
THAT'S MUCH MORE POSITIVE, DON'T YOU THINK?

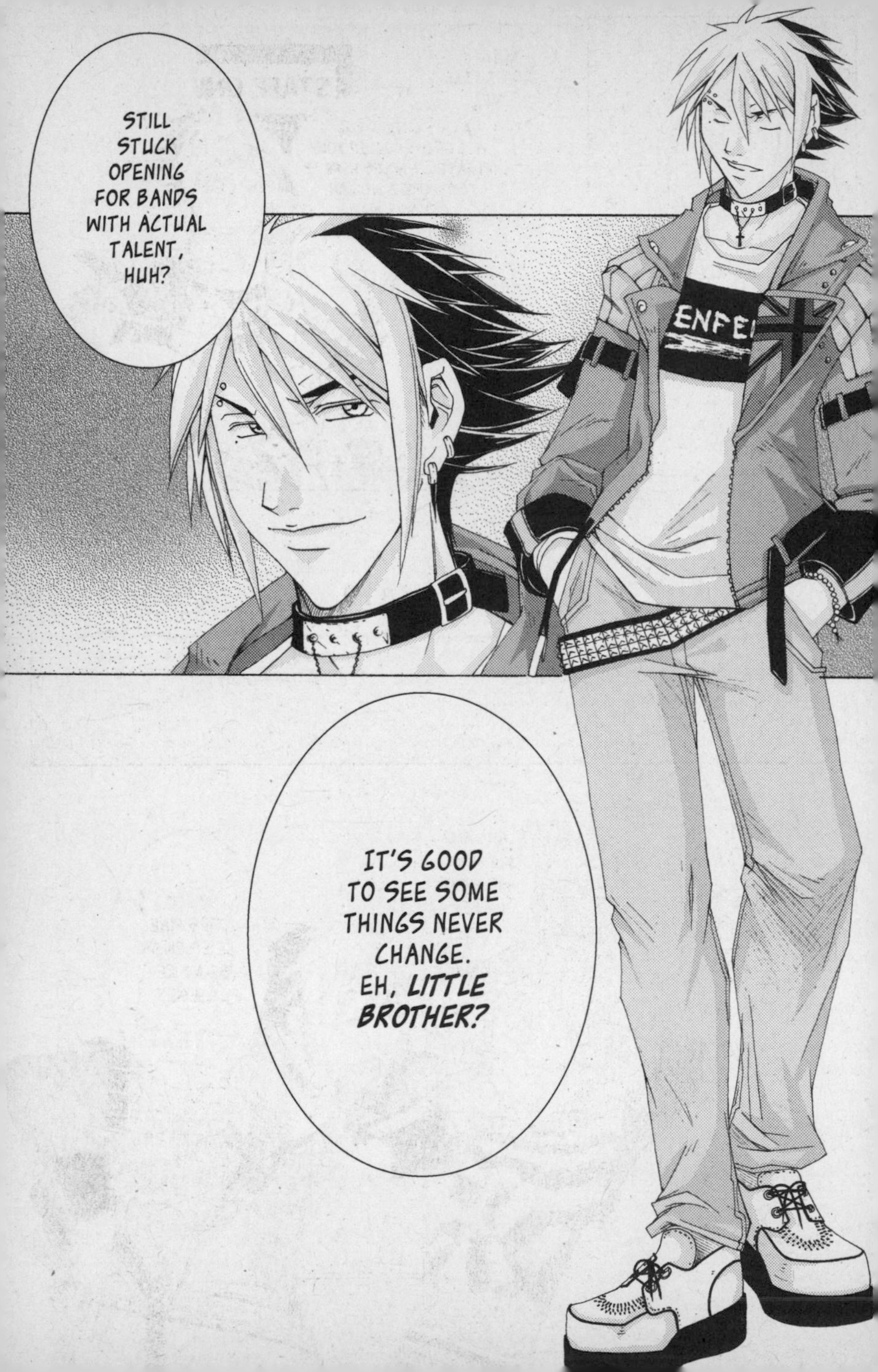
STILL STUCK OPENING FOR BANDS WITH ACTUAL TALENT, HUH?
IT'S GOOD TO SEE SOME THINGS NEVER CHANGE. EH, *LITTLE BROTHER?*

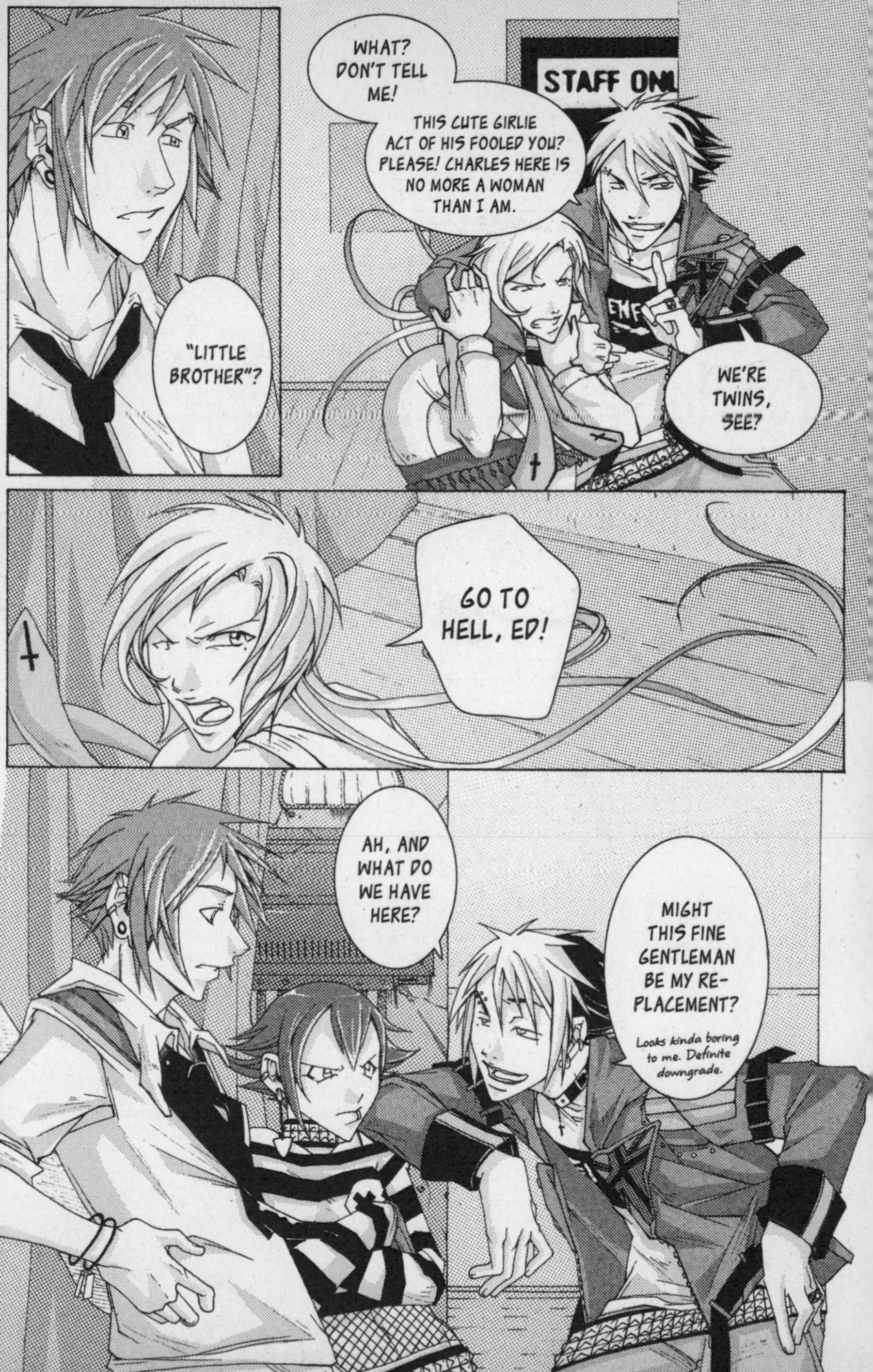
WHAT? DON'T TELL ME!
THIS CUTE GIRLIE ACT OF HIS FOOLED YOU? PLEASE! CHARLES HERE IS NO MORE A WOMAN THAN I AM.
STAFF ONL
"LITTLE BROTHER"?
WE'RE TWINS, SEE?
GO TO HELL, ED!
AH, AND WHAT DO WE HAVE HERE?
MIGHT THIS FINE GENTLEMAN BE MY RE-PLACEMENT?
Looks kinda boring to me. Definite downgrade.

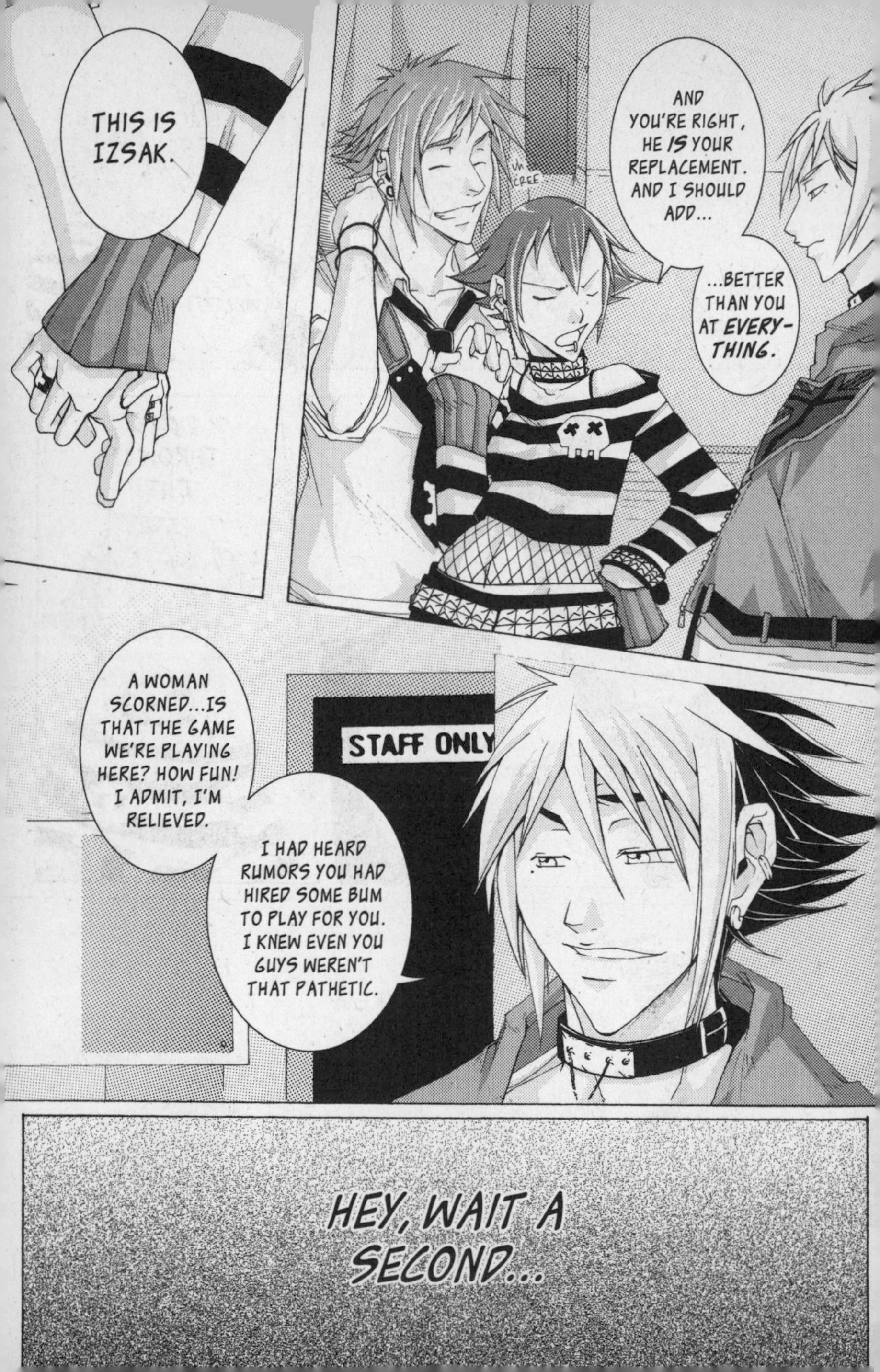
THIS IS IZSAK.
CREE
AND YOU'RE RIGHT, HE *IS* YOUR REPLACEMENT. AND I SHOULD ADD...
...BETTER THAN YOU AT *EVERY-THING.*
A WOMAN SCORNED...IS THAT THE GAME WE'RE PLAYING HERE? HOW FUN! I ADMIT, I'M RELIEVED.
STAFF ONLY
I HAD HEARD RUMORS YOU HAD HIRED SOME BUM TO PLAY FOR YOU. I KNEW EVEN YOU GUYS WEREN'T THAT PATHETIC.
HEY, WAIT A SECOND...

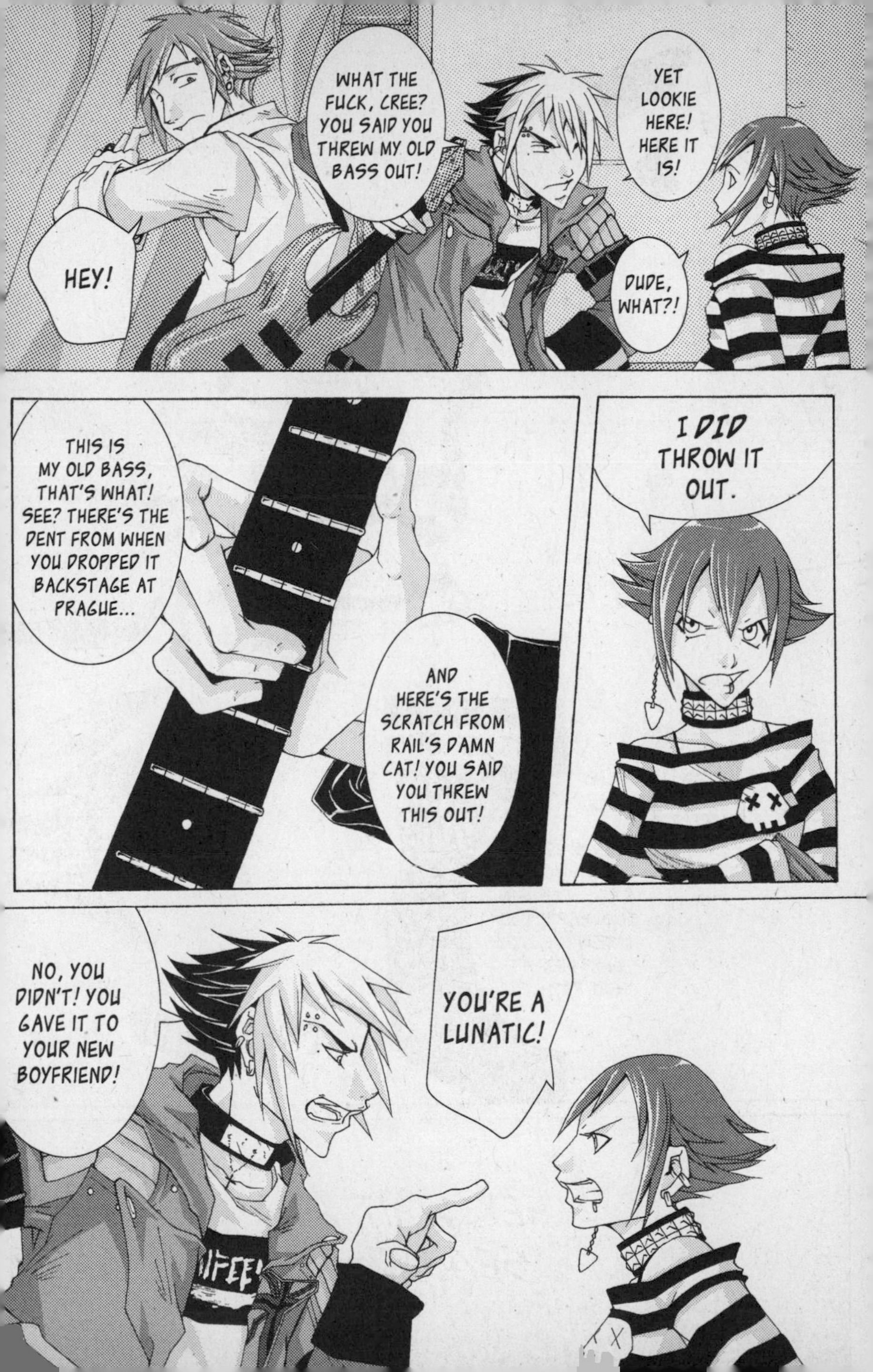
HEY!
WHAT THE FUCK, CREE? YOU SAID YOU THREW MY OLD BASS OUT!
YET LOOKIE HERE! HERE IT IS!
DUDE, WHAT?!
THIS IS MY OLD BASS, THAT'S WHAT! SEE? THERE'S THE DENT FROM WHEN YOU DROPPED IT BACKSTAGE AT PRAGUE...
AND HERE'S THE SCRATCH FROM RAIL'S DAMN CAT! YOU SAID YOU THREW THIS OUT!
I DID THROW IT OUT.
NO, YOU DIDN'T! YOU GAVE IT TO YOUR NEW BOYFRIEND!
YOU'RE A LUNATIC!

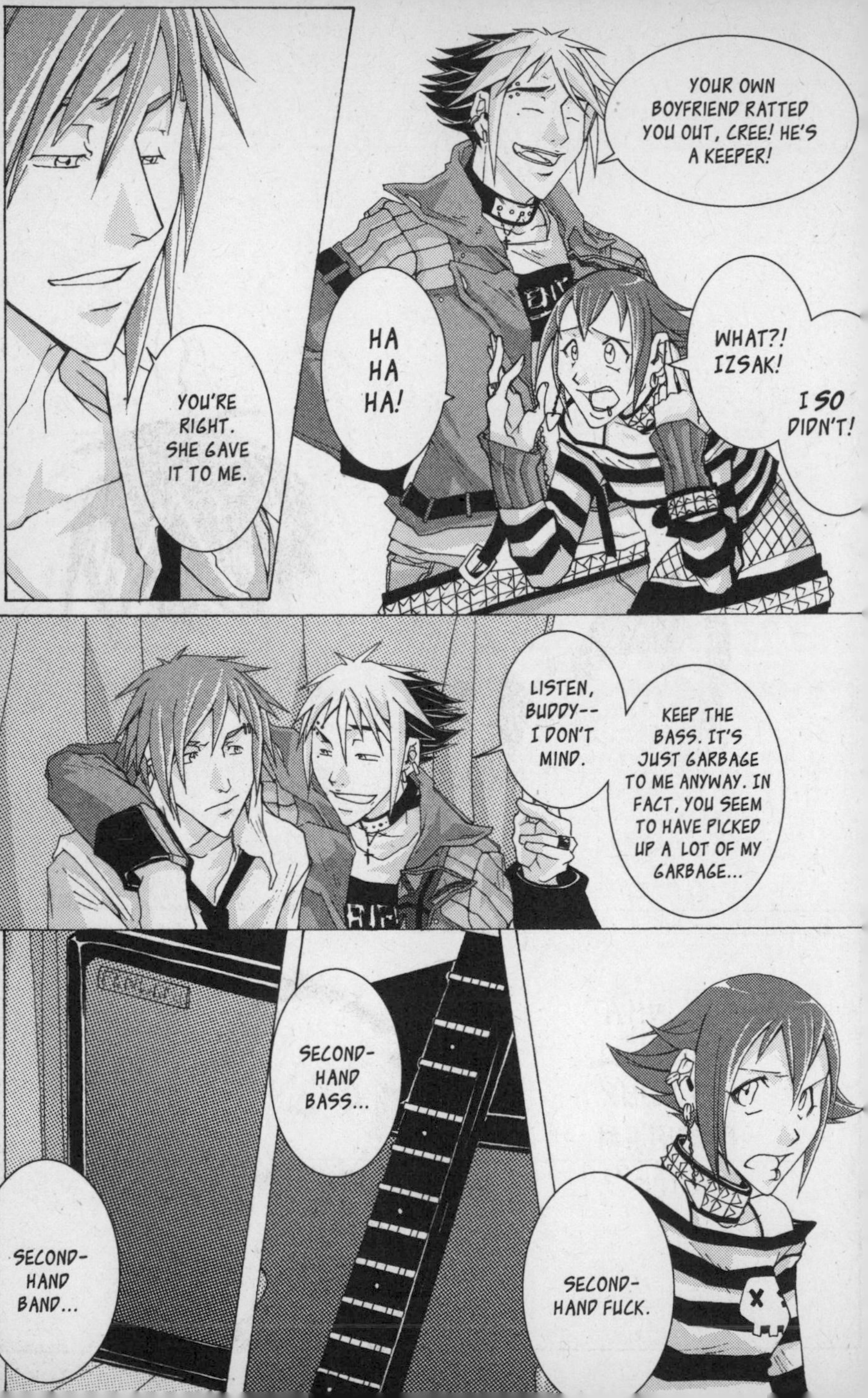
YOU'RE RIGHT. SHE GAVE IT TO ME.
HA HA HA!
YOUR OWN BOYFRIEND RATTED YOU OUT, CREE! HE'S A KEEPER!
WHAT?! IZSAK!
I SO DIDN'T!
LISTEN, BUDDY-- I DON'T MIND.
KEEP THE BASS. IT'S JUST GARBAGE TO ME ANYWAY. IN FACT, YOU SEEM TO HAVE PICKED UP A LOT OF MY GARBAGE...
SECOND-HAND BASS...
SECOND-HAND BAND...
SECOND-HAND FUCK.

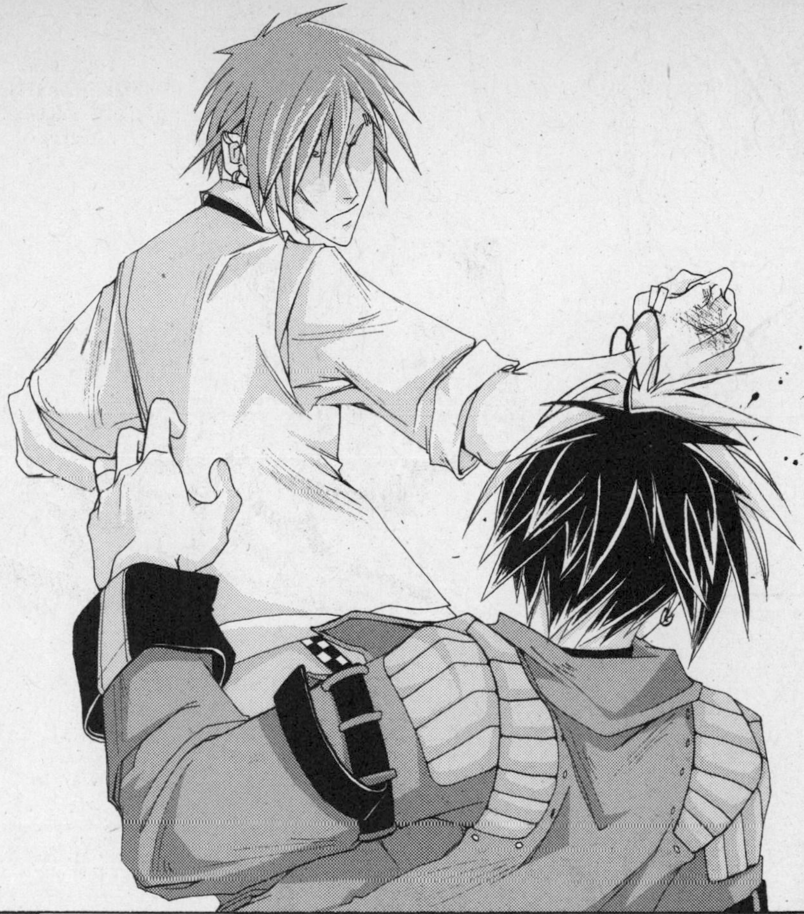
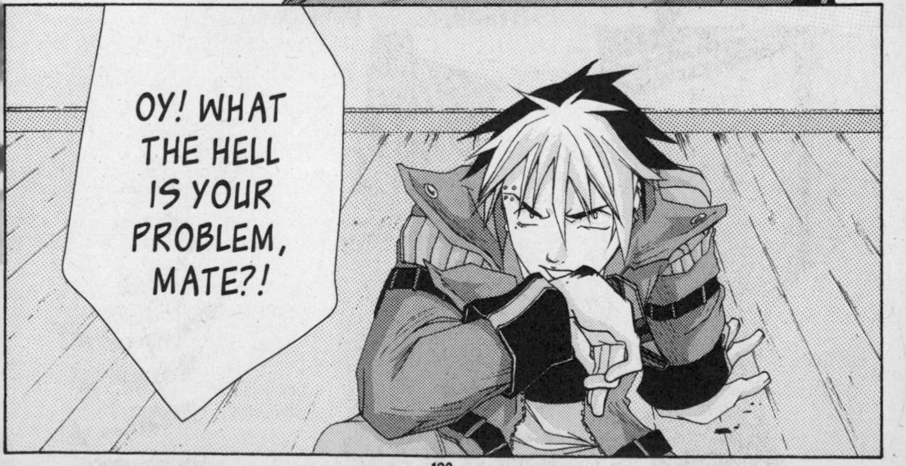
OY! WHAT THE HELL IS YOUR PROBLEM, MATE?!

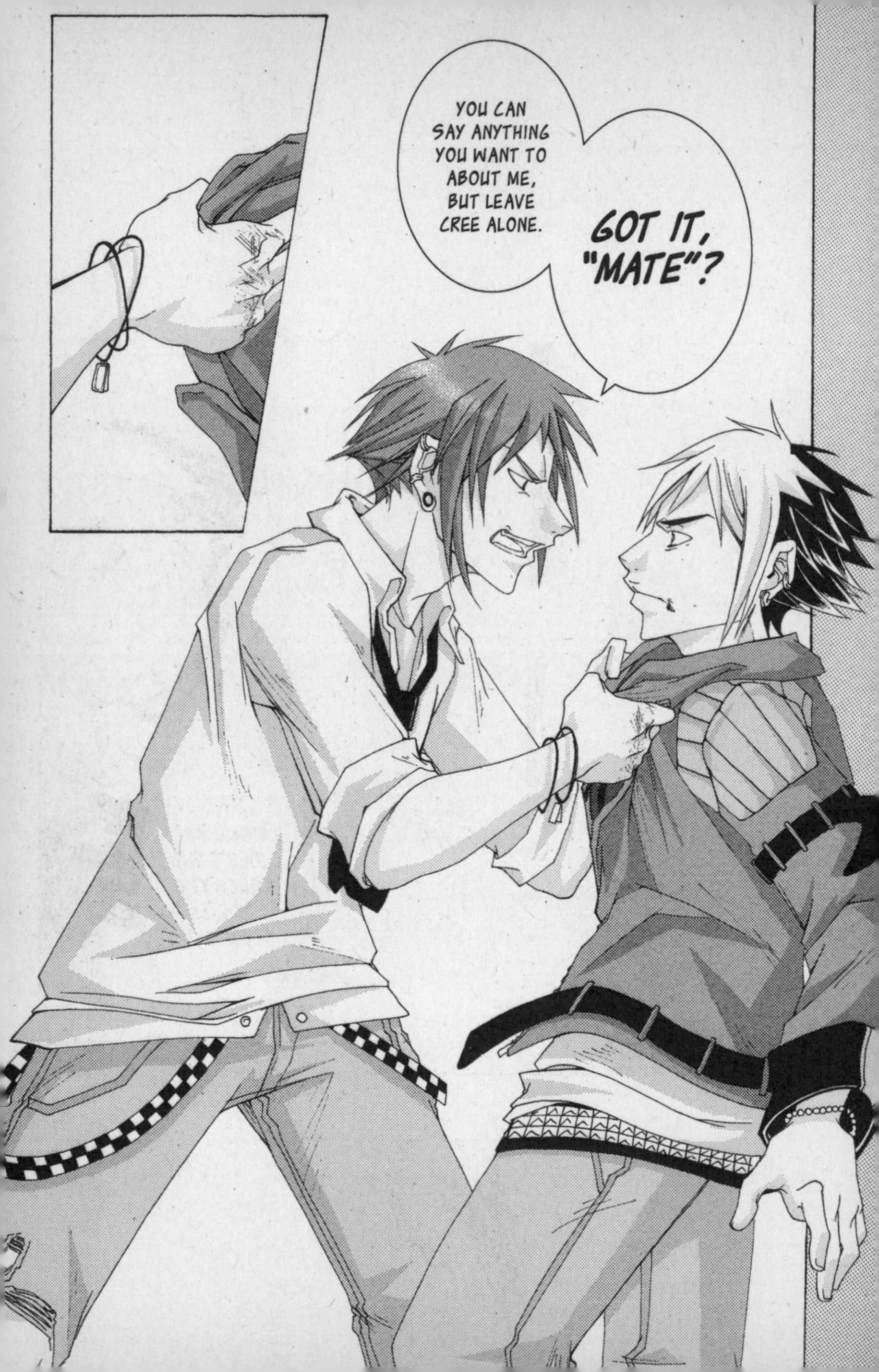
YOU CAN SAY ANYTHING YOU WANT TO ABOUT ME, BUT LEAVE CREE ALONE.
GOT IT, "MATE"?

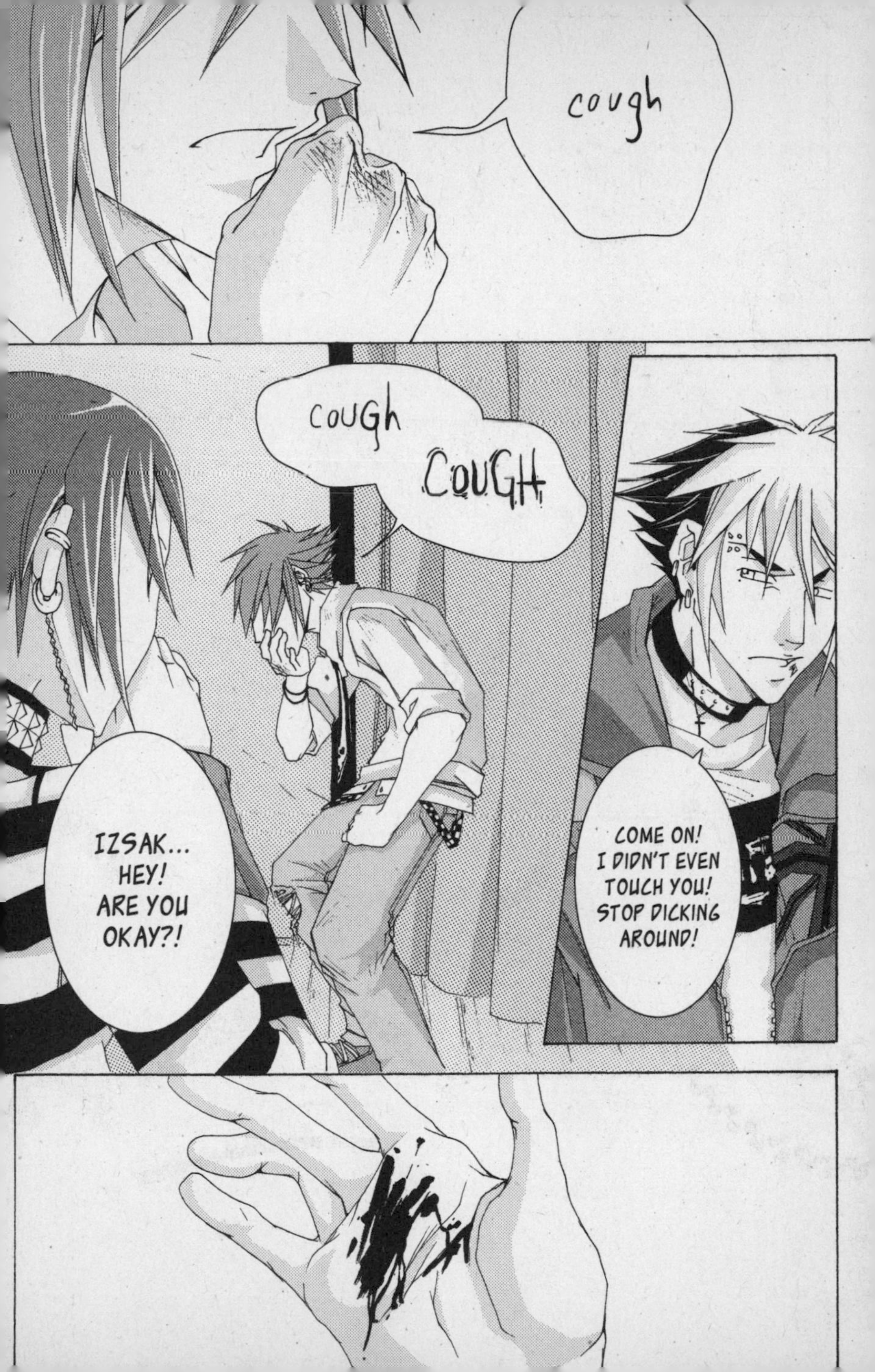
cough
cough
COUGH
IZSAK... HEY! ARE YOU OKAY?!
COME ON! I DIDN'T EVEN TOUCH YOU! STOP DICKING AROUND!

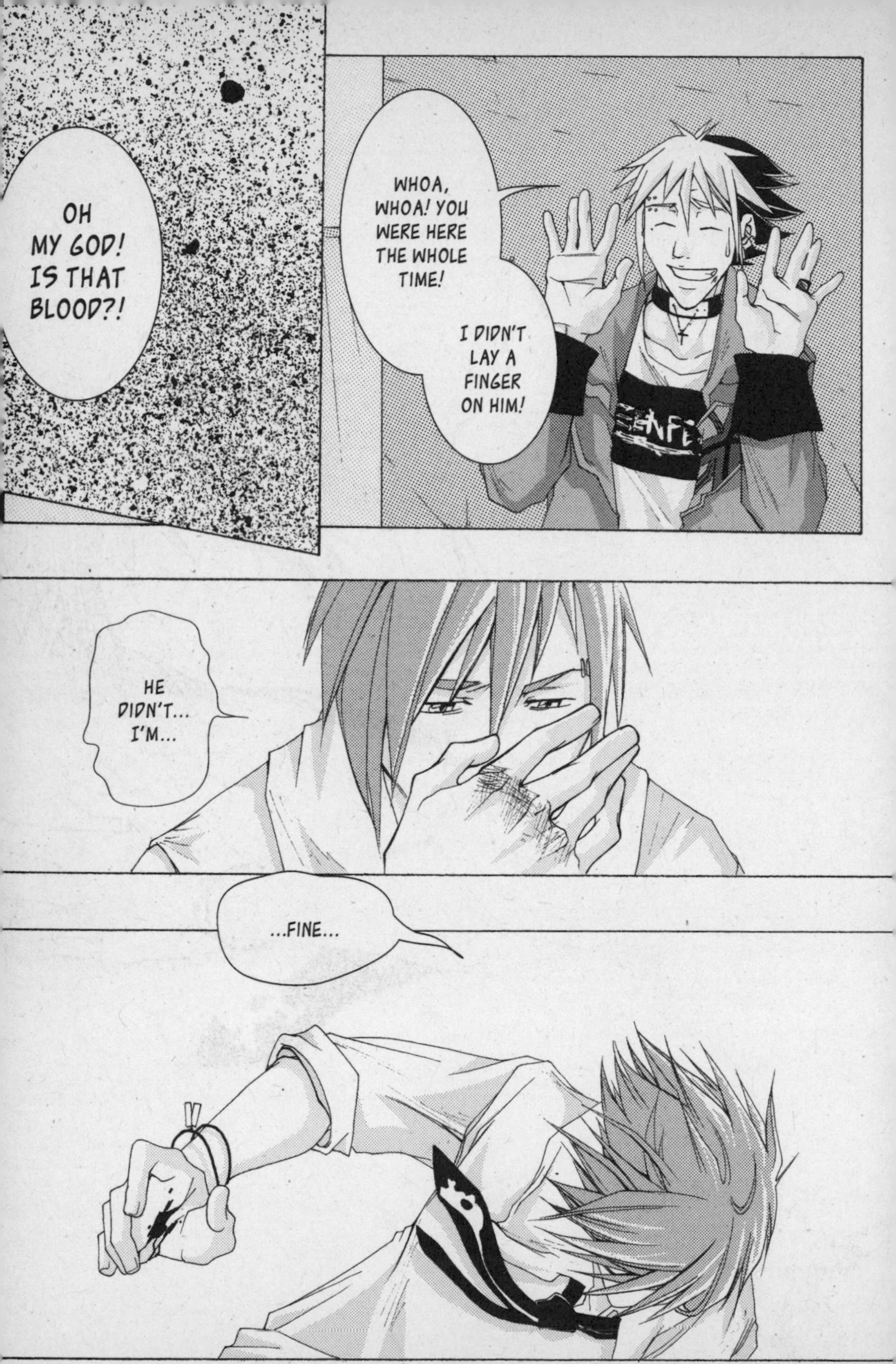
OH MY GOD! IS THAT BLOOD?!
WHOA, WHOA! YOU WERE HERE THE WHOLE TIME!
I DIDN'T LAY A FINGER ON HIM!
HE DIDN'T... I'M...
...FINE...

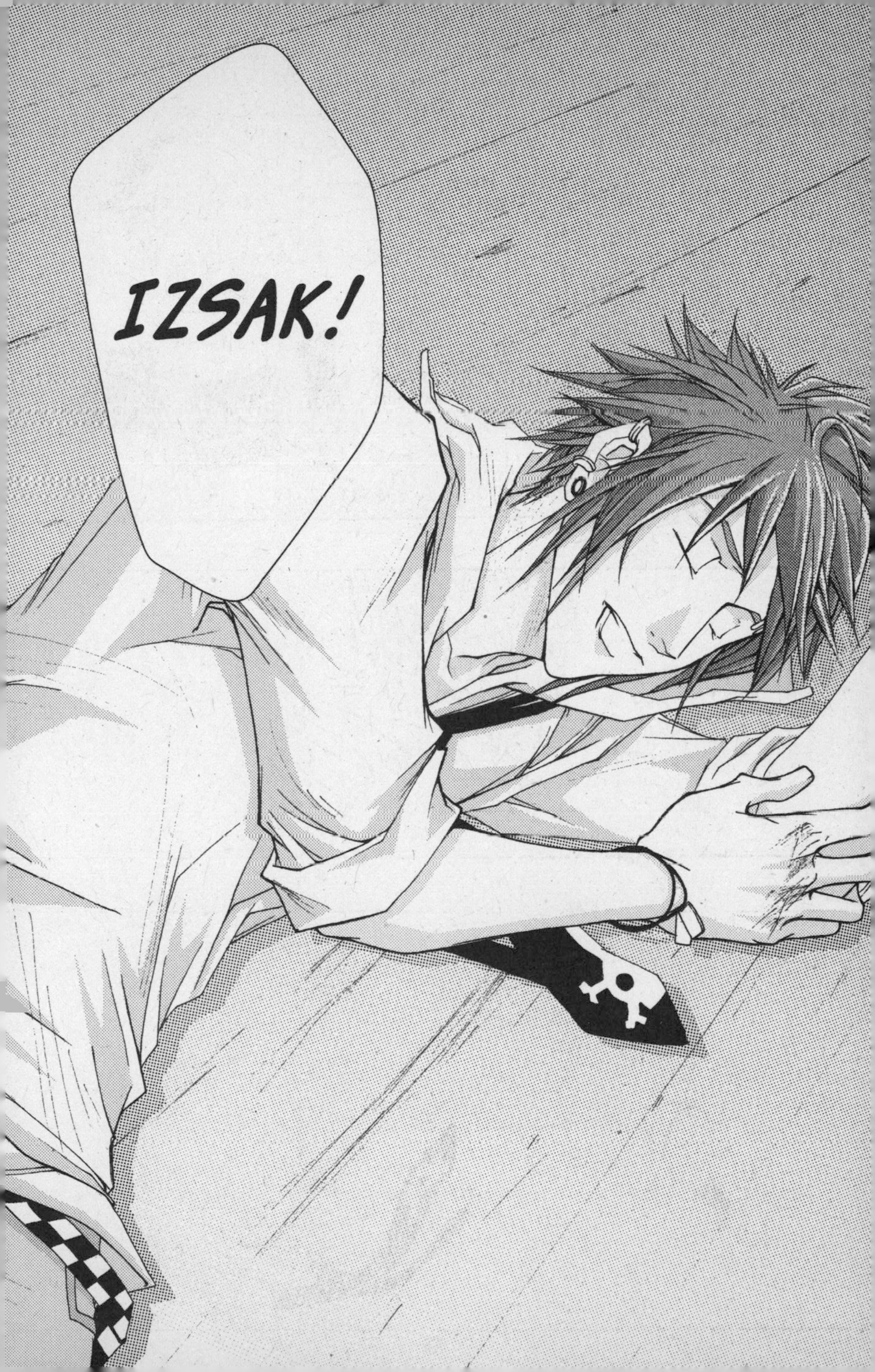
IZSAK!

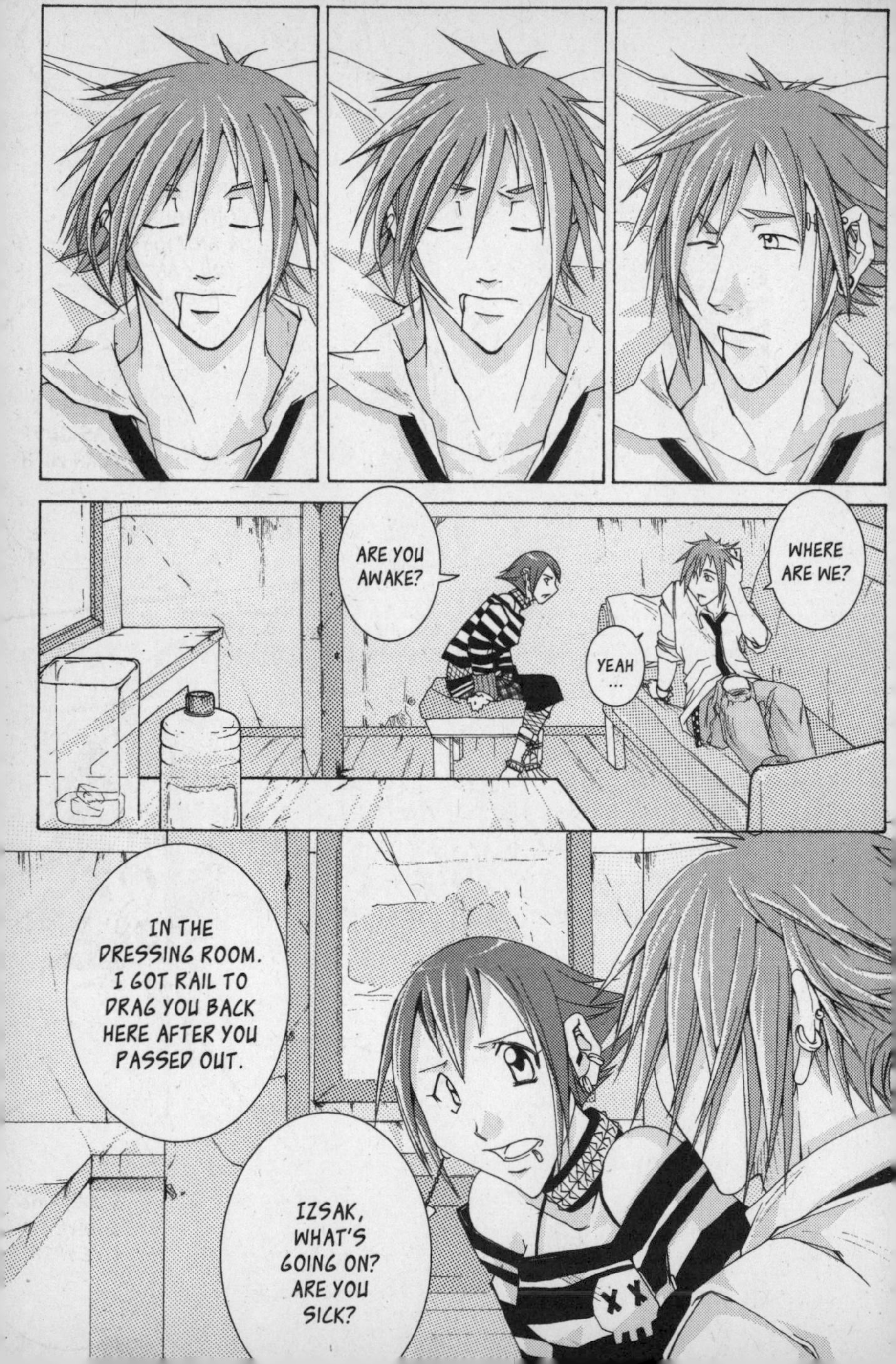
ARE YOU AWAKE?
YEAH ...
WHERE ARE WE?
IN THE DRESSING ROOM. I GOT RAIL TO DRAG YOU BACK HERE AFTER YOU PASSED OUT.
IZSAK, WHAT'S GOING ON? ARE YOU SICK?

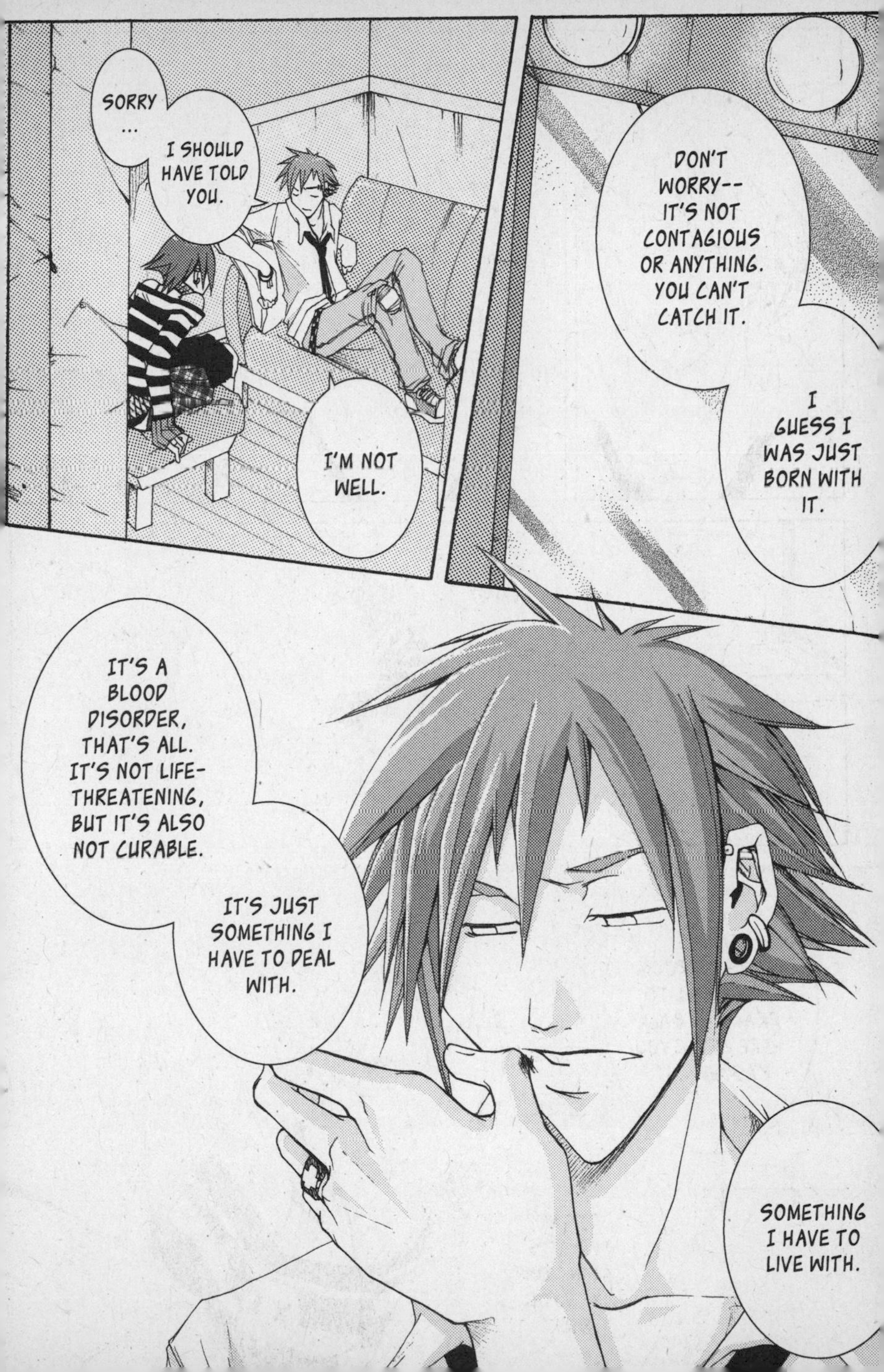
SORRY ...
I SHOULD HAVE TOLD YOU.
I'M NOT WELL.
DON'T WORRY-- IT'S NOT CONTAGIOUS OR ANYTHING. YOU CAN'T CATCH IT.
I GUESS I WAS JUST BORN WITH IT.
IT'S A BLOOD DISORDER, THAT'S ALL. IT'S NOT LIFE-THREATENING, BUT IT'S ALSO NOT CURABLE.
IT'S JUST SOMETHING I HAVE TO DEAL WITH.
SOMETHING I HAVE TO LIVE WITH.

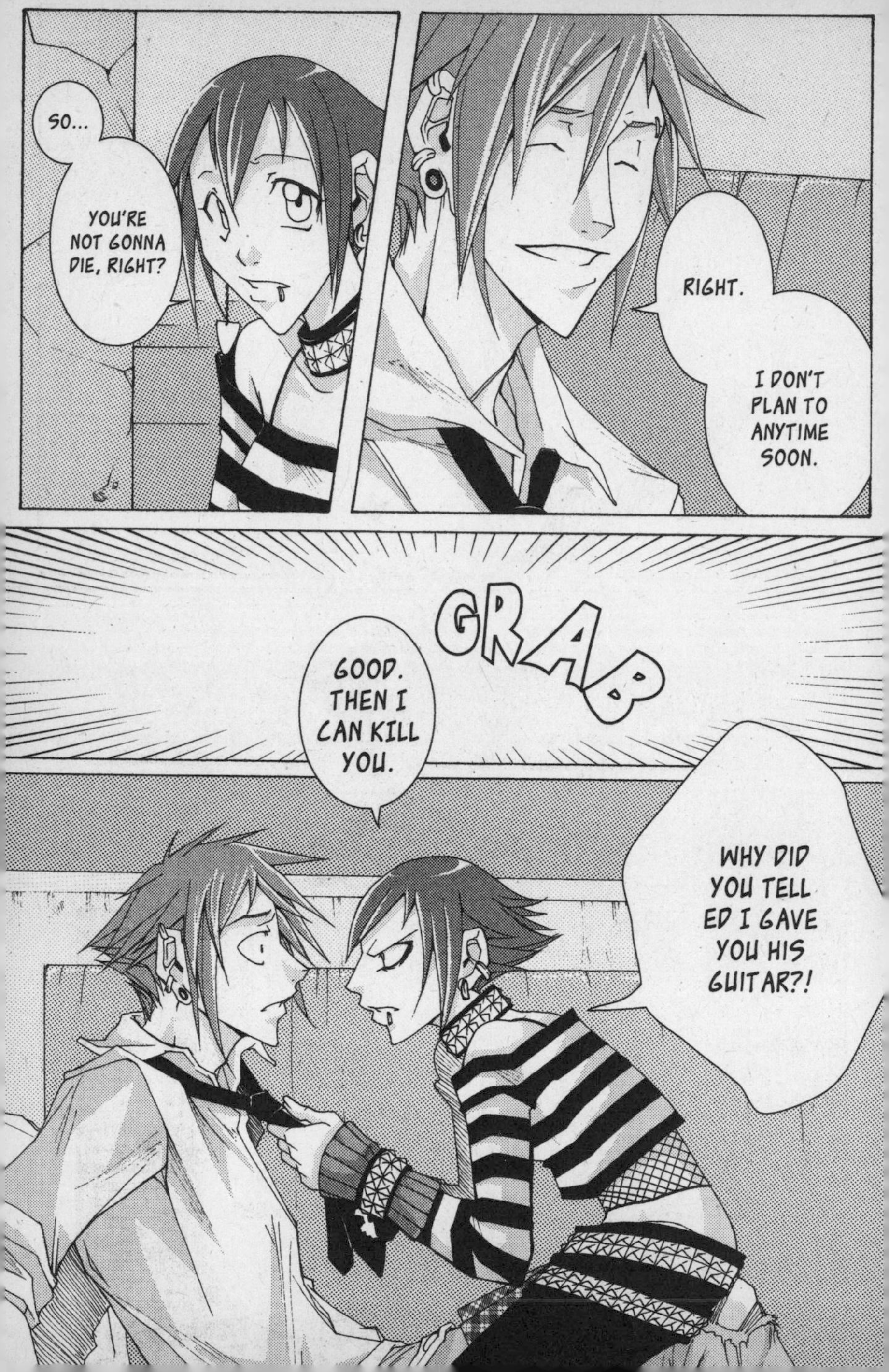
SO...
YOU'RE NOT GONNA DIE, RIGHT?
RIGHT.
I DON'T PLAN TO ANYTIME SOON.
GOOD. THEN I CAN KILL YOU.
GRAB
WHY DID YOU TELL ED I GAVE YOU HIS GUITAR?!

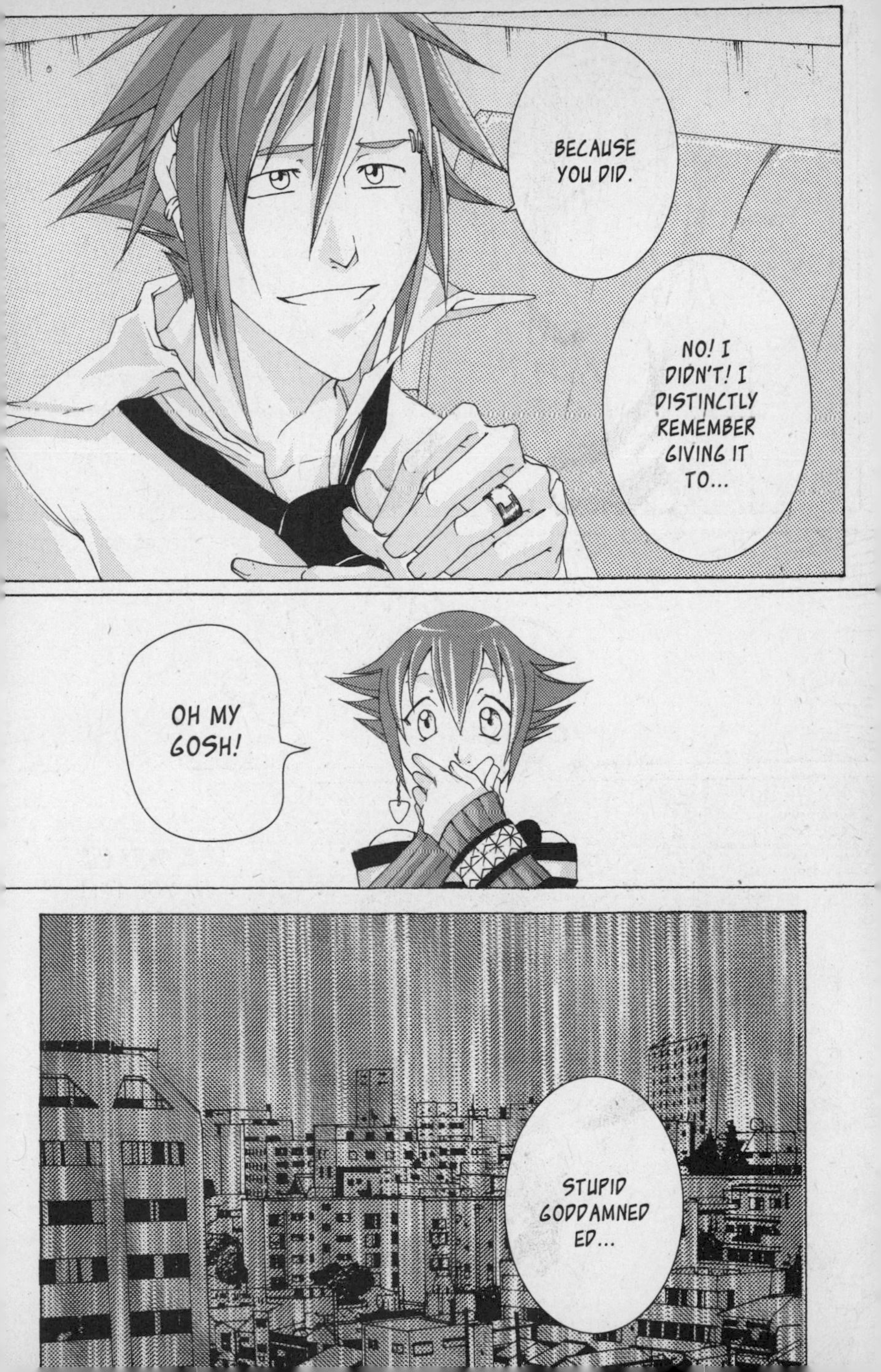
BECAUSE YOU DID.
NO! I DIDN'T! I DISTINCTLY REMEMBER GIVING IT TO...
OH MY GOSH!
STUPID GODDAMNED ED...

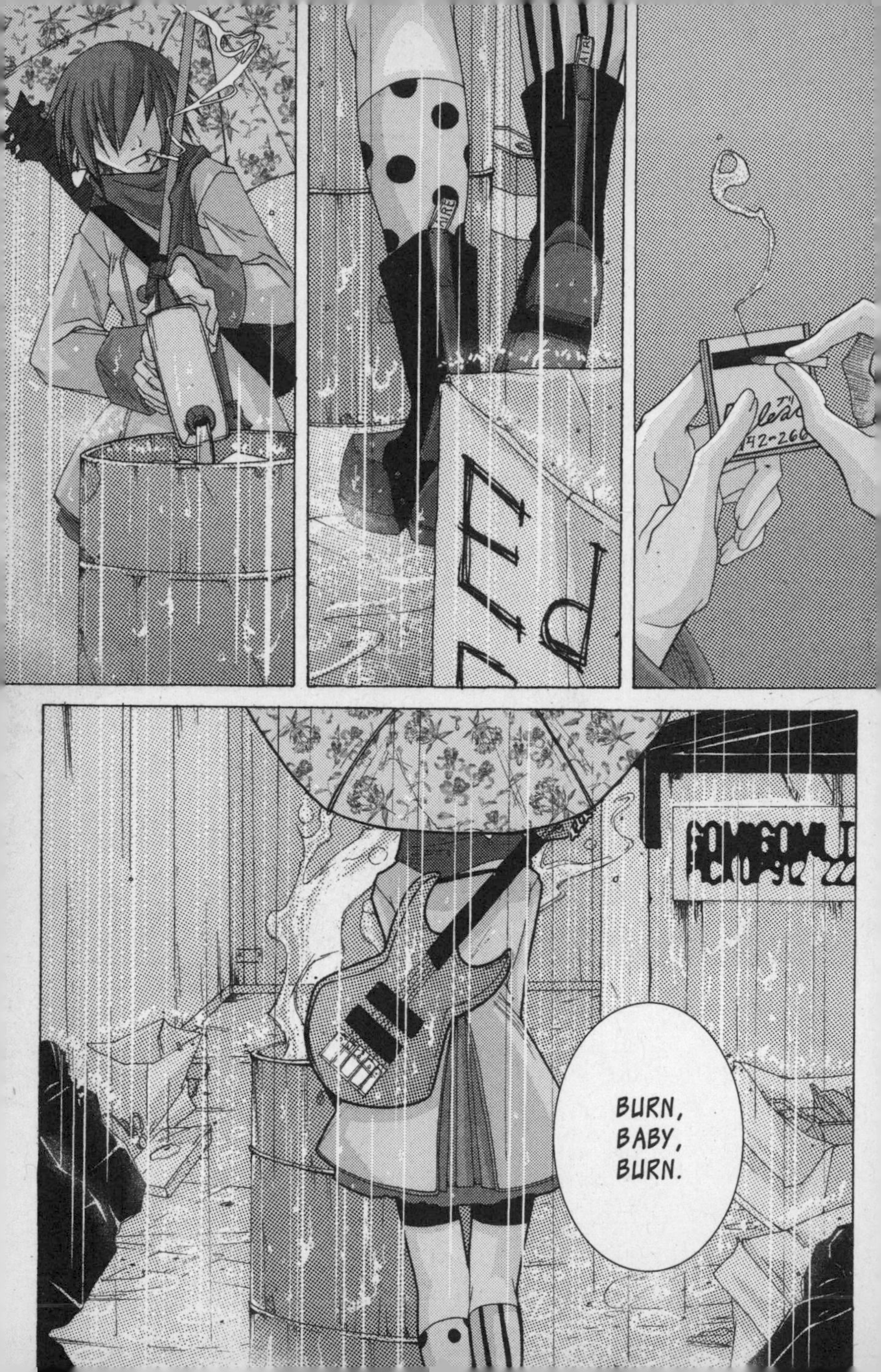
BURN, BABY, BURN.

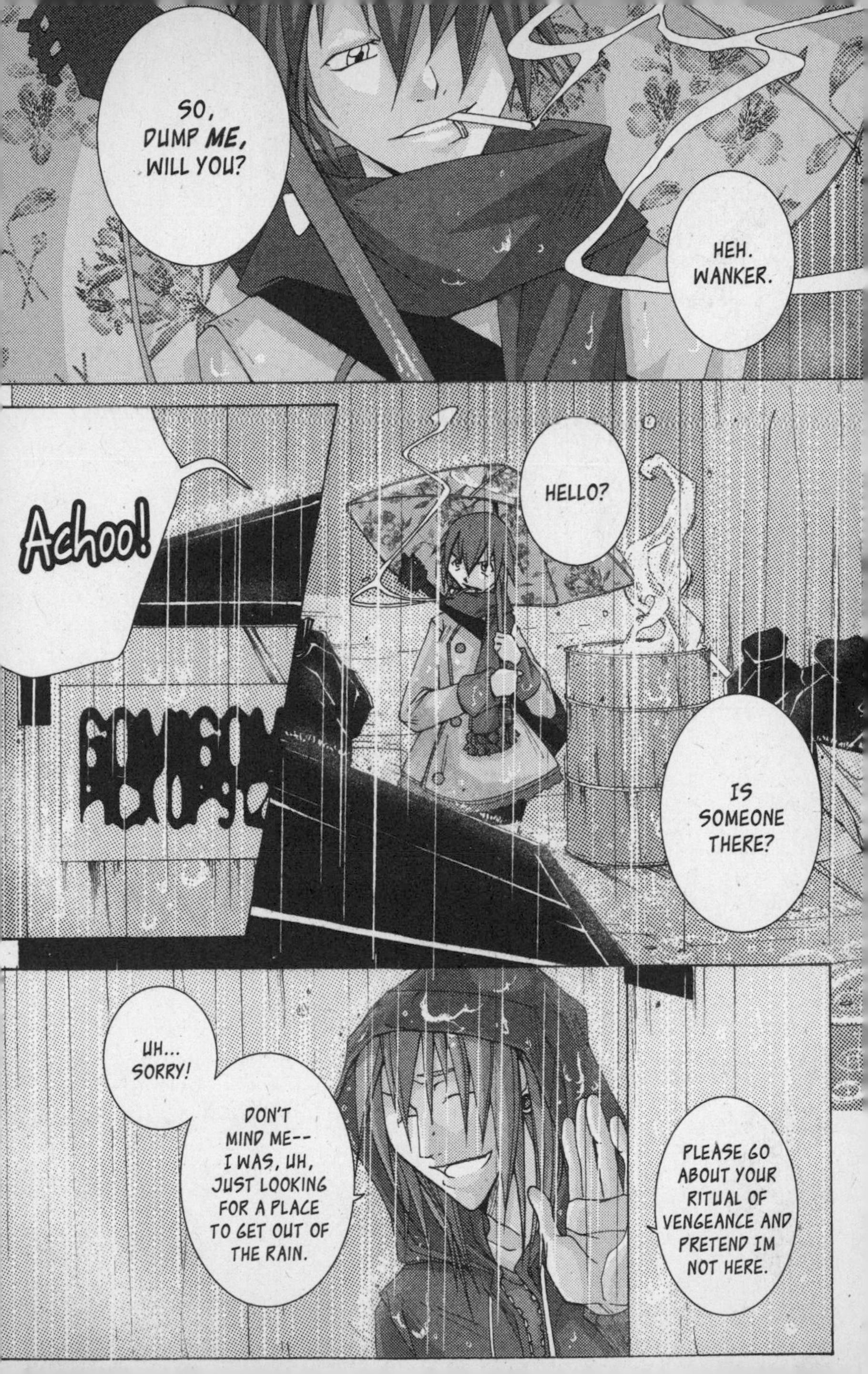
SO, DUMP *ME*, WILL YOU?
HEH. WANKER.
Achoo!
HELLO?
IS SOMEONE THERE?
UH... SORRY!
DON'T MIND ME-- I WAS, UH, JUST LOOKING FOR A PLACE TO GET OUT OF THE RAIN.
PLEASE GO ABOUT YOUR RITUAL OF VENGEANCE AND PRETEND IM NOT HERE.

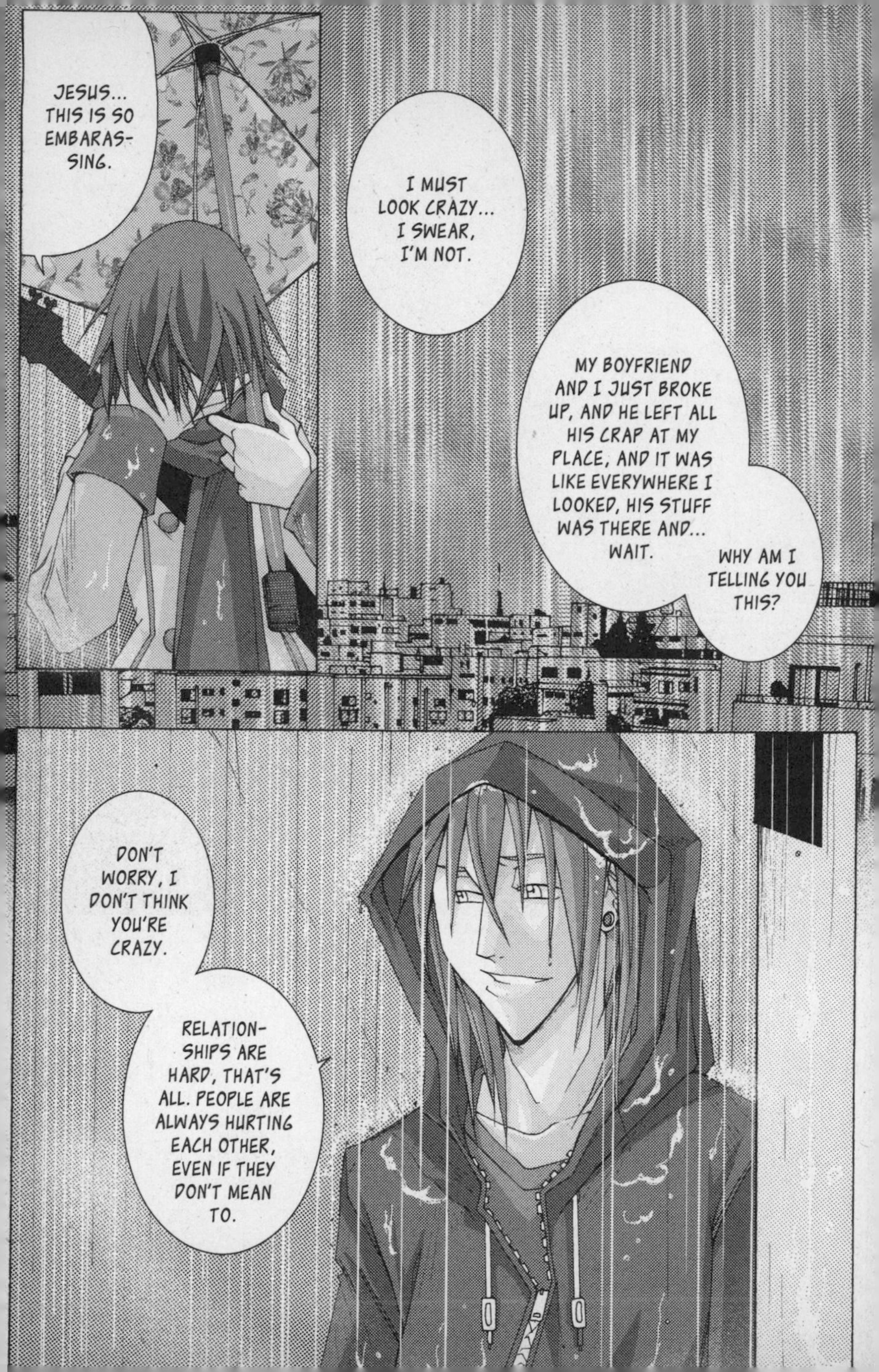
JESUS... THIS IS SO EMBARAS-SING.
I MUST LOOK CRAZY... I SWEAR, I'M NOT.
MY BOYFRIEND AND I JUST BROKE UP, AND HE LEFT ALL HIS CRAP AT MY PLACE, AND IT WAS LIKE EVERYWHERE I LOOKED, HIS STUFF WAS THERE AND... WAIT.
WHY AM I TELLING YOU THIS?
DON'T WORRY, I DON'T THINK YOU'RE CRAZY.
RELATION-SHIPS ARE HARD, THAT'S ALL. PEOPLE ARE ALWAYS HURTING EACH OTHER, EVEN IF THEY DON'T MEAN TO.

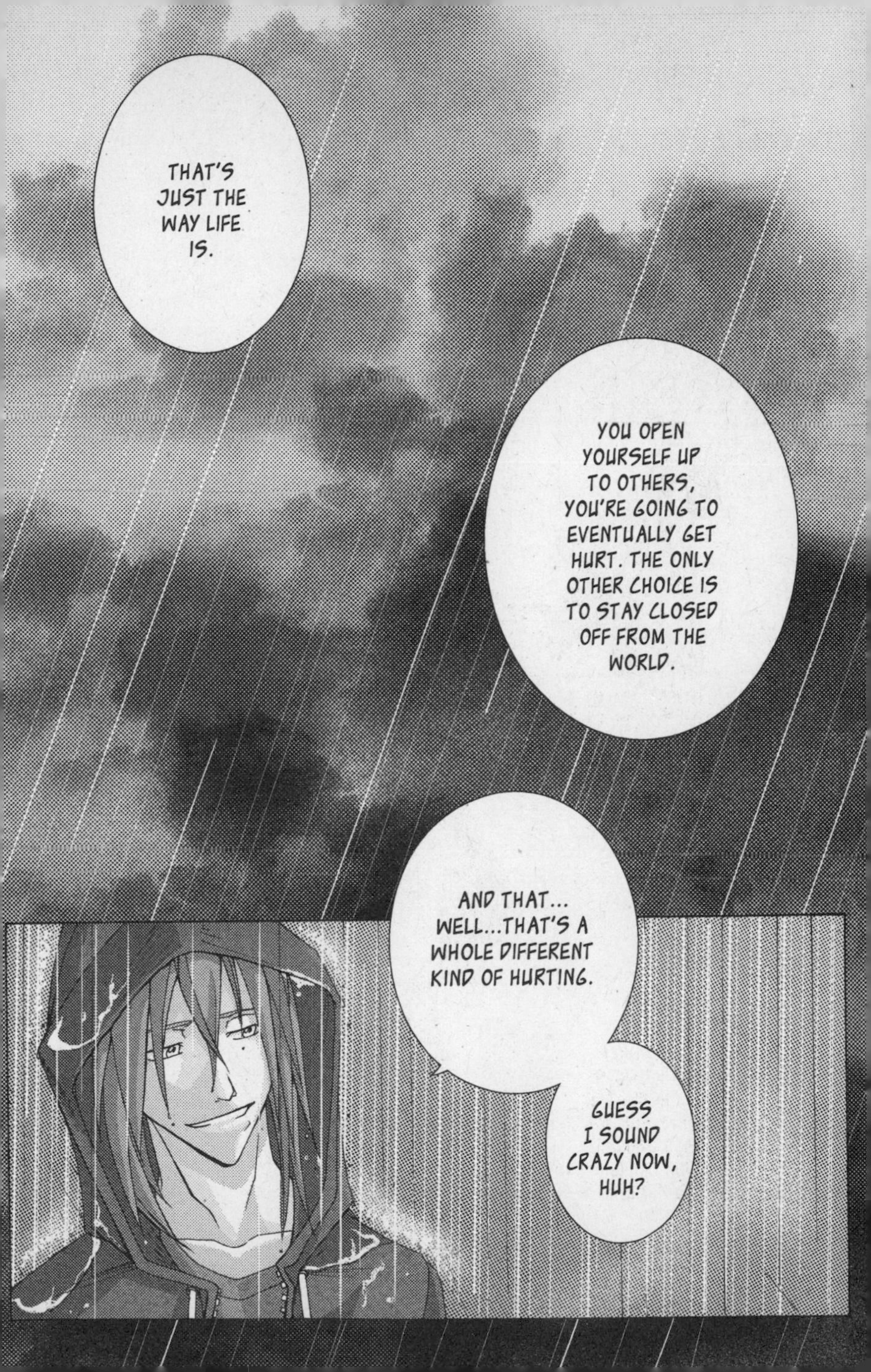
THAT'S JUST THE WAY LIFE IS.
YOU OPEN YOURSELF UP TO OTHERS, YOU'RE GOING TO EVENTUALLY GET HURT. THE ONLY OTHER CHOICE IS TO STAY CLOSED OFF FROM THE WORLD.
AND THAT... WELL...THAT'S A WHOLE DIFFERENT KIND OF HURTING.
GUESS I SOUND CRAZY NOW, HUH?

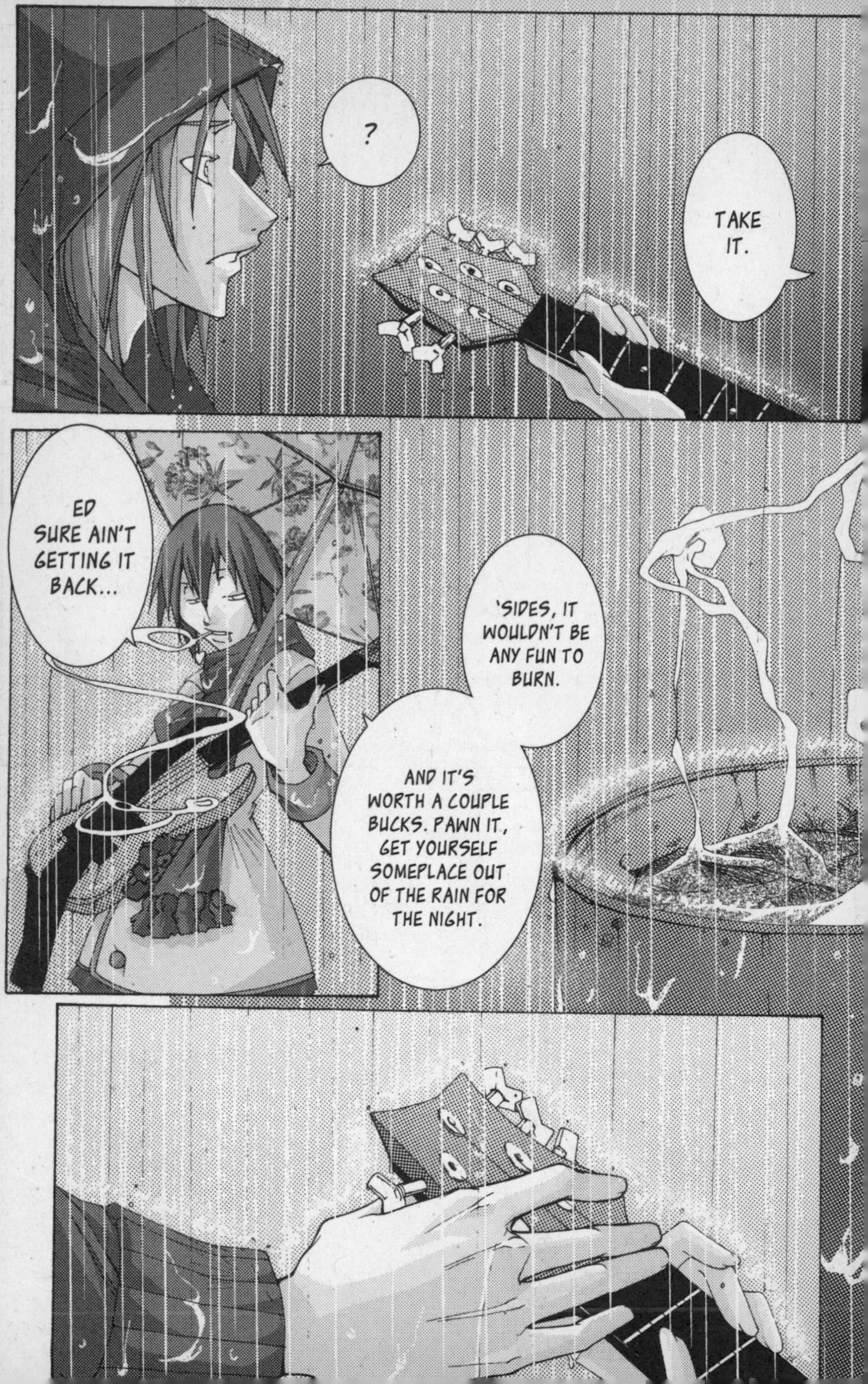
?
TAKE IT.
ED SURE AIN'T GETTING IT BACK...
'SIDES, IT WOULDN'T BE ANY FUN TO BURN.
AND IT'S WORTH A COUPLE BUCKS. PAWN IT, GET YOURSELF SOMEPLACE OUT OF THE RAIN FOR THE NIGHT.

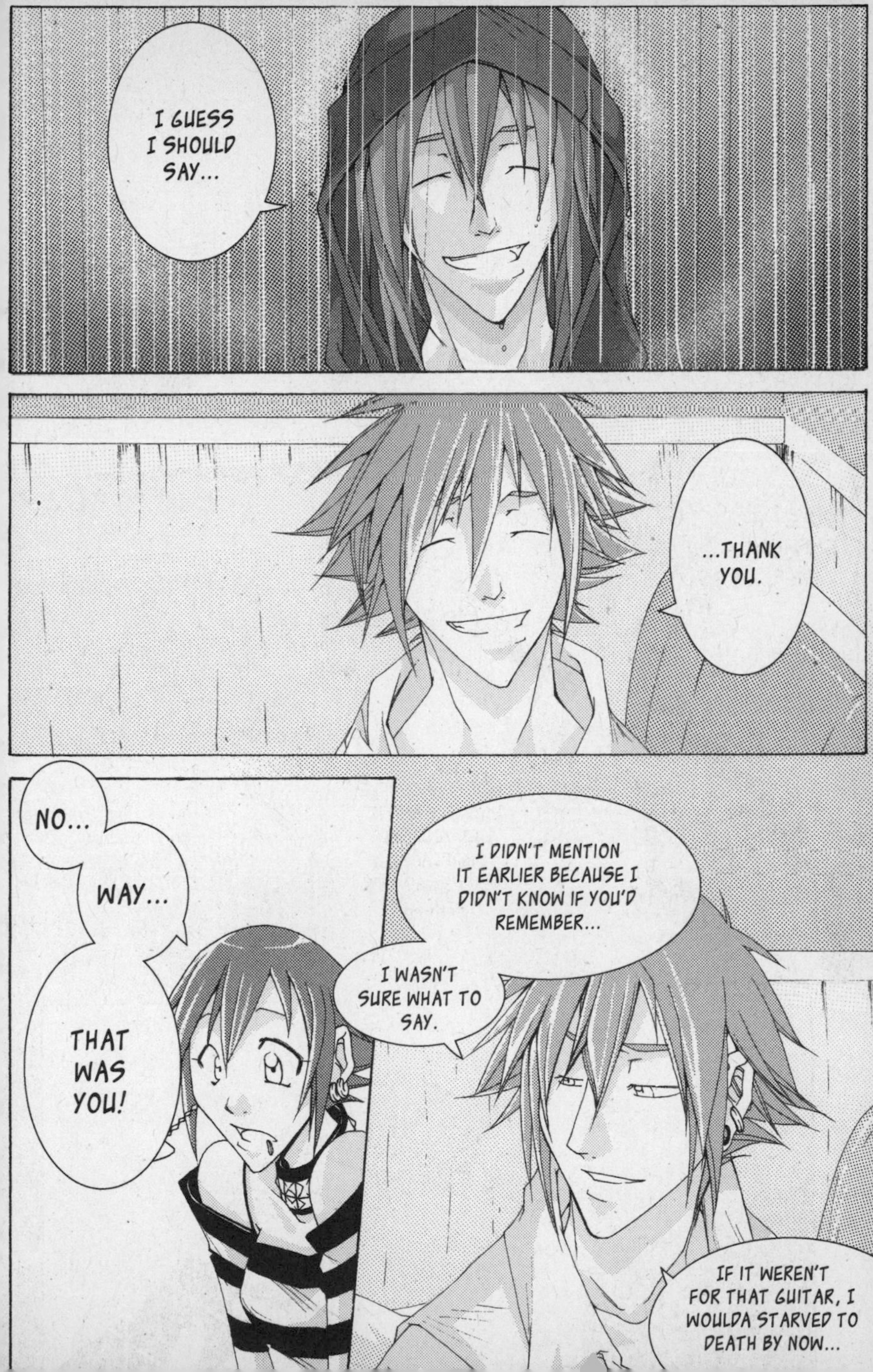
I GUESS I SHOULD SAY...
...THANK YOU.
NO...
WAY...
THAT WAS YOU!
I DIDN'T MENTION IT EARLIER BECAUSE I DIDN'T KNOW IF YOU'D REMEMBER...
I WASN'T SURE WHAT TO SAY.
IF IT WEREN'T FOR THAT GUITAR, I WOULDA STARVED TO DEATH BY NOW...

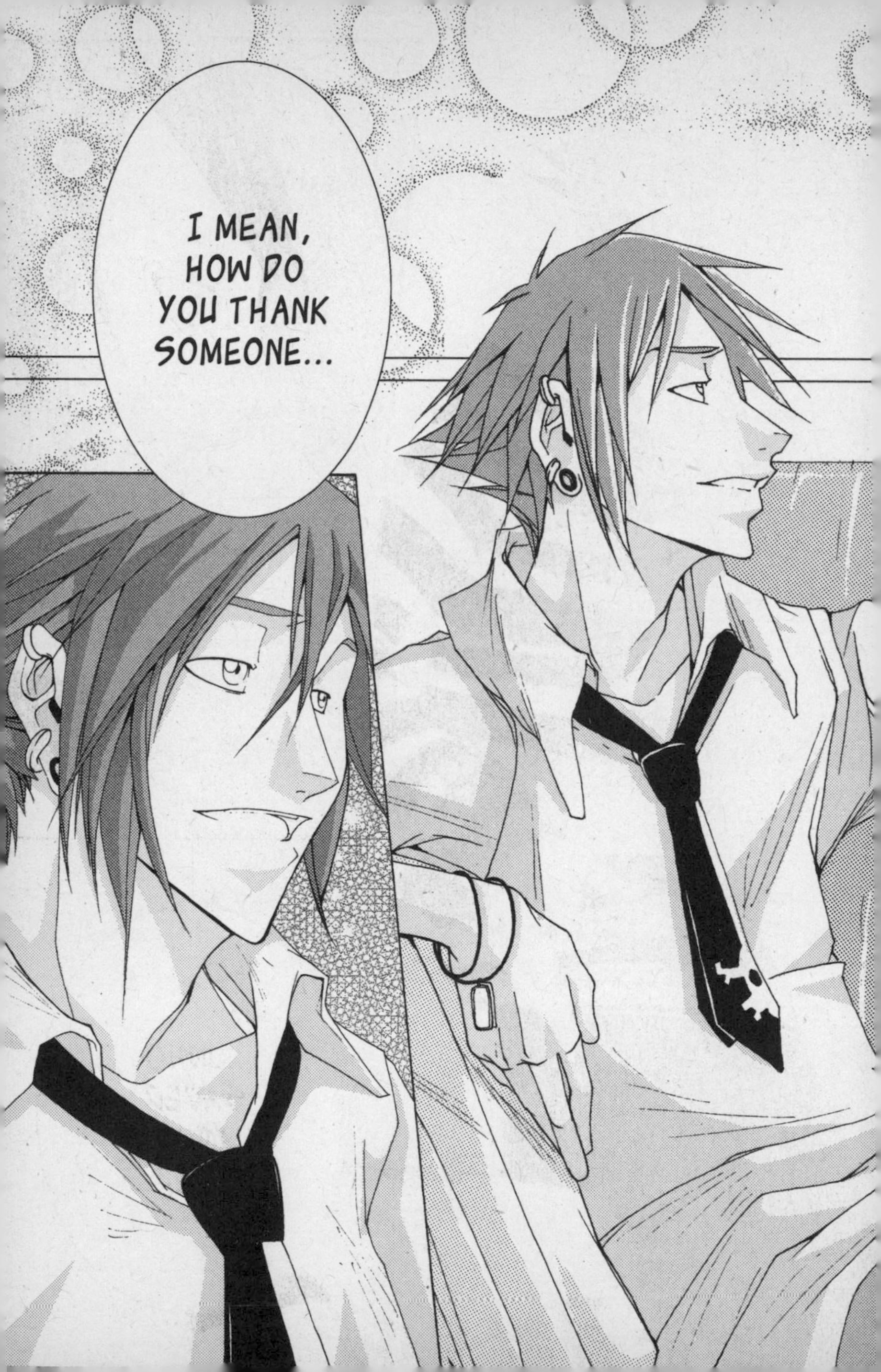
I MEAN, HOW DO YOU THANK SOMEONE...

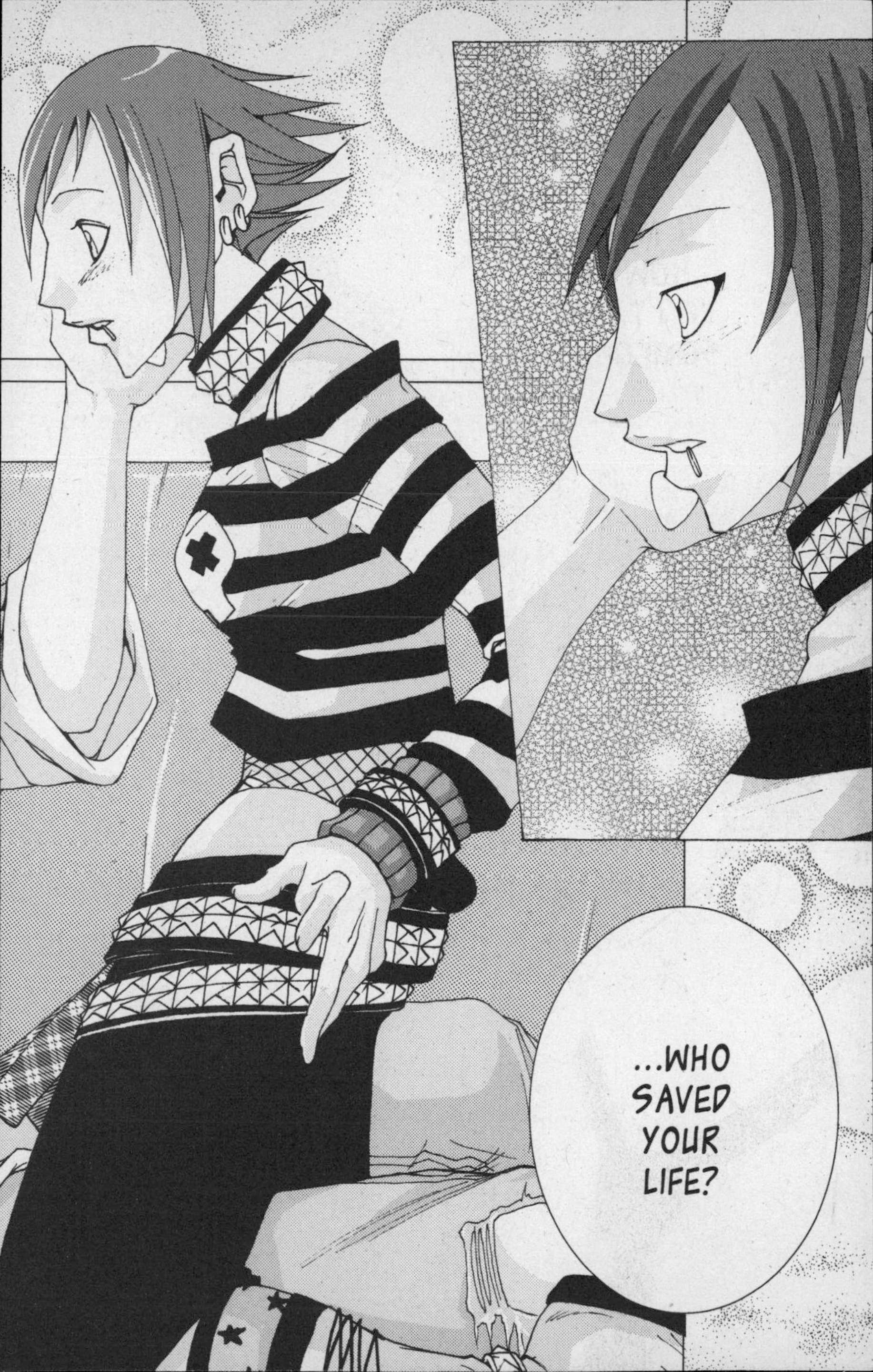
...WHO SAVED YOUR LIFE?

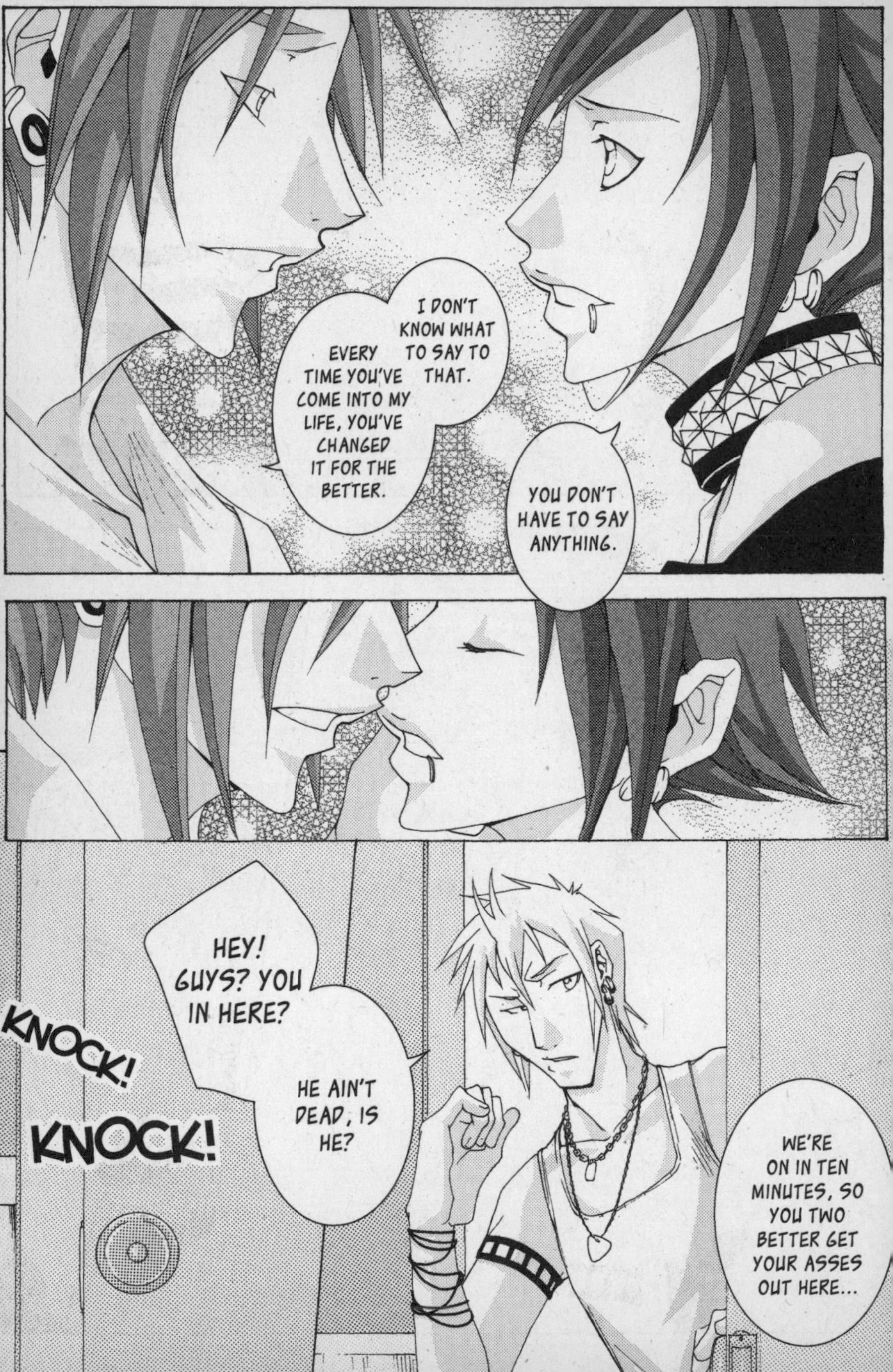
EVERY TIME YOU'VE COME INTO MY LIFE, YOU'VE CHANGED IT FOR THE BETTER.
I DON'T KNOW WHAT TO SAY TO THAT.
YOU DON'T HAVE TO SAY ANYTHING.
KNOCK!
KNOCK!
HEY! GUYS? YOU IN HERE?
HE AIN'T DEAD, IS HE?
WE'RE ON IN TEN MINUTES, SO YOU TWO BETTER GET YOUR ASSES OUT HERE...

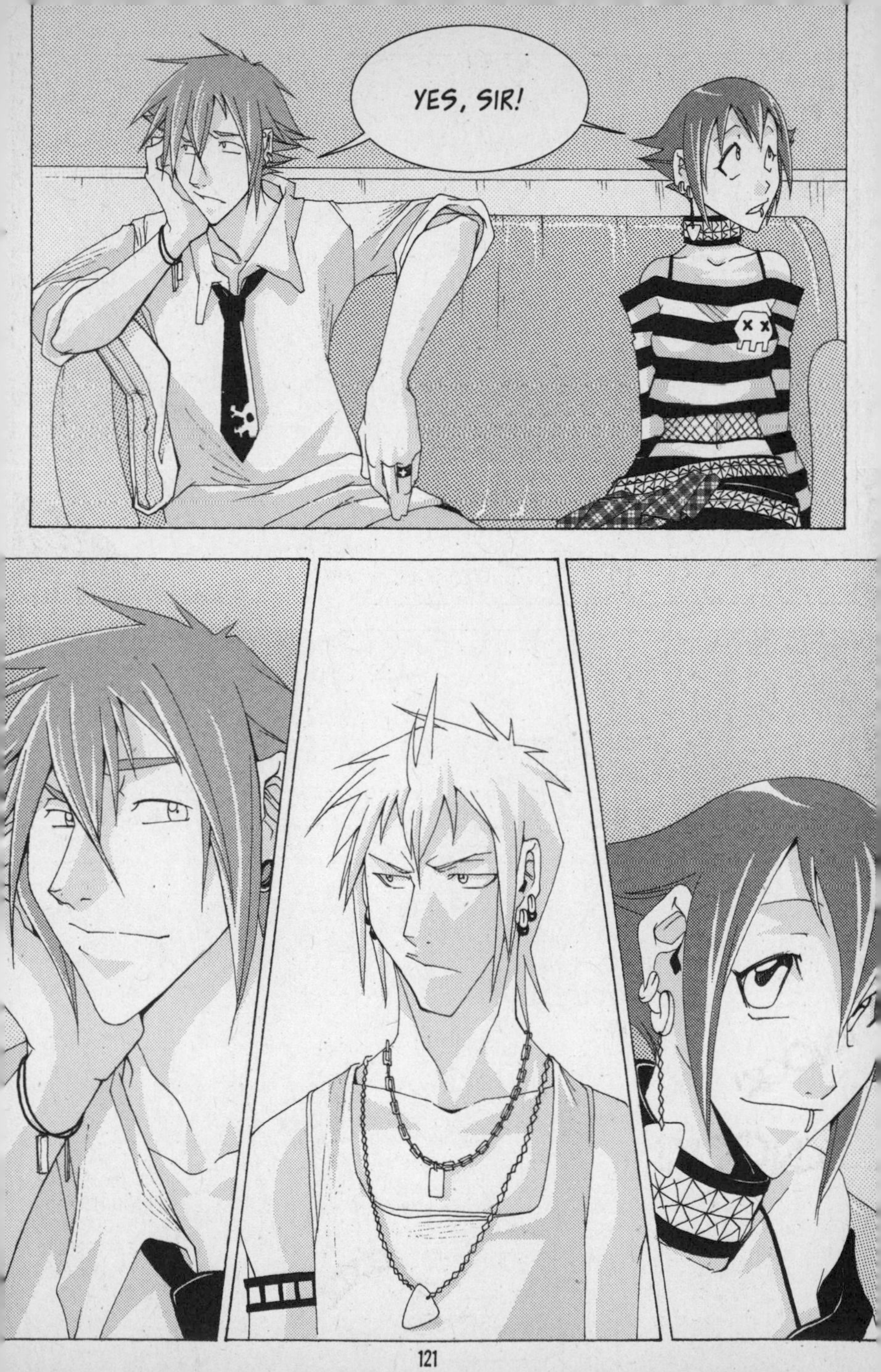
YES, SIR!

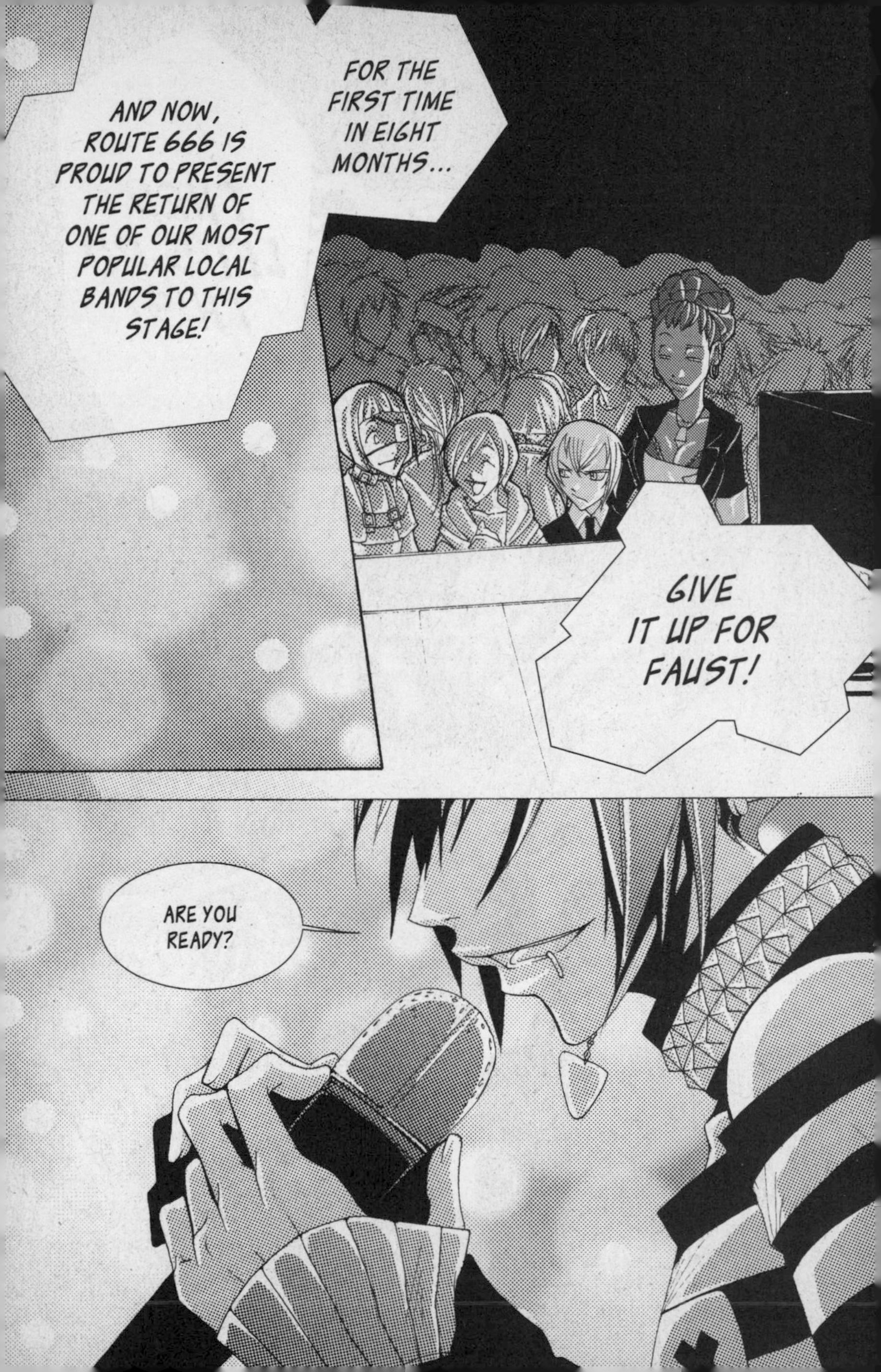
AND NOW, ROUTE 666 IS PROUD TO PRESENT THE RETURN OF ONE OF OUR MOST POPULAR LOCAL BANDS TO THIS STAGE!
FOR THE FIRST TIME IN EIGHT MONTHS...
GIVE IT UP FOR FAUST!
ARE YOU READY?

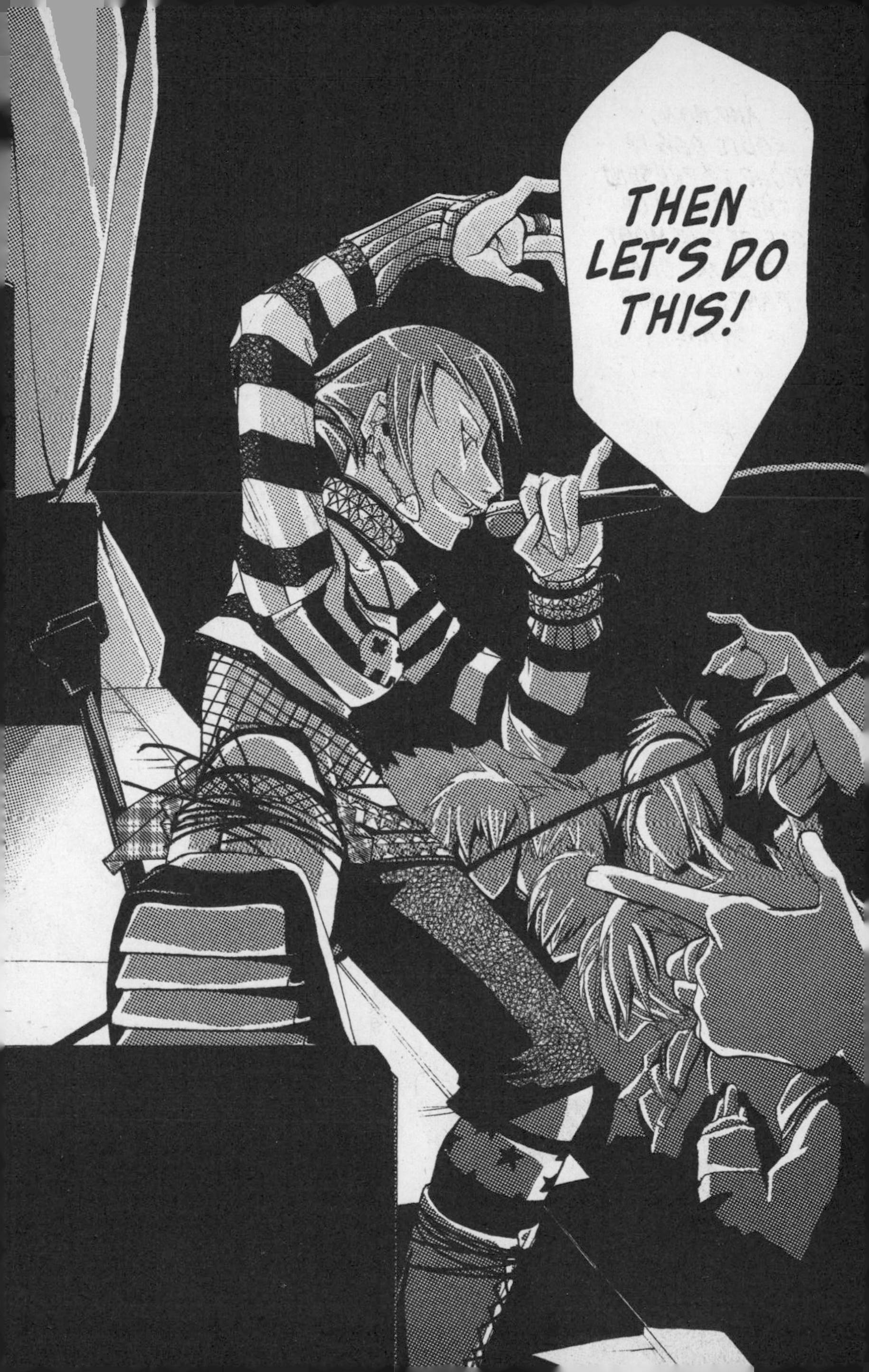
THEN LET'S DO THIS!

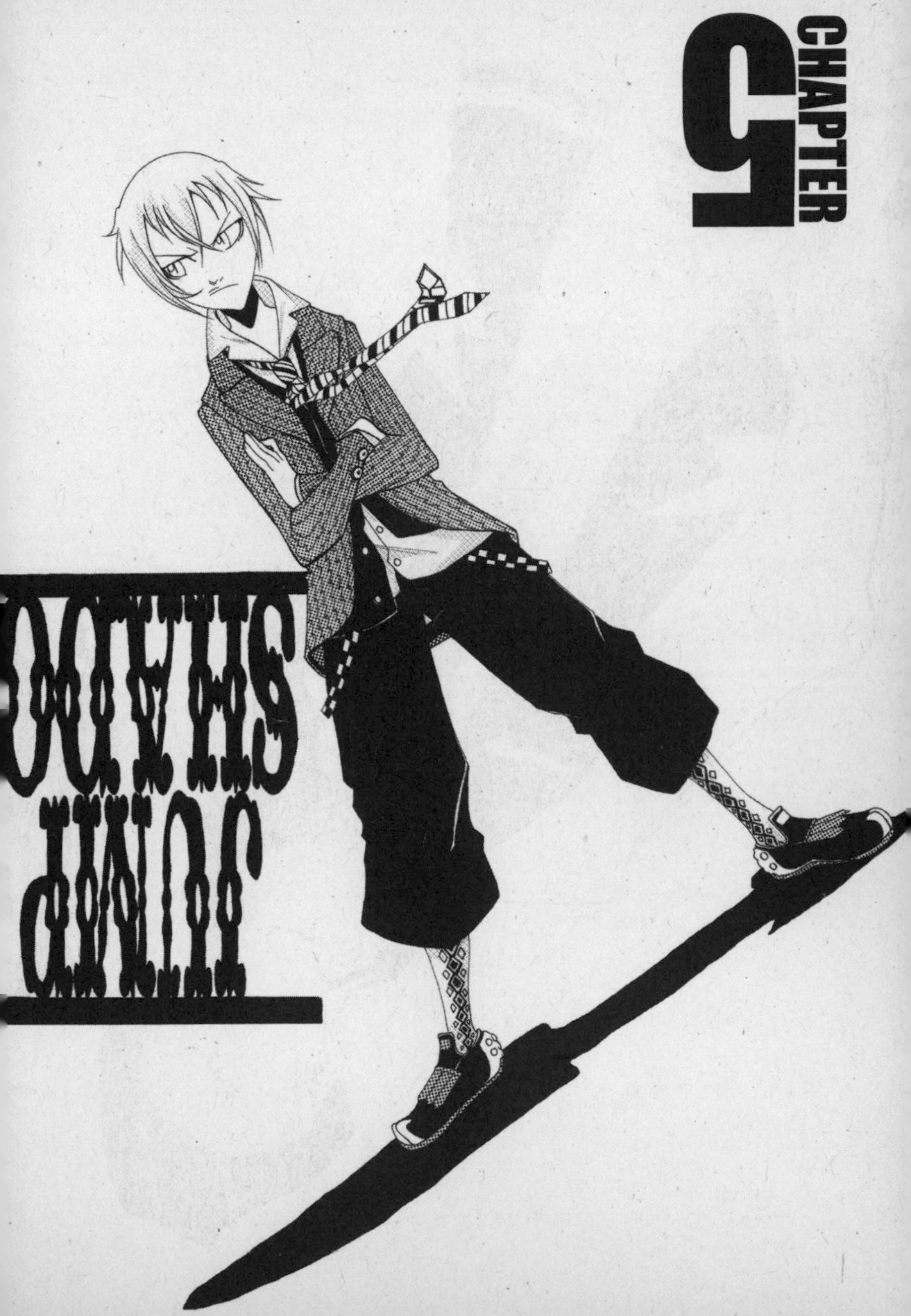
CHAPTER 5
JUMP SHADO

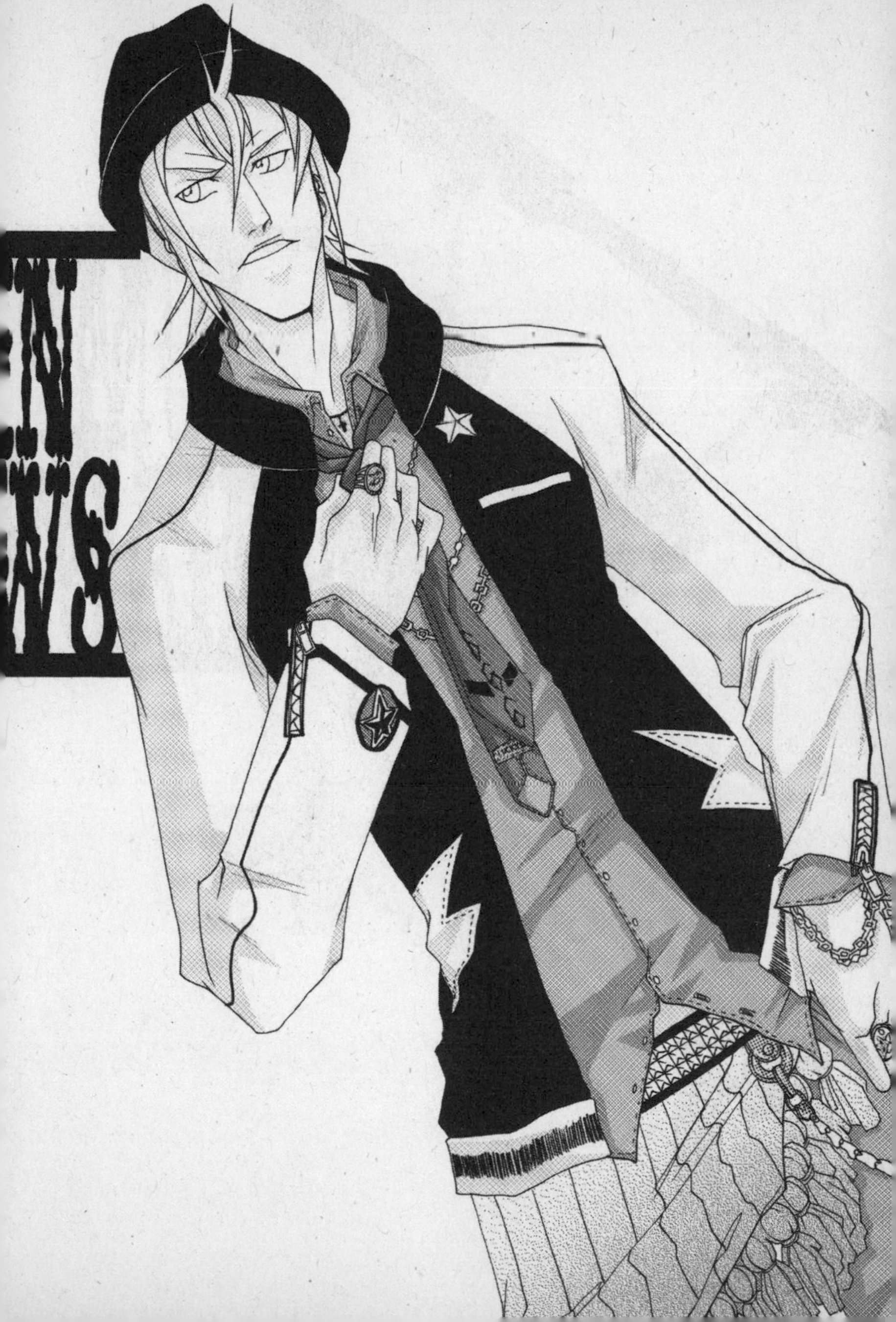
N
WS

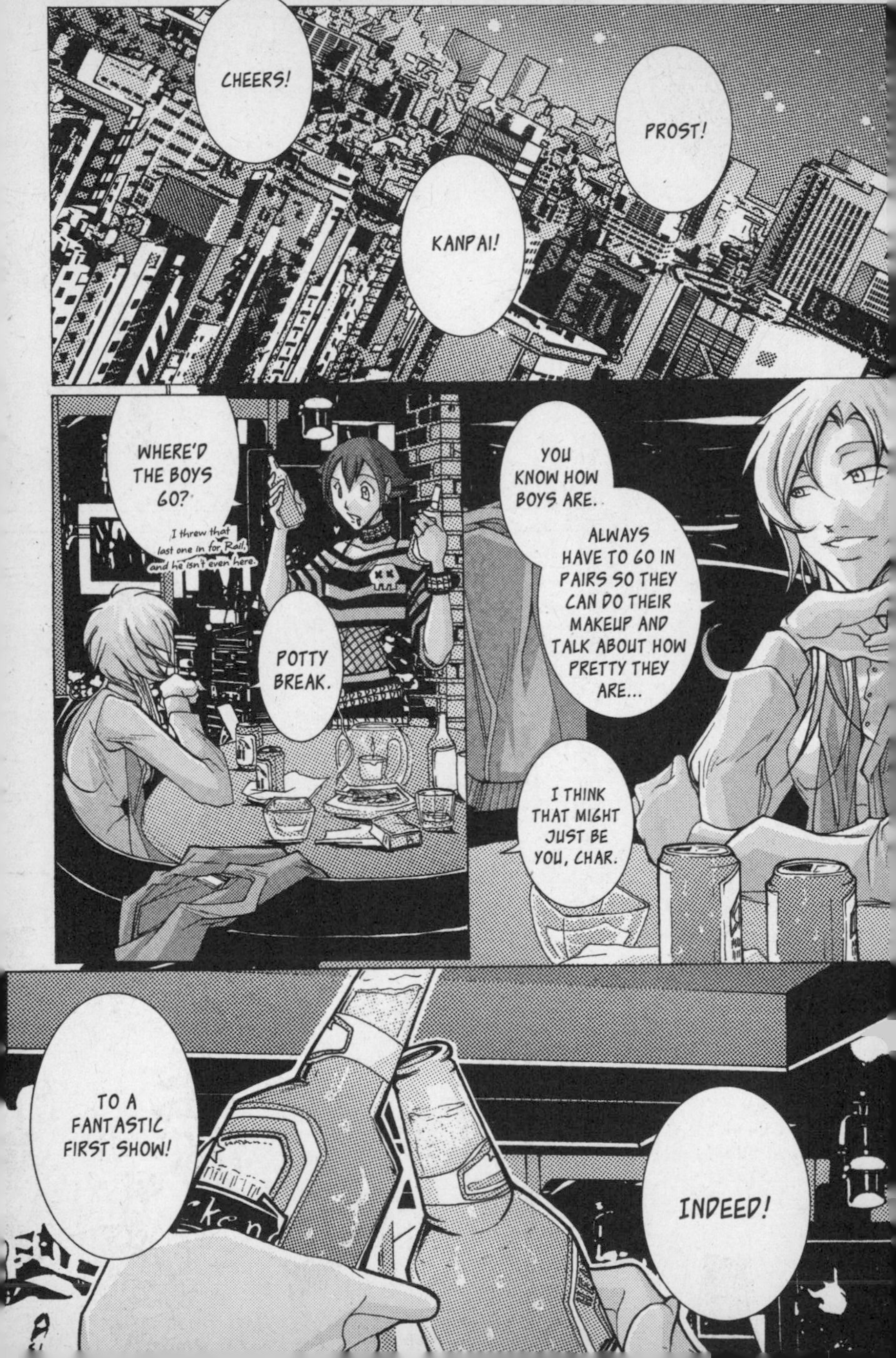
CHEERS!
KANPAI!
PROST!
WHERE'D THE BOYS GO?
I threw that last one in for Rail, and he isn't even here.
POTTY BREAK.
YOU KNOW HOW BOYS ARE.
ALWAYS HAVE TO GO IN PAIRS SO THEY CAN DO THEIR MAKEUP AND TALK ABOUT HOW PRETTY THEY ARE...
I THINK THAT MIGHT JUST BE YOU, CHAR.
TO A FANTASTIC FIRST SHOW!
INDEED!

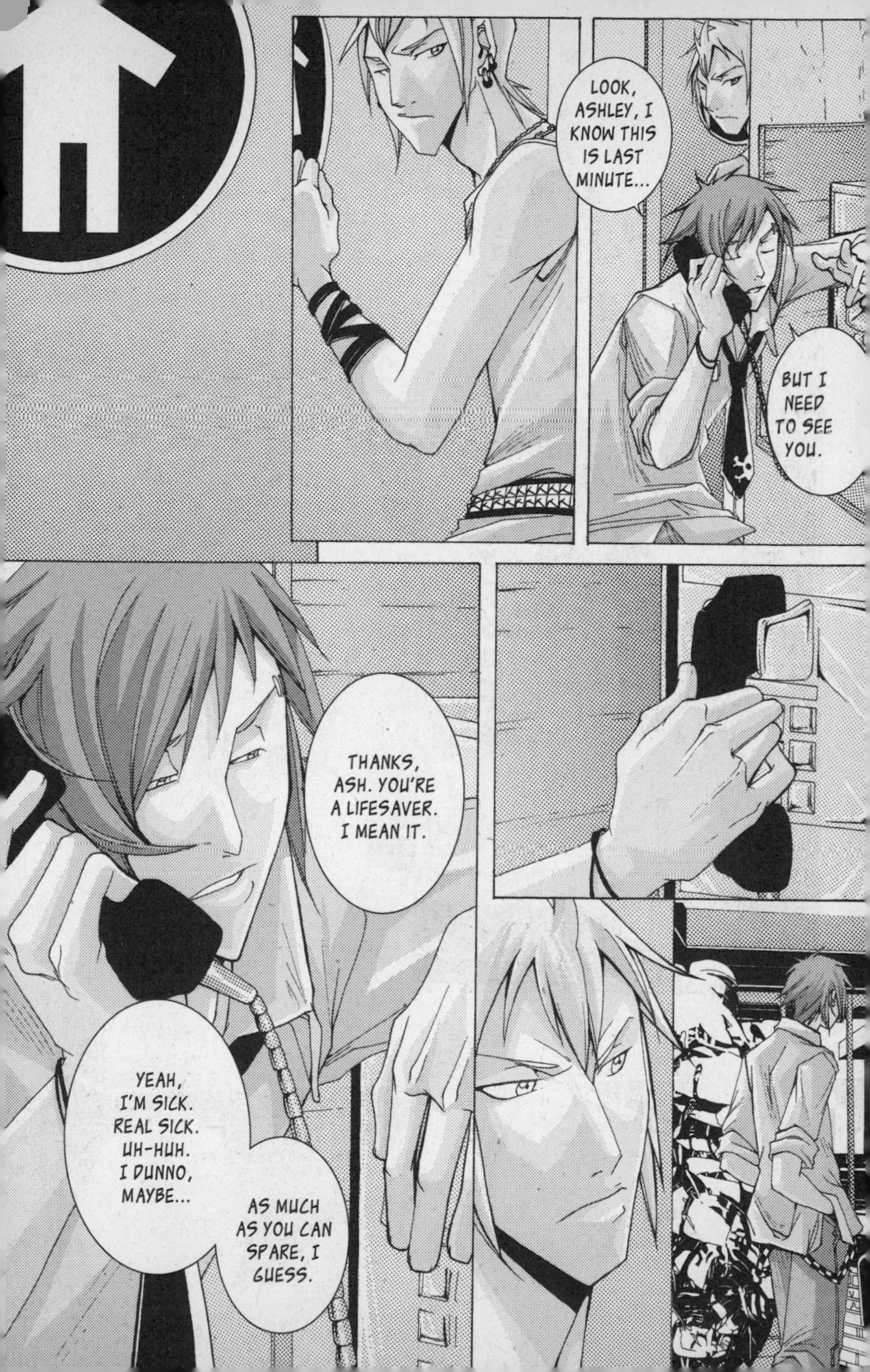
LOOK, ASHLEY, I KNOW THIS IS LAST MINUTE...
BUT I NEED TO SEE YOU.
THANKS, ASH. YOU'RE A LIFESAVER. I MEAN IT.
YEAH, I'M SICK. REAL SICK. UH-HUH. I DUNNO, MAYBE...
AS MUCH AS YOU CAN SPARE, I GUESS.

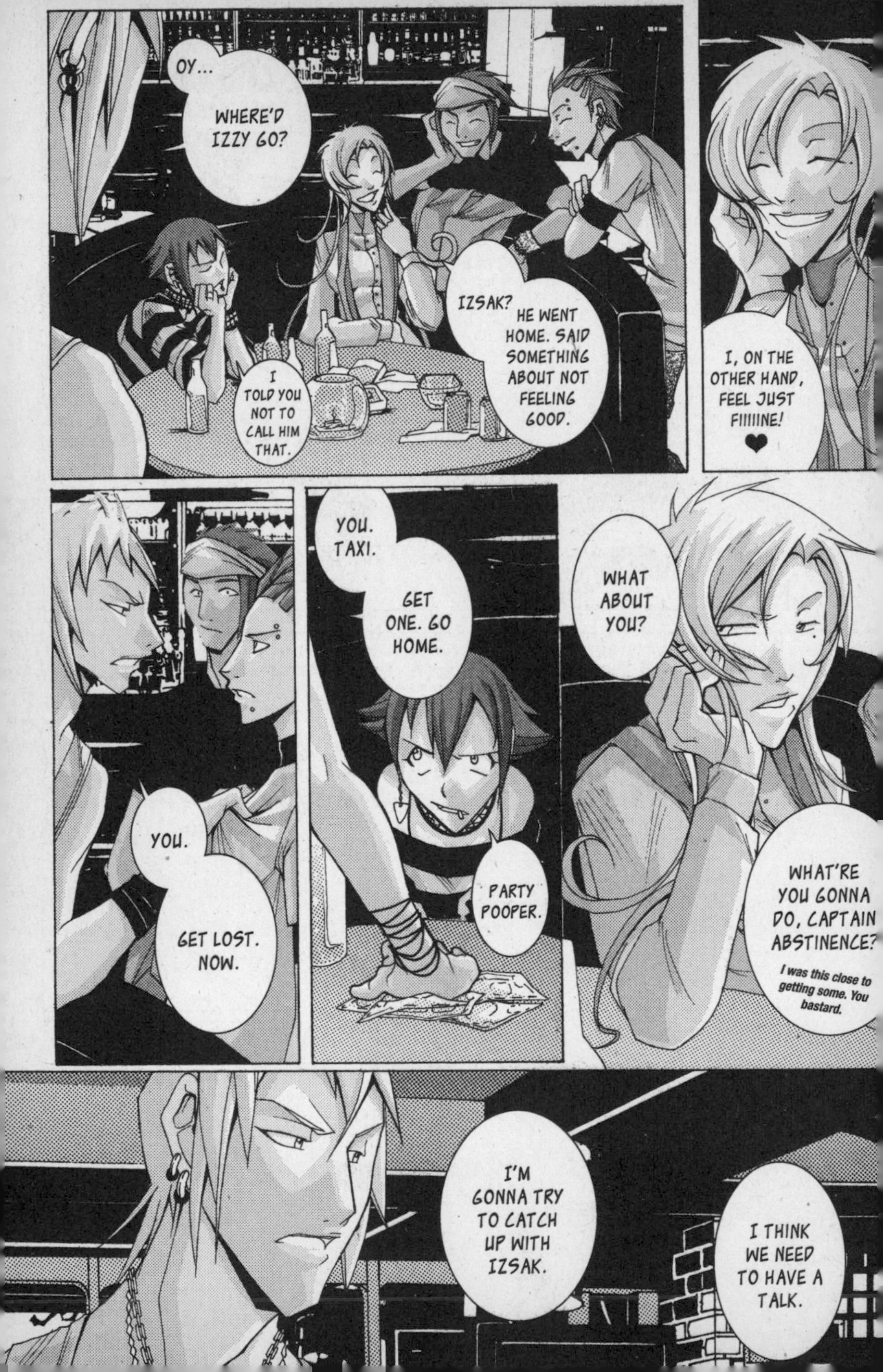
OY...
WHERE'D IZZY GO?
IZSAK? HE WENT HOME. SAID SOMETHING ABOUT NOT FEELING GOOD.
I TOLD YOU NOT TO CALL HIM THAT.
I, ON THE OTHER HAND, FEEL JUST FIIIIINE! ❤
YOU.
GET LOST. NOW.
YOU. TAXI.
GET ONE. GO HOME.
PARTY POOPER.
WHAT ABOUT YOU?
WHAT'RE YOU GONNA DO, CAPTAIN ABSTINENCE?
I was this close to getting some. You bastard.
I'M GONNA TRY TO CATCH UP WITH IZSAK.
I THINK WE NEED TO HAVE A TALK.

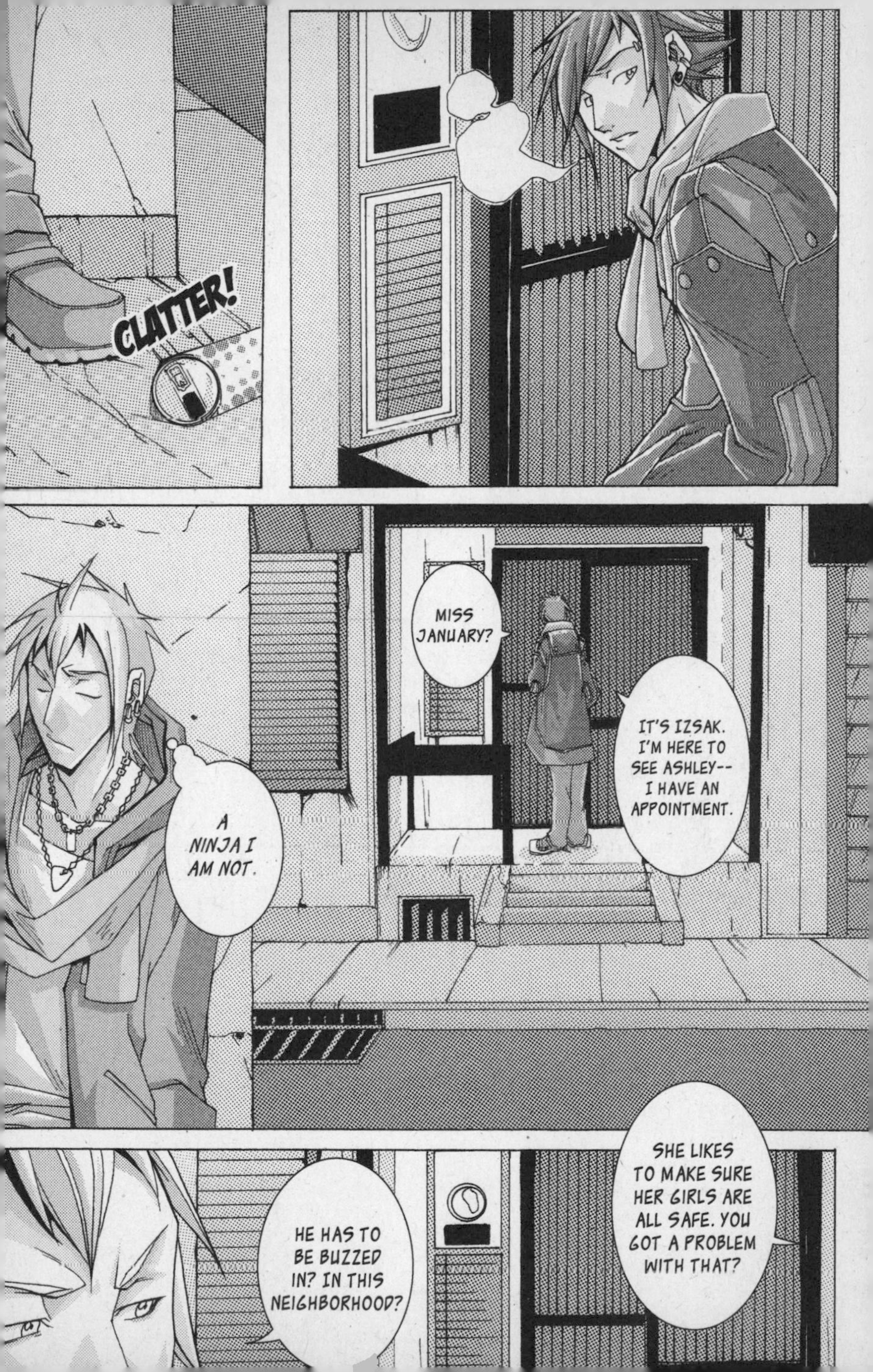

CLATTER!
A NINJA I AM NOT.
MISS JANUARY?
IT'S IZSAK. I'M HERE TO SEE ASHLEY-- I HAVE AN APPOINTMENT.
HE HAS TO BE BUZZED IN? IN THIS NEIGHBORHOOD?
SHE LIKES TO MAKE SURE HER GIRLS ARE ALL SAFE. YOU GOT A PROBLEM WITH THAT?

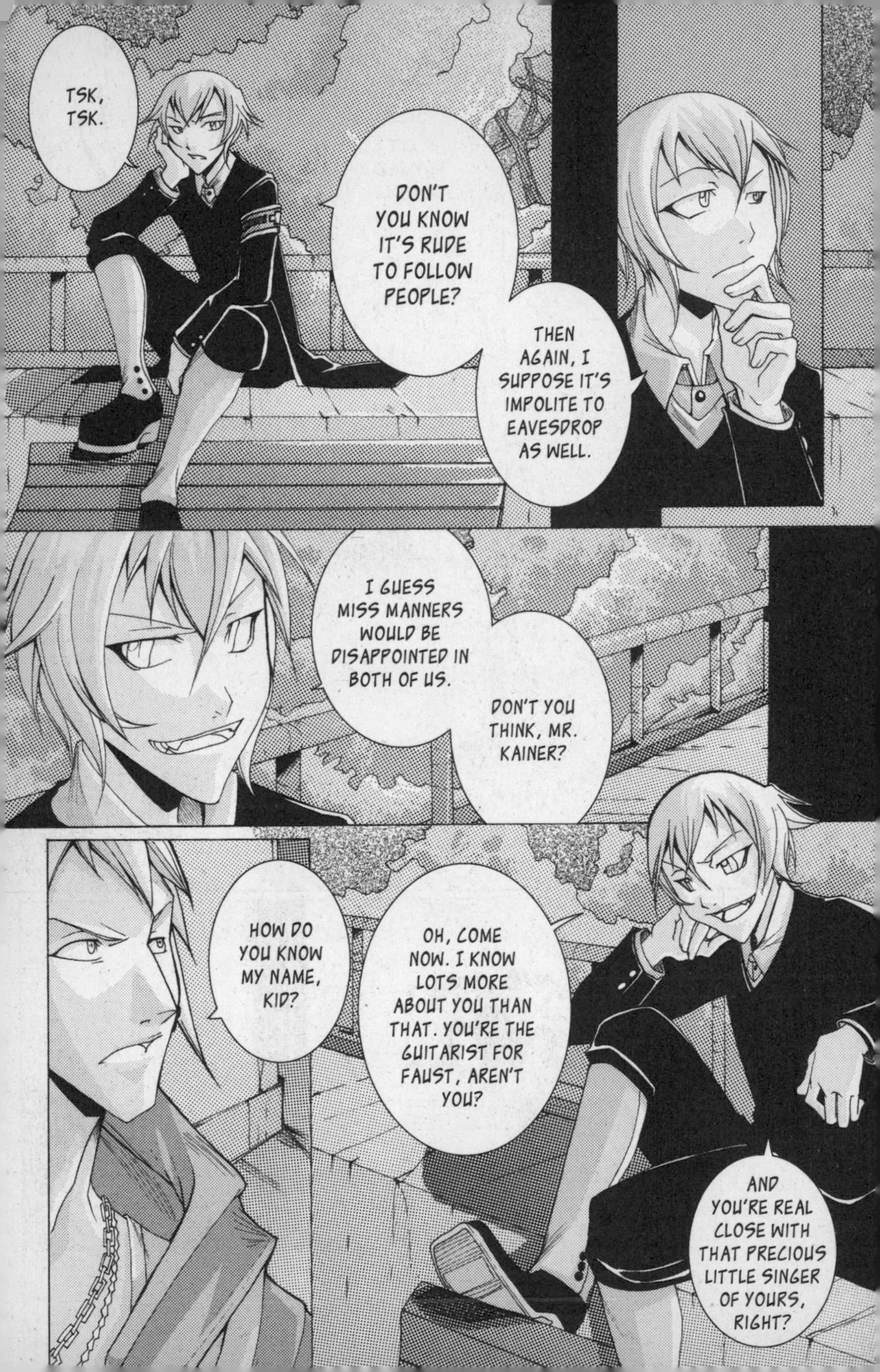
TSK, TSK.
DON'T YOU KNOW IT'S RUDE TO FOLLOW PEOPLE?
THEN AGAIN, I SUPPOSE IT'S IMPOLITE TO EAVESDROP AS WELL.
I GUESS MISS MANNERS WOULD BE DISAPPOINTED IN BOTH OF US.
DON'T YOU THINK, MR. KAINER?
HOW DO YOU KNOW MY NAME, KID?
OH, COME NOW. I KNOW LOTS MORE ABOUT YOU THAN THAT. YOU'RE THE GUITARIST FOR FAUST, AREN'T YOU?
AND YOU'RE REAL CLOSE WITH THAT PRECIOUS LITTLE SINGER OF YOURS, RIGHT?

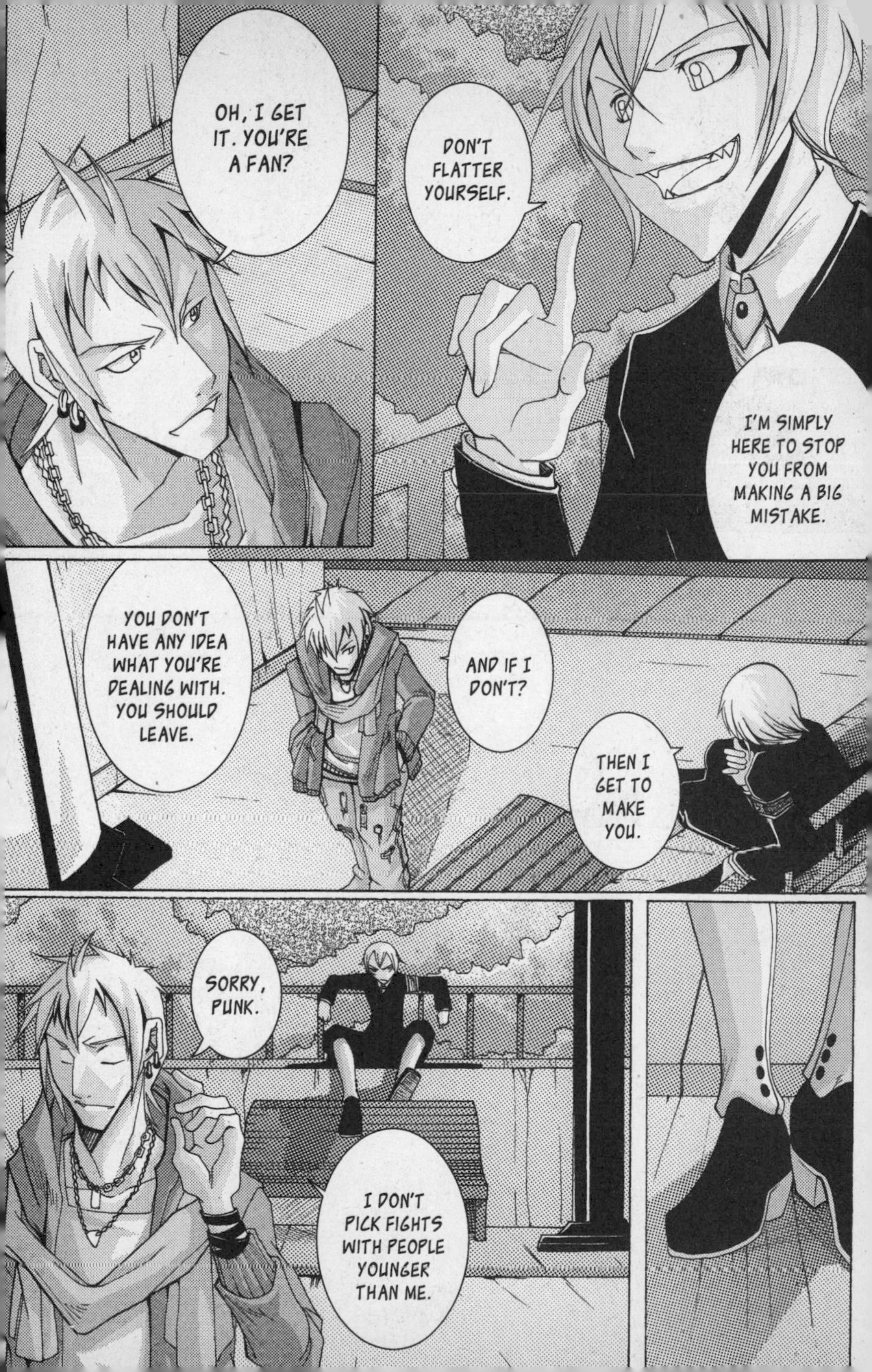
OH, I GET IT. YOU'RE A FAN?
DON'T FLATTER YOURSELF.
I'M SIMPLY HERE TO STOP YOU FROM MAKING A BIG MISTAKE.
YOU DON'T HAVE ANY IDEA WHAT YOU'RE DEALING WITH. YOU SHOULD LEAVE.
AND IF I DON'T?
THEN I GET TO MAKE YOU.
SORRY, PUNK.
I DON'T PICK FIGHTS WITH PEOPLE YOUNGER THAN ME.

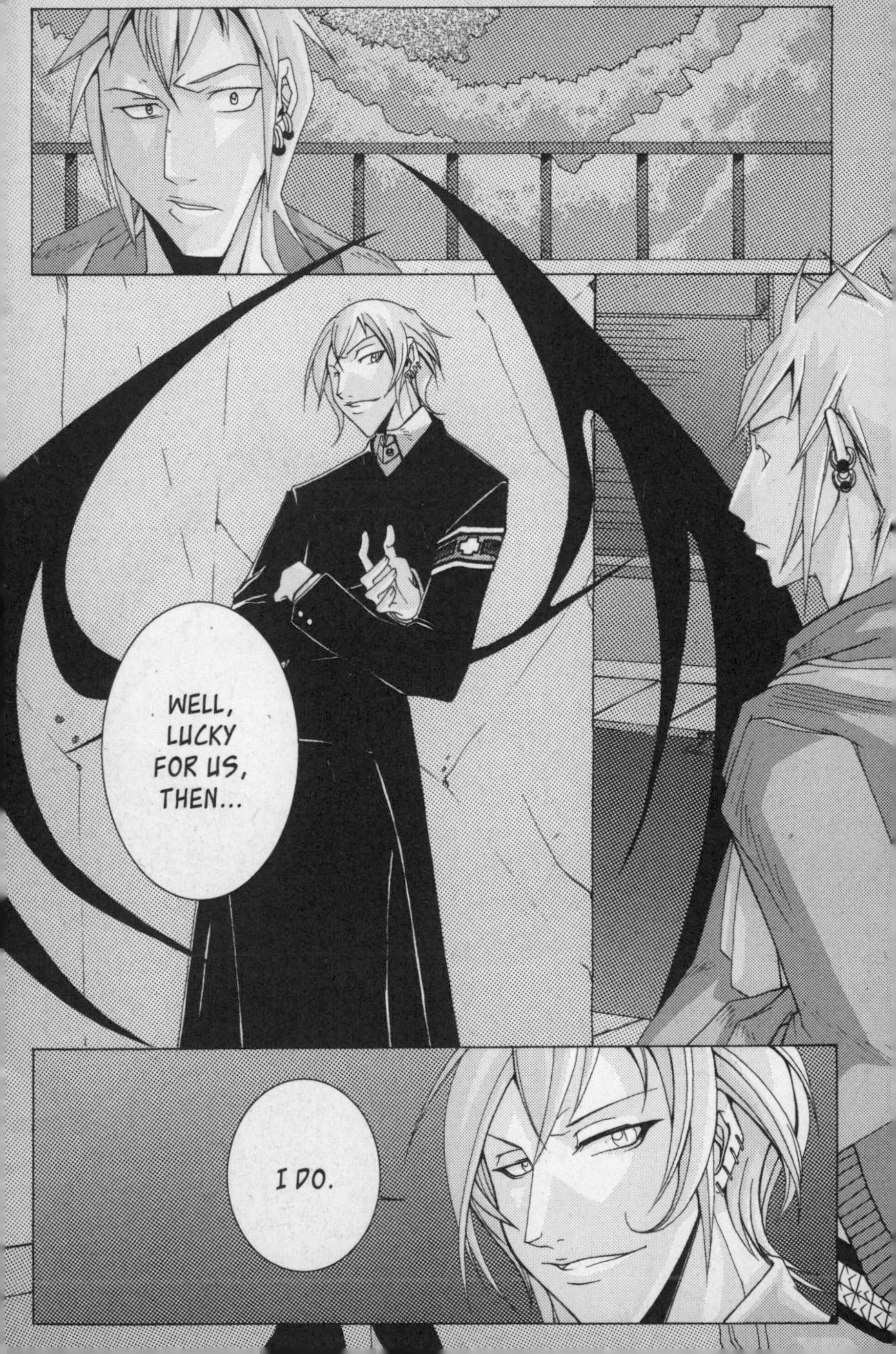
WELL, LUCKY FOR US, THEN...
I DO.

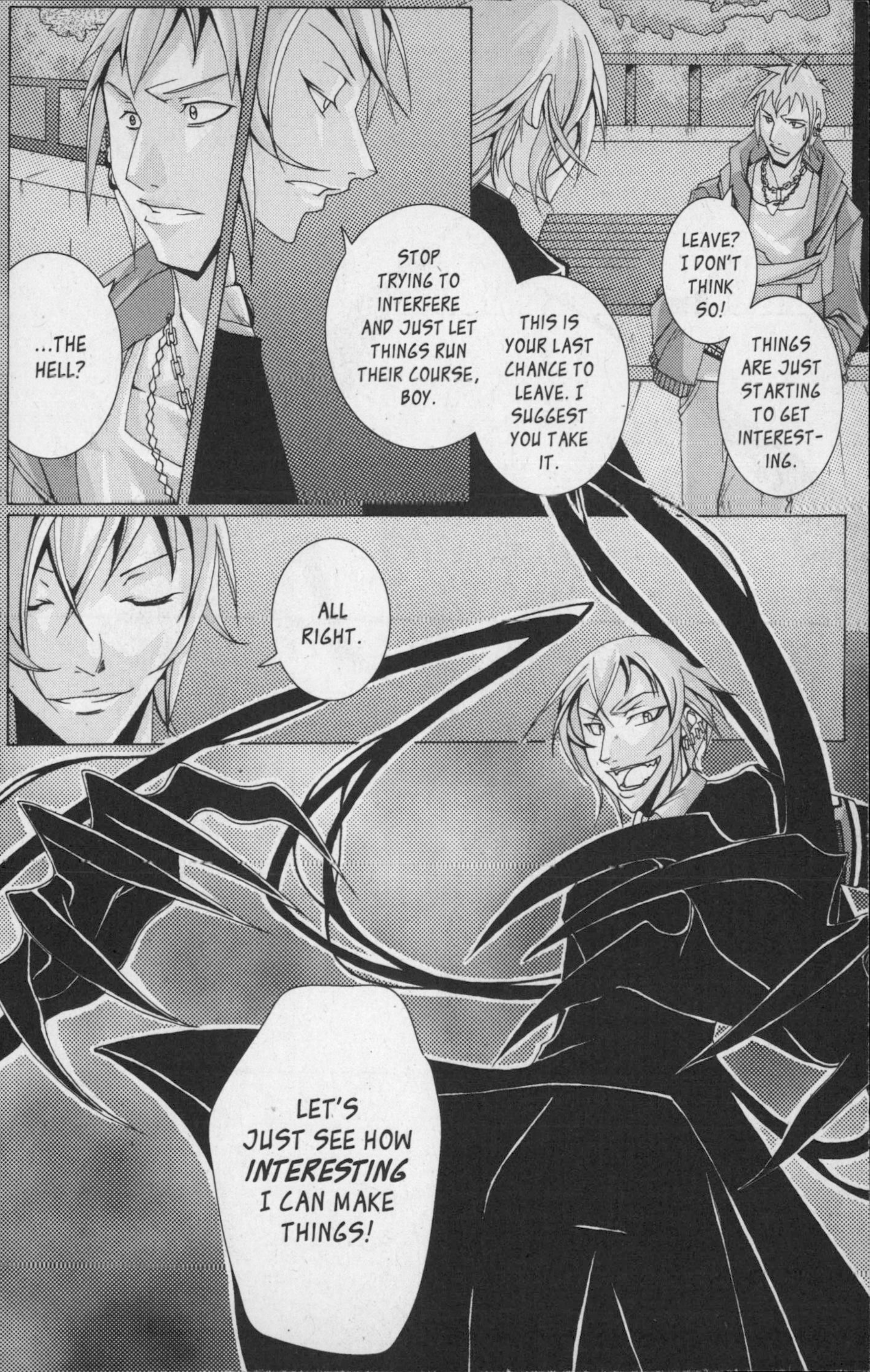
...THE HELL?
STOP TRYING TO INTERFERE AND JUST LET THINGS RUN THEIR COURSE, BOY.
THIS IS YOUR LAST CHANCE TO LEAVE. I SUGGEST YOU TAKE IT.
LEAVE? I DON'T THINK SO!
THINGS ARE JUST STARTING TO GET INTEREST-ING.
ALL RIGHT.
LET'S JUST SEE HOW *INTERESTING* I CAN MAKE THINGS!

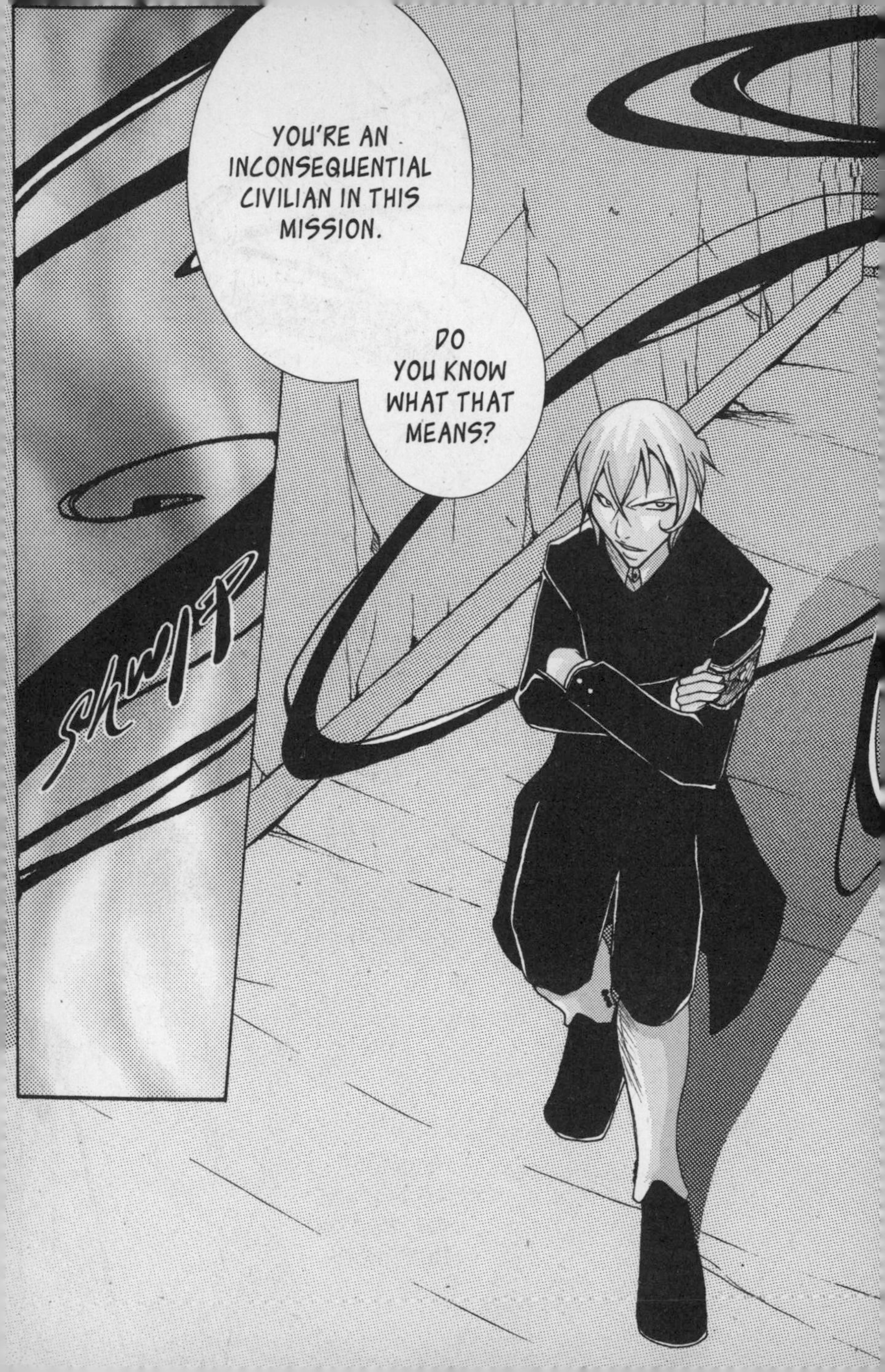
YOU'RE AN INCONSEQUENTIAL CIVILIAN IN THIS MISSION.
DO YOU KNOW WHAT THAT MEANS?
shwff

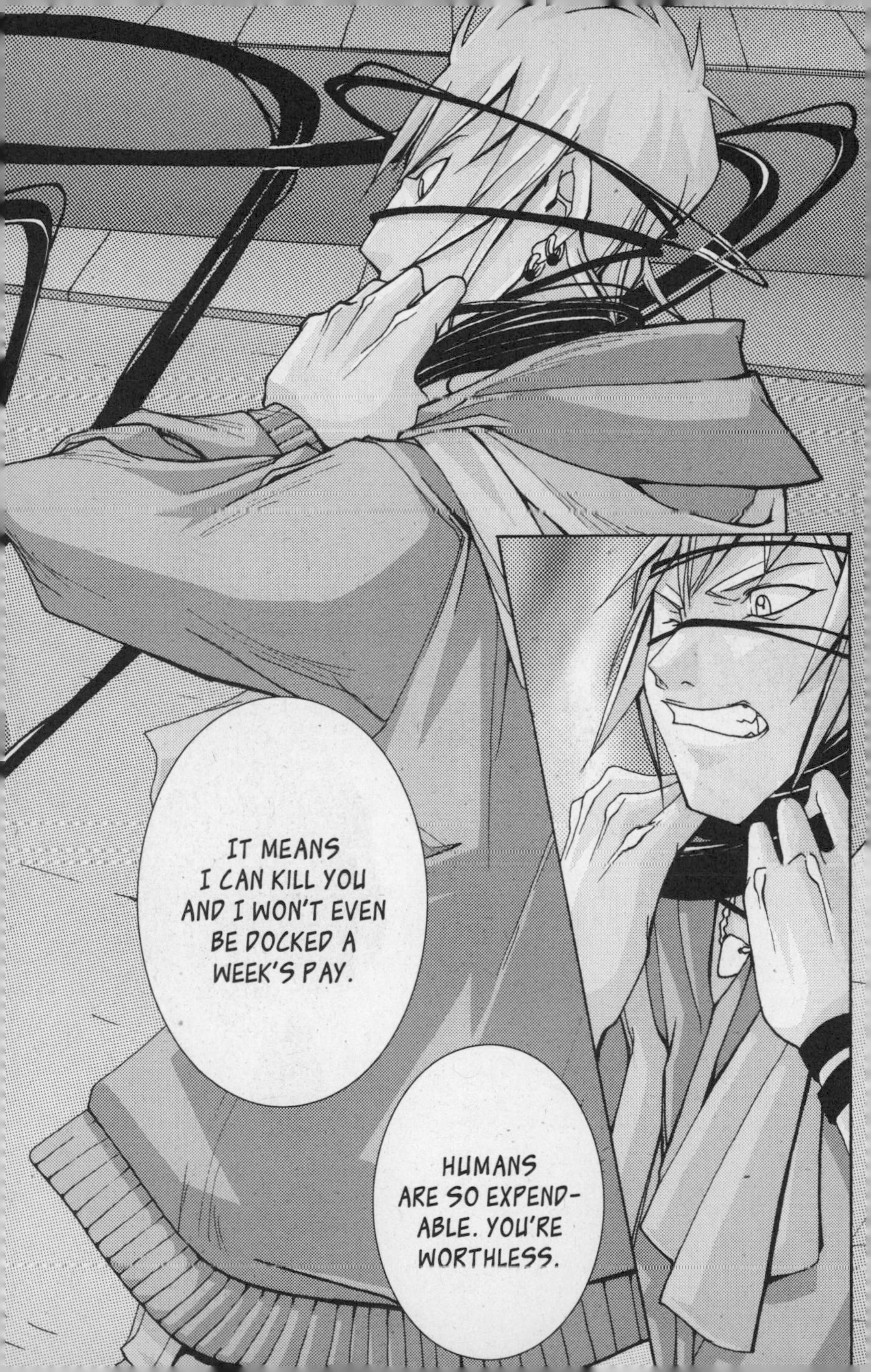
IT MEANS I CAN KILL YOU AND I WON'T EVEN BE DOCKED A WEEK'S PAY.
HUMANS ARE SO EXPEND-ABLE. YOU'RE WORTHLESS.

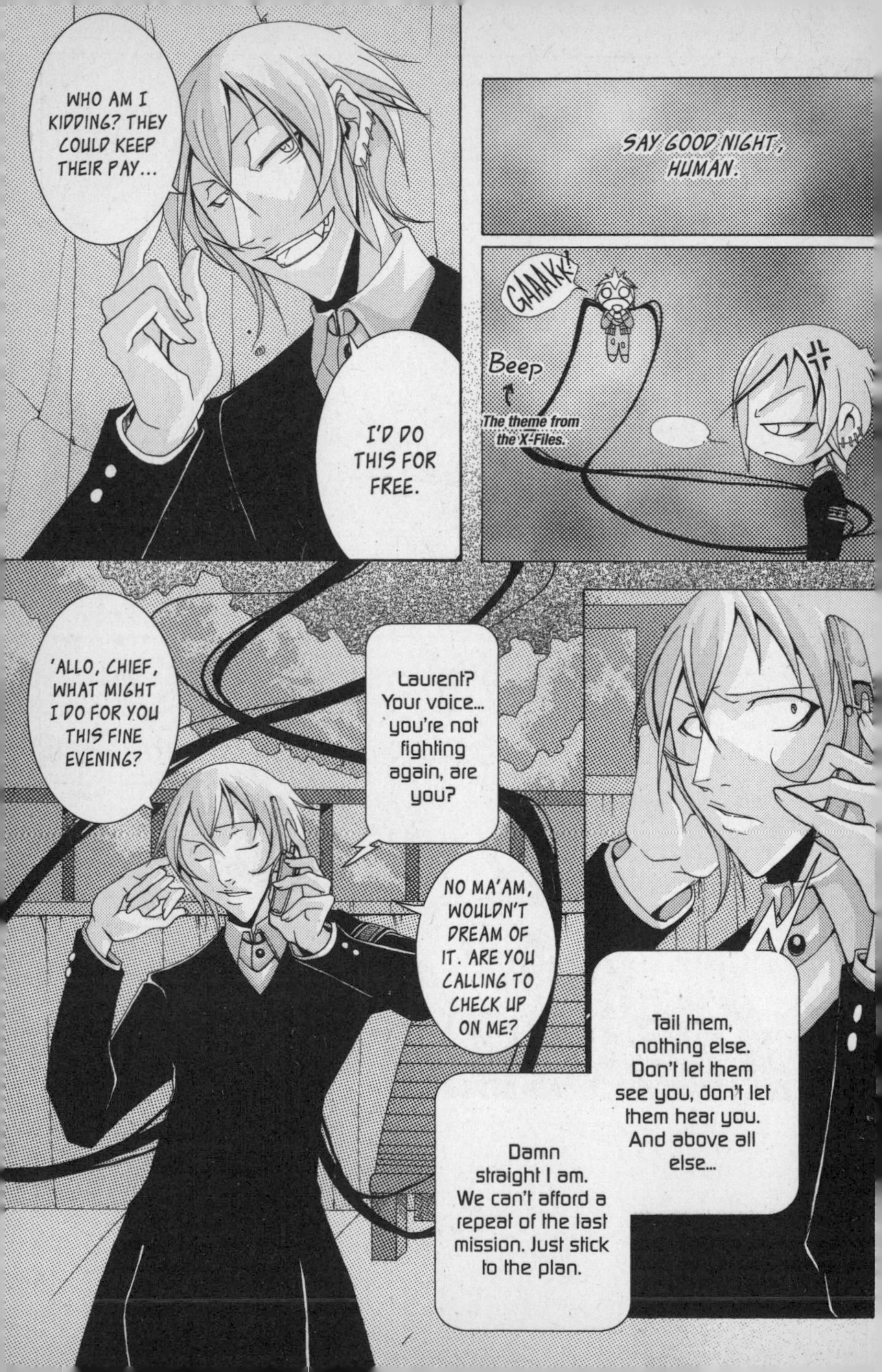
WHO AM I KIDDING? THEY COULD KEEP THEIR PAY...
I'D DO THIS FOR FREE.
SAY GOOD NIGHT, HUMAN.
GAAAKK!
Beep
The theme from the X-Files.
'ALLO, CHIEF, WHAT MIGHT I DO FOR YOU THIS FINE EVENING?
Laurent? Your voice... you're not fighting again, are you?
NO MA'AM, WOULDN'T DREAM OF IT. ARE YOU CALLING TO CHECK UP ON ME?
Damn straight I am. We can't afford a repeat of the last mission. Just stick to the plan.
Tail them, nothing else. Don't let them see you, don't let them hear you. And above all else...

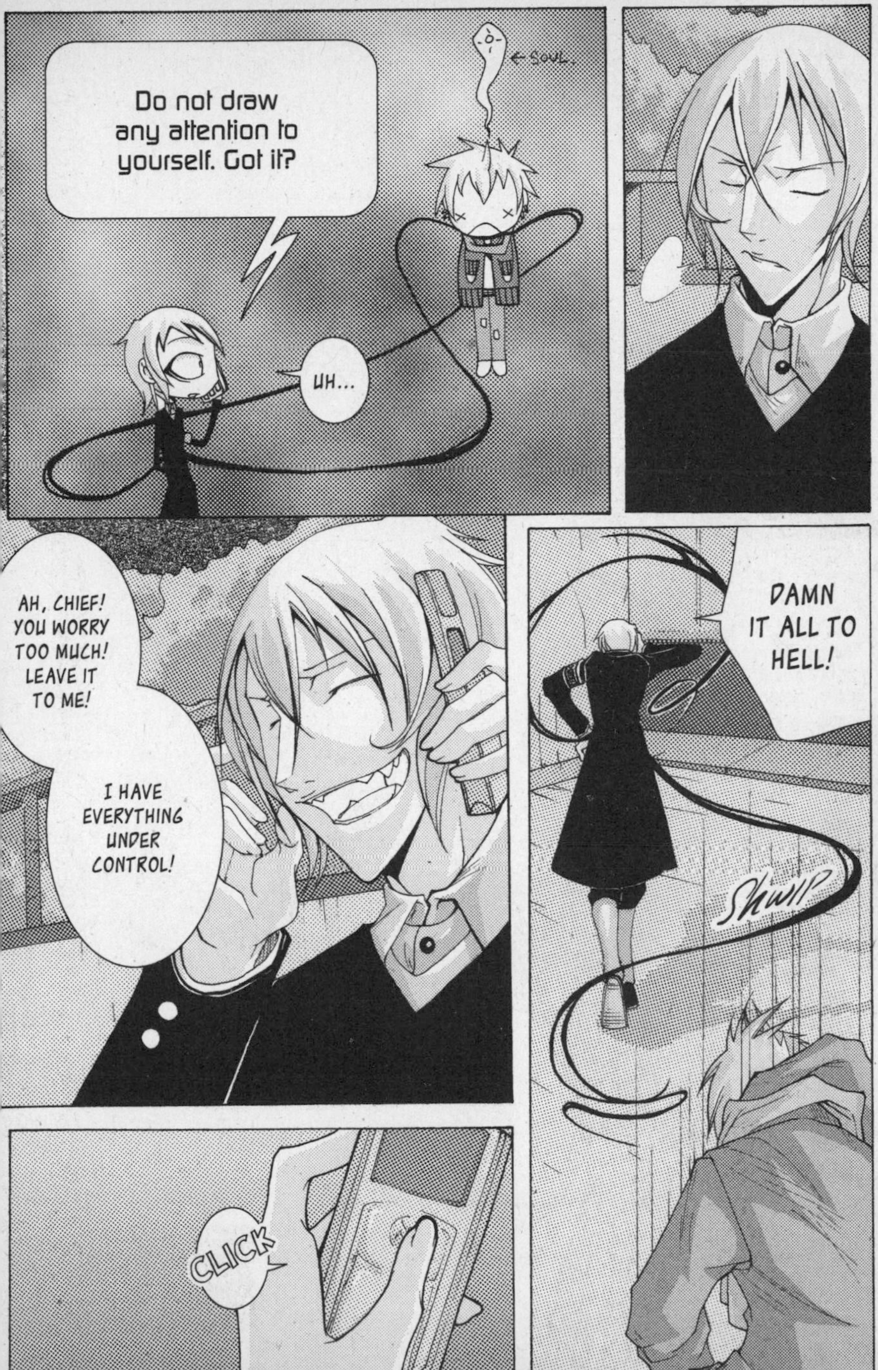
Do not draw any attention to yourself. Got it?
← SOUL.
UH...
AH, CHIEF! YOU WORRY TOO MUCH! LEAVE IT TO ME!
I HAVE EVERYTHING UNDER CONTROL!
CLICK
DAMN IT ALL TO HELL!
SHWIP

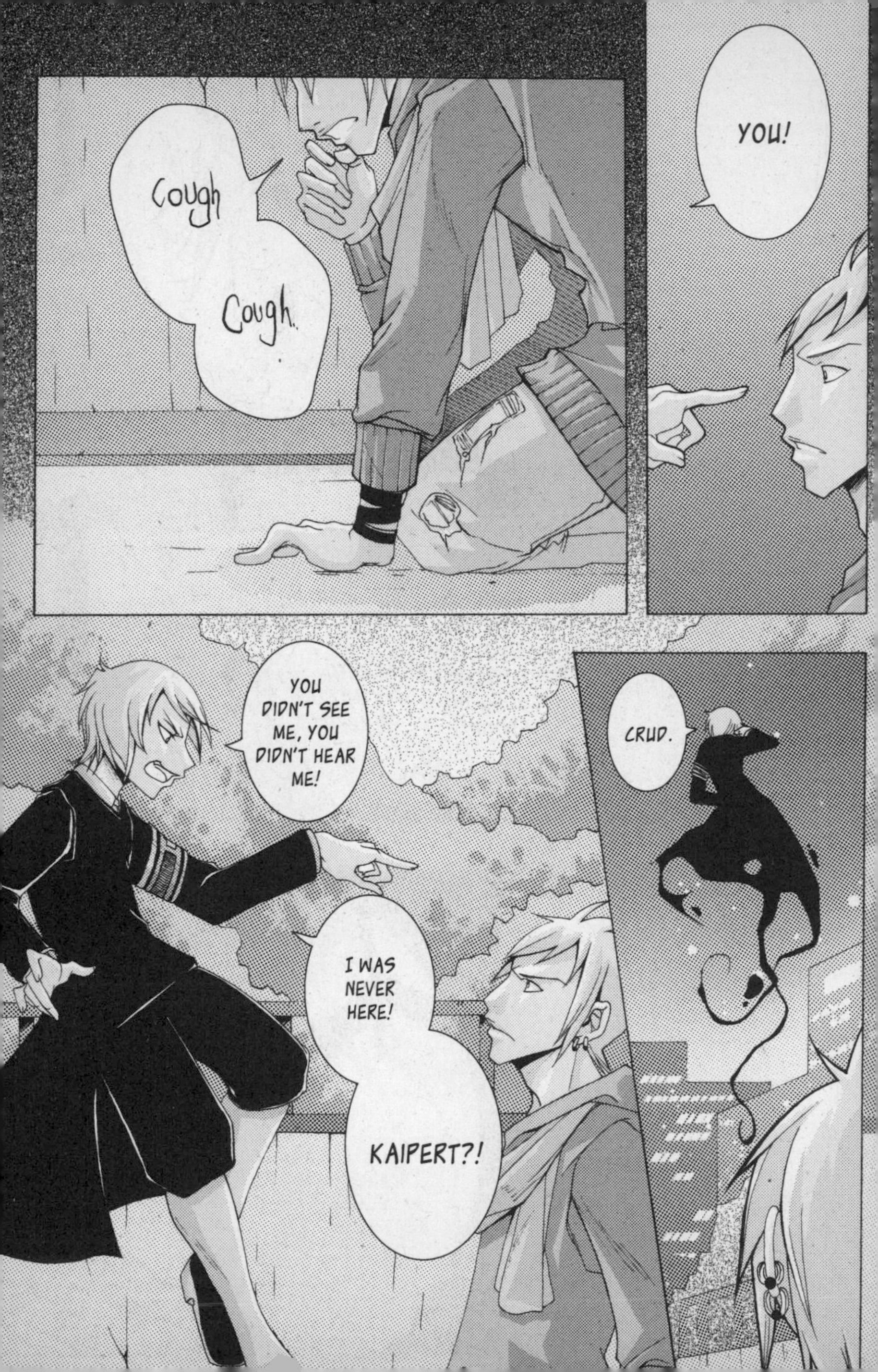
Cough
Cough.
YOU!
YOU DIDN'T SEE ME, YOU DIDN'T HEAR ME!
I WAS NEVER HERE!
KAIPERT?!
CRUD.

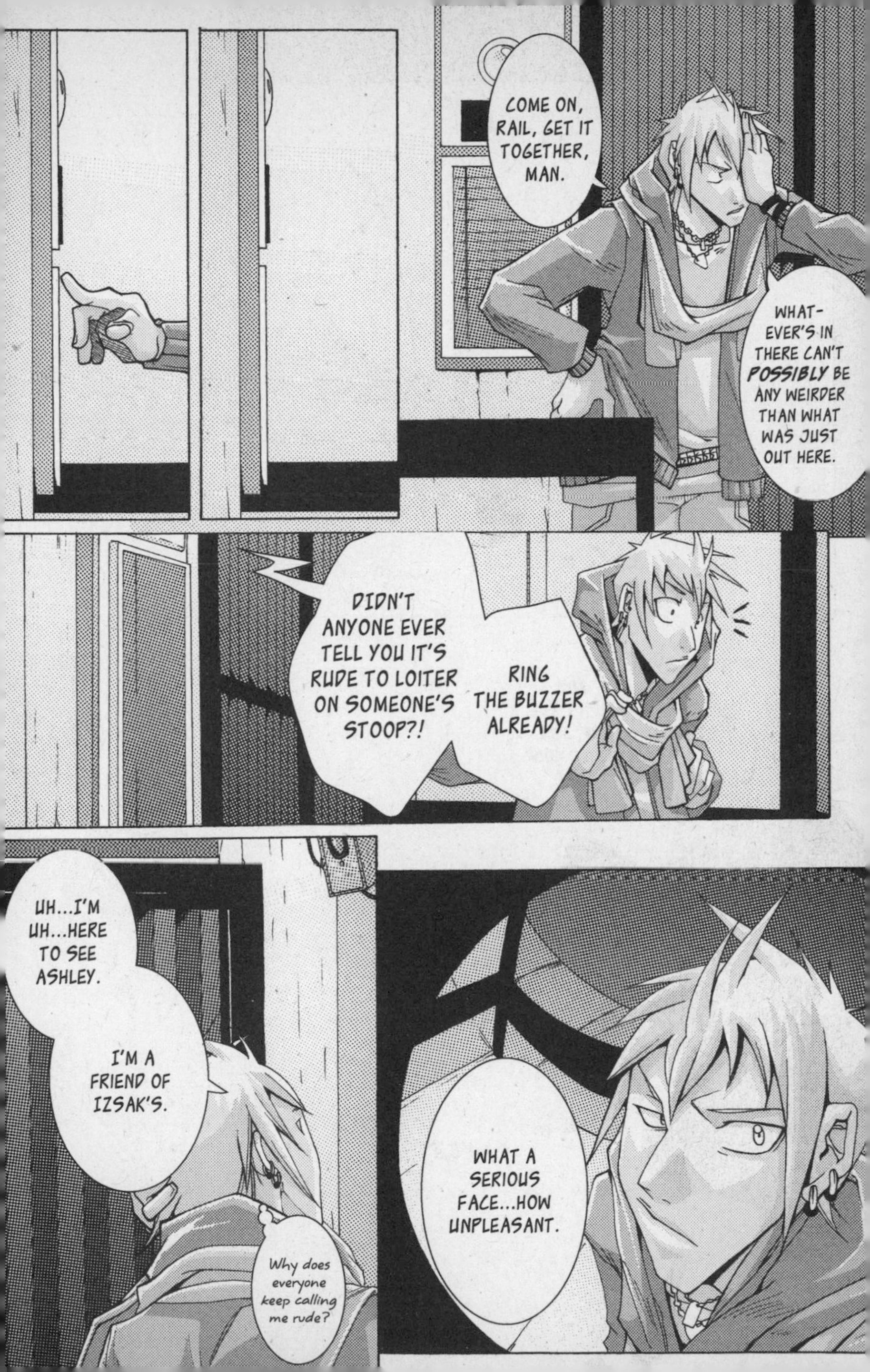
COME ON, RAIL, GET IT TOGETHER, MAN.
WHAT-EVER'S IN THERE CAN'T POSSIBLY BE ANY WEIRDER THAN WHAT WAS JUST OUT HERE.
DIDN'T ANYONE EVER TELL YOU IT'S RUDE TO LOITER ON SOMEONE'S STOOP?!
RING THE BUZZER ALREADY!
UH...I'M UH...HERE TO SEE ASHLEY.
I'M A FRIEND OF IZSAK'S.
Why does everyone keep calling me rude?
WHAT A SERIOUS FACE...HOW UNPLEASANT.

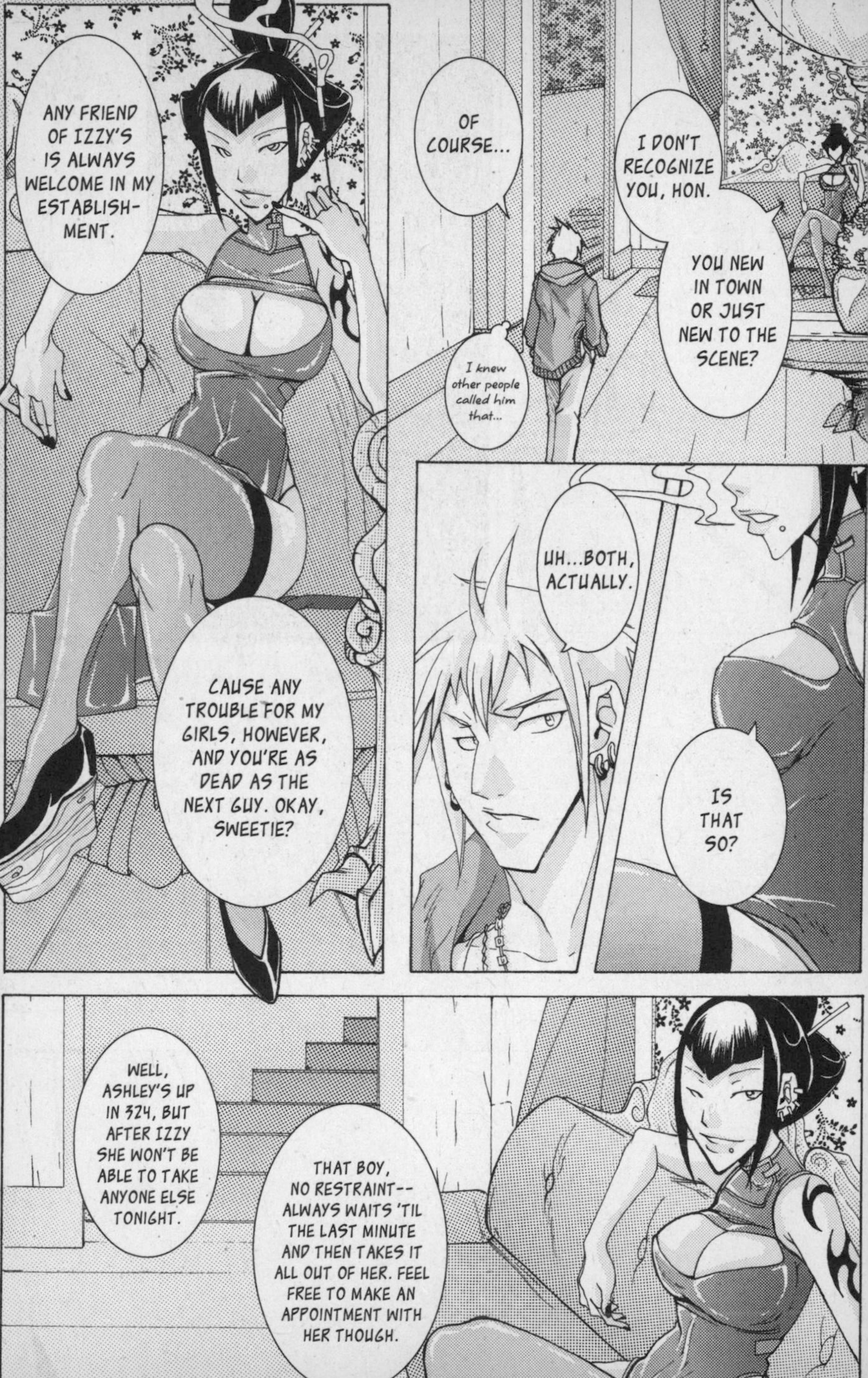
ANY FRIEND OF IZZY'S IS ALWAYS WELCOME IN MY ESTABLISH-MENT.
CAUSE ANY TROUBLE FOR MY GIRLS, HOWEVER, AND YOU'RE AS DEAD AS THE NEXT GUY. OKAY, SWEETIE?
OF COURSE...
I knew other people called him that...
I DON'T RECOGNIZE YOU, HON.
YOU NEW IN TOWN OR JUST NEW TO THE SCENE?
UH...BOTH, ACTUALLY.
IS THAT SO?
WELL, ASHLEY'S UP IN 324, BUT AFTER IZZY SHE WON'T BE ABLE TO TAKE ANYONE ELSE TONIGHT.
THAT BOY, NO RESTRAINT--ALWAYS WAITS 'TIL THE LAST MINUTE AND THEN TAKES IT ALL OUT OF HER. FEEL FREE TO MAKE AN APPOINTMENT WITH HER THOUGH.

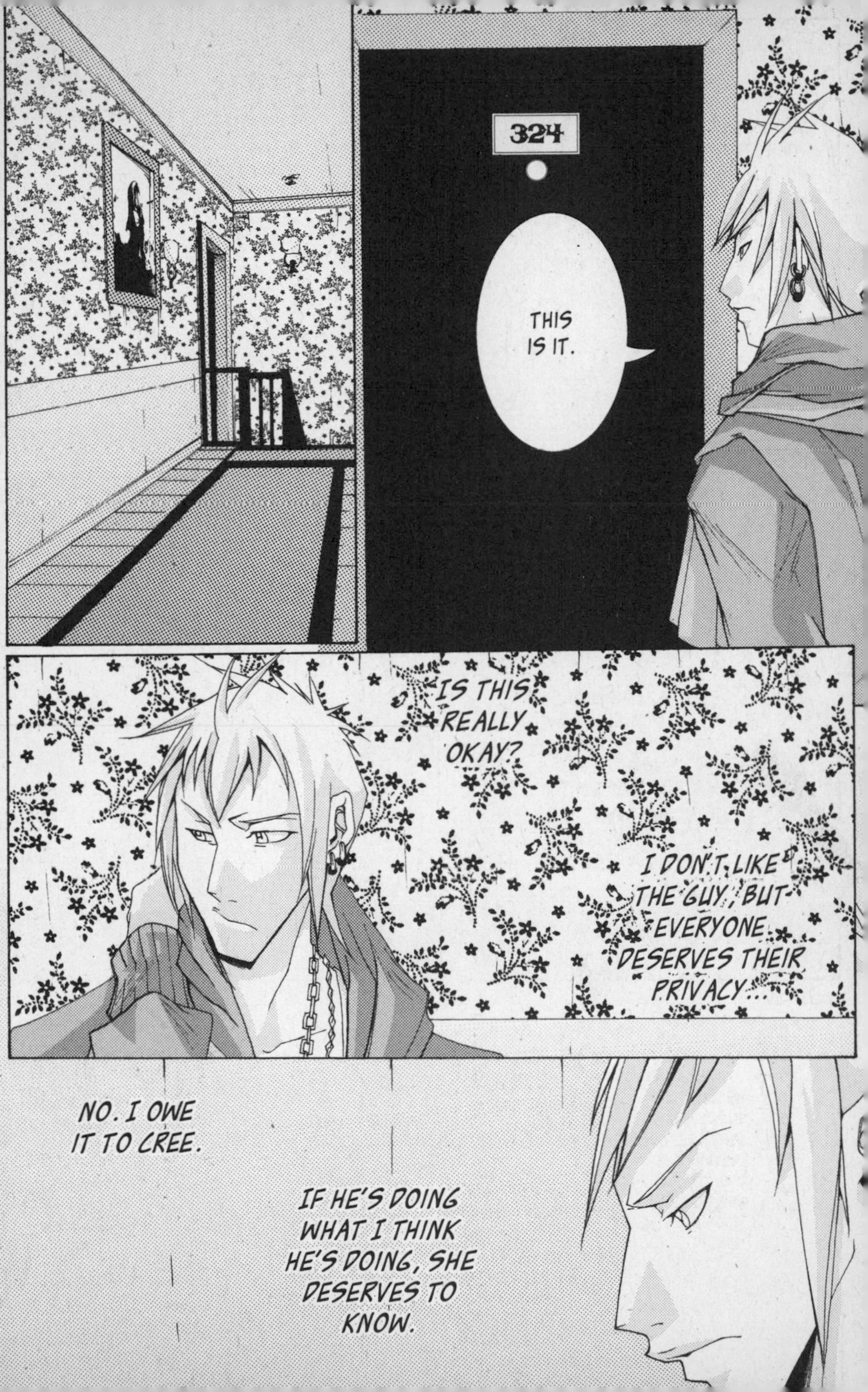
324
THIS IS IT.
IS THIS REALLY OKAY?
I DON'T LIKE THE GUY, BUT EVERYONE DESERVES THEIR PRIVACY...
NO. I OWE IT TO CREE.
IF HE'S DOING WHAT I THINK HE'S DOING, SHE DESERVES TO KNOW.

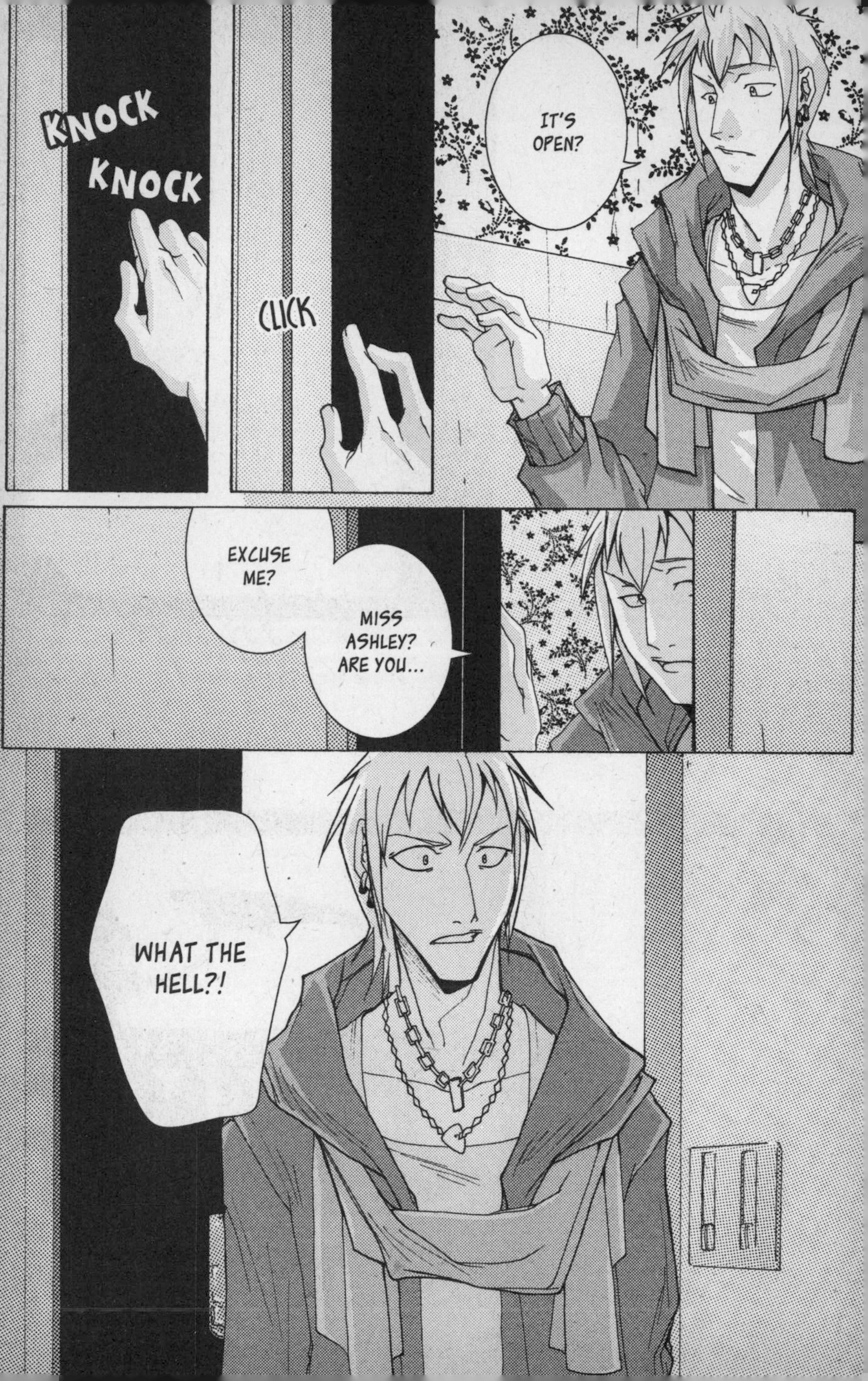
KNOCK
KNOCK
CLICK
IT'S OPEN?
EXCUSE ME?
MISS ASHLEY? ARE YOU...
WHAT THE HELL?!

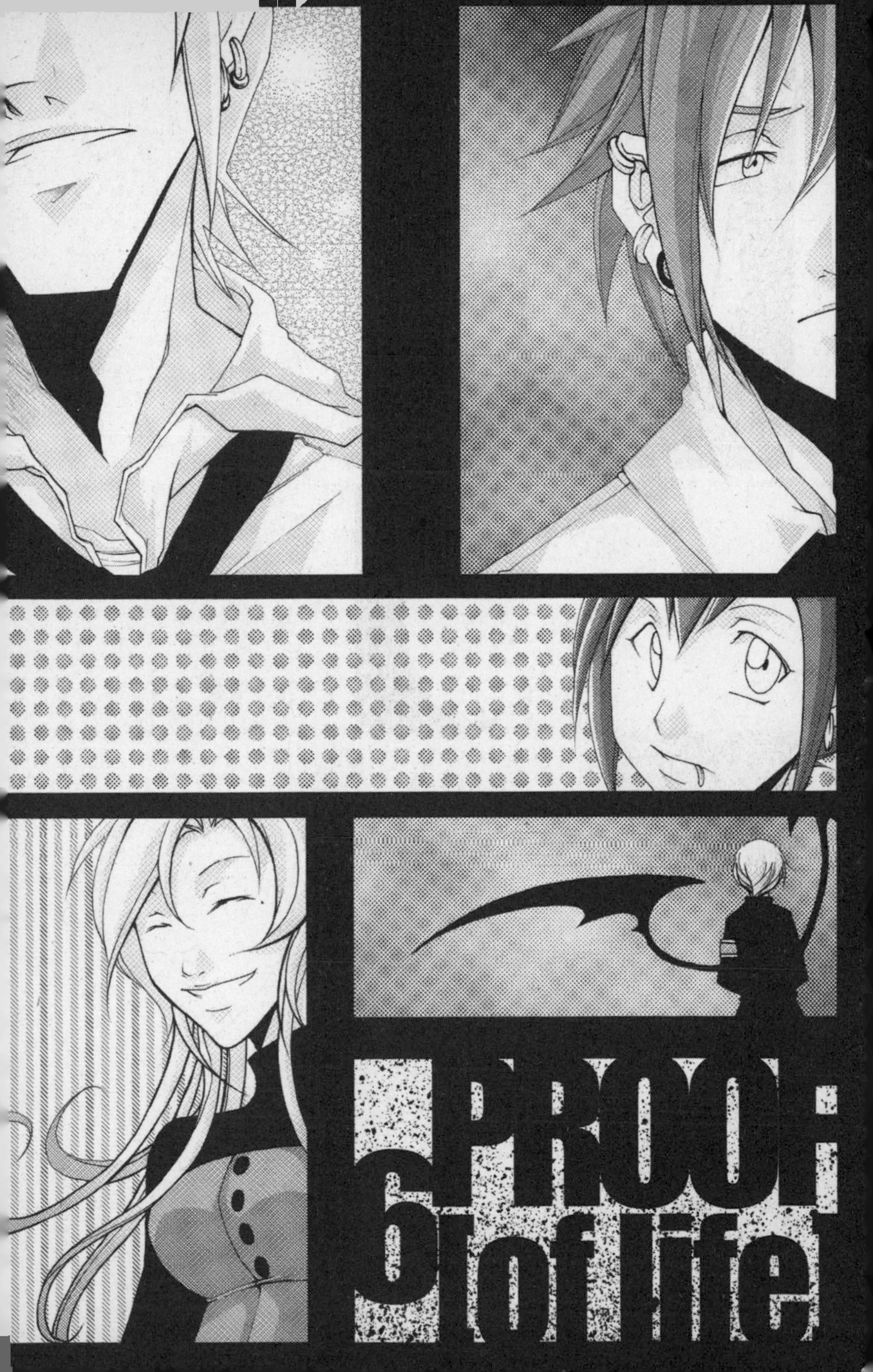
6 PROOF of life

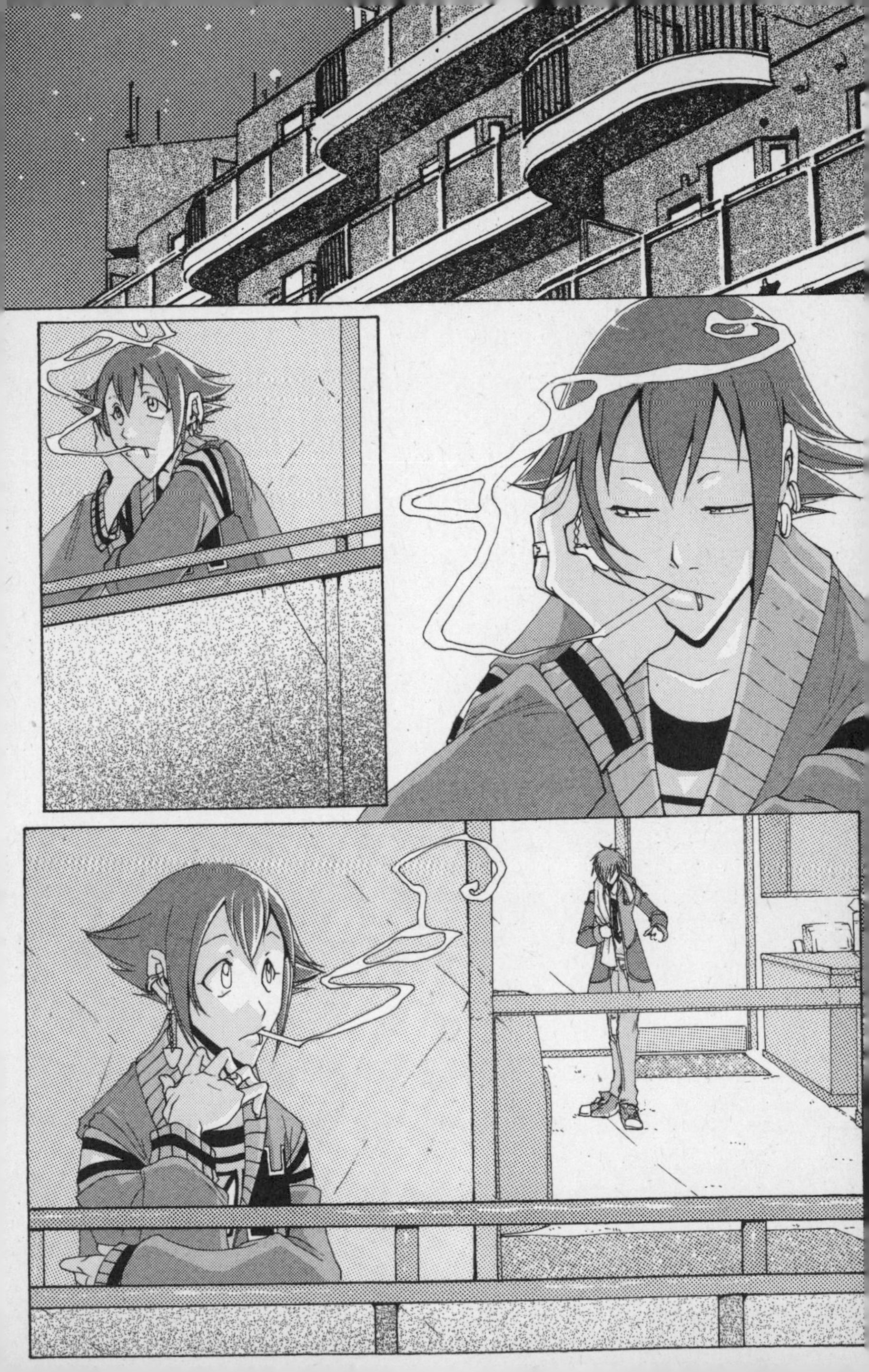

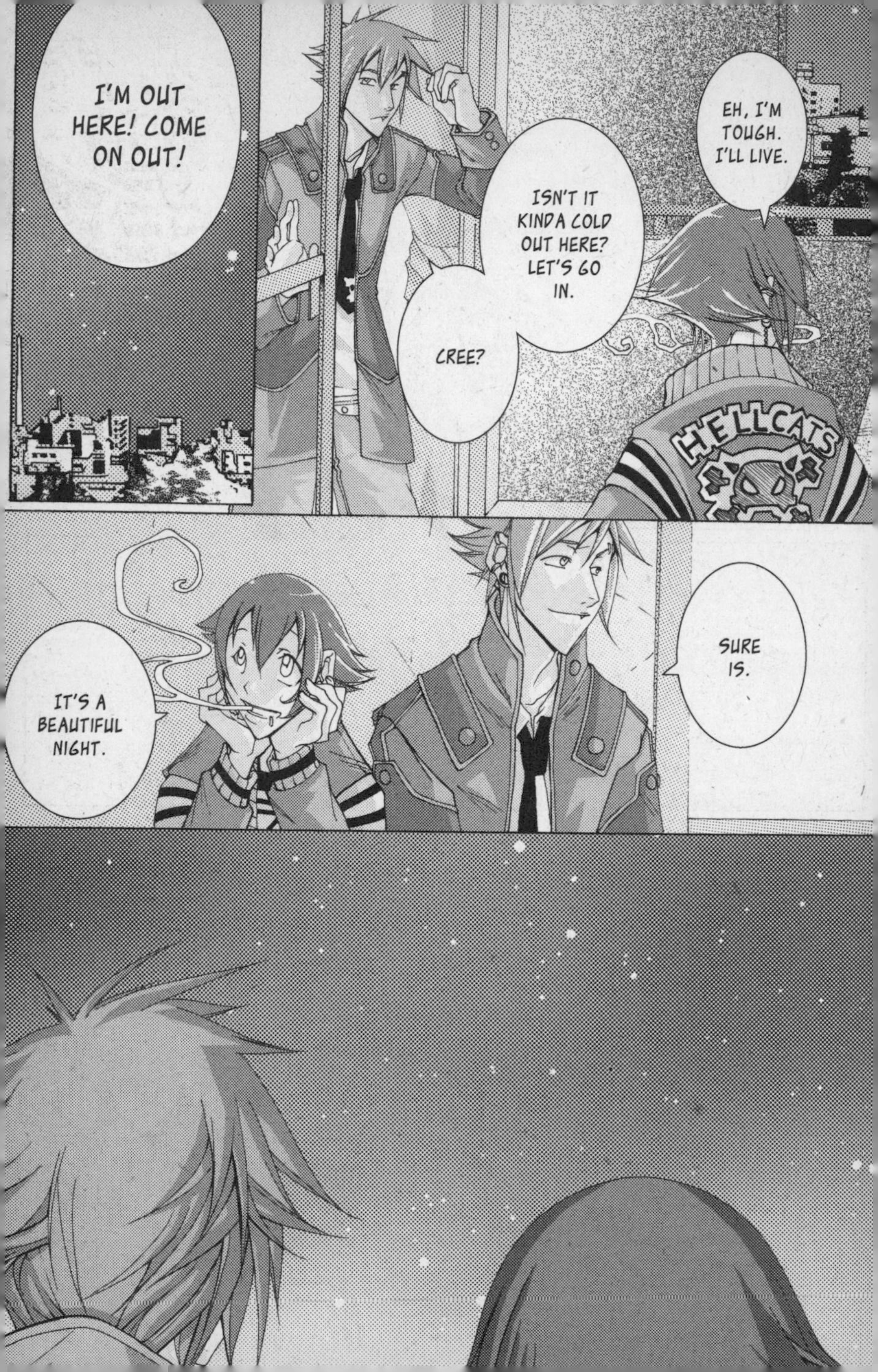
I'M OUT HERE! COME ON OUT!
CREE?
ISN'T IT KINDA COLD OUT HERE? LET'S GO IN.
EH, I'M TOUGH. I'LL LIVE.
HELLCATS
IT'S A BEAUTIFUL NIGHT.
SURE IS.

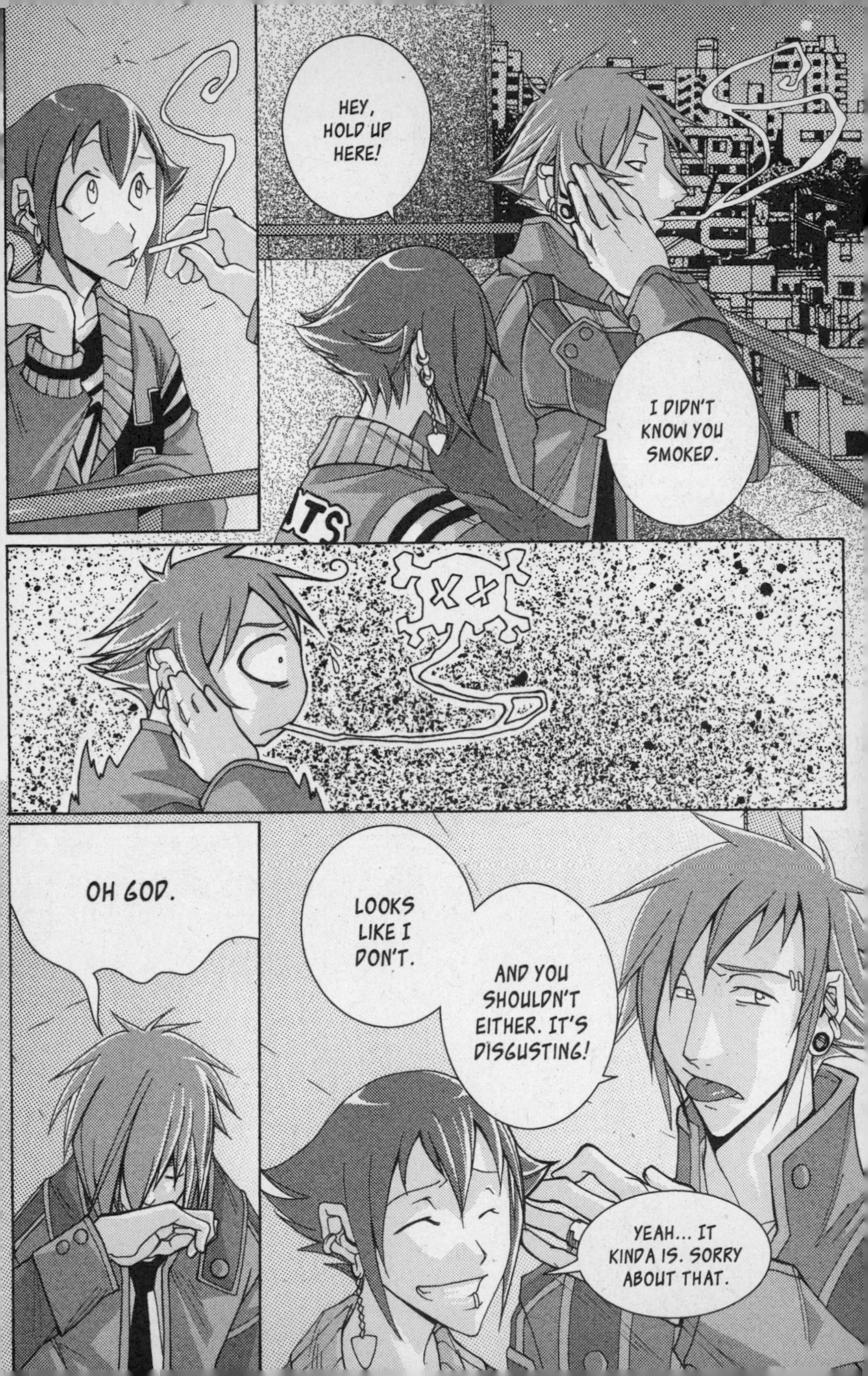
HEY, HOLD UP HERE!
I DIDN'T KNOW YOU SMOKED.
OH GOD.
LOOKS LIKE I DON'T.
AND YOU SHOULDN'T EITHER. IT'S DISGUSTING!
YEAH... IT KINDA IS. SORRY ABOUT THAT.

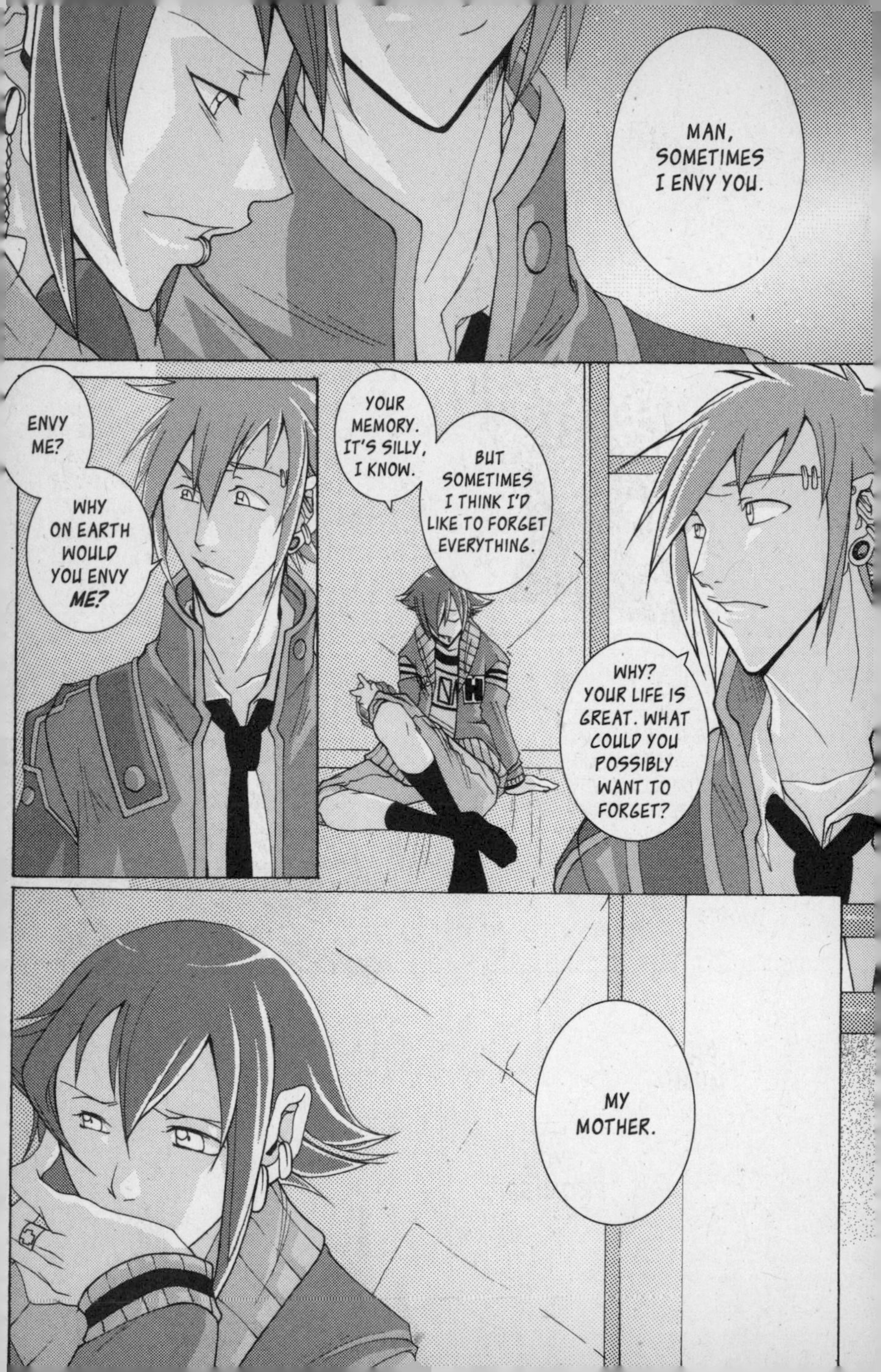
MAN, SOMETIMES I ENVY YOU.
ENVY ME?
WHY ON EARTH WOULD YOU ENVY *ME?*
YOUR MEMORY. IT'S SILLY, I KNOW.
BUT SOMETIMES I THINK I'D LIKE TO FORGET EVERYTHING.
WHY? YOUR LIFE IS GREAT. WHAT COULD YOU POSSIBLY WANT TO FORGET?
MY MOTHER.

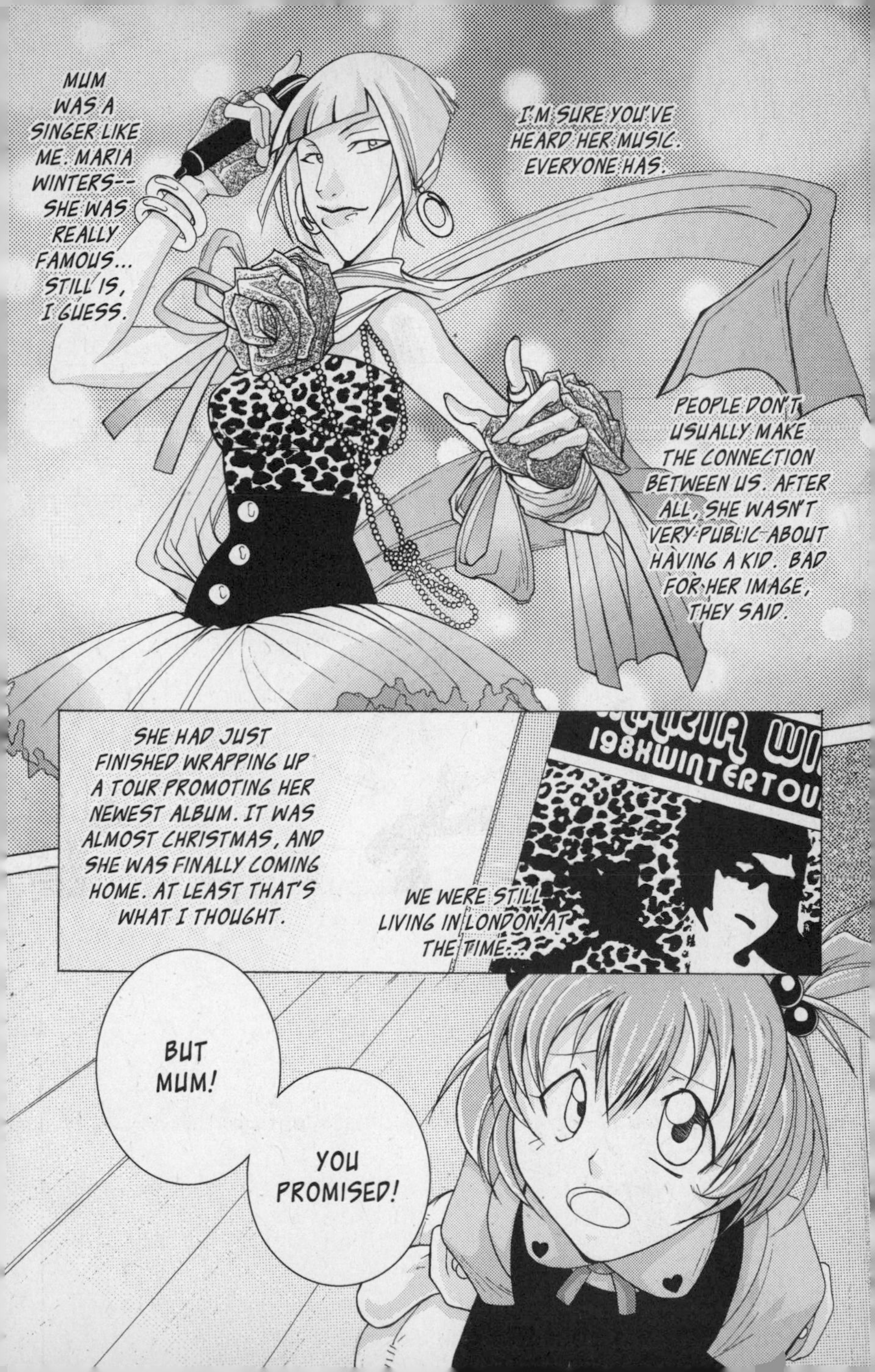
MUM WAS A SINGER LIKE ME. MARIA WINTERS-- SHE WAS REALLY FAMOUS... STILL IS, I GUESS.
I'M SURE YOU'VE HEARD HER MUSIC. EVERYONE HAS.
PEOPLE DON'T USUALLY MAKE THE CONNECTION BETWEEN US. AFTER ALL, SHE WASN'T VERY PUBLIC ABOUT HAVING A KID. BAD FOR HER IMAGE, THEY SAID.
SHE HAD JUST FINISHED WRAPPING UP A TOUR PROMOTING HER NEWEST ALBUM. IT WAS ALMOST CHRISTMAS, AND SHE WAS FINALLY COMING HOME. AT LEAST THAT'S WHAT I THOUGHT.
WE WERE STILL LIVING IN LONDON AT THE TIME...
BUT MUM!
YOU PROMISED!

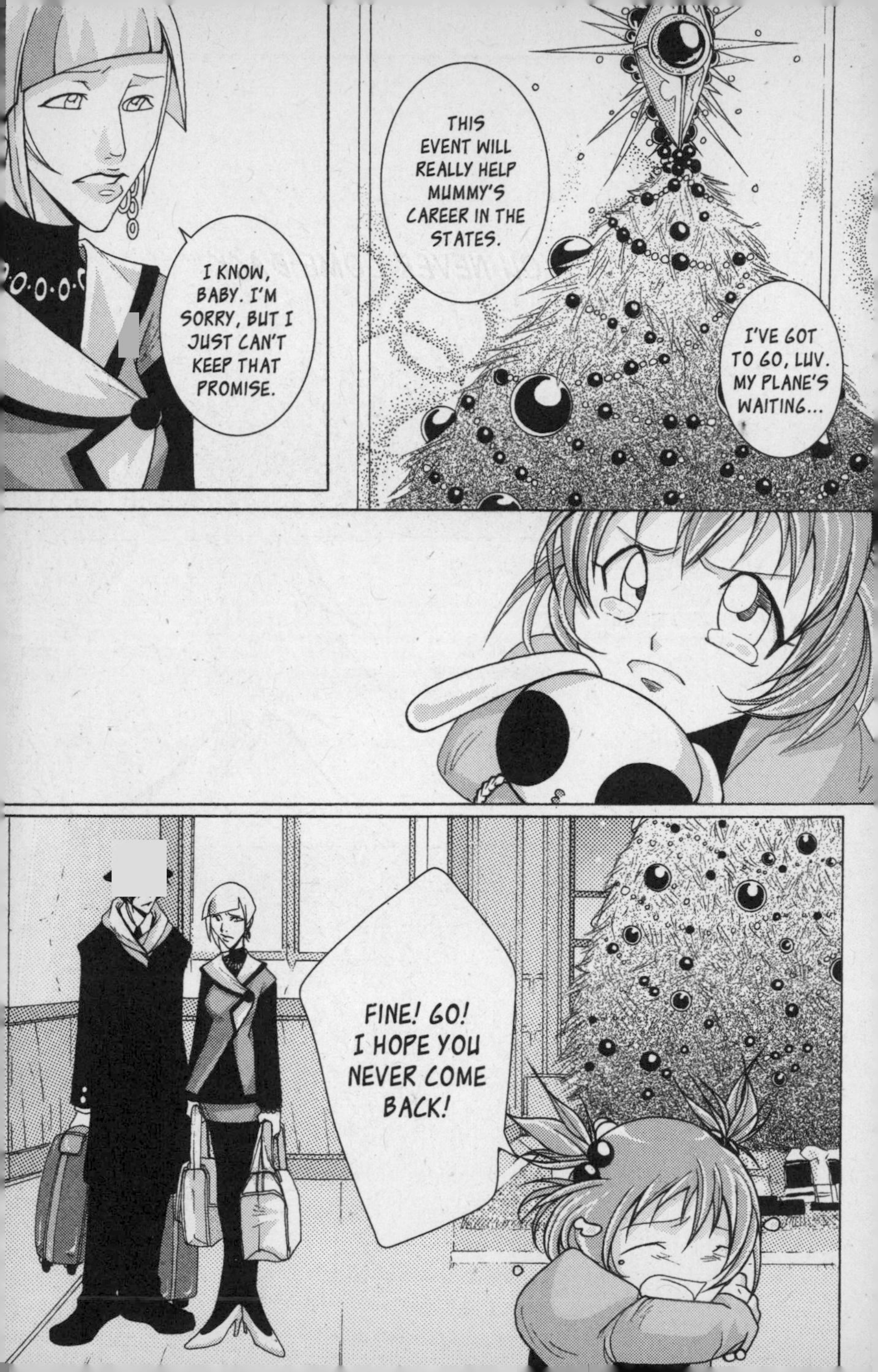
I KNOW, BABY. I'M SORRY, BUT I JUST CAN'T KEEP THAT PROMISE.
THIS EVENT WILL REALLY HELP MUMMY'S CAREER IN THE STATES.
I'VE GOT TO GO, LUV. MY PLANE'S WAITING...
FINE! GO! I HOPE YOU NEVER COME BACK!

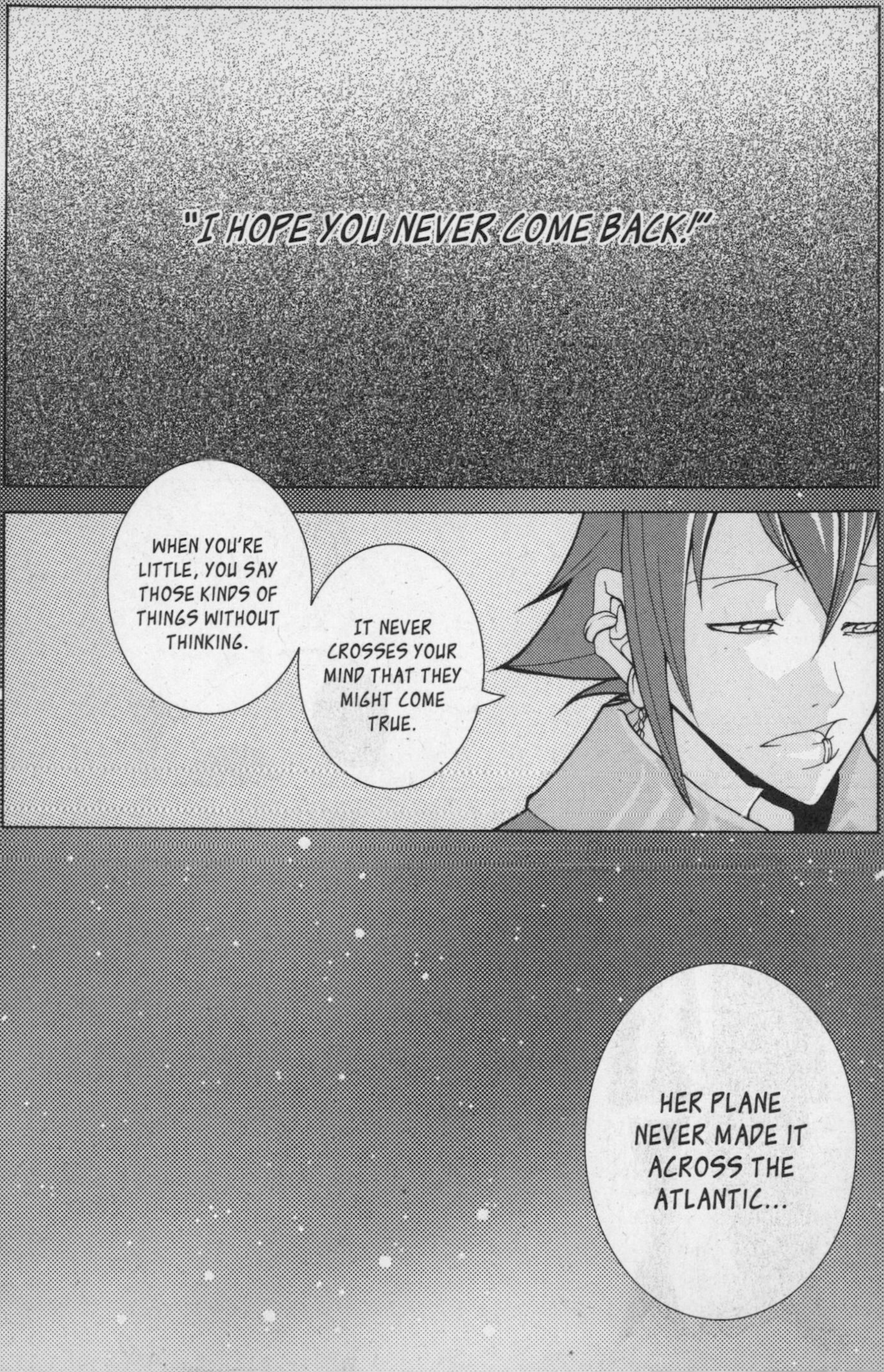
"I HOPE YOU NEVER COME BACK!"
WHEN YOU'RE LITTLE, YOU SAY THOSE KINDS OF THINGS WITHOUT THINKING.
IT NEVER CROSSES YOUR MIND THAT THEY MIGHT COME TRUE.
HER PLANE NEVER MADE IT ACROSS THE ATLANTIC...

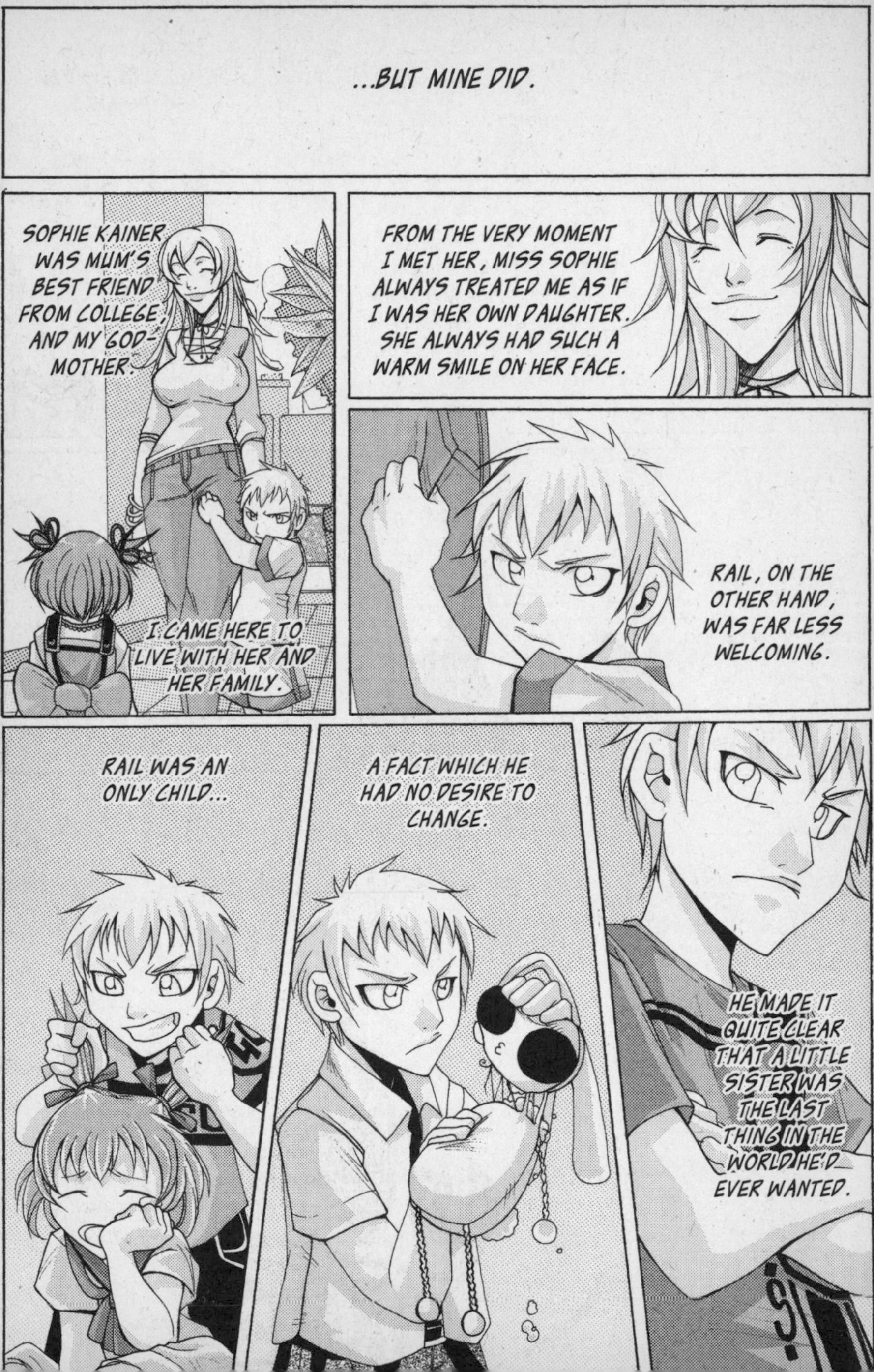
...BUT MINE DID.
SOPHIE KAINER WAS MUM'S BEST FRIEND FROM COLLEGE, AND MY GOD-MOTHER.
I CAME HERE TO LIVE WITH HER AND HER FAMILY.
FROM THE VERY MOMENT I MET HER, MISS SOPHIE ALWAYS TREATED ME AS IF I WAS HER OWN DAUGHTER. SHE ALWAYS HAD SUCH A WARM SMILE ON HER FACE.
RAIL, ON THE OTHER HAND, WAS FAR LESS WELCOMING.
RAIL WAS AN ONLY CHILD...
A FACT WHICH HE HAD NO DESIRE TO CHANGE.
HE MADE IT QUITE CLEAR THAT A LITTLE SISTER WAS THE LAST THING IN THE WORLD HE'D EVER WANTED.

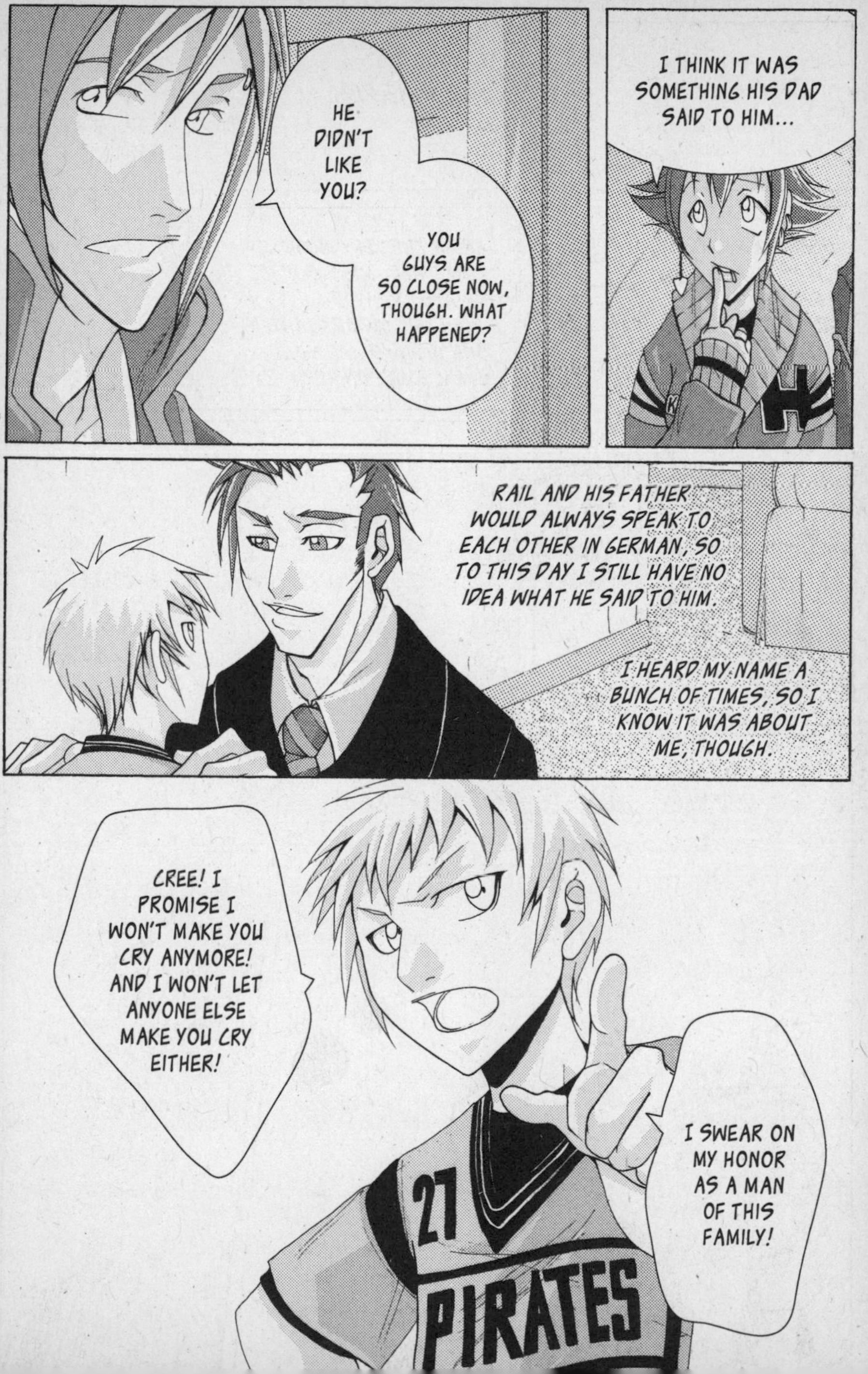
HE DIDN'T LIKE YOU?
YOU GUYS ARE SO CLOSE NOW, THOUGH. WHAT HAPPENED?
I THINK IT WAS SOMETHING HIS DAD SAID TO HIM...
RAIL AND HIS FATHER WOULD ALWAYS SPEAK TO EACH OTHER IN GERMAN, SO TO THIS DAY I STILL HAVE NO IDEA WHAT HE SAID TO HIM.
I HEARD MY NAME A BUNCH OF TIMES, SO I KNOW IT WAS ABOUT ME, THOUGH.
CREE! I PROMISE I WON'T MAKE YOU CRY ANYMORE! AND I WON'T LET ANYONE ELSE MAKE YOU CRY EITHER!
I SWEAR ON MY HONOR AS A MAN OF THIS FAMILY!
27
PIRATES

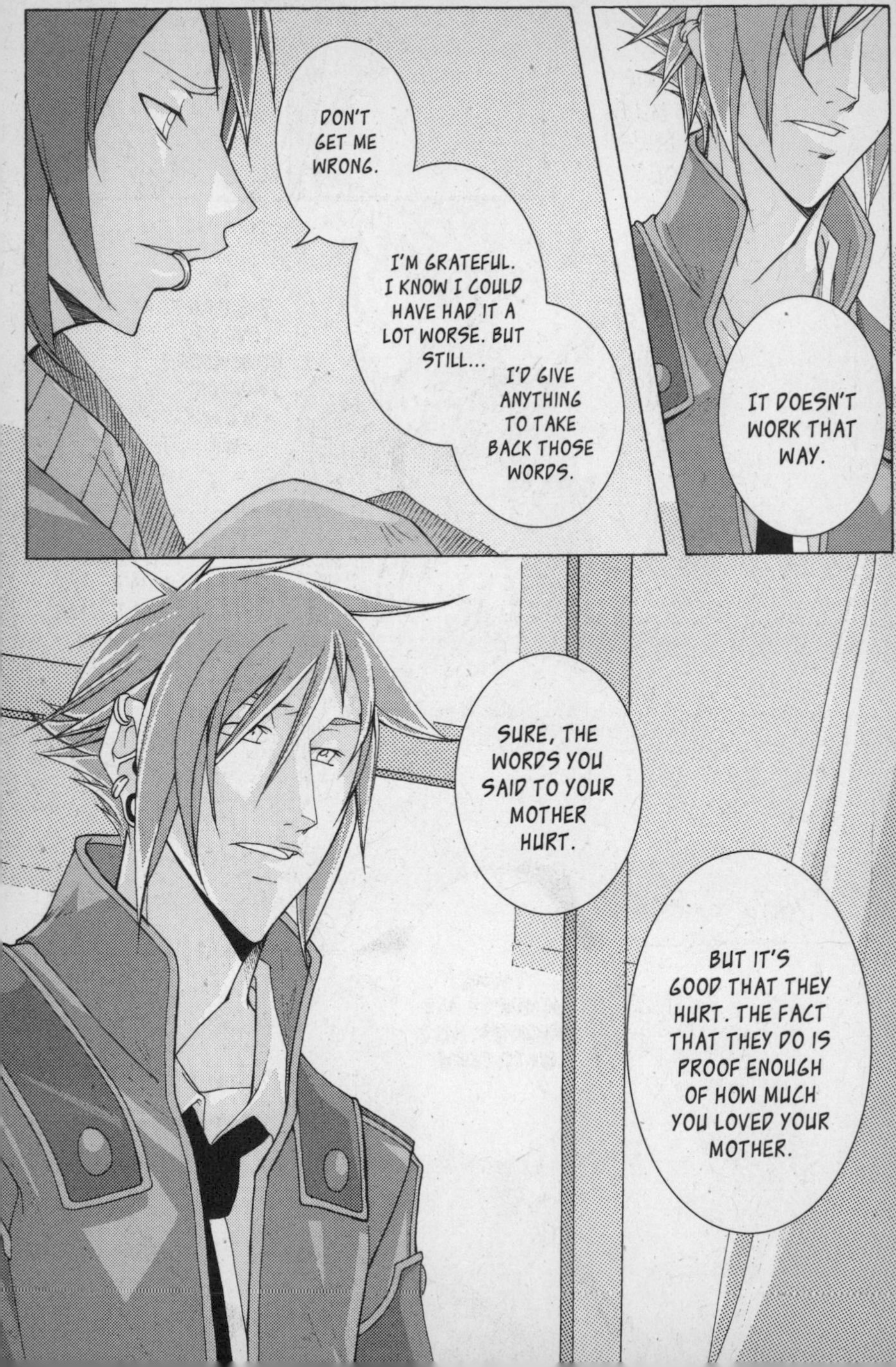
DON'T GET ME WRONG.
I'M GRATEFUL. I KNOW I COULD HAVE HAD IT A LOT WORSE. BUT STILL...
I'D GIVE ANYTHING TO TAKE BACK THOSE WORDS.
IT DOESN'T WORK THAT WAY.
SURE, THE WORDS YOU SAID TO YOUR MOTHER HURT.
BUT IT'S GOOD THAT THEY HURT. THE FACT THAT THEY DO IS PROOF ENOUGH OF HOW MUCH YOU LOVED YOUR MOTHER.

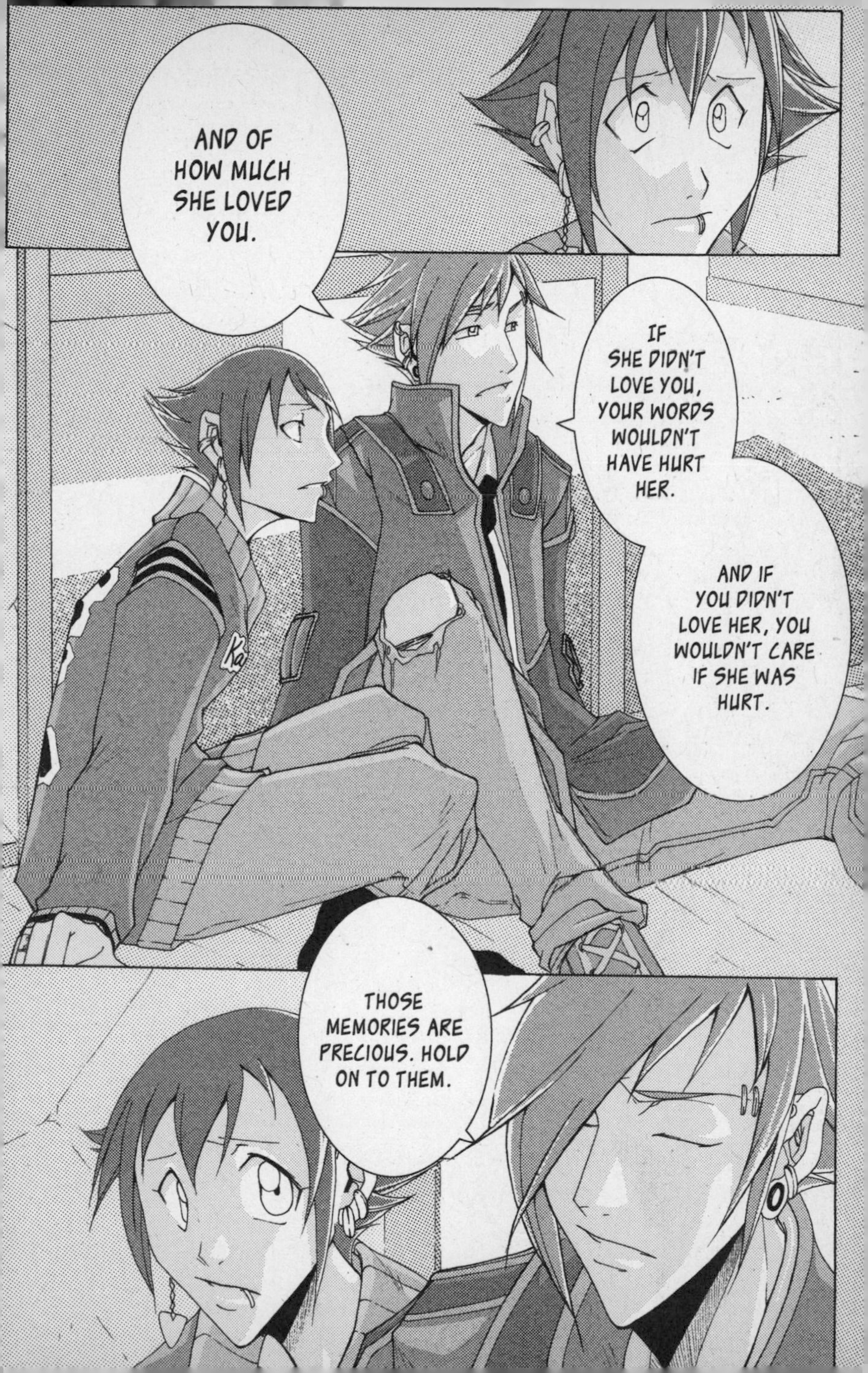
AND OF HOW MUCH SHE LOVED YOU.
IF SHE DIDN'T LOVE YOU, YOUR WORDS WOULDN'T HAVE HURT HER.
AND IF YOU DIDN'T LOVE HER, YOU WOULDN'T CARE IF SHE WAS HURT.
THOSE MEMORIES ARE PRECIOUS. HOLD ON TO THEM.

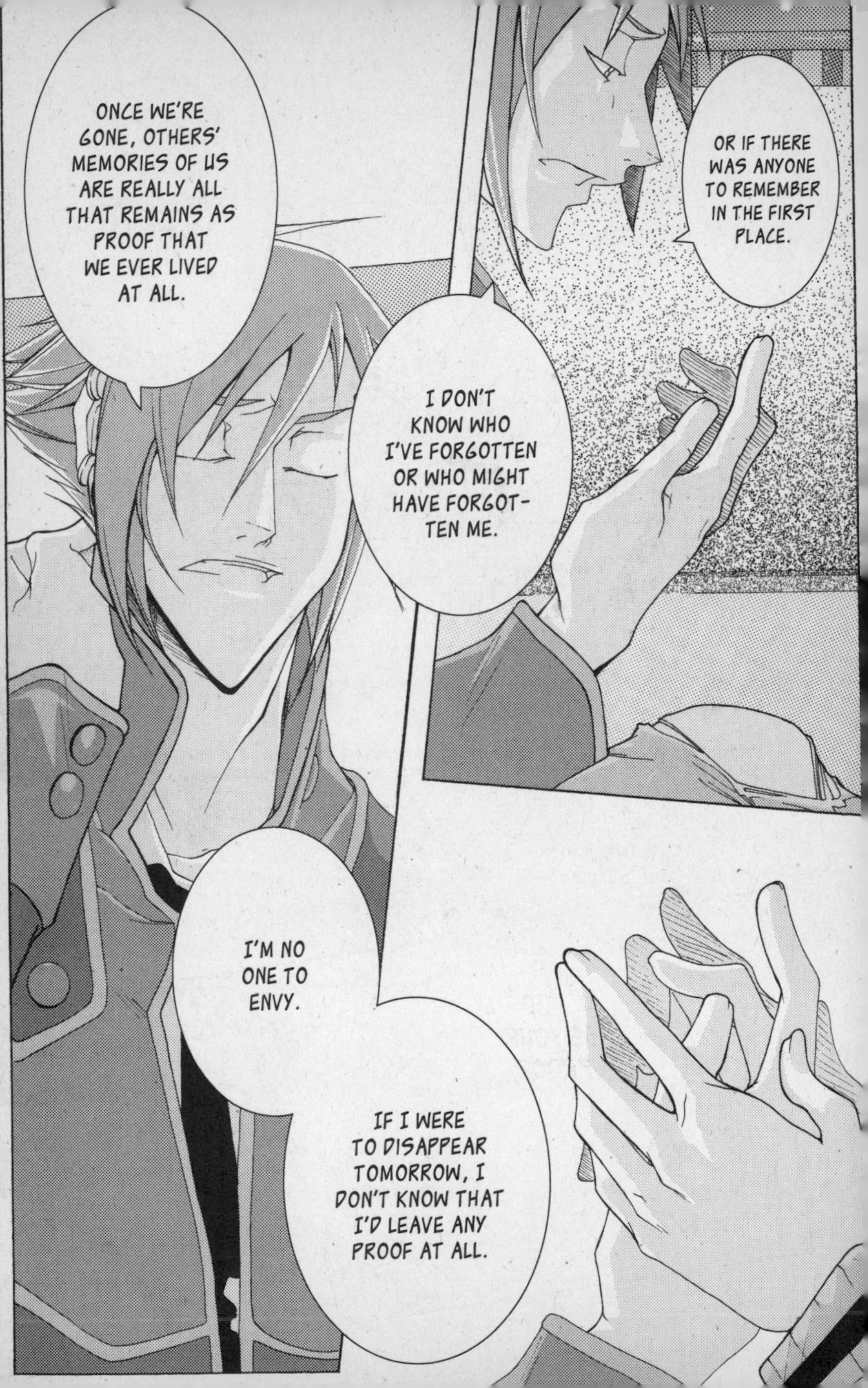
ONCE WE'RE GONE, OTHERS' MEMORIES OF US ARE REALLY ALL THAT REMAINS AS PROOF THAT WE EVER LIVED AT ALL.
I DON'T KNOW WHO I'VE FORGOTTEN OR WHO MIGHT HAVE FORGOT-TEN ME.
OR IF THERE WAS ANYONE TO REMEMBER IN THE FIRST PLACE.
I'M NO ONE TO ENVY.
IF I WERE TO DISAPPEAR TOMORROW, I DON'T KNOW THAT I'D LEAVE ANY PROOF AT ALL.

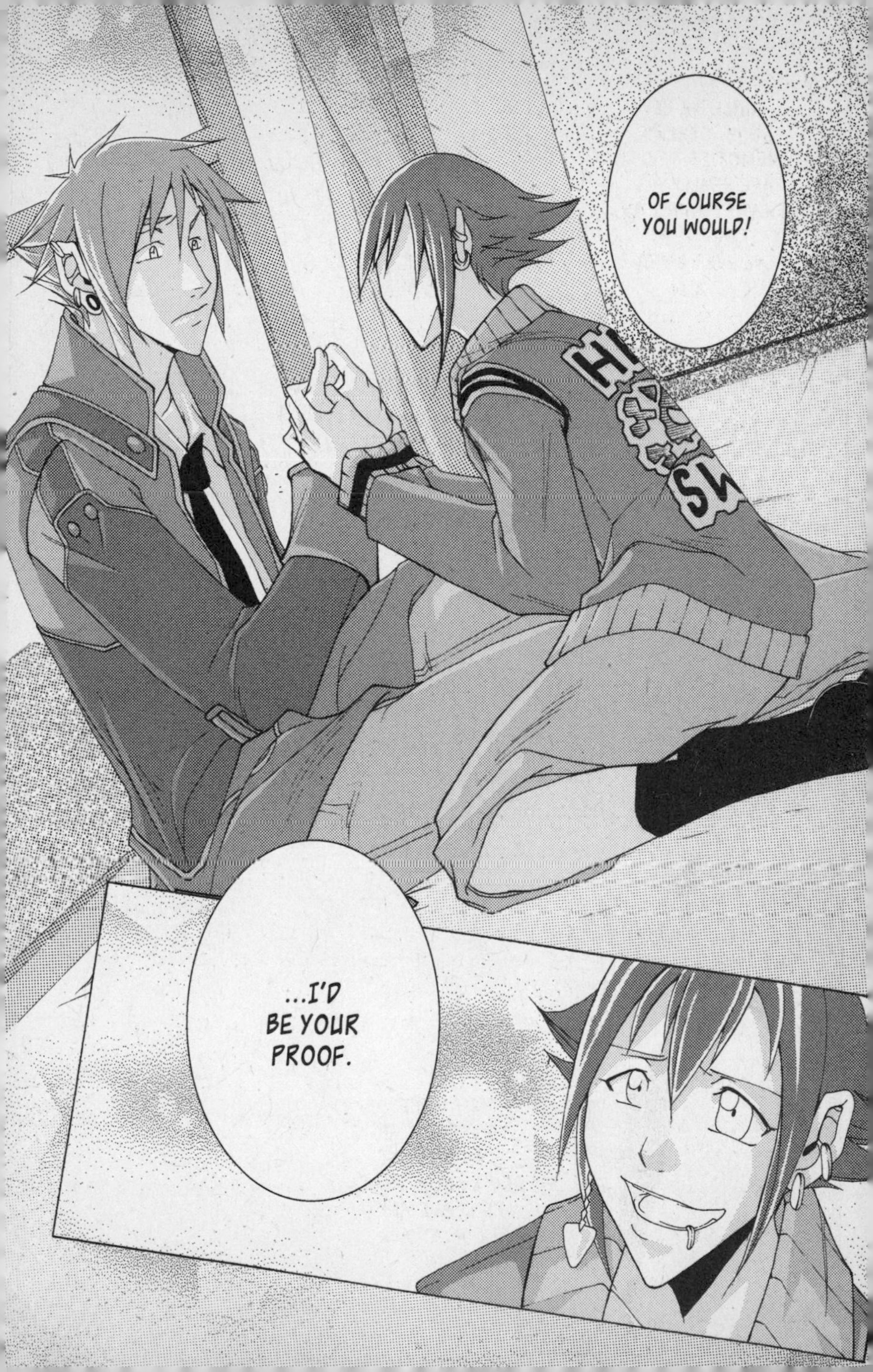
OF COURSE YOU WOULD!
...I'D BE YOUR PROOF.

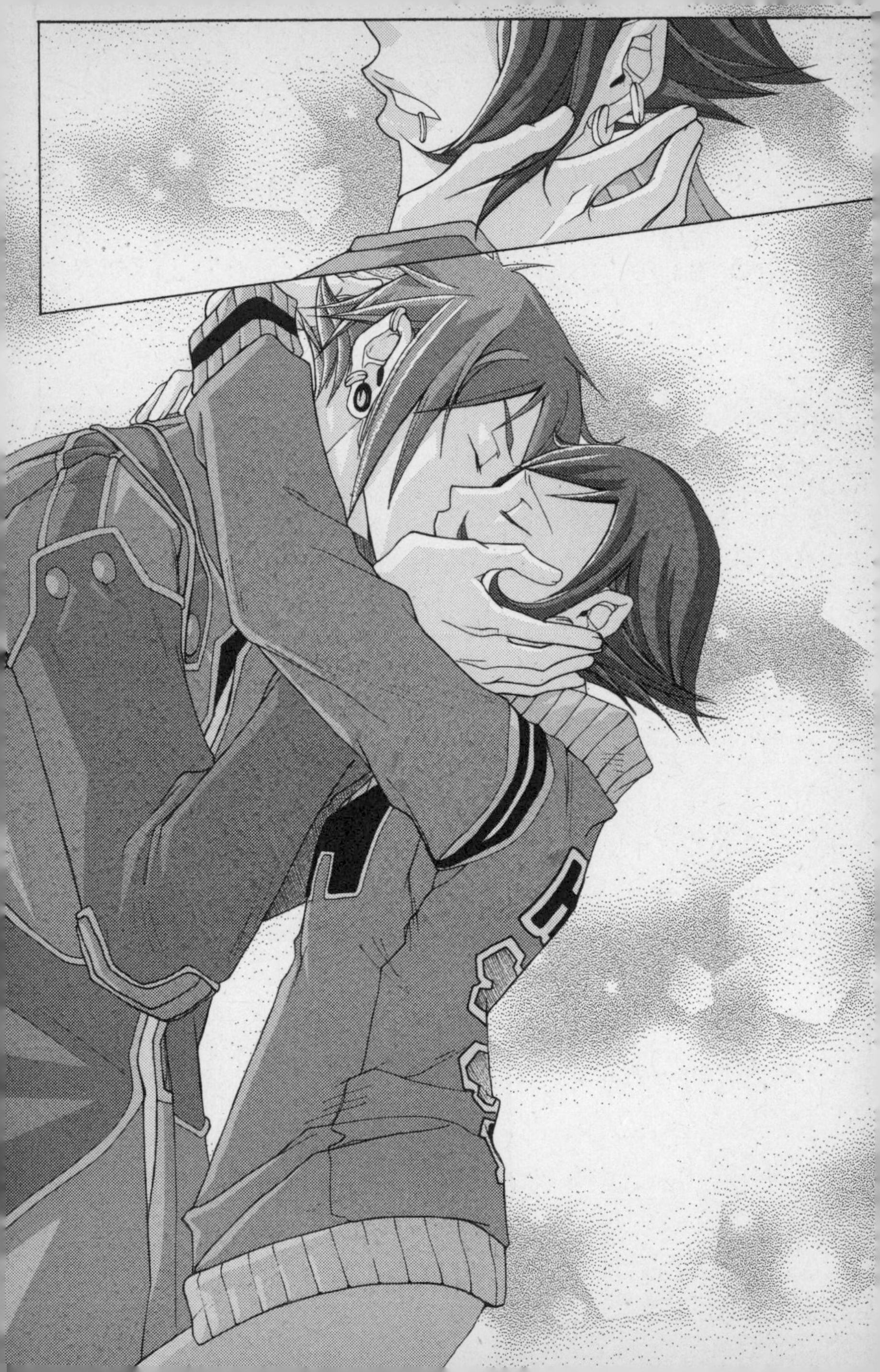

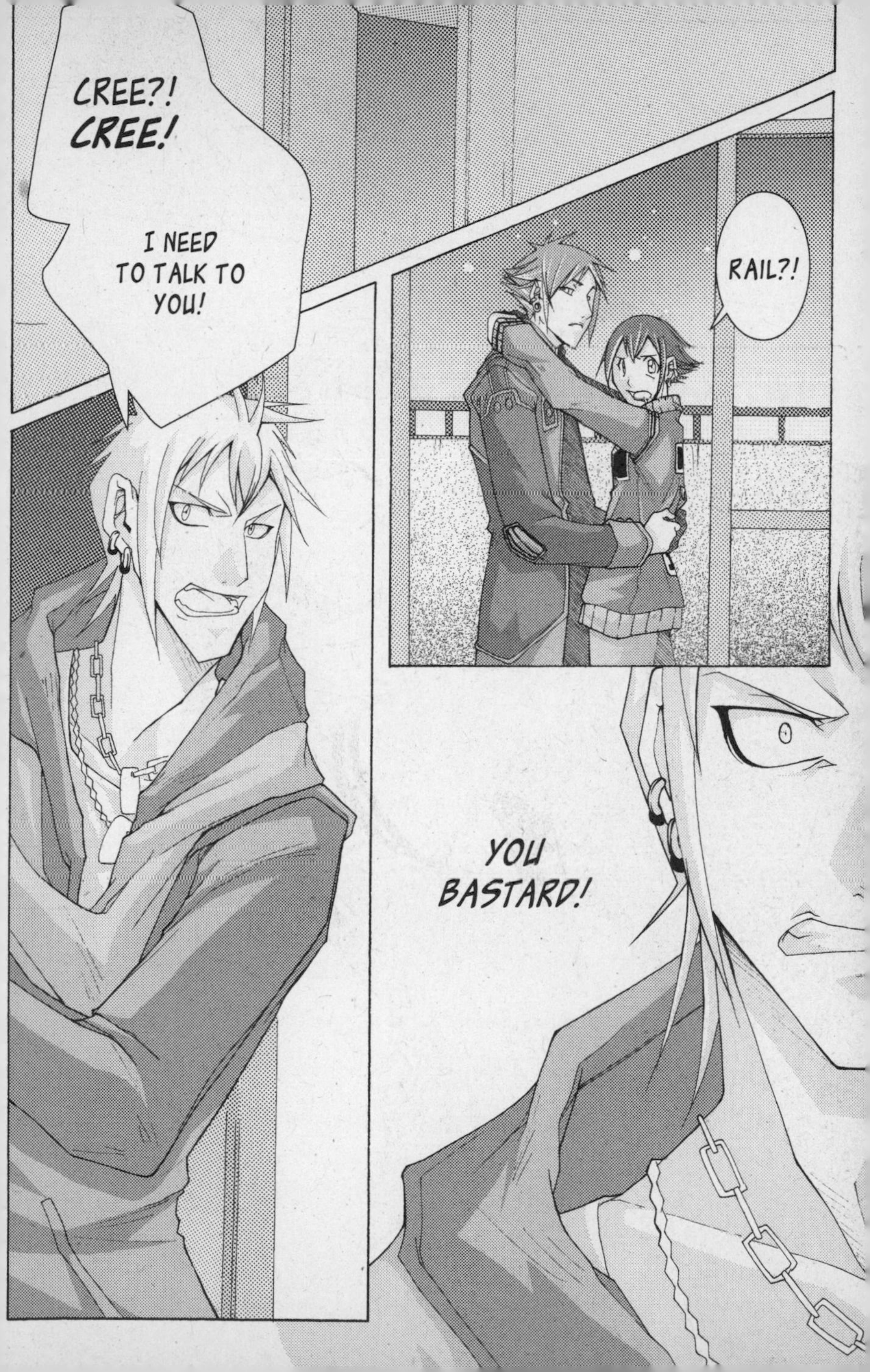
CREE?! CREE!
I NEED TO TALK TO YOU!
RAIL?!
YOU BASTARD!

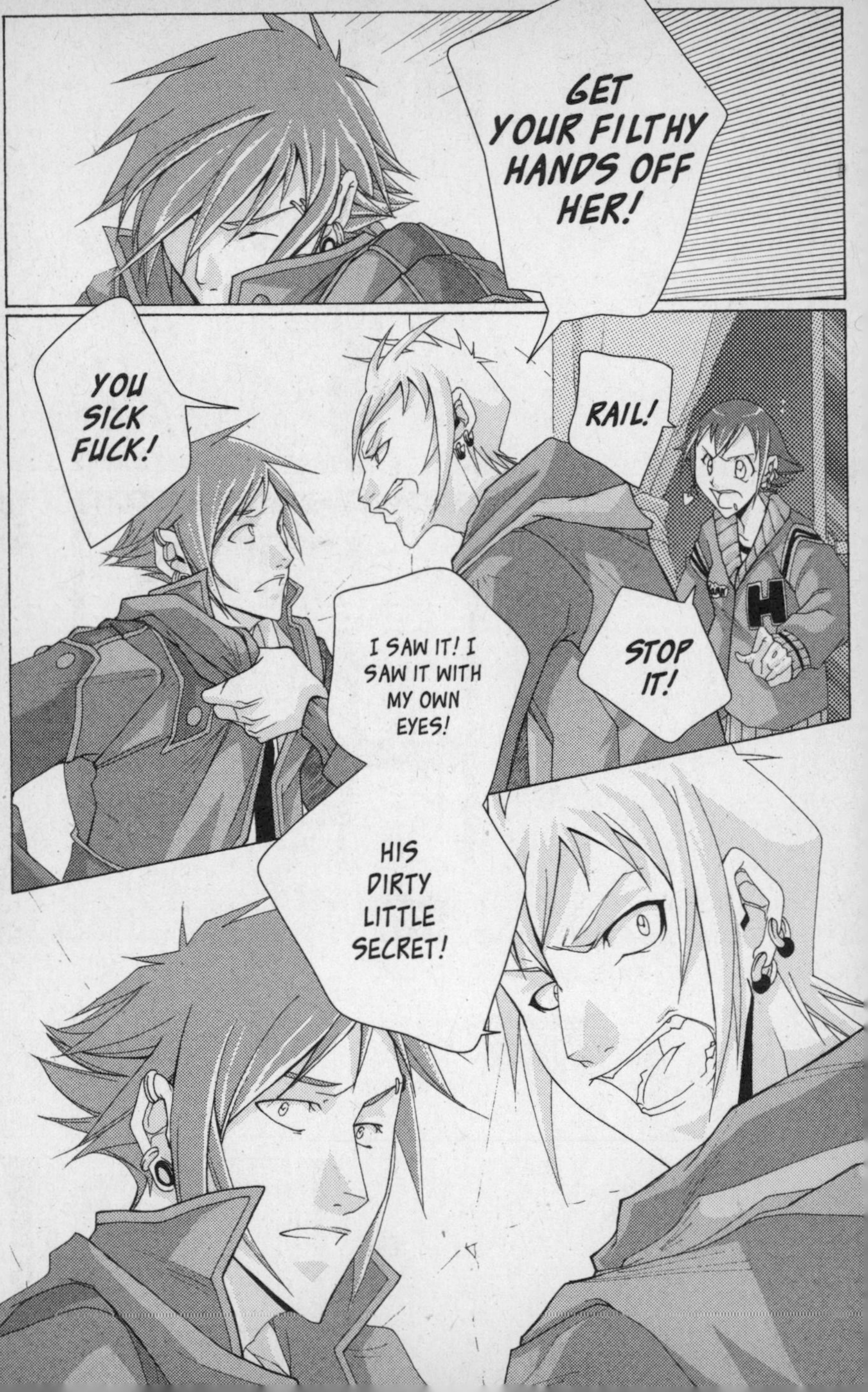
GET YOUR FILTHY HANDS OFF HER!
YOU SICK FUCK!
RAIL!
I SAW IT! I SAW IT WITH MY OWN EYES!
STOP IT!
HIS DIRTY LITTLE SECRET!

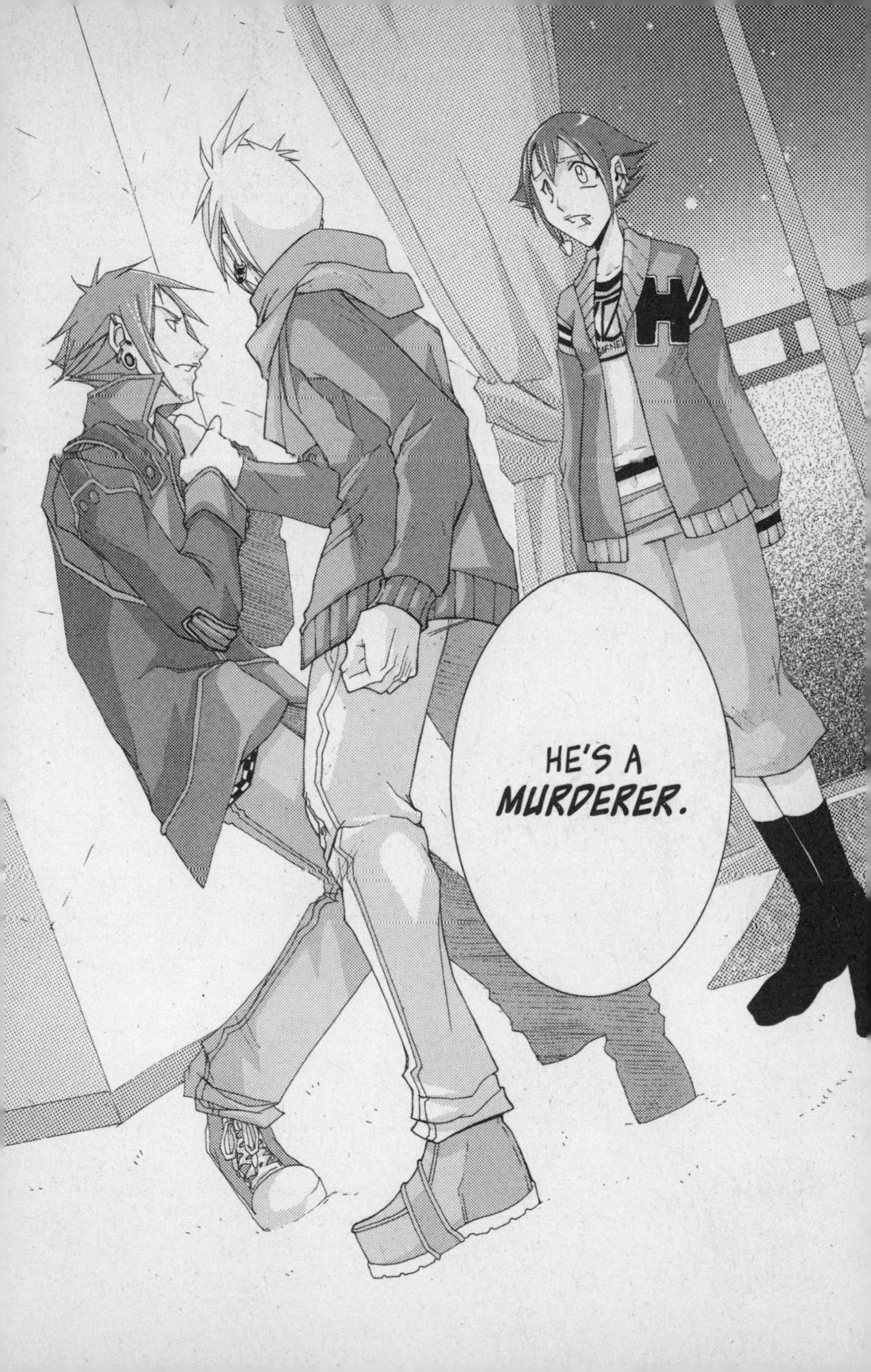
HE'S A MURDERER.

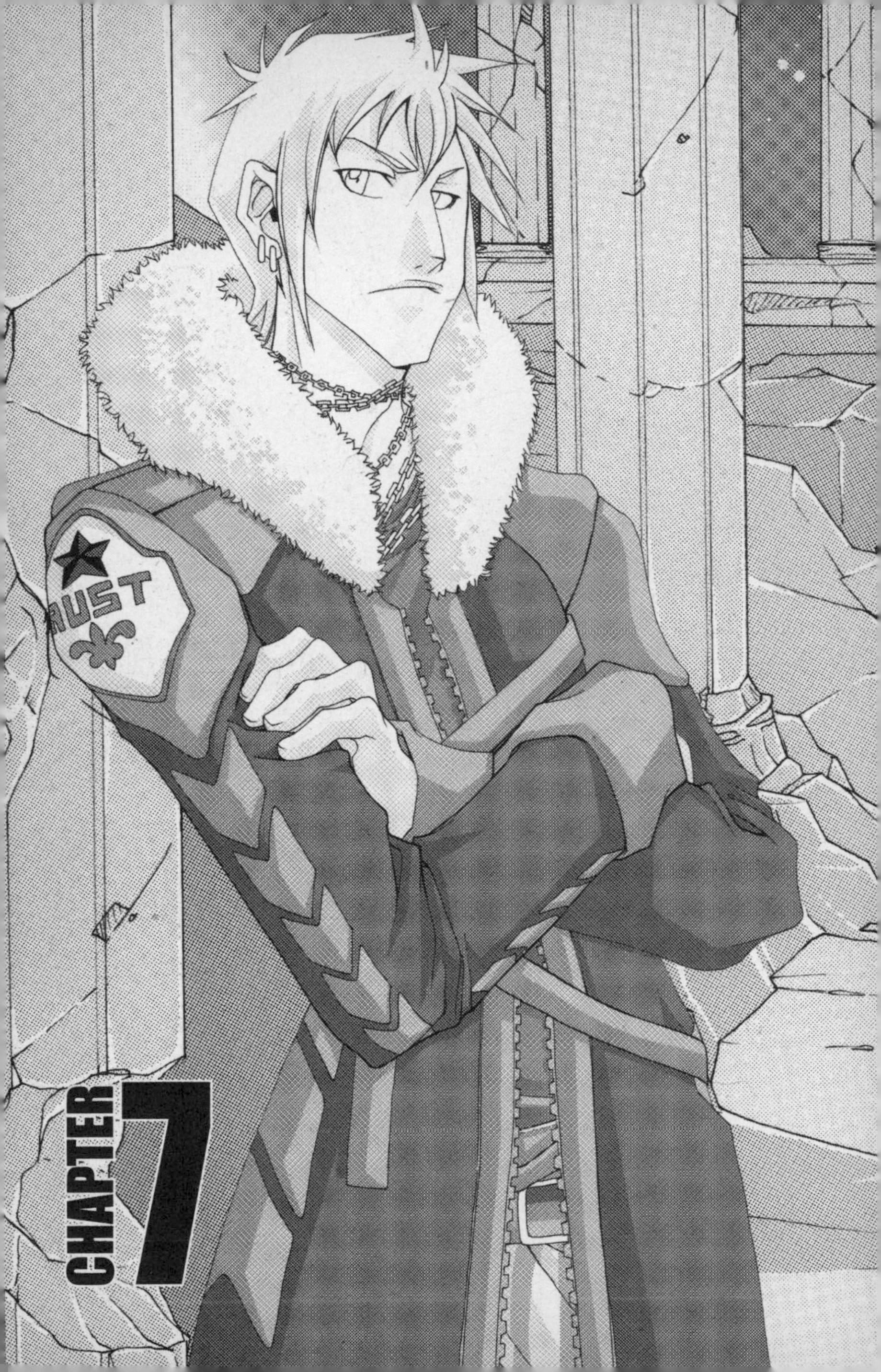
CHAPTER 7

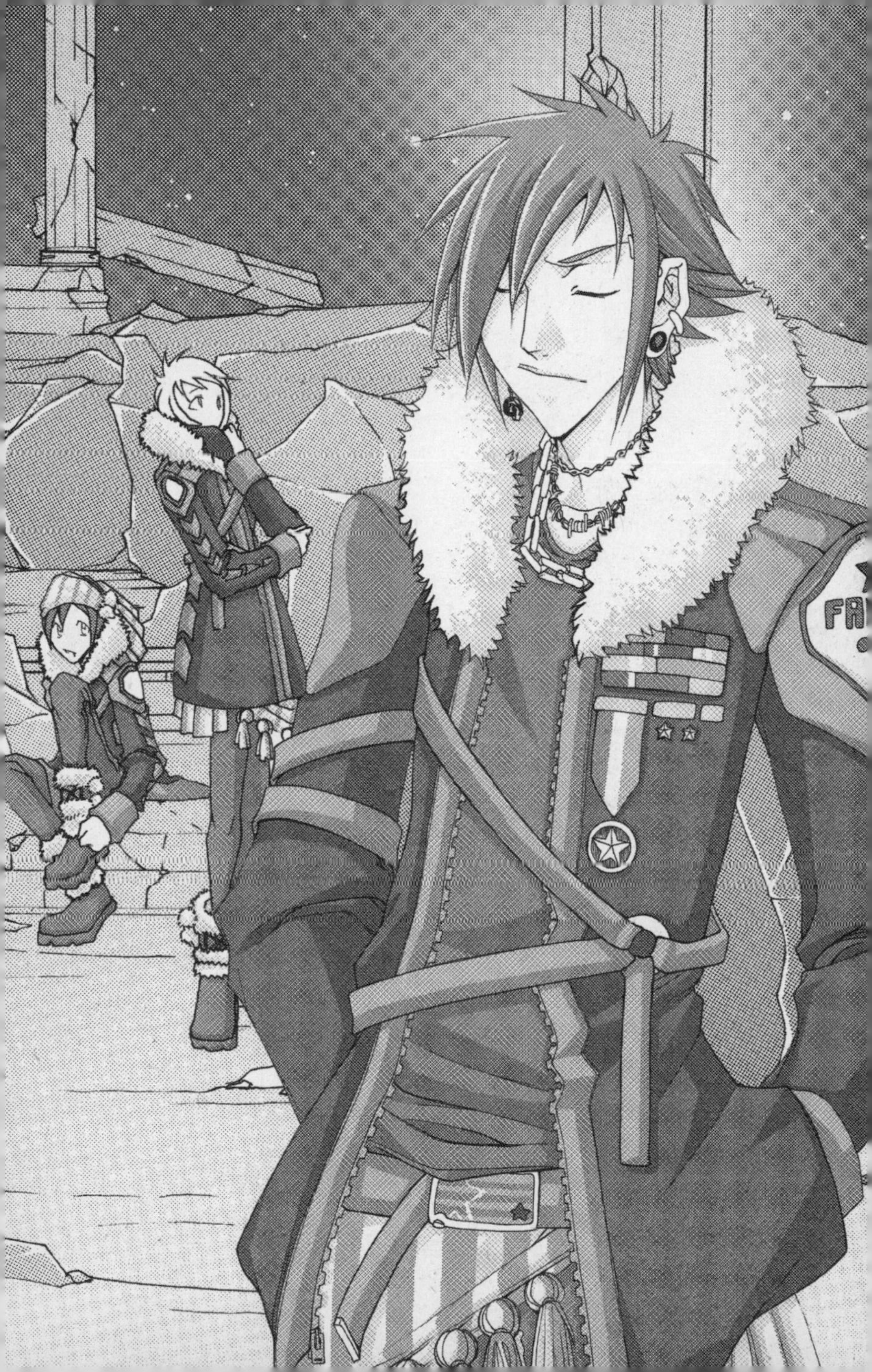

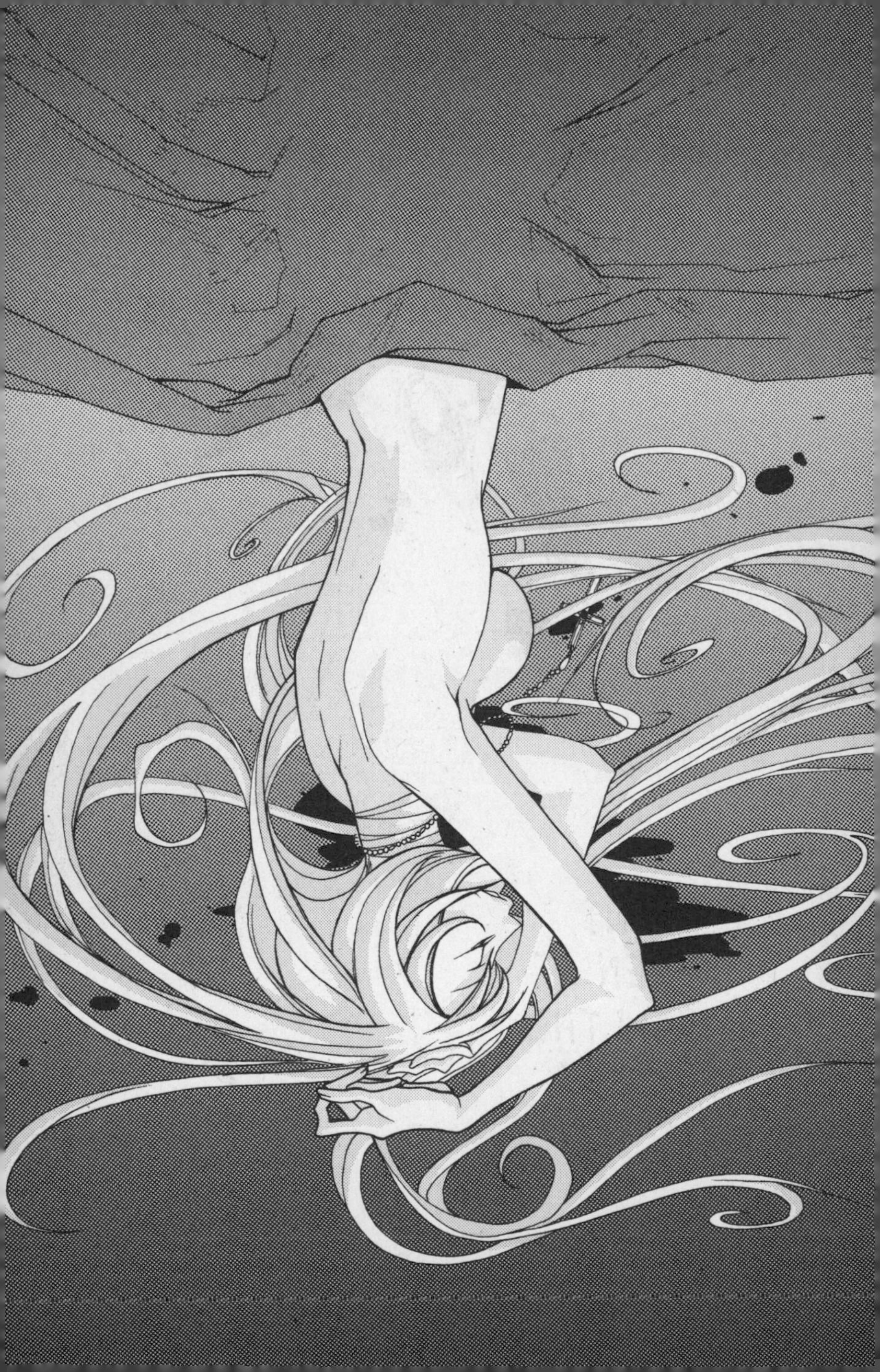

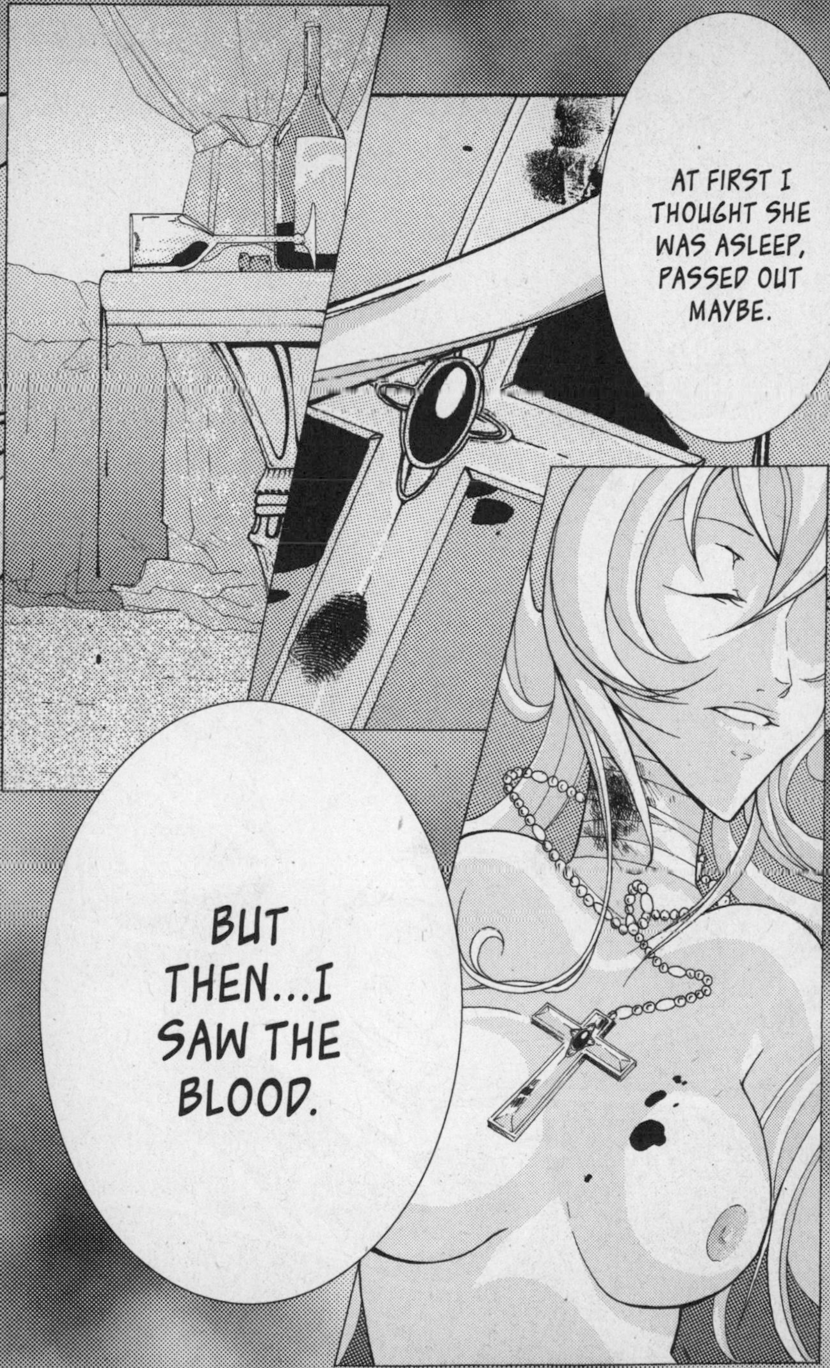
AT FIRST I THOUGHT SHE WAS ASLEEP, PASSED OUT MAYBE.
BUT THEN...I SAW THE BLOOD.

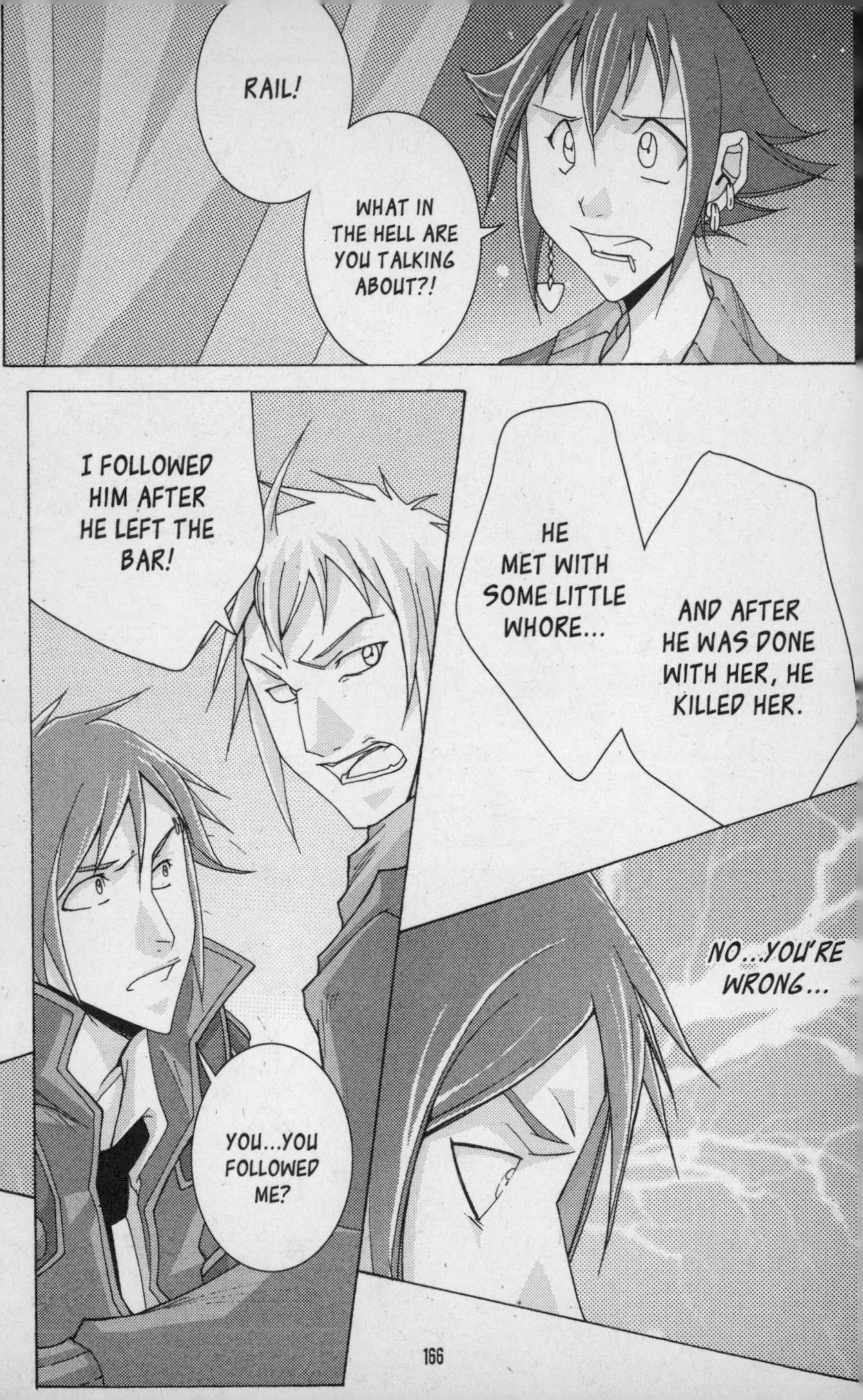
RAIL!
WHAT IN THE HELL ARE YOU TALKING ABOUT?!
I FOLLOWED HIM AFTER HE LEFT THE BAR!
HE MET WITH SOME LITTLE WHORE...
AND AFTER HE WAS DONE WITH HER, HE KILLED HER.
YOU...YOU FOLLOWED ME?
NO...YOU'RE WRONG...

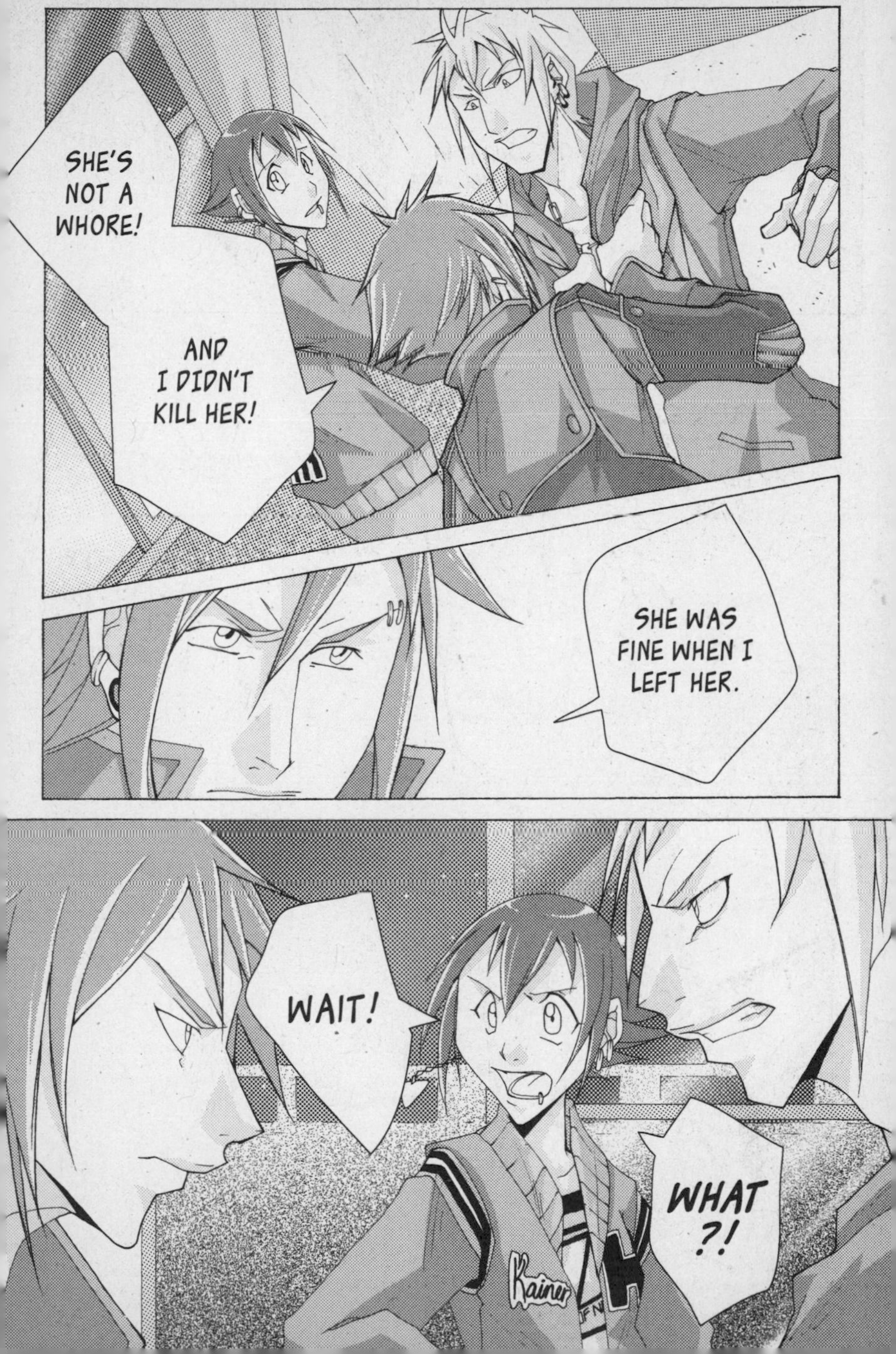
SHE'S NOT A WHORE!
AND I DIDN'T KILL HER!
SHE WAS FINE WHEN I LEFT HER.
WAIT!
WHAT ?!
Kainer

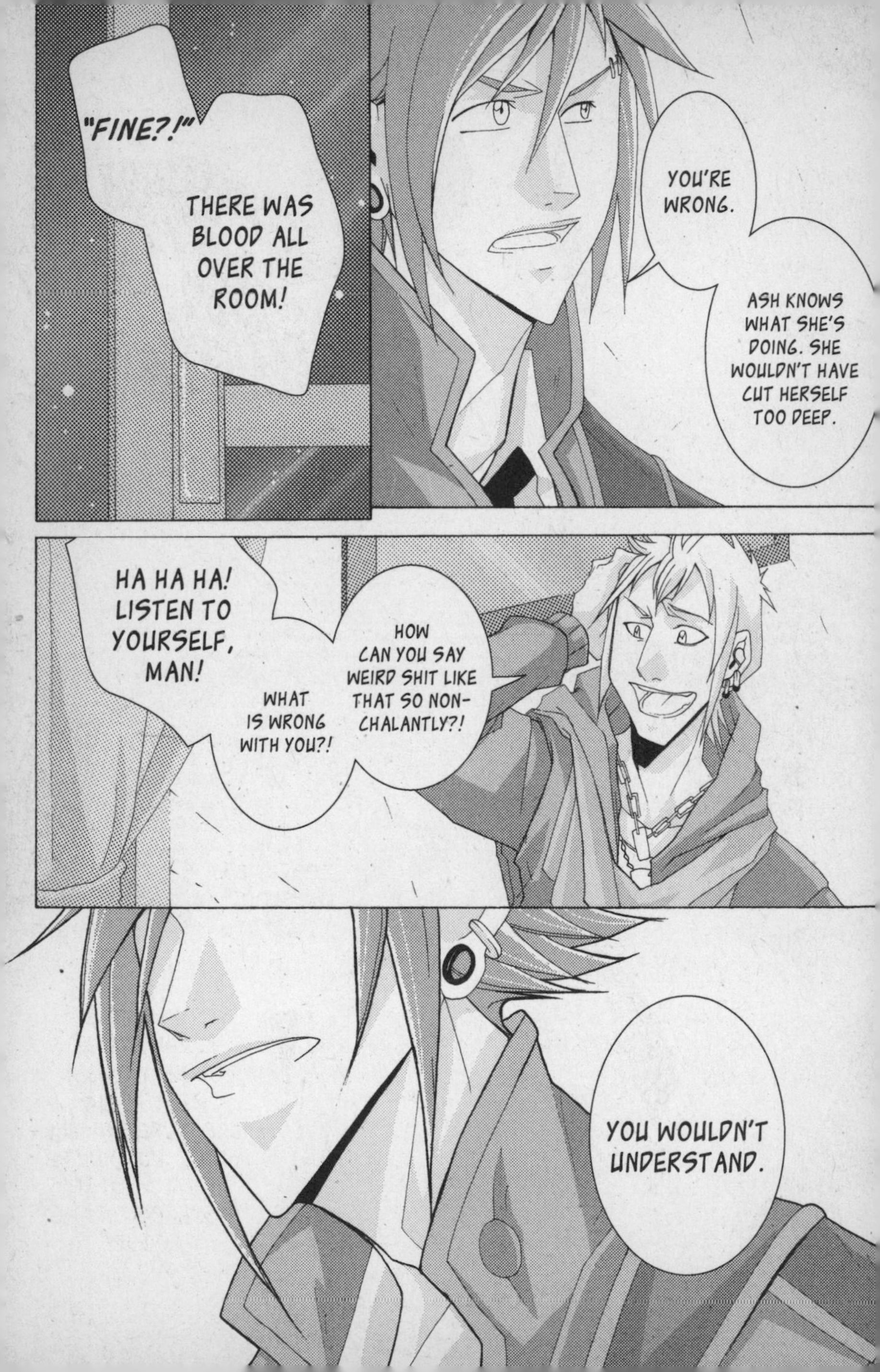
"FINE?!"
THERE WAS BLOOD ALL OVER THE ROOM!
YOU'RE WRONG.
ASH KNOWS WHAT SHE'S DOING. SHE WOULDN'T HAVE CUT HERSELF TOO DEEP.
HA HA HA! LISTEN TO YOURSELF, MAN!
WHAT IS WRONG WITH YOU?!
HOW CAN YOU SAY WEIRD SHIT LIKE THAT SO NON-CHALANTLY?!
YOU WOULDN'T UNDERSTAND.

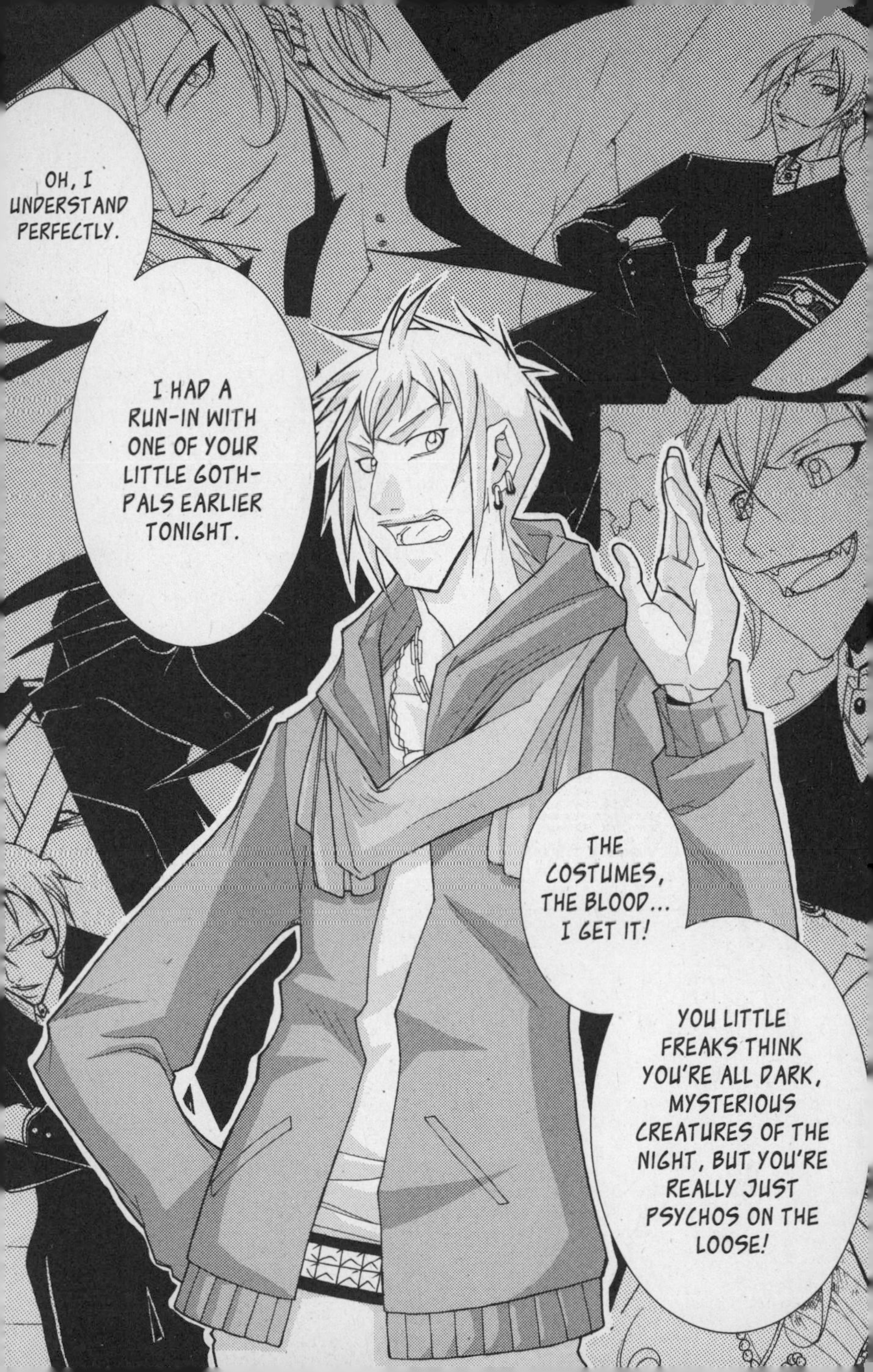
OH, I UNDERSTAND PERFECTLY.
I HAD A RUN-IN WITH ONE OF YOUR LITTLE GOTH-PALS EARLIER TONIGHT.
THE COSTUMES, THE BLOOD... I GET IT!
YOU LITTLE FREAKS THINK YOU'RE ALL DARK, MYSTERIOUS CREATURES OF THE NIGHT, BUT YOU'RE REALLY JUST PSYCHOS ON THE LOOSE!

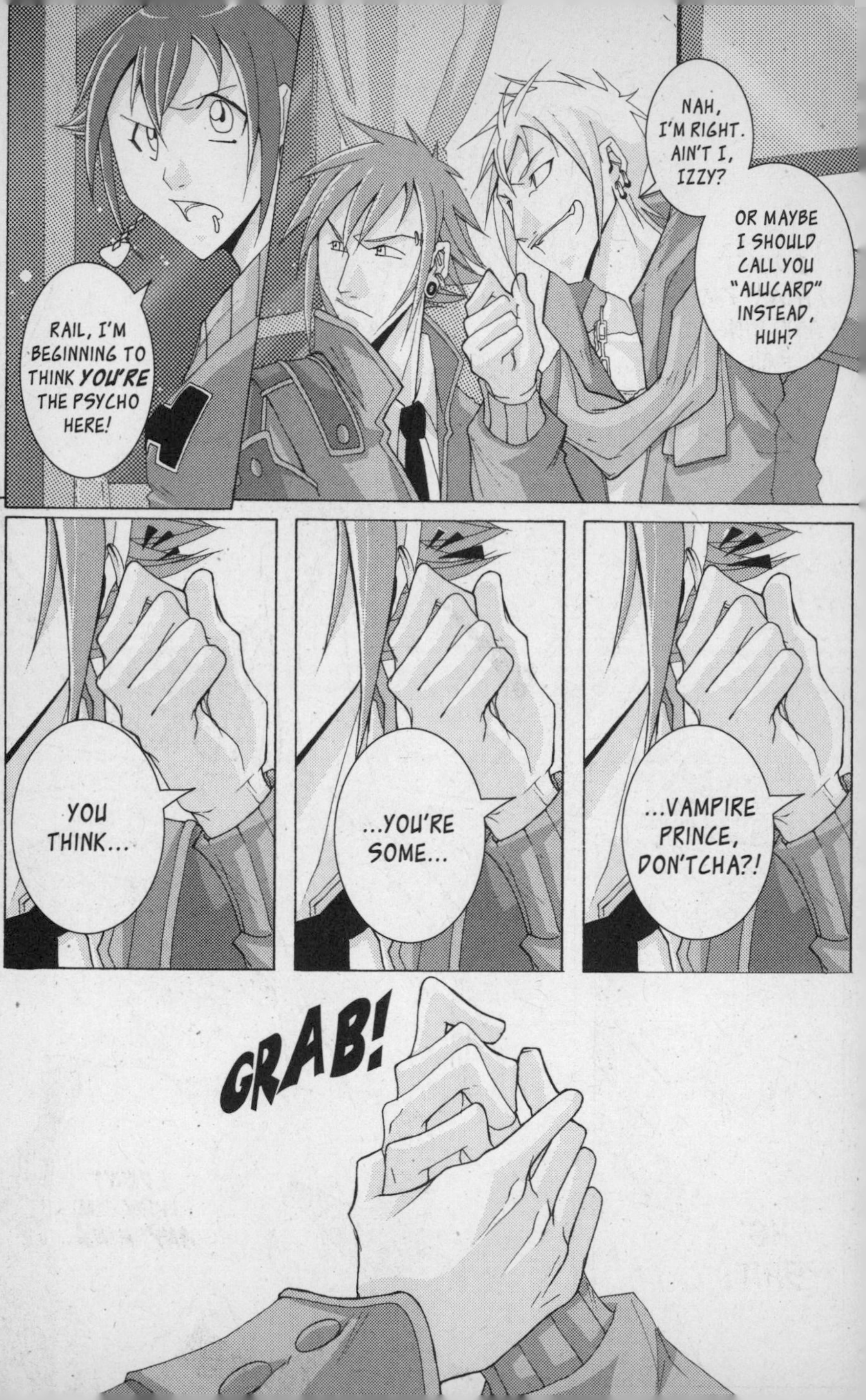
RAIL, I'M BEGINNING TO THINK YOU'RE THE PSYCHO HERE!
NAH, I'M RIGHT. AIN'T I, IZZY?
OR MAYBE I SHOULD CALL YOU "ALUCARD" INSTEAD, HUH?
YOU THINK...
...YOU'RE SOME...
...VAMPIRE PRINCE, DON'TCHA?!
GRAB!

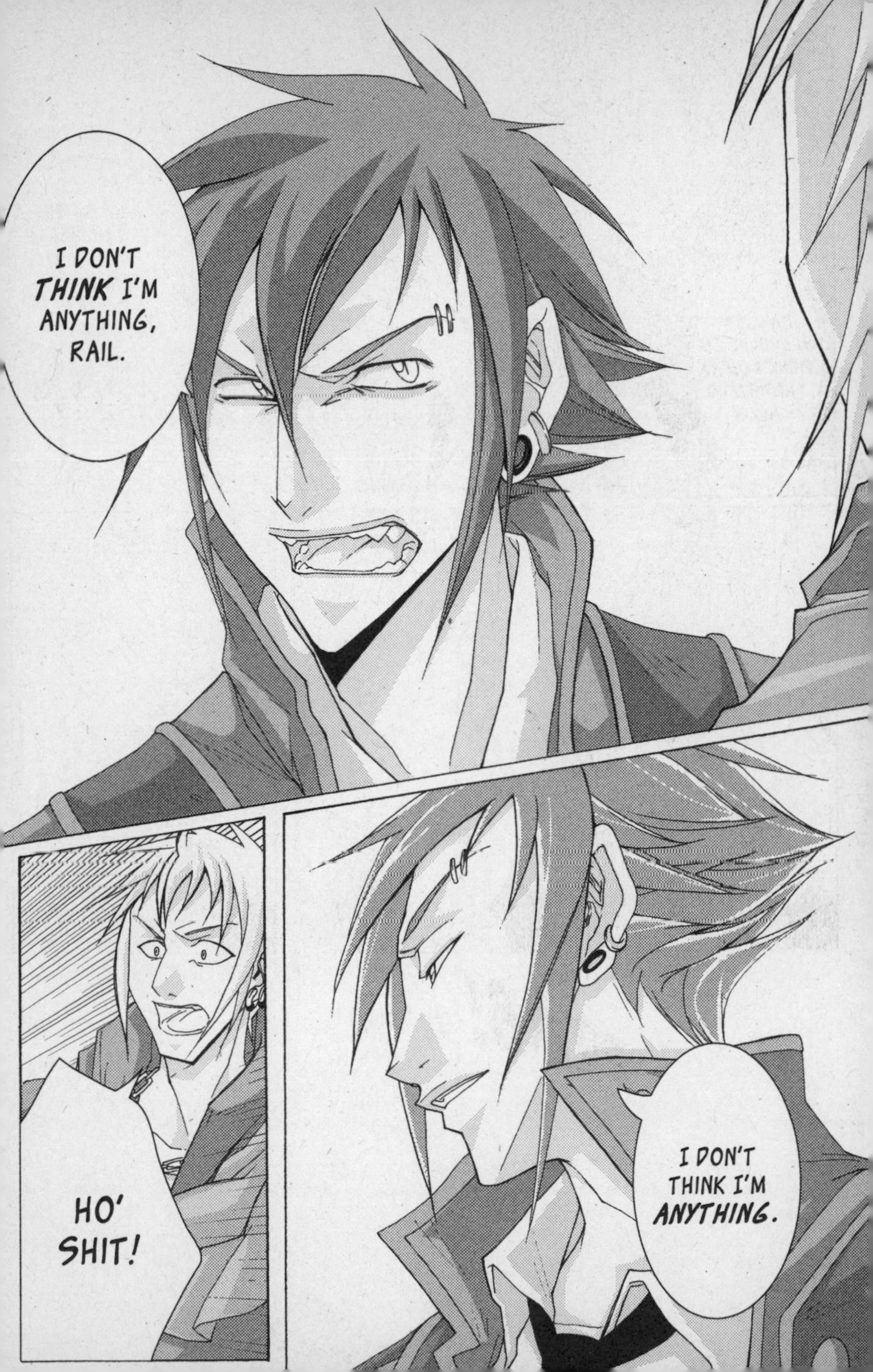
I DON'T THINK I'M ANYTHING, RAIL.
HO' SHIT!
I DON'T THINK I'M ANYTHING.

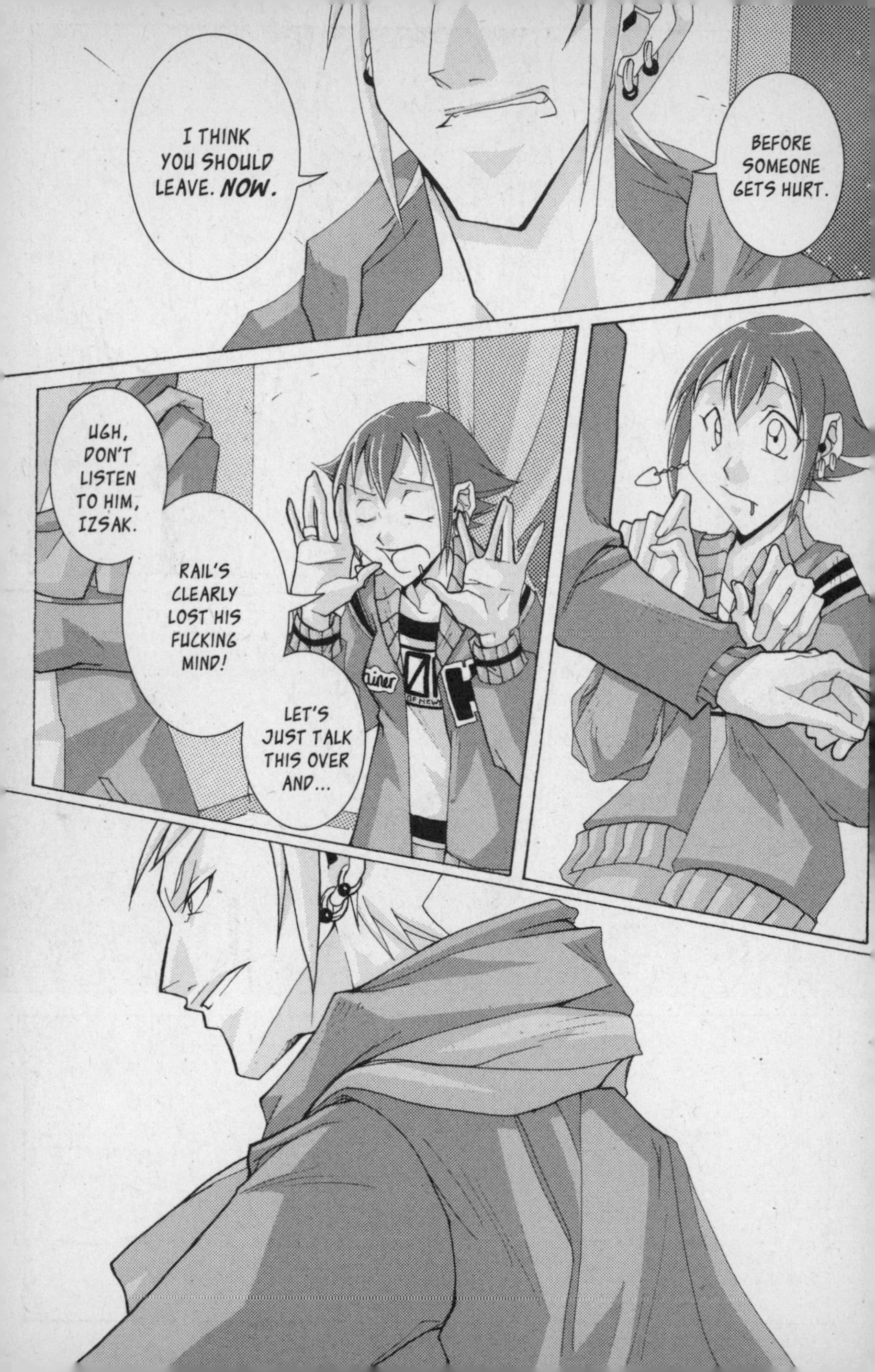
I THINK YOU SHOULD LEAVE. **NOW.**
BEFORE SOMEONE GETS HURT.
UGH, DON'T LISTEN TO HIM, IZSAK.
RAIL'S CLEARLY LOST HIS FUCKING MIND!
LET'S JUST TALK THIS OVER AND...

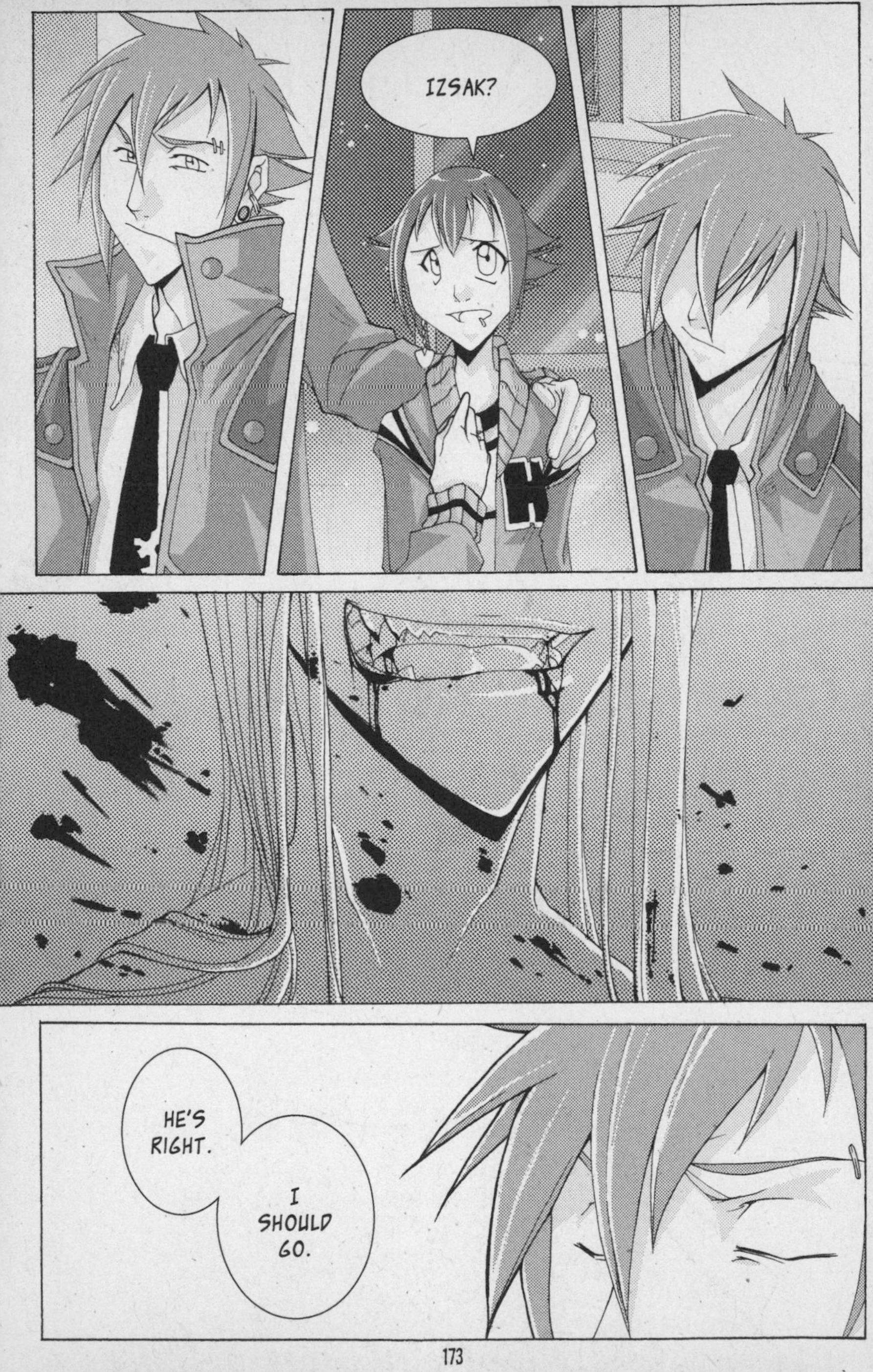
IZSAK?
HE'S RIGHT.
I SHOULD GO.

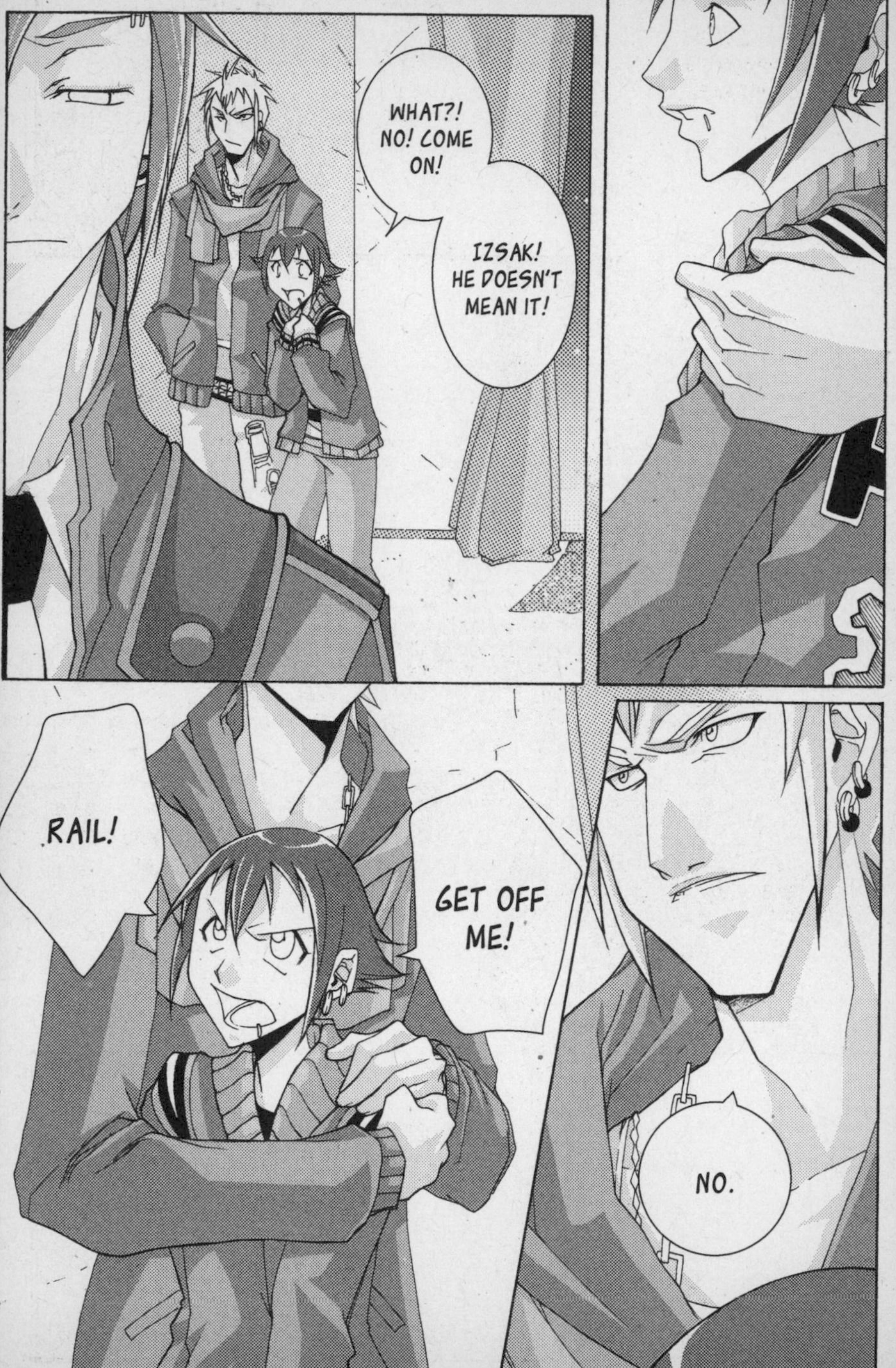
WHAT?! NO! COME ON!
IZSAK! HE DOESN'T MEAN IT!
RAIL!
GET OFF ME!
NO.

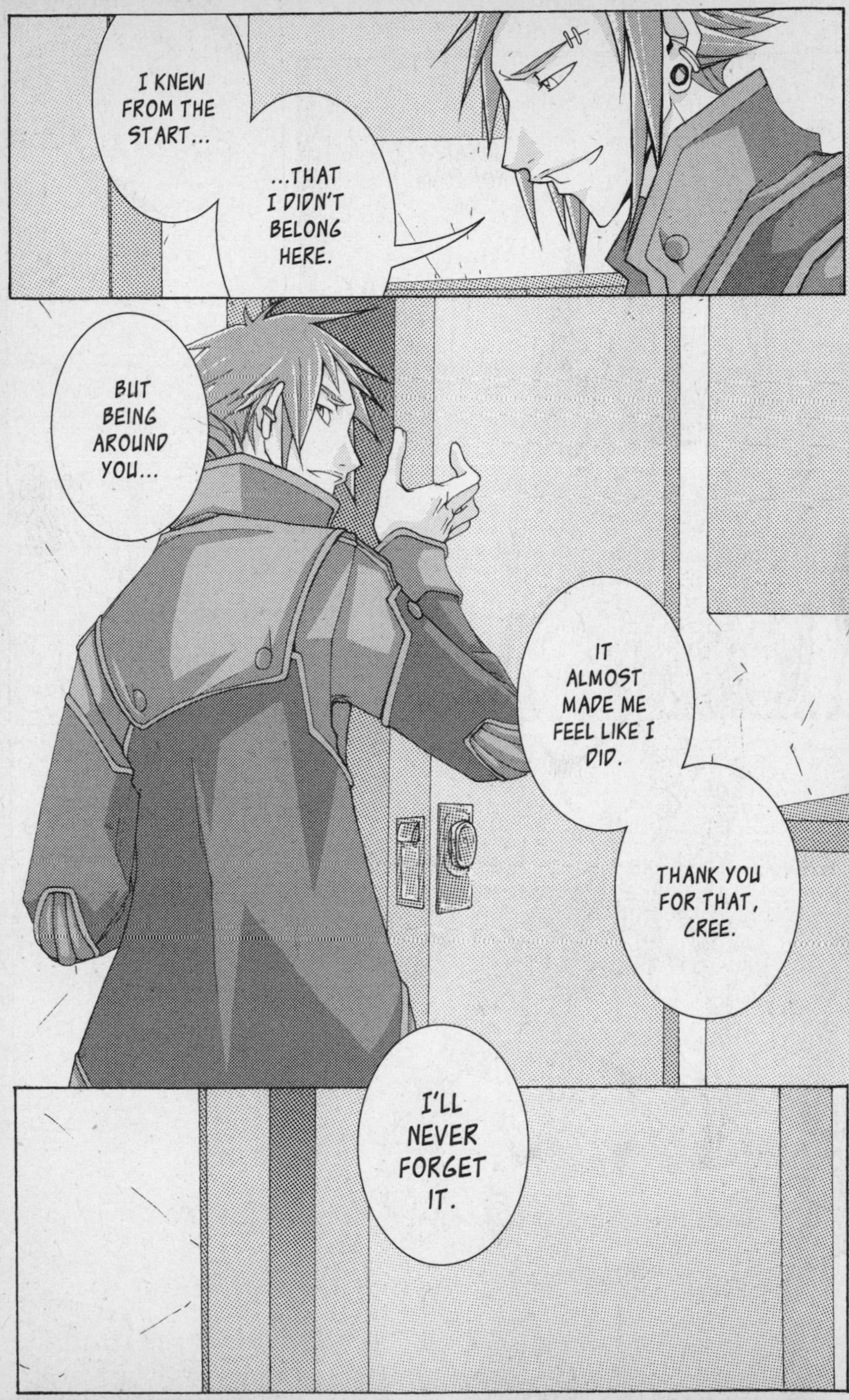
I KNEW FROM THE START...
...THAT I DIDN'T BELONG HERE.
BUT BEING AROUND YOU...
IT ALMOST MADE ME FEEL LIKE I DID.
THANK YOU FOR THAT, CREE.
I'LL NEVER FORGET IT.

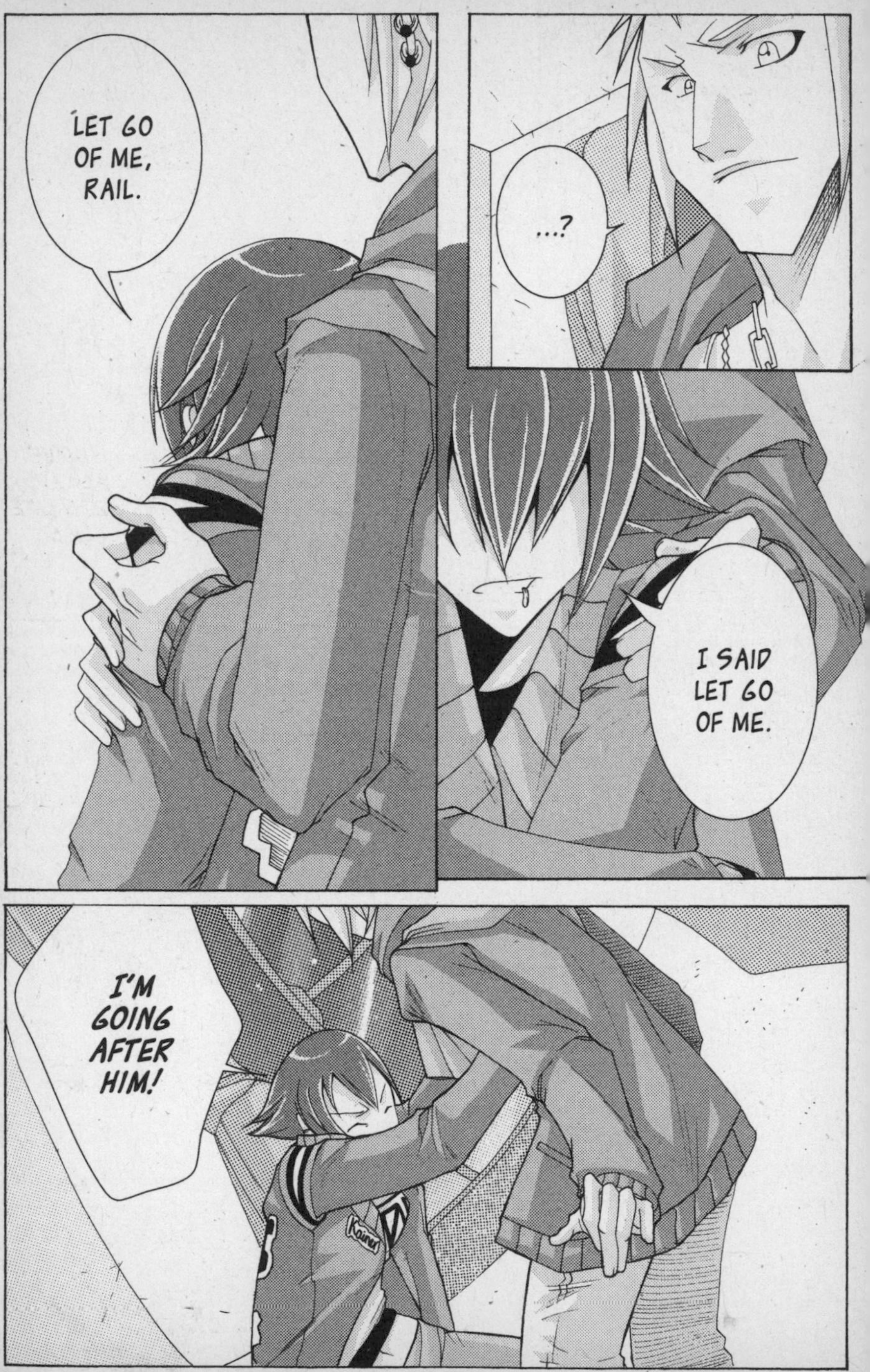
LET GO OF ME, RAIL.
...?
I SAID LET GO OF ME.
I'M GOING AFTER HIM!

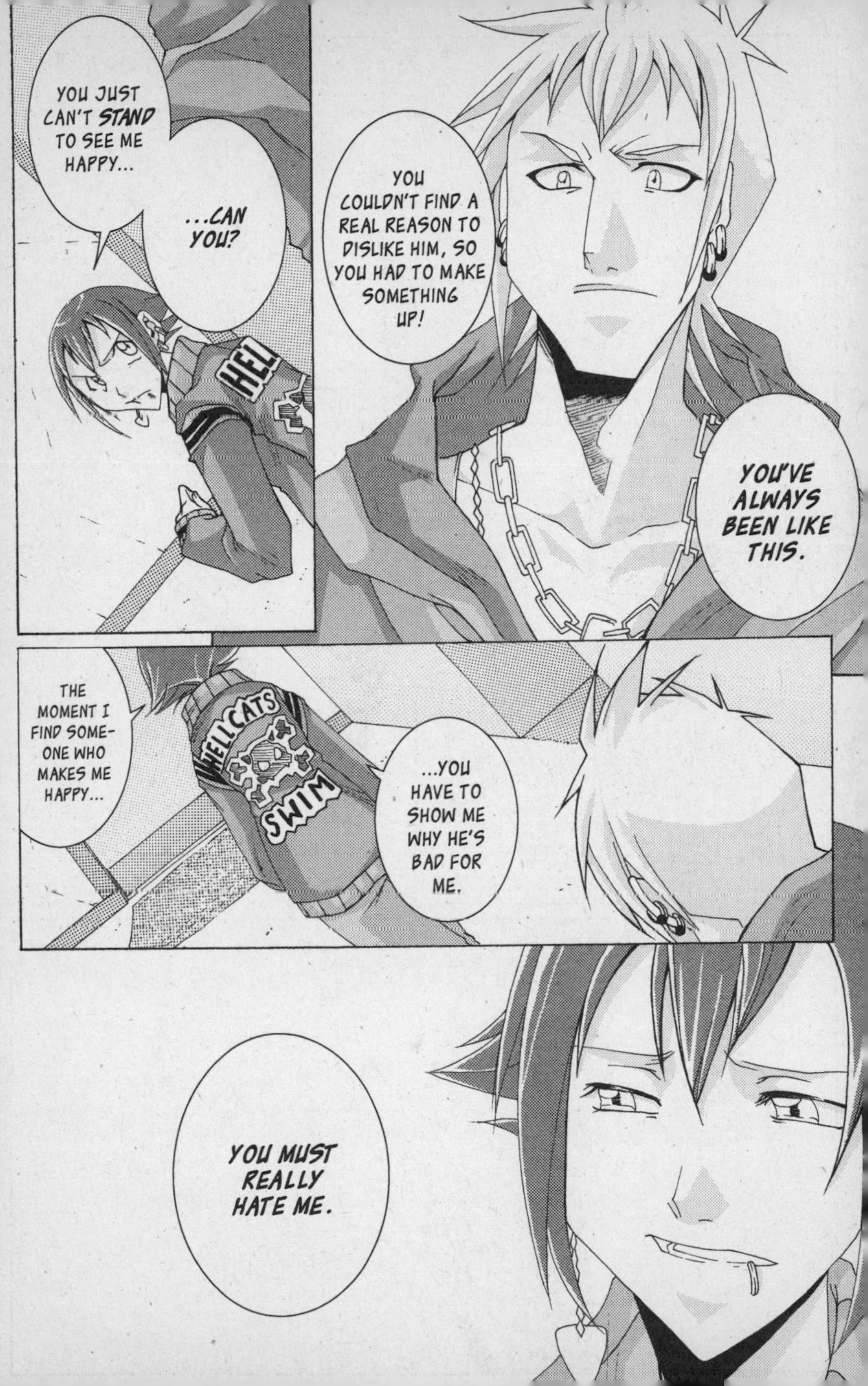
YOU JUST CAN'T STAND TO SEE ME HAPPY...
...CAN YOU?
YOU COULDN'T FIND A REAL REASON TO DISLIKE HIM, SO YOU HAD TO MAKE SOMETHING UP!
YOU'VE ALWAYS BEEN LIKE THIS.
THE MOMENT I FIND SOME-ONE WHO MAKES ME HAPPY...
HELLCATS SWIM
...YOU HAVE TO SHOW ME WHY HE'S BAD FOR ME.
YOU MUST REALLY HATE ME.

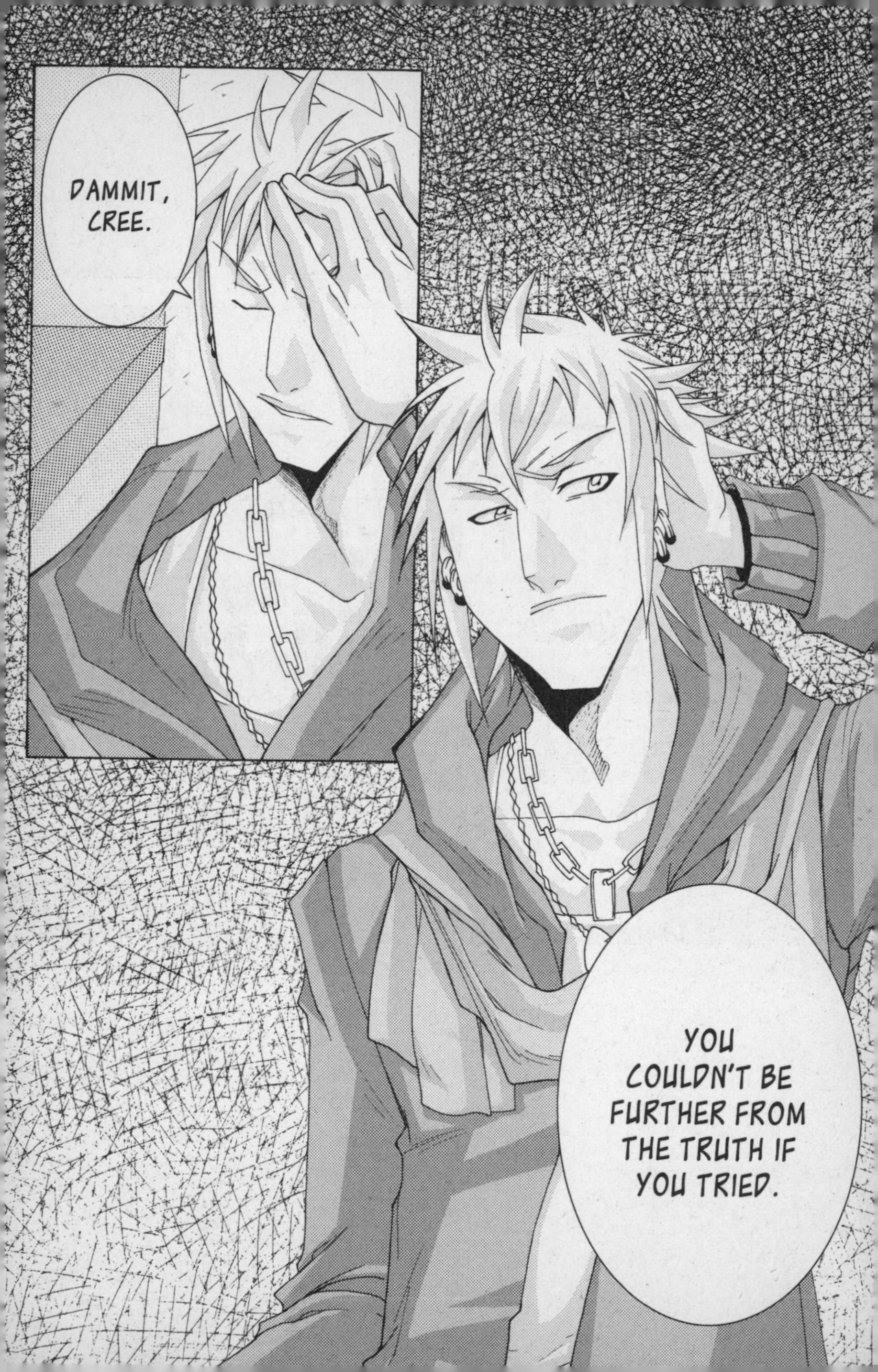
DAMMIT, CREE.
YOU COULDN'T BE FURTHER FROM THE TRUTH IF YOU TRIED.

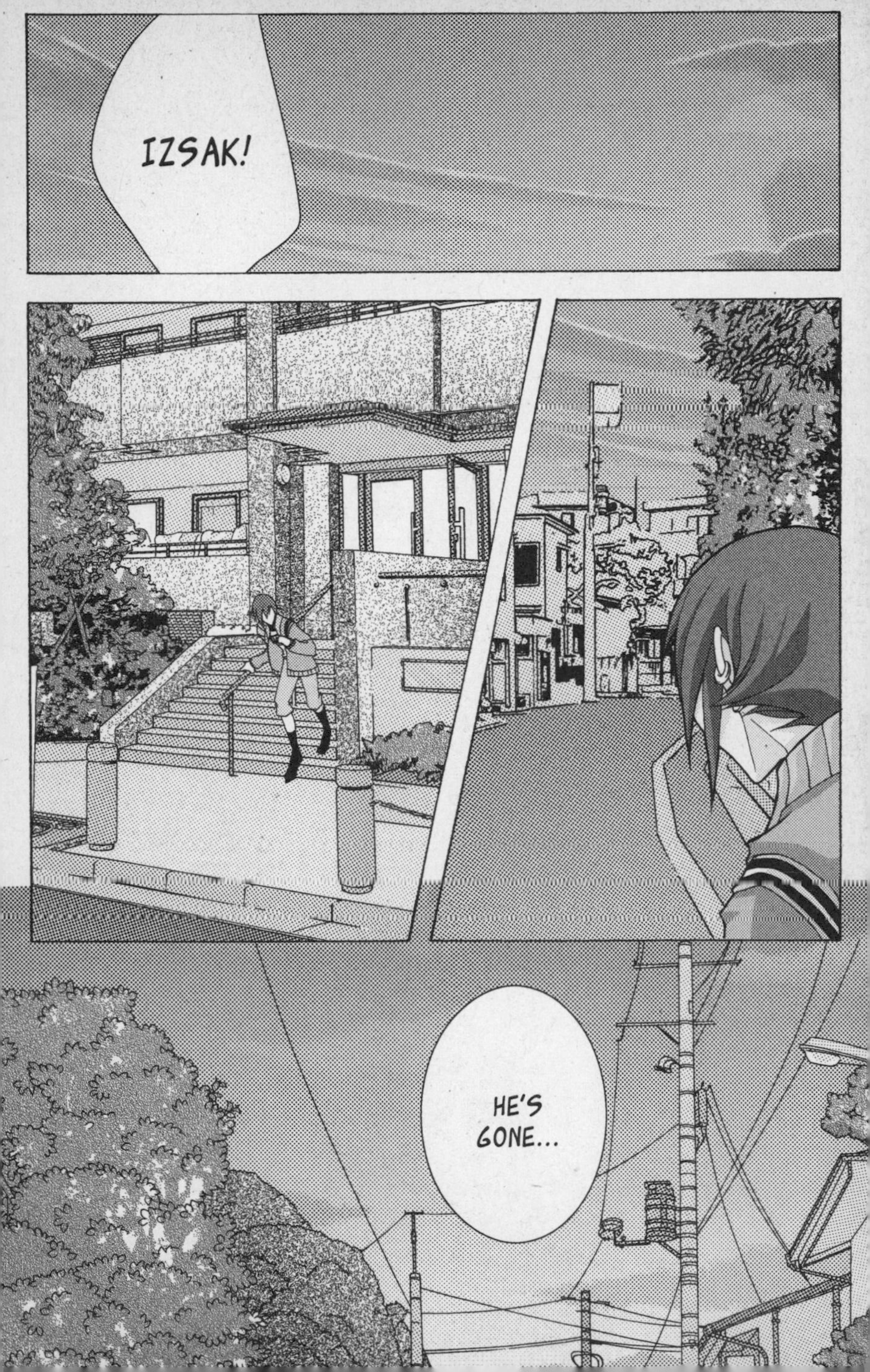
IZSAK!
HE'S GONE...

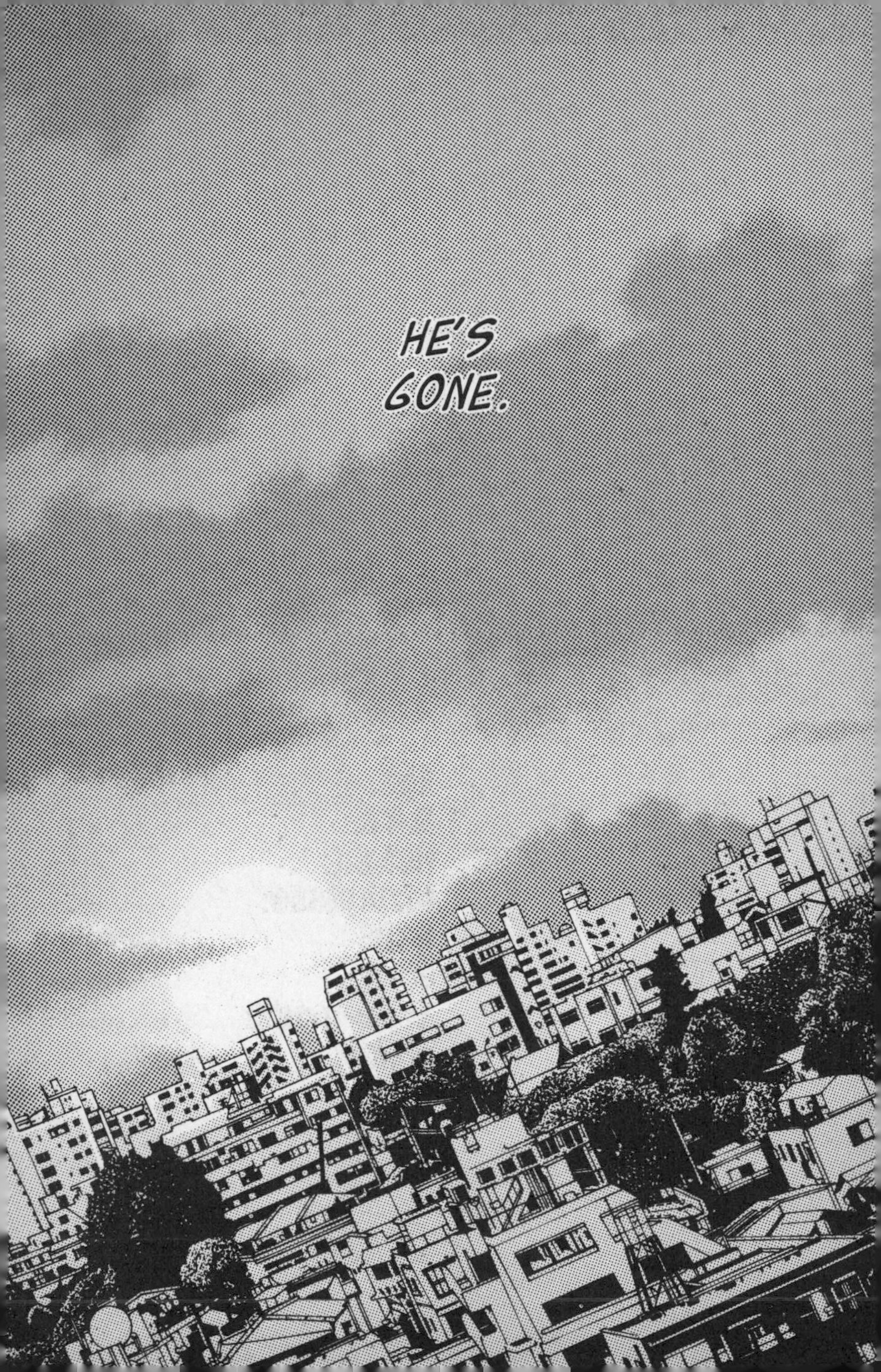
HE'S GONE.

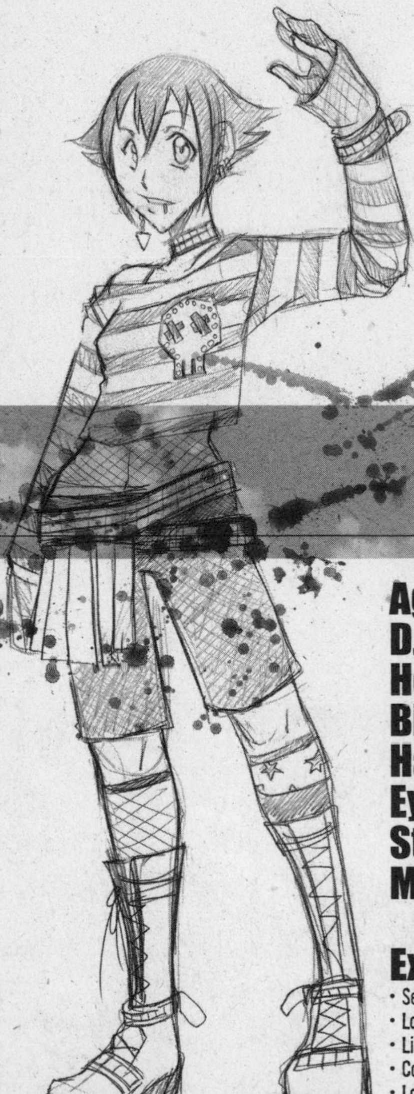

CREE

Name: Cree Winters

Age: 18
D.O.B.: 7/4
Height: 5 ft 1 in
Birthplace: London, England
Hair: (dyed) Royal blue
Eyes: Aqua blue
Style•mode: Algonquins/BananaFish
Major: not currently in school

Extra:

- Secretly loves tv dramas, particularly ones about lawyers
- Loves sweets, especially French pastries
- Likes platforms because they make her feel taller
- Collects skull goods, especially pink ones
- Loves fighting games

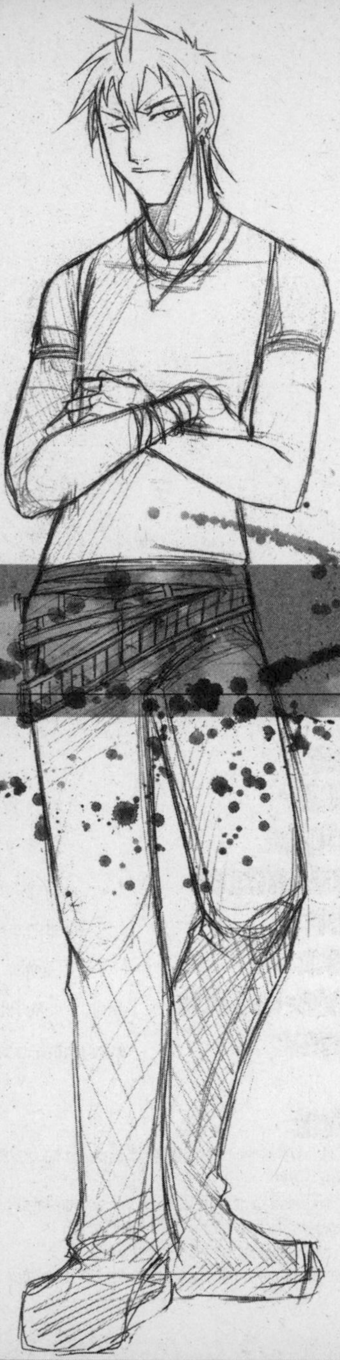

RAIL

Name: Rail Kainer

Age:	21
D.O.B.:	12/13
Height:	6 ft 4 in
Birthplace:	Hamburg, Germany
Hair:	Light orange
Eyes:	Clover green
Style•mode:	Hellcat Punks
Major:	Physics

Extra:

- Has a cat named Jehosephat
- Plays the violin & the cello as well as the guitar
- Is totally blind without his contacts
- Was the captain of his high school swim team
- Scored 10 points shy of perfect on his SATs

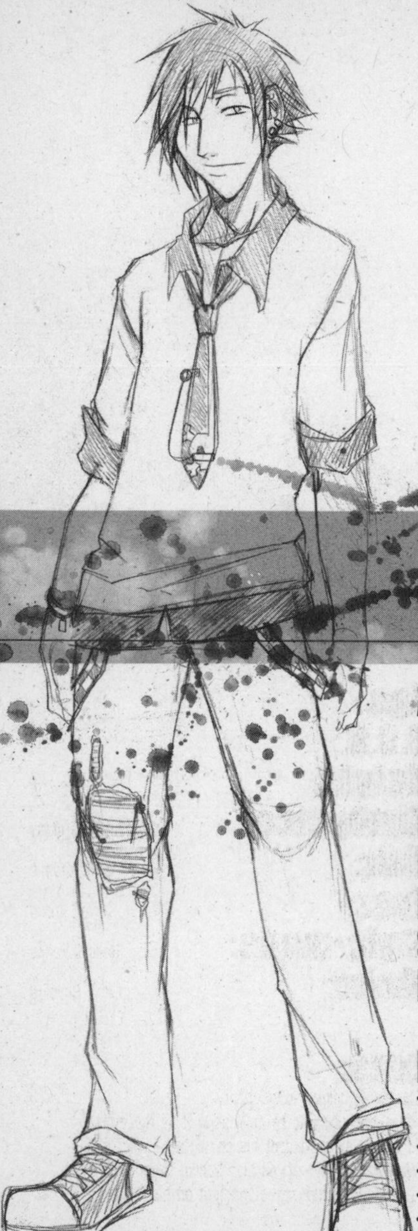

IZSAK

Name: Izsak ???

Age:	??
D.O.B.:	??-??
Height:	6 ft 1 in
Birthplace:	???
Hair:	Champagne gray
Eyes:	Copper red
Style•mode:	No Future
Major:	not currently in school

Extra:

- Doesn't have a very good sense of taste so he prefers strong flavors
- Can fall asleep in any position, in any surroundings
- Has never ridden in a car (that he knows of)
- Gets cold exceedingly easily, hates winter
- Is allergic to dogs, but if he sees one, he has to pet it.

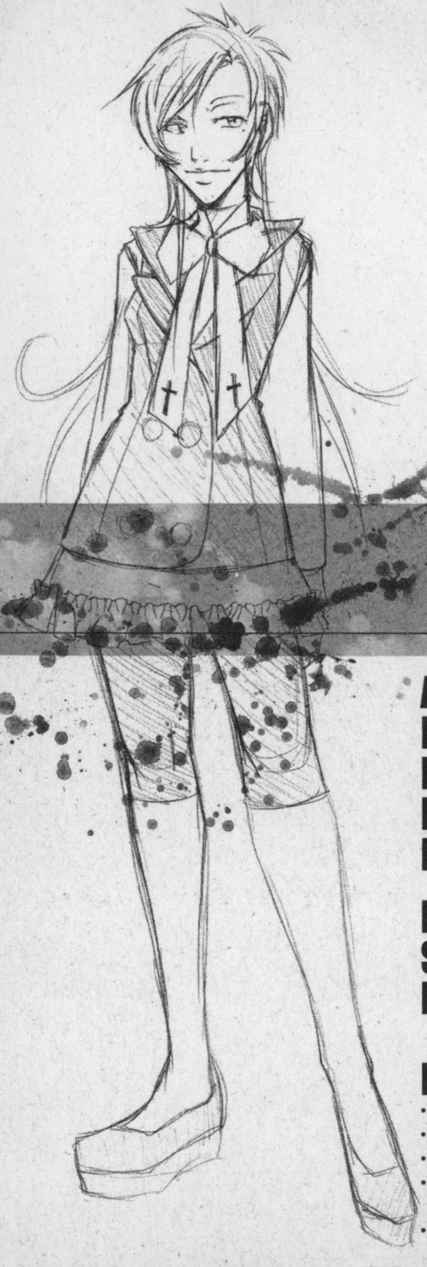

CHAR

Name: Char(les) Delphi

Age: 21

D.O.B.: 2/14

Height: 5ft 8in

Birthplace: New York City, USA

Hair: Strawberry blond with copper highlights

Eyes: Pale blue

Style•mode: Miho Matsuda

Major: Fashion design

Extra:

- Doesn't know how to drive
- Mother owns the building she lives in
- Has a half sister from her father's 2nd wife
- Consults a personal psychic and has her palm read once a week
- Can't swim, but once dated a lifeguard; thinks that's close enough

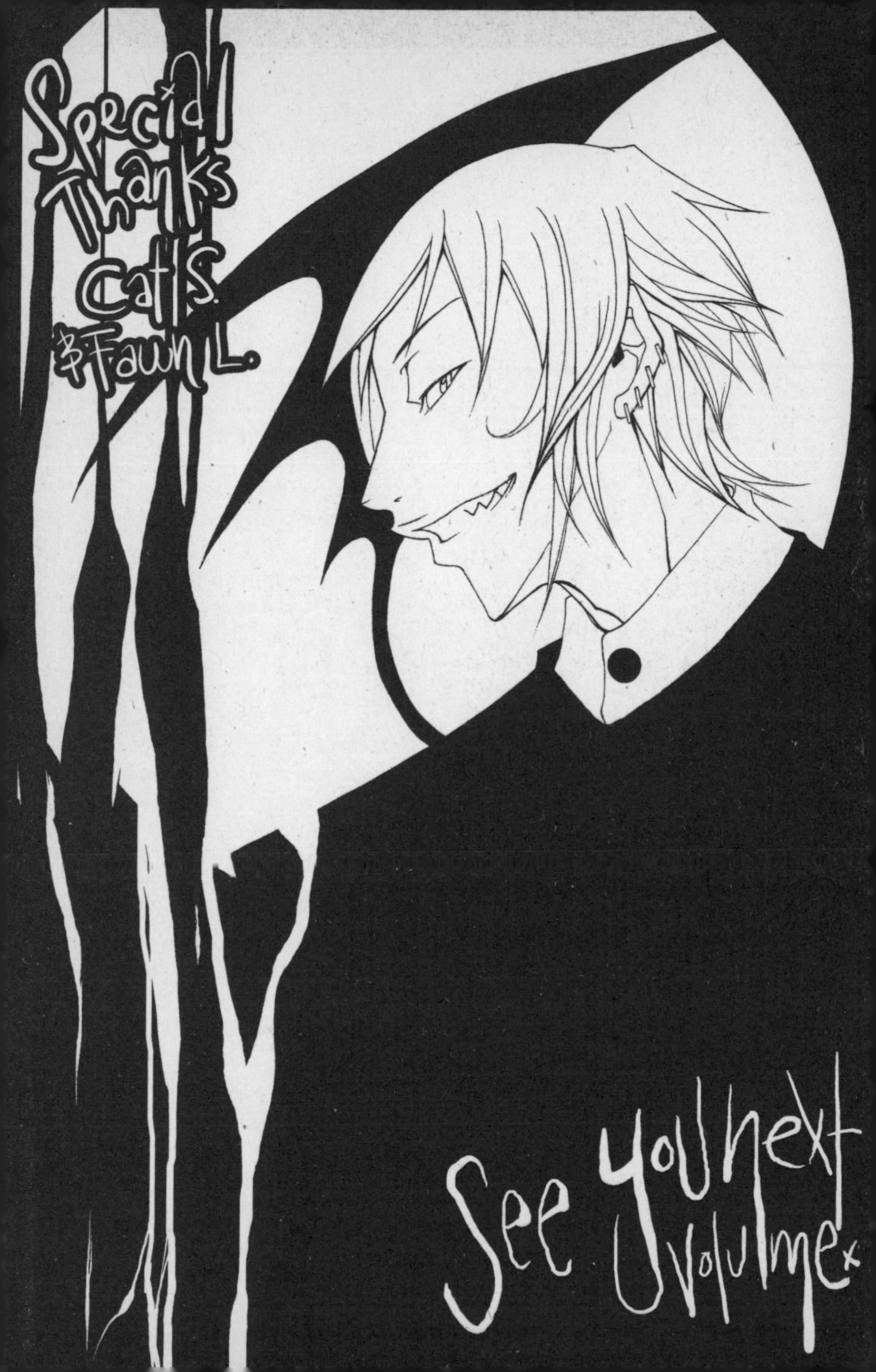
Special Thanks
Catls.
& Fawn L.
See you next volume

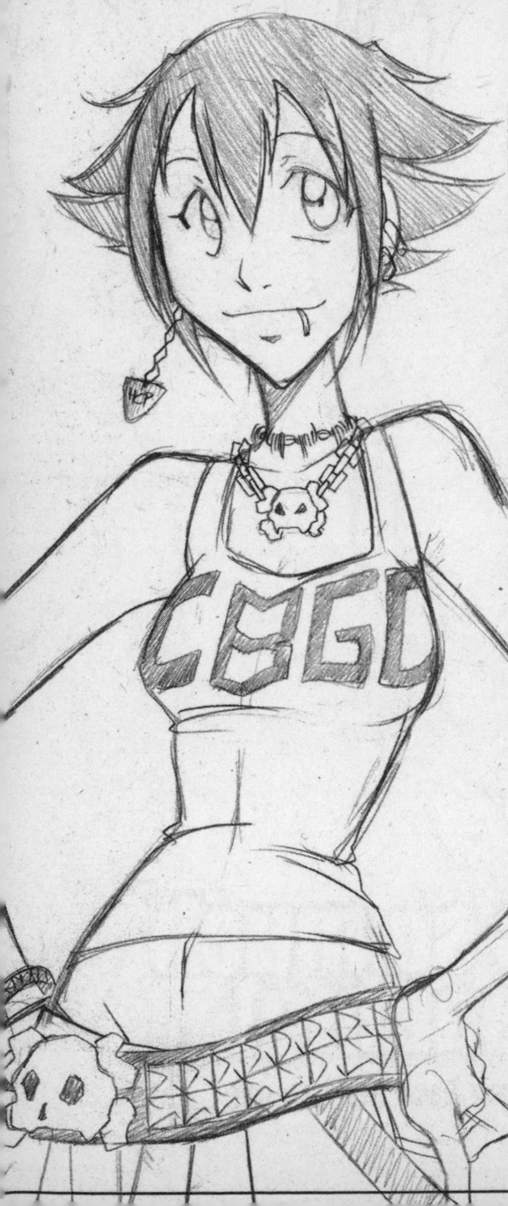
CBGB

So the first volume of RE:Play is finally here! It seems like forever and a day since I started on this project... it's a relief to finally be holding it in my hands! (In fact, it feels like ages since I drew these two in these costumes! Ha ha ha-- well, it's been almost two years X_X) This was the first graphic novel project I've worked on. I'm used to doing a monthly comic series, so it took a little getting used to. It was also the first time I had worked with an assistant tonist. In the beginning, it was a little rough and she and I each were still falling into the look we each wanted to bring to this comic, so I hope you'll excuse a few hiccups here and there! After a few chapters went by, however, it was like we totally fell in sync and understood each other a lot better. It's like she can read my mind now! I can't imagine what I'd do without her!

I've wanted to write this story for a long while now, and I'm really excited to get the chance to do so! I can't wait to get to the next book now that things have finally started rolling, and I promise there'll be a lot more surprises in store in the next volume!

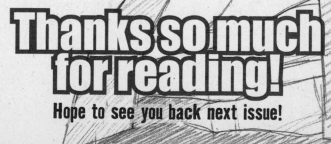

When I work I always listen to music, and since this comic is music-flavored, as I worked I jotted down songs that came on that reminded me of the characters and the comic. I'll include my own little playlist in the next volume, but until then I'd love to hear from anyone out there as to what your own music selections for RE:Play might be! So please, if you have any tracks you want to share, send them my way! I'll be sure to include some next volume!

Music, fan art, letters and pretty little red-haired boys can be sent to:

E-MAIL: NyankoChan@gmail.com

SNAIL MAIL
TOKYOPOP
RE:Play Fanart
5900 Wilshire Blvd. Ste 2000
Los Angeles, CA 90036

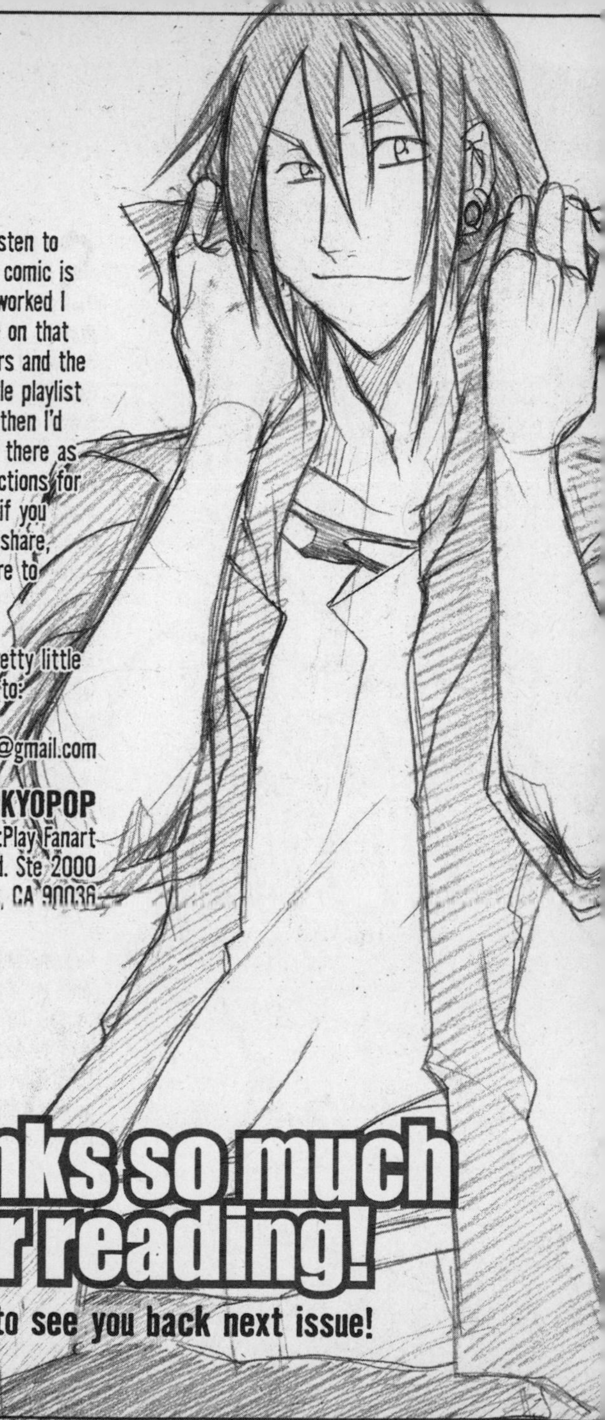

Thanks so much for reading!

Hope to see you back next issue!

RE:play

Volume TWO

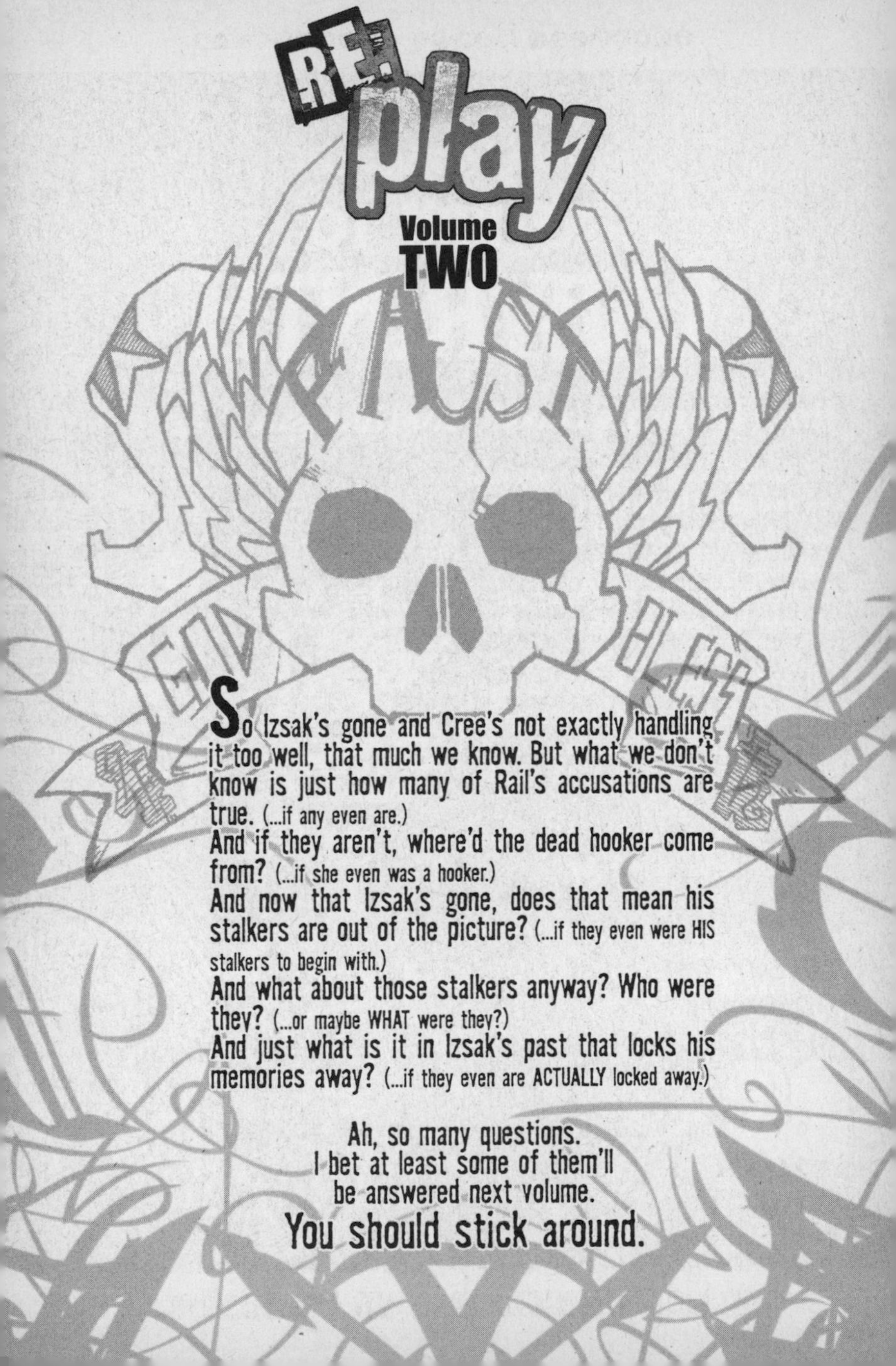
PAST

So Izsak's gone and Cree's not exactly handling it too well, that much we know. But what we don't know is just how many of Rail's accusations are true. (...if any even are.)
And if they aren't, where'd the dead hooker come from? (...if she even was a hooker.)
And now that Izsak's gone, does that mean his stalkers are out of the picture? (...if they even were HIS stalkers to begin with.)
And what about those stalkers anyway? Who were they? (...or maybe WHAT were they?)
And just what is it in Izsak's past that locks his memories away? (...if they even are ACTUALLY locked away.)

Ah, so many questions.
I bet at least some of them'll
be answered next volume.

You should stick around.

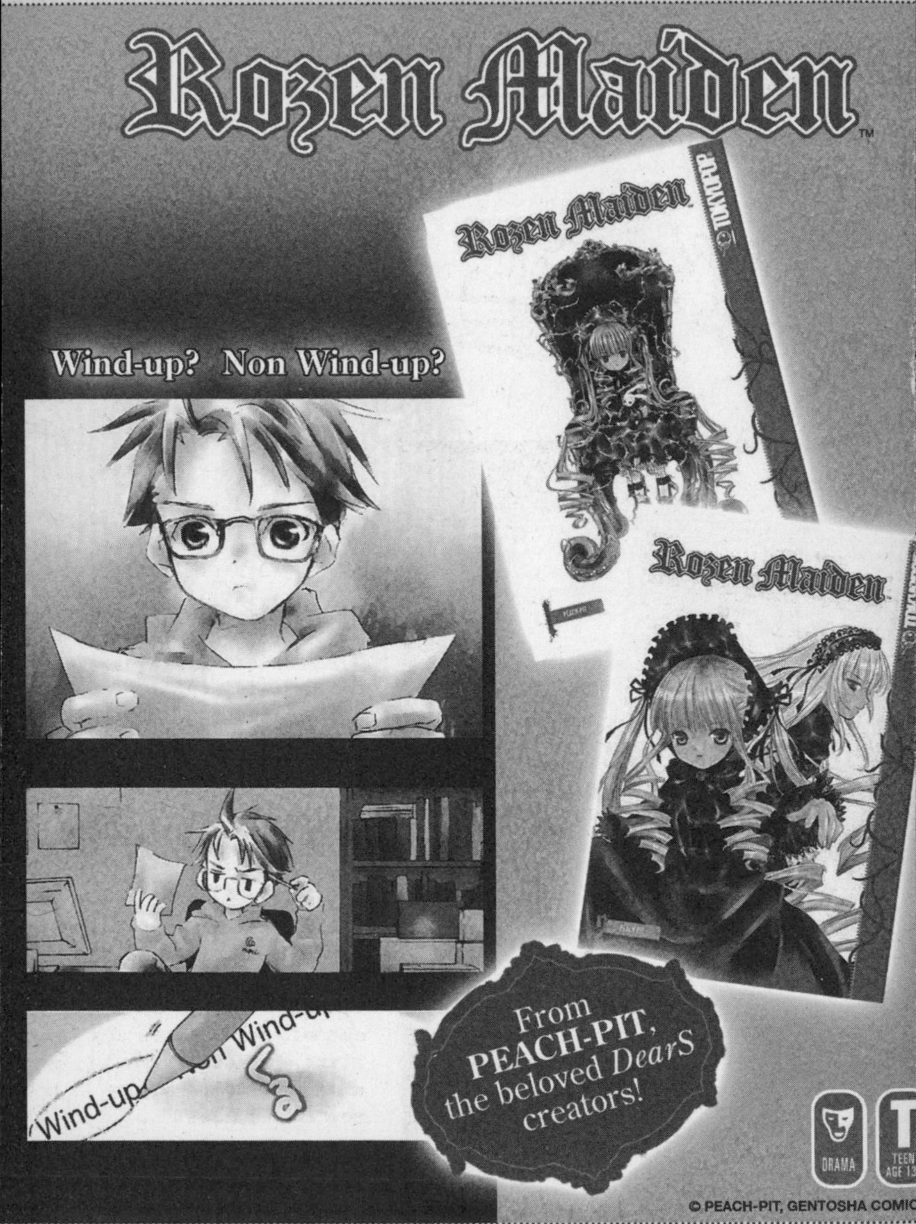
Rozen Maiden™
Wind-up? Non Wind-up?
Wind-up
Non Wind-up
From PEACH-PIT, the beloved *DearS* creators!
DRAMA
TEEN AGE 13
© PEACH-PIT, GENTOSHA COMIC

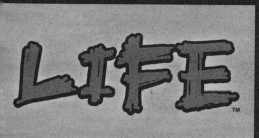

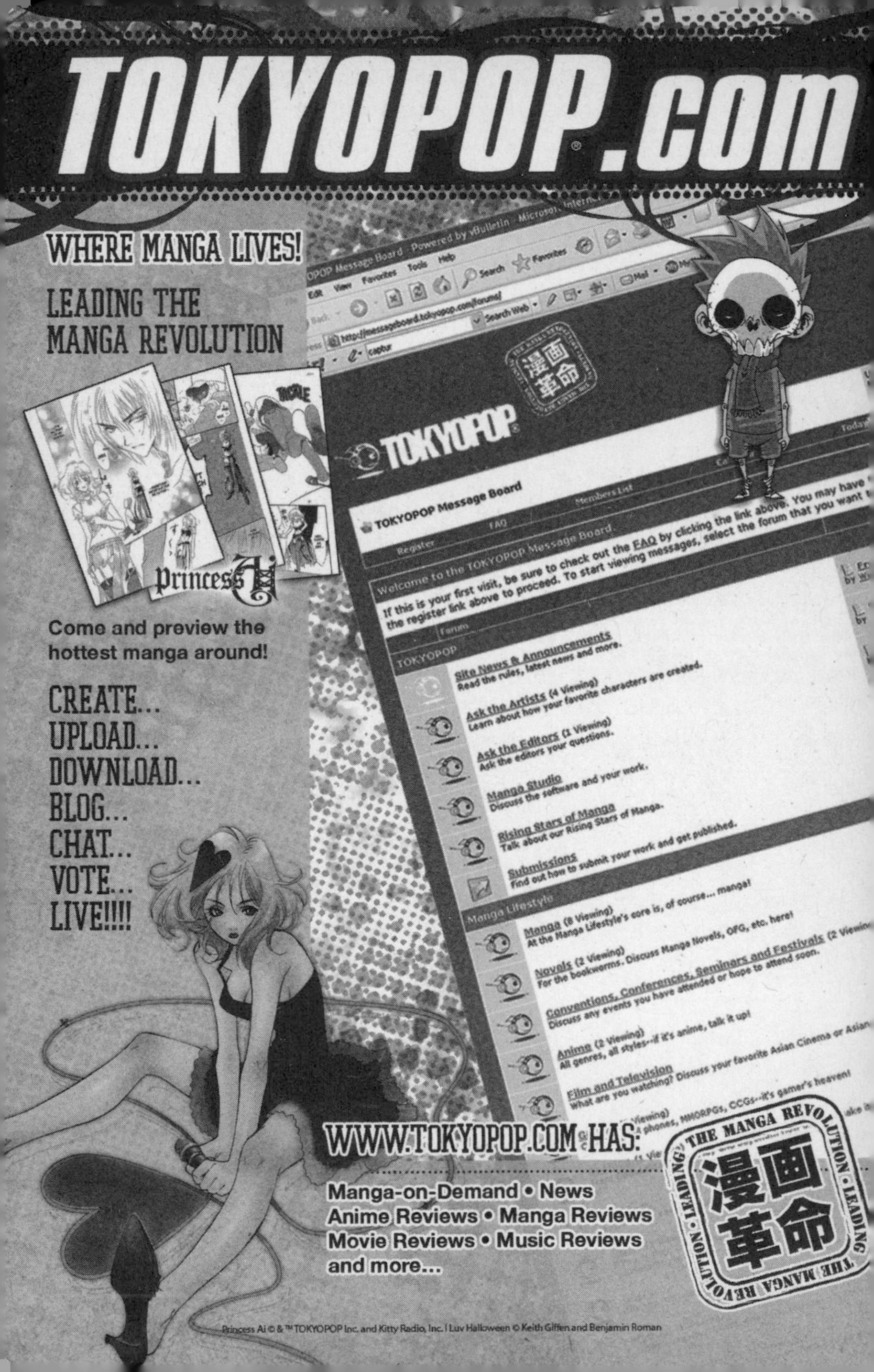
TOKYOPOP.com
WHERE MANGA LIVES!
LEADING THE MANGA REVOLUTION
Princess Ai
Come and preview the hottest manga around!
CREATE...
UPLOAD...
DOWNLOAD...
BLOG...
CHAT...
VOTE...
LIVE!!!!
TOKYOPOP
TOKYOPOP Message Board
Welcome to the TOKYOPOP Message Board.
Site News & Announcements
Ask the Artists
Ask the Editors
Manga Studio
Rising Stars of Manga
Submissions
Manga Lifestyle
Manga
Novels
Conventions, Conferences, Seminars and Festivals
Anime
Film and Television
WWW.TOKYOPOP.COM HAS:
Manga-on-Demand • News
Anime Reviews • Manga Reviews
Movie Reviews • Music Reviews
and more...
LEADING THE MANGA REVOLUTION
漫画革命
Princess Ai © & ™ TOKYOPOP Inc. and Kitty Radio, Inc. I Luv Halloween © Keith Giffen and Benjamin Roman